KIDNAPPED BY THE BILLIONAIRE

JACKIE ASHENDEN

St. Martin's Paperbacks

KIDNAPPED BY THE BILLIONAIRE

For information address St. Martin's Press, 175 Fifth Avenue, New York, NY 10010.

ISBN: 978-1-250-07785-1

Printed in the United States of America

St. Martin's Paperbacks edition / March 2016

St. Martin's Paperbacks are published by St. Martin's Press, 175 Fifth Avenue, New York, NY 10010.

10 9 8 7 6 5 4 3 2 1

Praise for Jackie Ashenden and her sizzling novels

"With a distinct voice and fresh, complex characters, *Mine To Take* is a sexy, emotional read that gripped me from page one. I can't wait to see what Ashenden brings us next."

—Laurelin Paige, *New York Times* bestselling author

"A scintillating, heart-pounding love story. A dark, sinfully sexy hero with a tortured past. I loved it!"

—Opal Carew, *New York Times* bestselling author

"The sex is dirty-sweet, with a dark lick of dominance and the tantalizing potential of redemption, and an explosive ending provides the perfect closure to Gabe and Honor's story while setting up the next installment."

—*Publishers Weekly* (starred review) on *Mine To Take*

"Intriguingly dark and intensely compelling . . . explosive."

—*RT Book Reviews* on *Mine To Take* (Top Pick!)

"Powerfully suspenseful and, above all, sensual and meaningful . . . not to be missed."

—*RT Book Reviews* on *Make You Mine* (Top Pick!)

"Ms. Ashenden is an incredible storyteller."

—*Harlequin Junkies*

"Sexy and fun." —*RT Book Reviews*

"Truly a roller coaster of a ride . . . well worth it."

—*Harlequin Junkies*

"Steamy." —*Guilty Pleasures Book Reviews*

ALSO BY JACKIE ASHENDEN

***Nine Circles* series**

Mine To Take
Make You Mine
You Are MIne

E-Novella series *The Billionaire's Club*

The Billion Dollar Bachelor
The Billion Dollar Bad Boy
The Billionaire Biker

Available by St. Martin's Press

To all my fantastic readers.
If I could take you all out for coffee I would.

ACKNOWLEDGMENTS

Once again thanks to Monique Patterson, my wonderful editor, and to Helen Breitwieser, my equally wonderful agent. To my family for bearing with the endurance event that is Jackie writing a book. And as always to Maisey, my critique partner and friend, who thought Elijah was one of her favorites.

CHAPTER ONE

Seven years ago Elijah Hunt lost everything that gave his life meaning.

Now, he'd lost it again.

This fucking bullshit was starting to get old.

The subway car rattled through the dark tunnel as he sat there with his fingers curled around the Colt in the pocket of his overcoat, watching the woman who sat opposite and a couple of seats down the car from him.

She hadn't seen him, hadn't recognized him. But then he'd made damn sure she wouldn't.

She looked like she was in her own little world anyway, staring down at the fringed leather purse she held tightly in her hands as if it contained the secrets of the universe.

Violet Fiztgerald. Daughter of the biggest prick God had ever put on this earth. The prick he'd spent the last seven years serving.

Not anymore. That prick was now dead and so was everything Elijah had worked toward.

He wasn't just pissed. He'd gotten beyond that. Way, way beyond it.

He was now in the cold zone, the dead place. Where only one thing had any meaning anymore: Take them down. Take them *all* down.

There was just one thing he needed in order to make that happen. Violet. His handy little backup plan.

She shifted in her seat, glancing distractedly at the drunk sitting a couple of seats away, an expression of distaste flickering across small, precise features heavily masked by the makeup she wore. Thick black eyeliner and dark blue mascara. Full red mouth. Her long blonde hair in its ridiculous dreadlocks was pulled back in a ponytail, and as she changed her hold on her battered-looking purse, the many silver bracelets she wore around her wrist made chiming sounds.

She was wrapped in a long and completely over-the-top dark blue coat of worn velvet, belted tightly around her waist. The boots on her feet were black and scuffed, lacing right up under the bright fall of her Indian silk skirt. In addition to the bracelets around her wrists, she wore heavy silver hoops in her ears and a little blue sapphire that glittered in her nose.

Ever since he'd become Fitzgerald's right-hand man, Violet had been dressing like she'd stumbled over a box of theater costumes and just put them all on.

She looked ridiculous. A poor little rich kid trying rebellion on for size. When he'd first met her, she'd just come back from college after studying psychology against the express wishes of her parents. Then, not a couple of months after being back, she'd left again to pursue yet more study. She was one of those perpetual students, without a goal or purpose, substituting academia for a proper job. He despised her. Especially when not long after she'd come back with her master's degree, she'd then taken off to India and Europe, claiming she needed some "me time." And all on her father's dime.

Spoiled, that's what she was. Unfortunately for her though, the days of swanning around doing whatever the hell she wanted were now at an end.

The lights flickered as the train went around a corner, then began to slow as it approached the station.

Keeping an eye on her and her mother had been one of his jobs, so he had an idea where she was going. And if he was right, she'd be getting off here.

Sure enough, as the train drew up to the platform, Violet got to her feet.

Time to go.

People were beginning to crowd around the doors, but he had no problem making sure they moved out of the way as he came up behind her. She was a full head shorter than he was and smelled faintly of some kind of hippie shit perfume. Sandalwood possibly.

Filing the observation automatically away, he brought the Colt out discreetly and bent his head so his mouth was near her ear. Then he jammed the muzzle against her back and said coldly, "Scream and I'll kill you."

She stiffened, jerking around to face him, shock written all over her pretty features.

He allowed her a glance, since one look into his eyes would be all she needed to know he meant business, and gave her an icy smile. "You don't want to die, do you, Violet?"

Eyes the color of fine turquoise widened, her pupils dilating. Her gaze flickered all over his face, probably taking in the bruises and cuts left by fucking Zac Rutherford's fists. He probably looked like he'd gone ten rounds with Muhammad Ali, but that was a good thing. The more terrified she was, the less likely she'd fight him—and he really couldn't be bothered with yet another fight right now. He'd rather shoot her and be done with it.

Elijah pressed the gun firmly into her back. "Eyes front. We're getting out right here."

A visible tremble shook her, and for a minute he wondered if she'd be stupid enough or afraid enough to ignore him and scream. Which would put a major fucking wrench in the works.

He cocked the gun. Kept the cold smile on his face. "Make the right decision, princess."

She paled. Her gaze flickered again, then abruptly she turned back to the doors.

Excellent. At least one thing was going right for him today.

The train stopped and the doors opened, and Violet got out with him close behind her. "Head for the exit," he murmured as they moved through the crowded platform. "Nod if you understand."

She didn't turn this time, but gave a jerky nod.

Keeping the gun pressed firmly into her back, he stayed close as they made their way to the escalators, people oblivious around them, all the while keeping an eye out for anyone tailing them. He wasn't fool enough to believe that just because he'd lost the men Rutherford had sent out after him, he was safe. No, not after the fight the other man had put up back at Fitzgerald's apartment.

His shoulder ached at the memory, but Elijah ignored the pain. Focused instead on the massive, black, volcanic rage that filled him. Rage at seeing the man he'd been chasing for seven years die from a gunshot wound to the head.

Everything he'd done, everything he'd worked for, gone in the blink of an eye.

Because that fucking bitch Eva King had taken his revenge from him.

He should have killed her up in that apartment, but he hadn't. He'd let her go to catch Fitzgerald off guard, to break the impasse Rutherford and King had gotten themselves into.

He'd expected Rutherford to go for Eva to protect her, but none of them had done what they were supposed to do. Eva wasn't supposed to shoot Fitzgerald in the head. She was supposed to collapse in a heap of fear and Rutherford was supposed to protect her while Elijah took the shot at Fitzgerald instead.

But none of it had gone to plan. Eva had taken up the gun and shot Fitzgerald, and then Rutherford had turned on him. Then Rutherford had shot him.

Fucking prick.

The bullet had gone through his shoulder and it hurt like a bastard, but Elijah was used to ignoring pain. After picking up the Colt from the dead body of the security guard on his way out of the building, he'd found an alley to hide in, ripping his shirt apart to use as a makeshift bandage while he put his coat on over the top. Then he'd had to think on the fly, try to remember what his backup plan was supposed to be if everything turned to shit.

He'd had to work fast, find Violet quickly, because once her father's death was discovered, the police would be all over it and not only would his element of surprise be gone, but she'd be protected. And not only by the police.

Violet Fitzgerald's best friend was Honor St. James, a member of the group who'd fucked up his revenge plans, and once Honor knew Fitzgerald was dead, she'd be running to her friend to make sure she was okay.

Which wasn't going to happen. At least not now at any rate.

As they came up out of the subway station, the icy wind of a late New York winter crawled under the overcoat he wore, sending tendrils of cold over the bare skin of his torso. He considered the sensation, then discarded it. He would have to get inside and out of the wind to deal with his wound soon enough, but he could manage for now. It wasn't as if his hostage was any danger to him.

Almost as soon as the thought crossed his mind, Violet made a sudden lunge to the left.

Stupid girl. Even with a gunshot wound his reflexes were better than most Navy SEALs.

He shot out a hand and grabbed her arm, hauling her back against him while jamming the muzzle of the Colt hard into her side.

"Bad move, princess," he hissed in her ear. "Do it again and I'll shoot you right here and now."

She was trembling, he could feel it. "W-W-Why are you doing this?" she stammered, her voice hoarse and ragged with fear. "W-What did I do?"

"Just shut up and do as you're told and you won't get hurt." Keeping a hold on her arm, he forced her to walk to the edge of the sidewalk near the street. "Now, flag down a cab. We're going for a little drive."

"My father will—"

"Your father, Violet, is dead. And if you want to live, you'll do whatever the fuck I say, understand?"

She'd gone totally still at that. "No . . ." It was a quiet, almost inaudible whisper.

But he had no time for her grief or her shock or her pain. He knew Fitzgerald had loved his daughter in his own twisted way and that Violet had no idea what her father was. That this news would come as a complete shock to her.

Too fucking bad. Life was short, then you died. And she was going to find that out the hard way.

"Get. A. Cab." He made each word as hard and as cold as a bullet. He'd let her collapse once they'd gotten back to the apartment he'd maintained for this very purpose. An apartment that no one knew about, that no one would find. The perfect bolt-hole he could disappear into while he formulated his escape route.

Or at least that had been the old plan, for after he'd taken his revenge and killed Fitzgerald.

Now, though, he'd have to think of something else. A use for his little bargaining chip, a way to bring it all down.

He wasn't going to let the past seven years all be for nothing. He fucking *refused.*

It took Violet a while to flag down a cab, and when one finally stopped, Elijah could feel the cold starting to settle down through his skin, going deeper. The gunshot wound ached and so did his hands, and his face was no doubt bruised as well; Zac Rutherford was a mean bastard who knew how to throw a punch.

Shit. He was probably going into shock, which he sure as hell didn't need right now.

Jerking open the cab door, he pushed Violet inside, following in closely behind her. The driver did a double take—probably due to the bruising on Elijah's face—but one hard look soon had the man turning right back to the front again. Just as well. Elijah didn't need any questions at this particular point in time.

He gave the driver the address then leaned back against the seat, keeping the gun jammed against Violet's side. She sat beside him, unmoving, her head turned away, her attention on the street outside. Her hands still clutched her silly little fringed purse, knuckles white.

He'd probably just shattered her entire world. Well, welcome to the club.

Seven years ago he'd have felt bad about that. Would have regretted giving her the news and would have delivered it at a better time, in a more appropriate setting. He would have comforted her. Certainly he wouldn't have kidnapped her at gunpoint.

But Marie was dead, and since then nothing mattered much to him anymore.

Except for Evelyn Fitzgerald's death. The death that he should have taken for himself.

The volcanic rage inside him shifted and he tightened his grip on it, letting its icy heat warm him, using it to combat the effects of physical shock.

Violet remained silent and he didn't bother to speak either, concentrating all his energy on merely staying upright and keeping that gun right where it was.

New York traffic being what it was, it took them longer than he wanted to get to the West Village address he'd given the cabbie. When they finally stopped and he got out, dragging an unresisting Violet with him, he found the ground unsteady beneath his feet, shivers starting to wrack him.

Fuck. He did *not* need this. Not now.

Throwing some money at the cabdriver, he tugged his overcoat more firmly around him then pulled Violet close. That musky perfume of hers made his head cloudy and the warmth of her body far more attractive than it had any right to be. But only because he was cold.

He hadn't wanted a woman in seven years and he had no intention of wanting one now.

Revenge was more important. Revenge had *always* been more important.

Hustling her down the sidewalk, he debated about whether this was wise, bringing her to his personal little bolt-hole. If he hadn't been shot and had to grab her on the fly, he'd have brought a blindfold or knocked her out or something so she wouldn't know where they were. But obviously he couldn't do that now.

It won't matter. It's not like you're going to be letting her go anytime soon.

Excellent point.

It wasn't far to the old brick factory that sat next to the river. It had been converted to apartments years ago, and Elijah had bought the entire building back before his world had fallen apart. Back when he'd been the owner of a very successful venture capital company and making shitloads of cash. When he'd been married and desperately in love with his wife.

Christ, he couldn't even remember what that feeling was like anymore. Being happy. Being in love. Not that he wanted to of course; the more you cared about something, the more it hurt when you lost it. Life was full of interesting little lessons like that.

He'd jettisoned nearly everything of that life after Marie had disappeared, but he'd kept the old factory building. Not because he liked having a big fuck-off apartment all to himself, but because he'd needed somewhere safe to go that no one—especially not Fitzgerald and his operations—knew about.

To keep up appearances, he'd leased out the first couple of floors, but the top floor he'd kept entirely empty so he could come and go as he pleased without any neighbors being nosy.

He got Violet to the front of the apartment building and keyed in his code to unlock the door before pushing her inside.

Her face was a mask as he pulled her over to the elevators and punched the button, her wide, generous mouth gone tight with some kind of suppressed emotion. Grief and shock probably.

The doors opened and he made her go in first then hit the button to the top floor. He resisted the urge to lean against the back wall of the elevator because if he did that, he wasn't sure he'd be able to stand upright again.

Violet stared rigidly at the doors in front of her, making no move to speak or to do anything else. She looked turned to stone.

Excellent. That would make his life a shitload easier.

As the doors opened, he urged her across the hallway to his apartment door, keeping his gun pressed to her back as he keyed in another code.

The door unlocked and he pushed her inside, kicking it shut.

For a second he allowed himself a moment to relax, lowering the gun and leaning back against the closed door, the pain and the cold starting to bite deep. He'd probably lost more blood than he'd thought. This could be a bitch to recover from if he wasn't careful.

It was only when he heard movement that he realized he'd closed his eyes for a moment.

Opening them with a start, he was just in time to see Violet's fist heading straight for his face.

She knew she had no chance, that she'd never win against a man like Elijah Hunt. But dammit, she had to do something because sitting back and taking it had never been her style.

He'd closed his eyes and sagged against the door, and she'd managed to shake off her shock enough to launch the heel of her palm up against his chin the way she'd learned to do in the self-defense classes she'd taken at college.

Unfortunately his head did not snap back the way it was supposed to.

Instead his hand came up—far quicker than it had any business doing—and fingers like iron clamped her wrist in a vice. Then before she quite knew what was happening, her arm was being twisted around and her body along with it, until she was jerked hard against him, her arm pulled up behind her and pinned agonizingly between her shoulder blades.

She tried struggling, unwilling to let the moment go where she might have, in a different universe, had a chance at fighting him and perhaps winning. But her struggles made no difference at all to the iron hold he had on her and when something even harder than the body up against her back pushed into her side, she knew the moment had gone utterly.

Violet stilled, panting. Fear sat in her chest, so large and sharp she could barely deal with that let alone the other thing he'd whispered in her ear back out on the sidewalk outside the subway station.

Your father is dead.

The words echoed in her head, meaningless syllables all jumbling together.

Her father. Evelyn Fitzgerald. She didn't even begin to comprehend it. He'd always seemed invulnerable, untouchable. A cool, clever man who prized control in all things. A cool, distant parent.

Now he wasn't either of those things. He wasn't anything.

How did Elijah Hunt know? And did he have something to do with it? Was he even telling the truth?

Okay. So. First things first. Pull yourself the fuck together.

"What the hell are you doing with me?" she forced out, her voice thin and tight. "If you're going to rape me then just get it over and done with, you prick, because the suspense is killing me." All bravado of course, but it was better than whimpering like a child.

He made a sound of disgust at that and suddenly she was free as he shoved her forward. She stumbled, going down on her hands and knees to the hard wood floorboards beneath her feet. Shaking, she turned over, raising her arms to fight.

But he didn't come any closer. He only pushed himself away from the door and pointed the muzzle of that nasty-looking gun in her direction.

The fear turned over in her chest, making her want to cower on the floor.

Elijah had always been a frightening man, right from the moment her father had first taken him on as his new bodyguard five years earlier. Her father never went anywhere without him, and Violet had hated the way the man seemed to hang around all the freaking time, like a gargoyle, all scarred face and cold black eyes. He never smiled. Never seemed to have any expression other than "don't fuck with me."

She didn't like him. And yet for some reason she couldn't ever quite put her finger on, she found him vaguely fascinating too. He was like a blade she wanted to test the edge of, just to make sure he really was as lethally sharp as she'd thought. Or a tiger she wanted to poke a stick at to see if he was as dangerous as he seemed.

But those urges had fled now. Because yes, he really was as sharp and as dangerous as he seemed, and if she wasn't careful she was going to get herself either cut or killed and eaten.

"That was a pretty fucking stupid move." His voice was so cold, like the rest of him, yet with an oddly rough, sensual edge that sounded like he'd spent one too many nights drinking whiskey and smoking cigarettes. Except of course she'd never seen him do either. His idea of a fun night out was probably polishing his knives and checking over his guns.

"I had to do something." She sat up slowly, rubbing her trembling hands together, her palms stinging. "Can't blame a girl for trying."

He shifted, the fabric of the overcoat he wore parting and giving her a glimpse of bronze skin.

How odd. What the hell happened to his shirt?

"A girl could get herself killed if she's not careful." He gestured with the gun. "Get up."

"So, no rape then?" She had no idea why she was talking like this. She was clearly being stupid.

Something flickered over his impassive features. Yeah, definitely disgust. "I'm a cold, hard bastard and I'll kill you if you try that little stunt again, but no, I'm not going to rape you. That's not why you're here."

Perhaps it was the ice in his voice that eased the sharpest edges of her fear. Ridiculous when there was a gun pointed right at her and he was threatening to kill her. As if death was better than rape.

Slowly, she got to her feet, her heart thumping around inside her chest like a bird throwing itself against the unyielding glass of a windowpane. "Then why am I here? And what did you mean about Dad being dead? Why would you say that?"

"All in good time, princess. Right now I need you to do something for me."

"Why the fuck would I do anything for you?"

"Because if you don't, I'll put a bullet through you." He reached over to the door frame and hit a button on the control panel next to it. Some lights on the panel flickered. Then he lowered the gun and smiled, a terrifying, cold smile that only seemed to make the black holes that were his eyes even darker. "Now, before we get to anything else, you have to understand that there is no way out of this apartment. You can only open this door with the code and only I have the code. The windows are bulletproof, so there's no way you can smash them. Are we clear?"

The brief thoughts she'd had of somehow rendering him unconscious, grabbing his gun, and smashing her way out of the apartment died stillborn.

Not that she would have gotten far anyway. Apart from those self-defense classes, she had no fighting skills to speak of and she'd never even touched a gun let alone fired one. She'd probably end up shooting herself rather than him. Not to mention the fact that he was a trained bodyguard who probably knew how to kill people with his bare hands.

A bodyguard with an apparently deep bank account.

She didn't take her eyes off him, but she'd caught a glimpse of the apartment as he'd shoved her inside all the same. Lots of exposed brick and wood floors, a high ceiling crossed with heavy, dark beams. A West Village loft this size had to be horrendously expensive, which was surely well above his pay grade. Then again, who knew? Her father was a man of many secrets and maybe he paid Elijah shitloads of cash.

"We're clear." She tightened her jaw against an incipient wave of panic. "Am I going to get any explanations then?"

"Not yet. You're going to do that little task I mentioned first." He inclined his head. "Behind you. Head through the door and into the bathroom."

"Why? What do you want me to do?" She was being an idiot continuing to push him. What the hell was she thinking?

Maybe that you don't have anything to lose?

But no, that was stupid. She had plenty to lose. Her life being the main thing, but also the first lead she'd had on Theo since she'd gotten back to New York two months earlier.

Sixteen years ago her brother had disappeared, ostensibly a suicide into the Hudson, his body never found. A verdict she'd never accepted, no matter what the coroner said.

And then fifteen years later, while she'd been living in Paris, she'd gotten the first sign that maybe she'd been right all this time. That Theo hadn't died. That he was alive. She'd scoured Paris trying to find information—any information—as to his whereabouts, and yet had come up with nothing.

So she'd come back to New York to see if she could turn up anything there. And today, just before she'd gotten on that wretched subway, she'd finally found the lead she was looking for.

The high-security storage facility where Theo had stored some of his belongings before his supposed death had gotten in touch with her, informing her that someone had accessed his storage locker. She'd left instructions and a hefty bribe with them years before, when she'd tried to access it herself and been refused, that should anyone come and try to get in, they were to let her know.

And now they had. And there could be only person who'd accessed it.

Theo himself.

At least that was the only person who'd had authorized access according to them. Only the owner of the locker was allowed in, not even family members.

She didn't know what was in that locker or why he'd taken out storage in such a high-security facility—especially when all the rest of his stuff had been stored elsewhere by their mother—but she was sure only she knew about it. And some instinct had told her not to tell anyone else. So she hadn't.

But someone had accessed that locker, and it had to be Theo. Which meant he was alive and she wasn't going to rest until she'd found him. She just had to get away from Mr. Elijah Hunt first.

"You'll find out," Elijah said. "Come on. I haven't got time to piss around arguing with you."

Swallowing, Violet pushed down the fear and the grief, and turned around.

Ahead of her was a walled-off part of the echoing apartment with a door in the middle of it. The bathroom space clearly.

She walked over to it and pushed the door open. There was a hallway beyond, painted stark white, and then another door.

"Through there," he ordered.

Obediently she went through the second door into a stainless-steel and white-tiled bathroom. A massive free-standing tub faced one of the huge windows, a glass walled shower area that could have fit in a whole baseball team off to the right of it.

There was a vanity unit near the door, as minimalist and bare as the rest of the space, white porcelain and stainless steel, an unframed mirror hanging above it.

Elijah went past her and reached into a cupboard under the unit, bringing out a big white plastic box. Setting it on top of the vanity, he took the top off and began to pull out what looked like some first-aid stuff, all the while keeping the gun trained on her.

Briefly she debated seeing if she could take him by surprise and try to knock him out somehow, then discarded the idea. She'd probably only get herself hurt. If she was going to get out of this, she'd have to think of another way.

"What are you doing?" Her voice echoed weirdly off the hard surfaces in the room.

He didn't reply, shrugging out of the overcoat he still wore.

Violet swallowed again.

She'd been right about the glimpse of bare skin she'd seen earlier. He wasn't wearing a shirt. Or at least the remains of a dark gray business shirt that had been torn up and used as a bandage were still wrapped around one massively muscled left shoulder. Blood streaked the sharply cut and defined lines of his chest and abdomen, staining the waistband of the business trousers that sat low on his lean hips. The blood also partially obscured the tattoo inked into his skin just above his heart. A rose with a thorny stem, red ink drops of blood mingling with his real blood.

It seemed a strange image for a man so cold. Did it mean anything? Was it for anyone?

What the fuck are you thinking about his tattoo for?

He was now unwinding the remains of the shirt from around his shoulder, revealing the source of the blood. Holy shit. He'd been shot.

The cold bite of fear returned as she glanced from the bloody wound to his face, suddenly becoming aware of what she'd only half taken in before. That his face was bruised. He had the beginnings of a black eye and there was a raw gash in his lip, more bruises along his jaw.

He looked like he'd been in one hell of a fight and hadn't come out the winner.

Your father is dead.

Elijah Hunt was his bodyguard.

Oh fuck. What the hell had happened?

He looked up, his black gaze catching hers. "Come here."

"Why?" The fear was rising in her chest, making her feel sick. "What do you want me to do?"

In one hand he held the pistol, still steadily pointed at her. "As you can see, I have a gunshot wound." He reached for a pair of what looked like forceps with his free hand, then held them up. "And you're going to remove the bullet."

CHAPTER TWO

She felt even sicker. She'd never taken a bullet out of anyone in her entire life and she really didn't want to start now. "But I'm not—"

"I don't care what you're not. Get over here and get this bullet out."

"And if I don't, you'll shoot me?"

The muzzle of the gun didn't waver and neither did the hard certainty in his eyes. "Yes."

"But if you shoot me, you'll have no one to get the bullet out for you."

He lifted his uninjured shoulder. "Then I'll get it out myself."

"So why don't you do that now?"

"Stop fucking arguing with me and get over here."

Yeah. Stop fucking arguing and do what the man says. What the hell is wrong with you?

She didn't know. She wasn't usually this brave—or this stupid, the jury was still out on which. Yet still she held her ground. "Tell me what's going on," she said hoarsely. "Tell me why I'm here and what you want with me."

The look on his face was absolutely expressionless.

She didn't see the movement of his finger. There was only an explosion of sound and something hot whizzing by her ear. Behind her the window cracked, a hole punched clean through it.

He'd shot at her. The bastard had actually shot at her.

"Like I said." His voice was hard and flat. "Get over here, otherwise next time I won't miss."

She wanted to say something snarky, like how apparently not all of the windows in the apartment were bulletproof, but her sense of self-preservation must have finally kicked into gear because she managed to stop herself, moving toward the vanity instead, her knees weak, her heart thumping, her ears still ringing from the gunshot.

Really, she should have been on the floor in a puddle of terrified tears and yet she wasn't. Perhaps knowing Theo was alive had uncovered a determination she never realized she had. Or perhaps it was simply sixteen years of living with the niggling feeling that there was something not right about her brother's death. Something no one else seemed to understand. Not her mother. Not her father. No one.

That there was something not right about her entire family. Something she couldn't quite put her finger on but was there nonetheless.

It was a terrifying, isolating feeling. Pretty much the way she felt right now in fact.

Violet didn't want to get too close to him, especially not while he was holding that gun and especially not with that horrible, emotionless look on his face. As if he felt nothing. As if he was dead inside.

It terrified her. And fascinated her for reasons she couldn't even begin to fathom.

That's really why you don't want to get close.

She carefully pushed that thought away.

"Here." Elijah handed her the forceps. "I don't think the bullet's that deep. Shouldn't be too difficult to get out."

Reluctantly she looked at the hole in his shoulder. It was crusty with congealed blood, a nasty-looking wound. "I-I've never done this before. I don't know what to do."

"Just stick the forceps in the wound, find the bullet, pull it out."

Her jaw tightened. "If it's so easy, why don't you do it?"

"I could if I had to, but the angle's wrong."

She let out a breath. "It'll . . . hurt."

He smiled that empty, cold smile. "Does it look like I give a shit?"

"I just don't want you to shoot me."

The muzzle of the gun remained steady. "Don't ram those things through my chest and I won't have to."

Jesus. "Alrighty then," she muttered under her breath and glanced back down at the wound.

Her hands shook slightly as she lifted the forceps, biting her lip as she pushed the metal tips inside the torn flesh. He didn't move. He didn't even flinch.

She glanced up, unable to help herself, meeting his gaze.

There was no sign of pain on his face, no anguish twisting his features. His expression was blank, like a robot's. Except . . . deep in his eyes something blazed. A fierce, ebony flame. Dense as a black hole, sucking in light and heat, and crushing them flat.

Rage. It was rage.

An icy wave of shock swept over her and she looked hurriedly away, trying to still her shaking hands. The ever-present fear twisted in her gut, tightened a noose around her throat.

This man wasn't just dangerous. He was lethal. And she was his prisoner.

No, don't think about it. Pretend. That's what you're best at.

Yeah, that was what she had to do. Pretend the way she

always pretended with just about everyone she knew. That she was this rebellious, live-in-the-moment hippie chick. The one who made her mother so furious and yet had no effect at all on her father.

The girl who didn't care what was happening as long as it felt good and she was having fun. A girl at ease with herself and her sexuality, who went wherever the wind took her.

A girl she wasn't and never had been.

"That's got to hurt," she said as she probed the wound, feeling around for the bullet, her bracelets chiming with the movement.

"It's sweet that you care, princess." His voice was steady, betraying nothing, and the gun in his hand didn't waver.

" 'Princess,' " she echoed. "I thought you were only supposed to call me Miss Fitzgerald." At least, that's what he'd always called her as her father's bodyguard.

"Not anymore."

She resisted the urge to look at him, not wanting to glance into that terrifying, fathomless black gaze again. "I'd prefer you called me—"

"Stop talking."

Violet shut her mouth with a snap. Her palms were sweaty, her fingers trembling, and she couldn't seem to slow the frightened beat of her heart.

Blood slid slowly down over his dark olive skin that looked like the legacy of some Mediterranean ancestor, obscuring the strange rose tattoo. This close she could smell the heavy, metallic scent of blood, and something else. A darker, earthier scent, like a forest covered in snow.

He didn't speak, his breathing slow and even. The gun never wavering.

The silence in the room was so thick it felt like her ears were stopped with cotton balls.

And then just when she thought she was either going to burst into tears with fear or scream from the pressure, she felt the metal tips of the forceps close around something hard. Muttering a prayer in her head, she tugged and slowly drew the bullet out.

The only sound from Elijah was a short, barely audible intake of breath, and then he was taking the forceps from her suddenly nerveless fingers, dropping them with a clatter into the sink, and reaching for a bottle he'd gotten out earlier.

Putting the gun down, he opened the bottle and poured it directly onto the wound. Then he reached for a thick white pad as more blood began to slide down his chest.

Violet stood back, watching him, trying to still the tremble in her limbs. Now would be the time, of course, to see if she could grab that gun. Or maybe hit him over the head with something.

Yet she made no move. Even with a wound like that he'd probably be light-years faster than she was, not to mention about a thousand times stronger. And she really didn't want to test whether or not he'd actually shoot her.

Better to wait for another opportunity or think of a plan that didn't involve a physical fight.

"Press hard here," Elijah ordered, pointing at the white pad with his chin.

Reluctantly, Violet came back to the vanity and did as she was told, pressing her hands against the pad to stop the bleeding. She didn't really want to touch him; at least there was a whole lot of white wadding between her hand and his bare skin. Yet even so, she could feel the heat of his body burning through into her palm. Didn't seem right for a man who seemed so goddamn cold to be so goddamn hot, and it made her uncomfortable.

She looked down to the vanity instead, where the gun rested.

"Don't even think about it."

"I'm n-not."

"Bullshit."

There was a surgical needle and thread next to some bandages. With a series of brisk economical movements, he bit off a length of thread then threaded the needle. "I should give those hands of yours something to do."

Her fear spiked. "I won't . . . I m-mean, I-I'm not—"

"Sewing," he interrupted flatly. "Sex is the last thing I want from you, princess."

She should have felt relieved, and she did, because God knew it was the last thing she wanted from him too. But there was also a little flash of something else. Something she didn't want to examine closely.

You're fucking crazy.

Yeah, she was. She might have been fascinated with him when he was her father's bodyguard and she was completely safe from him. But all bets were off now.

Shifting her hands on the pad at his shoulder, she said, "I can't sew to save my life."

"Fine." The word was uninflected. "You can stop pressing now."

Lowering her hands, Violet stepped back.

He peeled the pad from his shoulder and seemingly without any pain, began to sew up the wound.

Perhaps this was a good opportunity? While he was distracted?

The gun was too close to him, and she probably couldn't grab it without a fight. But . . . maybe she could hit him in the shoulder, where it hurt. Or push him. Or maybe even slip by him and run back into the lounge area of the apartment.

And then what? You can't get out the door without that code.

No, but her purse was out there, and inside her purse

was her phone. She could call the police, get help somehow. But then she'd have to wait until help arrived and he might very well shoot her in the interim. Not exactly the best plan.

Perhaps it would be better to wait until later, when he was asleep or something. So she could make a call or send a text without him knowing.

"Yeah, I know what you're thinking." The cold, rough sound of his voice was a shock. "You're thinking about how quickly it would take you to run for the phone in your purse."

Violet stared at him. "I wasn't . . . I mean I didn't—"

"You're a fucking hopeless liar too." He didn't look up from his wound, pushing the needle into his skin and drawing the thread through it. "Try it. I'll even time you."

She tensed. "What would you do if I did?"

"Shoot you."

A shiver swept through her. "That's kind of your response to everything, isn't it?"

"Then stop asking me what I'd do if you tried to escape."

She folded her arms, hugging herself. "I could take your gun. Shoot *you* instead."

He didn't even glance in her direction. "Be my guest. If you manage to get it, it's yours."

Of course she wouldn't be able to get it. Though maybe she should try for form's sake.

"I should add," he said casually, pulling the thread through another stitch, "that if you take one step toward this gun, I'll shoot you in the leg and save us both the bother of having to deal with this shit. I haven't got either the time or the patience for it."

Violet's jaw tightened. The fear had begun to dull in its intensity, leaving only a heavy, sick feeling in her gut. She had no doubt he'd do exactly what he said, so unless she wanted a nice gunshot wound to match his, she was going to have to sit tight and wait until he told her what he was going to do with her. If in fact he was going to do anything with her.

"Okay, so what do you want me to do?" She hugged herself tighter. "Just stand around admiring your sewing skills?"

Calmly, he finished the last stitch and knotted the thread, biting off the end. Then he put down the needle and looked at her. "You're not afraid of me." His gaze was blacker than space. "You should be."

She was already pretty white. Now she'd gone the color of new-fallen snow. Her gaze dropped from his, down to the floor, her arms wrapped tightly around herself as if she was cold.

Good. She should be fucking scared. He had no patience with a hostage who was going to give him grief. He had no patience left at all.

His shoulder throbbed, a deep ache settling into the wound, and he was starting to feel dizzy. Physical pain was easy to disregard once you knew how, but it was the shock that could be a killer. He needed to get warm and eat something, get his blood sugar back up again.

Fucking Rutherford shooting him with his own damn gun.

Elijah leaned surreptitiously against the vanity, eyeing the woman standing opposite him.

He had to admit, he was surprised by her responses to him. He didn't know her that well, only what he'd seen of her when she'd been wafting around the family home, all chiming bracelets, silk skirts, and musky perfumes, but he'd always had the impression of a pampered girl indulging in a bit of passive-aggressive rebellion, safe and secure of her own position.

He knew fear. Knew what it did to people. Had seen all the possible responses to it over the years. Some people cried or cowered or threw up. Some people became catatonic. And some people rose to the challenge.

He hadn't expected Violet to be one of those who rose to the challenge. Yet that's exactly what she'd done, getting all sarcastic, pushing him. If he hadn't lost everything he'd worked for these past seven years and been fighting the effects of a gunshot wound, he might have been more impressed.

But he had, and right now it only pissed him off.

She looked up at that moment, the color of her eyes intense in her pale face, the sapphire stud glittering in her nose. "Why should I be afraid of you again?" There was an edge in her voice, and he thought it was desperation. "I mean, you said you weren't going to rape me and if you were going to kill me you would have done so already, right?"

Another challenge. Well, that was one way of fighting fear. Perhaps he had to revise his opinion of her as being passive-aggressive.

He picked up the gun, held it casually in one hand. She was right, he wasn't going to kill her. Killing was a blunt instrument at best and besides, he hadn't gone through all the trouble of kidnapping her only to get rid of her. She'd always been his backup plan and perhaps that might still work. As for rape, well, that was for animals and cowards, and he was neither.

However, he had no problem incapacitating her if she was going to prove a nuisance, though hopefully the mere threat of it would be enough to get her to back off.

"Very astute," he said as he lifted the gun. "Though a nice bullet wound to match mine might have you rethinking that little scenario."

Her gaze dropped to the gun, then came back up to his again. "You'd really do that?"

"What do you think?"

There was fear in her eyes, he could see that much. And yet . . . something else. Something like anger. And why not? If someone had kidnapped him at gunpoint, he'd be pretty pissed about it too.

"I wouldn't if I were you," he warned softly, before she pushed him further. "You wouldn't like it, I guarantee."

For a second, a spark of deep blue flared in her gaze. Then she looked away. "Fine. Whatever. So are you going to tell me what I'm here for then?"

"Eventually." He pushed himself away from the vanity, the ground moving unsteadily under his feet. Gritting his teeth, he took a moment to will it still again then said, "Stay here."

She said nothing as he left the bathroom, going down the hallway and into the bedroom.

There was a chest of drawers in one corner and he pulled one of the top drawers open, finding what he was looking for. Heading back into the bathroom, he was mildly surprised to find her exactly where he'd left her, with her arms wrapped around her middle, a mutinous expression on her face.

"Hands out, princess."

Slowly, she did so and he pushed her bracelets back then snapped the handcuffs he'd found around her wrists.

"Wow, kinky," she said sarcastically. "I didn't know you had it in you."

He didn't bother to respond, gripping her arm, steering her out of the bathroom and back into the main living area of the apartment.

Over by the massive paneled windows was a black leather couch, and he pushed her down onto it. "Wait here."

She muttered something that was probably rude under her breath.

He ignored it, picked up the purse she'd dropped on the ground and rummaged around inside it, finding her phone among a pile of receipts and all sorts of feminine shit. Taking it out, he quickly extracted the SIM card, dropped the phone onto the floor, and stepped on it. Hard.

Glass cracked, electronics scattering everywhere.

"You asshole!" Violet had risen to her feet, staring at the broken piece of technology, fury stamped all over her pale, delicate features. "That was my phone!"

Interesting. Her response was anger rather than fear. Another little fact to file away for future reference.

"Not any more." He pocketed the SIM card for flushing down the toilet later. "I'm going to have a shower and get cleaned up. So sit down, shut up, and if you're very lucky, I might tell you what you're doing here."

She did as she was told, but there were wild, blue sparks in her eyes.

Again, interesting.

He'd witnessed a few altercations that Violet had had with her parents, and her responses had always been of the 'whatever, man' variety. She'd never been as openly furious as she was now.

As if, for a moment, he was seeing a different Violet.

Or maybe what you're seeing is the real *Violet?*

"Asshole," Violet repeated, her expression still furious.

Christ, what did it matter what he was seeing? She was merely his hostage, and he didn't give a shit what kind of person she was as long as she sat down, shut up, and did what she was told.

Elijah ignored her, turning and heading back toward the bathroom.

After he'd gotten rid of the SIM card, it took him a while to get clean, the pain making the shower a lesson in agony as he washed off the blood. Then he had to bind up the wound and get rid of his dirty, bloodstained clothes. It wasn't until he pulled on a clean T-shirt, jeans, and a thick, black hoodie, that the pain began to subside from a shriek to a dull roar and he began to feel moderately human again.

It helped that the plan on how he could use Violet was coming together in his head.

He was still turning the details over, but he thought it might work. In fact, it fucking better since he really had no other options, thanks to Eva goddamn King, a really piss-poor decision, and lack of planning on his part.

He'd never expected Rutherford to not protect her. He'd never expected her to pick up the gun and shoot Fitzgerald herself.

Bitch.

Let it go. You can't change it now and anyway, you have bigger fish to fry.

His anger coiled like a snake, shifting and turning.

Since losing Marie, he'd managed to divest himself of every single emotion. Anything that could hurt, anything that could undermine, he'd gotten rid of. Everything except anger. And that he'd kept sharp and bright, and most of all cold. He'd had to. After all, revenge took its time and hot rage burned itself out soon enough. Cold rage though, that kept going, kept sustaining.

And he was going to need all of it if he wanted to go through with the plan he was forming in his head right now. A plan that was bigger than merely crushing Fitzgerald.

A plan that took it right back to the source.

To Jericho.

Back out in the lounge, he found Violet frantically going through her purse, bits of crap strewn all over the couch. As he approached her, she had her hands in her lap and was bent over them, one hand twisted over, something clutched in her fingers.

It took him a moment to realize she was trying to get the handcuffs open with a hairpin.

He stopped not far from the couch and folded his arms, watching her. There was no way she was going to succeed, but a tiny part of him was vaguely impressed with her tenacity. Especially since it was clear by her movements that she'd never picked a lock in her entire life.

After a moment she stopped what she was doing and looked up. Color crept into her pale cheeks. Then she tossed the hairpin away and leaned back against the couch cushions, her expression changing from steely determination to barely masked boredom.

Ah, that's the Violet he knew.

"It would never have worked," he said flatly. "You don't know what you're doing."

"Yeah, well, that's pretty fucking obvious." Her turquoise gaze met his, then flickered away again. "So what am I supposed to do? Just sit here? Wait until you deign to tell me what you're going to do with me?"

He ignored the questions, studying her instead. She was definitely scared, he could see little flashes of it leaking out from underneath the mask of sarcasm and anger she was desperately trying to hide behind.

Good. He was doing his job properly then.

"Yes. That's pretty much exactly what you're going to do." He turned toward the kitchen area, sectioned off from the rest of the apartment by a big white wall.

"Tell me why I'm here." Again the edge of desperation in her voice. "Tell me about Dad."

"All in good time." He had to get himself something to eat, something that would get rid of this fucking dizziness.

"No," Violet demanded. "Now."

He didn't know what it was in her voice that made him stop and turn around, but he did.

She was sitting bolt upright on the couch, the look on her face blazing. Fear was there, yes, definitely, but a healthy measure of anger too.

Jesus, she had some nerve. Handcuffed and his prisoner, she was sitting there demanding answers like she had a right to them. Like she wasn't merely the spoiled daughter of a man the Mafia would have been proud to call their own. A woman oblivious to the monster who'd given her life.

A poor little rich girl whose life had never been touched by darkness. An innocent.

The volcanic rage inside him flared.

Why should she remain untouched? What made her special? When her father had been the one who'd destroyed Elijah's life. Who'd killed everything that made him human, everything he'd loved.

Why should she be spared anything?

"Your father died a few hours ago," Elijah said coldly. "He was shot in the head."

Violet blinked. "But . . . but, I—"

"You don't understand, do you? You don't know what he was."

"What *who* was?" Her throat moved. "What are you talking about?"

There was no room for mercy in him anywhere. "Your father ran one of New York's biggest crime rings. He had a string of drug dealers, ran underground casinos, and had been making it big in sex trafficking too."

Her eyes went huge and black, her mouth falling open. "What?" she whispered faintly. "No, I don't believe it."

"Think about it, princess. Where do you think he got all his money from?" Elijah smiled. "Why do you think he had someone like me guarding him all the fucking time?"

She was starting to shake her head, all the fight draining from her eyes. "No . . . I don't . . . I mean, I can't . . ."

"Believe it. It's all true. All that happening right under your pretty little nose. Your father was a murderer, princess. A rapist. A master manipulator. He was the devil himself." Elijah paused, watching her face, seeing the shock set in. Once he would have felt regret for hurting her like this, for hurting anyone like this. But regret was something he'd long ago ceased to feel.

"He had plans for you too, did you know that?" Elijah continued. "You were never going to escape. He liked to use anyone and everyone for power, no one was exempt."

She'd fallen silent, gone still, her only movement the rapid rise and fall of her chest as she breathed.

He wouldn't spare her. No one had spared Marie.

"Your father was going to use you, Violet. You were going to be the bargaining chip he used in exchange for more territory, so he could extend his human trafficking networks into Eastern Europe."

She kept shaking her head as if that alone would deny the truth.

Elijah kept talking. "He was going to give you to the biggest crime lord in Europe in return for his so-called 'trading links,' and whether you wanted it or not wouldn't have mattered in the slightest. Everyone was fair game to him and that included his daughter."

She stared at him.

He stared back. If she wanted to know the truth, he'd give it to her. "I was going to kill him, but Eva fucking King took that honor for herself. So instead, I'm going to use you. You're my bait, Violet. Jericho wants you, which makes you the perfect tool to flush him out." He smiled again. "Because since your prick of a father is already dead, I'm going to kill Jericho instead."

* * *

Violet sat on the couch as Elijah disappeared into the kitchen area, the sounds of cupboards being opened and food being prepared drifting out.

She felt frozen. Like she'd been thrown outside into a snowbank naked.

Your father is dead. Your father was a murderer. Your father ran one of the biggest crime rings in New York. . . .

No. No. No. It couldn't be. That wasn't true.

Oh sure. Like you never thought that something about Dad was wrong. That he was hiding something, concealing something. Something you could never put a finger on and were too frightened to want to find out.

She swallowed, staring down at the handcuffs around her wrists, glittering among the silver already there.

It was too much, too big to get her head around.

Grief thickened in her throat, because whatever else was true about what Elijah had said—if indeed any of it was true—her father had still been her father. Sure, he'd been kind of distant and closed off, never physical in the slightest, but he'd gone to all her school plays. Encouraged her with her homework. Supported her academic achievements, never pushed her to do more the way her precise and very particular mother had.

It wasn't until she'd been around twelve, about a year after they'd lost Theo, that she'd realized there was something about her dad that disturbed her. He'd get a cold look in his eye. A look that made her feel as if another man was looking out from behind those blue eyes she knew so well.

It had frightened her. But she'd thought it was grief and so had pretended not to see it.

Apparently she'd been wrong. Perhaps it hadn't been grief at all. Perhaps it had been there all along.

Nausea churned in her gut. She stumbled to her feet and

headed for the bathroom, shouldering through the door and staggering over to the toilet. Then she dropped to her knees on the white tiles and retched into the bowl as her stomach heaved.

Afterward she sagged to the side, closing her eyes and leaning her head against the tiled wall, shudders shaking her.

Maybe it wasn't true. Maybe Elijah had lied to her about everything. But then those marks on his face . . . He hadn't gotten those for the fun of it, that was for sure. And why would he lie anyway? He had nothing to gain from it, surely?

Tears slipped down her cheeks and she let them fall for a minute or two, needing to get rid of the heavy stone of grief and pain in some way.

Better to concentrate on one thing at a time, such as the loss of a father.

Anything else would have to wait.

She didn't know how long she sat there, but all of a sudden, strong fingers wound around her arm and she was being hauled ignominiously to her feet.

"Save your tears." Elijah's cold, rough voice in her ear. "He wasn't worth any of them."

Violet didn't say anything. She didn't want to talk to him right now. Didn't want to hear that voice of his hurling icy truths at her. Truths that hit her far harder than any bullet.

Really, it would have hurt less if he'd just shot her in the leg like he'd said.

"Yes," he said as he flushed the toilet and dragged her back out to the lounge area. "That would probably have been a lot less painful for all concerned."

Oh shit. She must have said it aloud.

He sat her once more on the couch, in among the detritus she'd pulled out from her purse, and she didn't have any energy to fight him. "Why didn't you then?" she only said. "I think I would have preferred it."

"The truth would have come out one way or another." He stepped back, giving her a cold look. "Anyway, why should I spare you? You've been successfully looking the other way for years now, just like your mother. You deserve the truth shoved in your face."

Behind the grief, guilt waited. Because hadn't she known? Hadn't she realized deep down that things weren't quite right?

"It's not my fault," she said tonelessly. "I didn't know what he was."

"Purposefully."

Of course it was purposefully. You didn't want to know.

She looked away. "He was my father."

"He was also a murderer."

A little flash of anger went through her at the sheer implacability in his tone. Turning back, she looked up at him, standing there all dressed in black, expressionless as a brick wall. "What the hell do you care? You worked for him. Didn't you know? And come to think of it, how do I know you're telling the truth about any of this in the first place?"

"Of course I knew." His gaze didn't waver from hers. "And you should believe me because I was his right-hand man."

CHAPTER THREE

She hadn't expected that, though why she had no idea, since if anyone looked like a criminal it was this cold, pitiless man. Yet she couldn't deny the shock that spread through her, already joining the acid still sitting in the pit of her stomach.

God, if she didn't get herself together, she was going to need to throw up again.

"Okay then," she said shakily. "So you're a monster just like Dad."

His scarred, bruised mouth turned up in another of those terrifying smiles. "We're all monsters deep down, princess. Even you."

Something lurched inside her at that, but she ignored it. "I thought you were just his bodyguard."

"I was his bodyguard, but I also did other things."

"I don't want to know."

"Don't worry. I'm not going to tell you."

"And yet you had no problem telling me that Dad was a—"

"That's because it concerned you. Whatever else I did, doesn't."

Her stomach twisted. "So, why haven't you killed me? What do you want with me?"

His fathomless black gaze was utterly unreadable. "I already told you why. Because I want to use you. And you're no good to me dead."

"But apparently incapacitated is fine."

"Yes."

Her stomach twisted in another knot. "Oh, Jesus, I'm going to be sick."

"No, you're not." He moved over to the low table beside the couch and picked up the glass of water sitting on it. Then he handed it to her, along with a small white pill. "Here, take this."

"What? You're going to drug me too?"

"Fine. Throw up if you want. But you'll be cleaning it up."

Bastard. Bastard. Bastard.

Violet grabbed the pill and put it in her mouth, then took the glass and a hefty swallow of water. Maybe, if she was lucky, it would be Valium. God knew, she could use one right about now.

"What was that?" She handed back the empty water glass to him, her mouth tasting marginally less vile.

"An antinausea pill."

"Great, so you're looking after me now?" A weird kind of euphoria had started to move through her and since the pill clearly hadn't been Valium, it must mean she was in shock. Or something. Whatever, the fear and nausea had started to drop away as if knowing the worst, she had nothing left to be afraid of. Except for a gunshot wound of course.

"You're an investment and I have to protect it." He gave her a once-over that was the very definition of impersonal. "Are you hungry?"

"No." Not a lie. The thought of food made her feel sick again, especially if he'd made it for her.

"Fine. I have to take care of a couple of things. I've left you some food on the counter in the kitchen. And for future reference, there's nothing sharp in there you can use as a weapon. But good luck if you want to use the frying pan."

He turned and started heading in the direction of the front door.

So he was leaving? Well, excellent. She wanted him to be gone. Maybe once he was, she could start trying to figure out how to escape, or at least how to contact someone who could help her.

"How long are you going to be?"

"I don't know. But don't worry, you'll be quite safe here."

"But not safe from you."

He stopped, as massive as a modern gladiator, the black cotton of his hoodie stretching over his wide shoulders, and turned his head, tar-black eyes sweeping over her. "Princess, no one is safe from me."

A shiver of fear broke through the weird euphoria.

Yeah, that she could believe.

The apartment door clicked shut five minutes later, leaving her mercifully alone; and for a long moment she just sat there as the pill he'd given her calmed her roiling stomach.

Then, once she was feeling a little better, she got to her feet to have a bit of a look around.

The apartment was huge, a great echoing space that seemed to occupy the whole top floor of the building. The kitchen was in one corner, an industrial, bare-looking affair that had the basic amenities but not much more, while the lounge where she'd sat occupied the whole right side of the apartment. Because the space was so massive, with a soaring ceiling, it made all the furniture seem far too small for the room, as if they too were cowering.

A couch, a low coffee table, and, most weirdly of all, a lonely thick, colorful rag-rolled rug. It looked like a setting from another room that had been plonked into the space without regard for the surroundings. A little island in the sea of the vast wood floor.

On the opposite side of the apartment was nothing but more bare floorboards and open space. A punching bag hung from a beam, a treadmill and stationary bike not far from it. Another little island of purpose.

There wasn't anything else of much interest or use, apart from a few bookshelves filled haphazardly with a strange collection of books. Classics and thrillers, sci-fi and romance, with a few cozy mysteries thrown in for good measure. She could see Elijah reading the thrillers, but he didn't strike her as an intellectual kind of guy for the classics. And there was no way he'd be reading the romances.

It was weird.

There wasn't anything personal hanging around either, apart from the books. No photos or pictures, no knick-knacks. Not even a potted plant.

Frustrated, she wandered over to the doorway that led to the bathroom and went down the little hall. After a quick search of the bathroom failed to turn up anything useful, she continued on down to the end of the hallway to where it opened up into a huge bedroom.

It was as bare as the rest of the apartment.

A massive bed was pushed into a corner up against a window, and it clearly hadn't been slept in. There were no creases in the crisp black sheets; they looked like they'd just been ironed.

Against the opposite wall stood a chest of drawers, but a cursory rifle through them turned up nothing but practical, plain male clothing.

Violet cursed as she slammed the drawer back.

Why couldn't there have been a handy gun just lying around? It didn't matter that she didn't know how to fire one, at least it would have given her an option.

Slowly, she walked over to the windows and looked out.

The cold, steel blue of the river flowed, snow falling in fat, white flakes. People moved on the sidewalks and traffic drove along the streets, the world going on as if nothing had happened. As if she wasn't the prisoner of some scary dude who'd kidnapped her at gunpoint and was going to use her as bait.

Your father is dead. Your father was a monster.

She leaned her head against the cold glass, the handcuffs heavy around her wrists.

Her eyes prickled with tears.

She'd known there was something wrong with him. Deep down, she'd known. But she'd ignored what her gut was trying to tell her because she hadn't wanted to face it. Her suspicions about Theo's death already haunted her; she didn't want to have suspicions about her father as well, not after she'd lost her brother, the one person in her life she could count on.

In fact, since Theo had disappeared—she'd always refused to believe he was dead—she'd had no one except Honor, her best friend since high school. She hadn't talked to Honor about Theo before, but the moment that lead had come through, she'd wanted to go straight to her friend and lay it all out for her. Because if she was going to track Theo down, she was going to need help. Perhaps Honor might even get Gabriel Woolf, her boyfriend, to help too..

She went still all of a sudden as she remembered something.

Hadn't she texted Honor? Yeah, she *had.* She hadn't gotten a return text, but hers at least had gone through. Which meant that Honor knew Violet wanted to talk to her and might be trying to contact her.

How long would it take for her to realize Violet wasn't answering her texts? How long before she realized she was missing?

Another thought struck her.

If her father was dead, then all hell would have broken loose.

Someone would be trying to get hold of her. Someone would be trying to find her.

Who? Your mother? Like she gives a shit . . .

Violet pushed the thought away. No, someone would. Honor would.

She swallowed, the small knot of fear beginning to loosen a little bit. It would probably take a day or two for Honor to realize she was actually missing, but then the hunt would be on. Of course actually finding her would be another story.

A wave of sudden exhaustion swept through her.

She'd been kidnapped at gunpoint, locked into an apartment, shot at, forced to take a bullet out of someone's shoulder, and she had thrown up. She was officially sick of being scared. Sick of being angry. Sick of the grief and the guilt that waited for her if she thought too much about it.

A person could only take so much before they just shut down.

She turned from the window, looked at the bed with its perfect black sheets and black velvet quilt. Seemed ridiculously sumptuous for a man like Elijah. A monster of a man.

She couldn't imagine him sleeping in it. But she could imagine herself sleeping in it just fine.

Violet took a couple of steps and sat down on the edge of the bed, sinking down into the softness of the quilt.

Screw him. She was going to sleep in his goddamn bed like Goldilocks. She'd gotten to the beyond-fear stage and was now approaching exhaustion. Besides, it wasn't like she could do anything else with those handcuffs on her wrists.

If he didn't like it, that was too fucking bad.

* * *

Elijah adjusted his hoodie further to shield his face, the snow swirling around him. No point scaring civilians with the marks of his fight with Rutherford still all over him.

He'd taken the subway a few stops then gotten out, walked into the first store he'd come across, and bought himself a cheap burner phone.

Now, as he walked back toward the subway station, he punched in the numbers he'd memorized six months back and lifted the phone to his ear. It was ringing, always a good sign. In fact it rang for a good long time before someone answered, a man's rough voice answering in French.

"It's Hunt," Elijah said in the same language. "Tell Jericho that Fitzgerald is dead and I have what he wants." He didn't bother waiting for a reply, hitting the disconnect button and sticking the phone in the pocket of his jeans.

Now all he needed to do was wait. Jericho would come to him, of that he had no doubt. The prick wanted Violet quite badly according to Fitzgerald, who'd been playing a dangerous game with the other man for months now. Using his daughter to try and get concessions and new "trade links" to bolster his growing empire.

Not anymore. All Elijah wanted to do was kill the bastard. If he couldn't have Fitzgerald, he'd have the man behind that particular throne—and this time nothing would go wrong.

He'd use Violet as bait to lure Jericho to New York, then he'd put a bullet in him. Simple.

Of course, it probably wouldn't prove to be simple since Jericho was Europe's biggest crime boss and no doubt protected by a small army. Elijah had never actually seen the guy, but Fitzgerald apparently had had meetings with him. No one knew anything about him—hell, Jericho was in all likelihood not even his real name—but that didn't matter.

The guy would come for Violet.

What if he doesn't? What if she's not as important to him as you thought?

Then he'd have to rethink his strategy, find something else to use. But that was a bridge he hadn't had to cross yet so no point thinking about it now.

Sirens blared, a cop car roaring past.

Elijah pushed his hands into his pockets.

It would be only a matter of time before someone found Fitzgerald's body and news of his death hit the media. Then the shit would really hit the fan. Violet's disappearance would be noted and they'd be out in force looking for her, which meant he was going to have to lay low for a while, at least until he'd heard from Jericho.

He returned to the apartment by a circuitous route just in case anyone was tailing him, and by the time he'd gotten inside, his wound was aching and he was cold again. Pausing at the door, he jacked the heat up a couple of notches, then gave the room a quick scan to see where his captive had gotten to.

She wasn't there.

Elijah gave the room a more thorough search. The food he'd left for her in the kitchen was untouched and the main living area was empty. Still, there weren't many places she could have gotten to. She couldn't have gotten out, not unless she had the skills to disarm his security system and, since that was top of the line, he was pretty sure she didn't.

Which meant she was either in the bathroom or in the bedroom.

He went down the hallway and glanced into the bathroom. Empty. Continuing down the hall, he came into the bedroom. And sure enough, lying curled up on his bed fast asleep was Violet.

A strange sensation turned over in his gut, though what it was he didn't quite know.

This apartment was full of the furniture from his old life, the life he'd had with Marie. Bits and pieces he hadn't been able to bring himself to get rid of. The rag-rug she'd bought for their first place together. The couch she'd given him as a surprise gift after he'd spent a good hour admiring it in the store. Their bed and the black velvet quilt she'd adored. The one he used to make love to her on . . .

The sensation clenched tight.

Fuck, what the hell was that? It had been years since the memories had forced any kind of emotion from him and he'd made damn sure it stayed that way.

Frowning, he walked slowly over to the bed, gazing down at the woman on it.

She looked very small curled up in the center of the black quilt, wrapped in her blue coat. Her face was relaxed in sleep, the delicate lines of it finely drawn. The sapphire stud in her nose glittered. Her hands were pillowed beneath her head, the metal of the handcuffs and all those silver bracelets pressing against one cheek. She looked like a doll, a hippie Barbie with her blonde dreadlocks all over the black velvet, her bracelets and nose stud. A very young doll.

She was also very pretty, so what the hell was she doing in that getup? What the hell kind of point was she trying to prove? And she was trying to prove a point, of that he had no doubt. He'd always gotten the impression that the face Violet Fitzgerald showed to the world wasn't her real one—and he should know, he'd hadn't shown the world his real face for years.

Perhaps she didn't know that if you wore a mask long enough it became part of you.

Violet shifted in her sleep, and he noticed the tear tracks under her eyes where her eyeliner had run, leaving black streaks on her cheeks.

The weird feeling inside him lurched. Shit, that was

starting to irritate him. And anyway, what the fuck was she doing on this bed? He hadn't had another woman in it since Marie, and he never would. Violet needed to get the fuck off it.

He was just about to shake her awake when her eyes opened and she looked straight at him.

And for a moment, all he could see was deep blue green, his stomach dropping away.

Then she said dully. "Oh. I thought I'd dreamed you."

The simmering irritation morphed into anger for reasons he couldn't quite identify and he had to concentrate to force it down. "Unfortunately, you didn't. Now get the fuck off the bed. If you want to sleep, there's a perfectly good couch in the living room."

She ignored him, closing her eyes again and nestling against the black velvet. "No thanks. I'm quite happy here."

His anger spiked. This wasn't her bed. It was Marie's. And she was fucking trespassing.

Reaching down, Elijah grabbed her upper arm and hauled her bodily off the bed.

Violet cursed. "What the hell are you doing?" She'd lifted her handcuffed hands in an instinctive attempt to grab at something to stop herself from falling, and had gotten a fistful of his T-shirt. The cotton pulled against the wound on his shoulder and he swore, grabbing her by her upper arms to keep her from tearing the material and to keep her hands away from the wound.

Her skin felt soft and very warm, and he was suddenly excruciatingly aware of her fingers gripping his shirt.

She was looking furiously up at him, little blue sparks in her eyes. "What the hell was that for?"

A shock of heat arrowed through him. A heat he hadn't felt for seven years.

Fuck.

Elijah released her, tore her clinging hands from his

shirt, and took a couple of steps back, his heart beating strangely fast. Christ, what had gotten into him?

"If I catch you on that bed again," he said roughly, "I'll put a bullet through you."

She frowned, brushing her dreadlocks away from her face. "Okay, okay. What's the big deal? It's just a bed."

"None of your fucking business." He gritted his teeth, forcing away the feelings that should never have been there in the first place. "Get into the living area. You need to eat something."

The crease between her fair eyebrows deepened. "But I—"

"Do as you're told. I'm not in the mood to be screwed with."

Slowly, she lowered her hands from her hair, bracelets chiming against the handcuffs as they slid down her wrist. Her gaze narrowed. "Why? Where did you go?"

Did she not see his don't-fuck-with-me look? "Again, none of your fucking business."

"Yeah? Well, I guess I don't have to eat."

"Suit yourself."

Her mouth tightened. "I thought you wanted me alive."

"Somehow, princess, I can't see you starving yourself to death."

Something steely entered her eyes. "You don't know a thing about me, *Eli*."

Eli. She'd always called him that the few times she'd addressed him directly, probably in an attempt to piss her mother off, who always insisted on the right form of address for people. Maybe she said it to annoy him too, because if there was one thing he'd seen of Violet, it was that she liked poking at people, liked getting a reaction.

The only person she never poked at though, was her father.

Maybe because some part of her knew who he was?

Well, whatever the hell the reason was, it didn't make him like her any better and he didn't give two fucks what she called him. Elijah wasn't his real name anyway.

"All I need to know is that you're my goddamn prisoner and that you'd better do what I tell you."

She looked him up and down, the delicate curve of her upper lip curling. "Or what? You'll shoot me? Go ahead, I could use something to relieve the boredom."

Did she really have no idea what he was capable of? There was a reason he'd been Fitzgerald's right-hand man for five years and it wasn't because he was good with people.

It was because he'd single-mindedly descended into the darkness right along with his boss.

Because the best way to get to know your prey was to become it.

Elijah put his hands in his pockets, held her furious gaze. Since she knew he wanted her alive, he was going to have to give her something else to be afraid of to keep her biddable. "Did you know I have a basement downstairs?" he said softly. "It's dark, but then you won't need any light because you won't need to see anything."

She paled a little. "I'm not afraid of the dark."

Bravado. He could see the small flash of fear that sparked in her eyes. "I'll keep you down there, Violet. And I'll lock the door." He kept his voice flat and uninflected. "If you don't want to eat, I'm sure you won't mind a couple of days without food."

Her gaze flickered, all the remaining color in her cheeks draining away. Then that steely determination flashed. "Someone's going to come for me," she said suddenly, fiercely. "They'll know you took me. They'll find you."

He gave a short, mirthless laugh. "And how are they going to do that? No one knows this place even exists. I know how to cover my tracks, believe me." He let her see the darkness inside him, gave her a little taste of the fear she should be feeling. "And anyway, who's going to come for you?"

Finally, a look of genuine fear crossed her face. "My mother. She'll—"

With the instinct of a hunter who knew he'd dealt a killing blow, Elijah took a slow step toward her. "Your mother?" he echoed. "Because she cares so much about you? No, princess. No one is coming for you. And that's what you're really afraid of, isn't it?

She backed away from him, her face white, the dark circles beneath her eyes stark against her skin. "I have my friend. I have Honor. She'll know I'm missing soon enough. She cares."

He knew about Honor. Knew the dangerous man she was with too. But neither Honor nor Gabriel Woolf was a threat because they wouldn't find him. No one would.

"But how long will it take before she knows you're missing? Perhaps she's too busy with other things. Perhaps she'll think you've left the country." He kept walking toward her, backing her up until she was against the exposed brick of the bedroom wall. "Perhaps she's too distracted with her new friends to notice that you're no longer around."

A spark of pain flared in Violet's eyes as she flattened herself against the wall and his hunting instincts sharpened. Yes, this was where she was weak, this was her vulnerability. It was a purely logical observation, that weird sensation in his gut entirely gone now, thank Christ.

"There's only one person coming for you, Violet," he went on, coldly, implacably. "And when he gets here, I'm going to give you to him." Elijah didn't come any closer, but then he didn't need to. He'd proved his point, shown her who was boss. "And then I'm going to kill him."

CHAPTER FOUR

Violet hated him. She honest to God hated him. And if she'd had a gun on hand and the chance of a free shot, she'd have put a bullet through that hard, scarred face of his without a second's hesitation.

Unfortunately she did not have either a gun or a free shot.

What she had was a crap night's sleep spent on the couch in a pair of handcuffs, nightmares about being thrown down a dark hole into a cave of tunnels and being forced to run through them with something horrible chasing her, and a clawing sense of panic sitting in her stomach.

On the coffee table in front of her was the breakfast of eggs and bacon and toast he'd cooked for her, that she'd only picked at since her appetite appeared to have vanished utterly, while Elijah himself sat at the glass-topped dining table not far away, all his attention bent on the laptop he had open on it.

He looked like he'd had a great night's sleep, the prick, the shadows gone from beneath his eyes, the drawn look from his face. Which made her hate him even more.

He'd scared her the day before, no question, and she hated being scared. But then when you were kidnapped at gunpoint and casually told that not only was your father a murdering sex trafficker and drug dealer, but also that he'd been killed, fear was a pretty natural response.

Still didn't mean she liked it.

He'd made her feel helpless as he'd towered over her, talking about shutting her up in the darkness in his basement, his black eyes cold, merciless. He was a psycho, that was all there was to it. And all because she'd dared to have a nap on his stupid. goddamn bed.

Not forgetting the part where he told you no one was coming for you. Remember that?

Violet stared down at the congealing eggs on the plate, any remaining appetite well and truly gone.

Yeah, not forgetting that part, or ignoring the sneaky doubt that threaded through her. The wondering about her mother and what she'd do now that her father was dead. Sure, she and her mother had had their run-ins, it was true. Like her husband, Hilary Fitzgerald wasn't exactly the world's warmest person—she held everyone at a distance, her children included. But still . . . she'd want to make sure her daughter was okay, wouldn't she?

A sudden thought struck Violet. Had her mother known what her father was? Had she known what he did? The secret life he'd had?

Oh God. What if she'd even been involved?

Violet shivered, staring around the apartment, a surge of desperation going through her. Jesus, she *had* to get out of here. Had to get away from Elijah and find out just what the hell was going on with her family. First her brother, then her father. Now her mother might be involved too. It was too much. Way, way too much.

Yeah, sure. Just get up and walk through the front door. That'll work.

She cursed silently and viciously in her head. Okay, so she didn't have a gun and didn't have the physical strength that would enable her to overpower Elijah. But she wasn't stupid. Clearly he wasn't going to hurt her or else he'd have done so already, plus he needed her alive. That gave her a few parameters to work with.

Pity she had no idea what was happening outside the apartment, but since there was no TV and he kept her away from the laptop, that couldn't be helped.

She got up from the couch and paced over to the bookshelf, looking at the books and pretending she was finding one to read.

"Stop." His hard tone came from behind her.

Violet didn't look at him, studying the spines on the books and trying not to shiver again at the rough sound of his voice. "What?"

"Get away from the bookshelf."

She threw a glance at him over her shoulder. He was still sitting at the table, but the black ice of his gaze was settled firmly on her over the top of the laptop screen. And there was no mistaking the anger and hostility radiating from him.

"Why?" It was probably stupid to be so demanding, especially given what he'd threatened her with the day before. But shit, she couldn't even read a book now?

"The books are not yours. Don't touch them."

"What the hell else am I supposed to do then? Just sit around with a pair of handcuffs on?"

The menacing expression on his face didn't soften one iota. "I don't care what you do as long as you sit down on the couch and shut the hell up."

It was annoying in the extreme to have to give in, but she wasn't stupid enough to push him. Not after yesterday.

Stepping back from the bookshelf, she nevertheless made herself hold his gaze. "Can I walk around at least. Is that okay with you?"

One massive shoulder lifted. "Just don't touch anything."

"Why not? You think I'm going to break something? I'm not a child, Elijah."

His scarred mouth twisted. "Of course you're a child, princess. You're a fucking babe in the woods. Now stop whining and don't disturb me again."

"But I didn't—"

"One more word and I'll put you downstairs, I swear."

Violet bit her lip. Hard. *Asshole.*

He looked away, back down at his screen, and she had the impression she'd almost ceased to exist for him.

Oh yeah, she hated him all right. God, she *had* to find a way out of here.

She paced around the coffee table for a bit, then went over to the little island of gym equipment, then back again, turning over ideas in her head one by one before discarding them.

After a while, Elijah pushed the laptop shut with an abrupt movement and rose from the table. He picked up the computer and disappeared down the hallway with it, then five minutes later, he was back again, tucking something into the pocket of his worn jeans.

"I'm going out," he said shortly, putting on the leather biker jacket he held in one hand. "Don't do anything stupid."

Violet stopped in the middle of the room, the heavy slide of the handcuffs on her wrists reminding her for the fifty millionth time she was a prisoner. They were starting to hurt now, not helped by her bracelets, and there were red welts circling her skin.

"Like what?" she said sarcastically. "Accidentally try to escape? Sure, I'll get right on that."

He stared at her. "Remember what I said about the basement."

"You're a fucking psycho."

He didn't even blink. "No, what I am is fucking determined."

"Why? What is it about this Jericho guy?"

"None of your goddamn business. Now . . ." The look he leveled at her froze her to the spot. "Don't touch my books. And stay the fuck away from my bedroom. If I find you've been a bad girl, the next meal you'll be having will be in the basement. In the dark."

Her heart gave a wild burst of fear at that, but she fought it down. Refused to let it show on her face. "Thank you, but I'd rather starve."

"That can be arranged." Without another word, he strode to the door and went out, the sound of it closing behind him as final and heavy as that of a bank vault.

Violet turned and began pacing again.

She had to get out and there was only one way that was going to happen: with him. But how to get him to take her? Obviously asking him wasn't going to work, and she had a feeling pleading and playing the female tears card wouldn't either. He was as hard as obsidian and twice as sharp. He'd probably put her in the basement for even suggesting it.

No, the only way she was going to get him to take her out was an emergency of some kind. Like . . . if she was hurt and needed medical attention.

Violet stopped pacing near the entrance to the kitchen, staring sightlessly into space, trying to ignore the cold clutch of fear.

If she managed to hurt herself badly enough, he'd have to take her to the doctor, even a hospital. And she had no doubts he'd do it since he seemed pretty keen on keeping her alive. The only question was whether she had the guts to do something like that.

But then again, what other choice did she have? She had to make a move and soon, take advantage of the fact people would be looking for her, because no matter what he said, people *had* to be looking for her. They had to.

The only other option was to stay here and wait for the right moment, whenever that was. But then that would risk her being all laid out for Jericho when he decided to come. And who knew what would happen then?

No, she couldn't wait. She needed to make a move and she needed to make it now. With her father dead it was even more important for her to find out what had happened to Theo.

She took a deep, steadying breath.

So. What to do? If she was going to hurt herself, she needed to do it badly enough that Elijah couldn't fix it himself, yet not so badly that she'd die if she didn't get treatment immediately. Tricky.

Turning she went into the kitchen and began looking through the cupboards. There were various different cleaning solutions but downing a bucket of bleach would only end up corroding her insides and she definitely didn't want that, especially not if she wanted to get away from the hospital or medical center quickly.

No, it had to be something like a wound. Painful but if it was stitched up she could still move around.

For a moment she paused, looking down at herself, thinking. Then her gaze went to her reddened wrists. A cut there, yes. If she did it right and timed it correctly, she'd bleed a lot and he'd have to get her to the hospital quickly, but if they stitched her up, she'd probably be okay sooner than if she'd poisoned herself.

What are you? A fucking idiot?

Yes, she probably was. A desperate fucking idiot.

Without letting herself think too deeply about it again, Violet started going through the kitchen drawers. He'd already told her there wasn't anything sharp there, but she searched anyway and sure enough, she turned up nothing.

Undeterred, she started searching the rest of the apartment. If there wasn't a handy knife, she'd find something else to cut herself with. There had to be something, for God's sake. Weren't people always being taken to the hospital for getting injured by seemingly innocuous things? Like tea cozies or chairs or stuff like that?

Yet half an hour later, she still hadn't turned up anything.

Cursing, she went back into the bathroom she'd already searched at least twice, upending the box of medical supplies Elijah had used the day before, and going through them once again. God, she'd even be happy with some nail clippers at this rate.

After pawing awkwardly through a whole lot of bandages and getting a whole lot of nothing, she eventually threw them at the wall in frustration.

A distinctive metallic sound chimed.

She blinked and looked down to see a tiny pair of scissors that must have gotten caught up with the bandages lying next to the shower cubicle.

Her heart thumping, Violet reached down and grabbed them.

Okay, so nail clippers weren't far off. These were nail scissors with small curved blades, and they didn't look sharp enough to do damage to anything. But then again, they were better than nothing.

She straightened, holding them in one hand, trying to figure out how she was going to cut herself while she was handcuffed. It would take some contortions but she thought she'd manage.

Yeah, you'll probably manage to cut your tendons or something. Are you really sure this is a good idea?

No. It was a really stupid idea. But she couldn't keep sitting around waiting to be put in a dark basement or to be handed over like a piece of meat to whoever this Jericho guy was.

"No, princess. No one is coming for you."

The doubt threading through her abruptly pulled tight. That was another thing she didn't want to wait for, the slow, terrible realization that he was right. That no one was going to come. That she was on her own.

Fuck that.

Right, so if she was going to do this, she needed to know when Elijah was going to return. Cutting herself too early could be a very bad thing indeed, yet cutting herself too late would mean nothing but pain, probably a dark basement, and definitely any further chance of escape gone.

She only had one shot at this so she had to get it right.

He'd been gone half an hour already so hopefully he wouldn't be too much longer. Because if she had to wait another half an hour or so, she wasn't going to be able to go through with it. Already the thought of cutting herself with a tiny pair of scissors was making her palms damp and nausea roil in her stomach.

Didn't sometimes people cut their wrists in the bath because warm water numbed the pain? Perhaps she should do that?

Violet turned and went over to the big, white claw-foot marble tub that stood near one of the windows, turning on the faucet.

Then she stood there, breathing deeply and slowly, the way she did when she wanted to annoy her mother with another pretense at meditation. All part of the hippie-chick act that drove Upper East Side Hilary crazy. Funnily enough it worked. After about ten minutes she was feeling better. More determined.

She might be a babe in the woods, but dammit, this babe was not going to let herself be eaten.

When the bath was partly full, she turned off the water and stood there looking down at it for a moment. Then taking one more breath, she stepped into the tub fully clothed.

It was warm, so that helped her relax, but unfortunately it made her palms get even damper, which did *not* help her grip on the scissors. Dammit, when should she do this?

She sat for a second, just listening. But there was no sound from the outside.

Okay, the longer she sat here, the more likely she'd lose her nerve. Which meant if she didn't do it now, she was screwed.

Violet took one last deep breath and gripped the scissors, angling her hands.

Then she brought the blades down hard across her wrist.

Elijah shook out the paper and stared at the newsprint in front of him. It hadn't made the front page, but there it was on page two. Evelyn Fitzgerald, found dead in his home yesterday, the victim of a professional hit.

People on the sidewalk brushed past him but he ignored them as he stared at the paper. It pretty much said the same thing as all the other stuff he'd gleaned from his media search of the web that morning. Two dead bodyguards, signs of a fight in Fitzgerald's private office, plus other evidence apparently pointed to a paid hit carried out by a business competitor.

Fucking Zac Rutherford must have cleaned everything up, including planting evidence.

Which all in all was extremely good since it meant the heat was off him. All he had to worry about was Violet, and with any luck it would be days before they realized she was missing.

How goddamn weird to think he had Rutherford to thank for that.

Satisfied, Elijah bunched up the paper and dumped it in the nearest trash can. As he did so, the burner phone in his pocket vibrated. He pulled it out, glancing down at the screen.

His sense of satisfaction deepened.

It was a text from an unknown number and all it said was *I need proof.*

Excellent. Jericho was interested. Not that Elijah had any doubt. From what Fitzgerald had told him, the man had been unshakable in his desire for Violet, which in turn had made Fitzgerald cocky about the concessions he'd planned to get from the guy.

Elijah didn't want concessions. All he wanted was Jericho personally coming to get Violet, at which point he'd figure out the best way to take the prick out. And he would take him out, that was absolutely certain.

But first, he had to get that proof.

I'll send a photo, he texted back.

There was a slight pause. *You have two hours.*

So Fitzgerald hadn't been wrong. The guy really was desperate.

Not bothering with a response, Elijah put his phone away and headed back toward the apartment. He'd take a couple of pics of Violet then send them on, no drama.

Ten minutes later, he unlocked the apartment door and stepped inside. Violet wasn't in the living area or, after a quick check, in the kitchen.

Jesus, if she'd gone into his damn bedroom again after he'd told her not to . . .

He stepped into the hallway and glanced down toward his bedroom. Then he heard a slight sound coming from the bathroom. Frowning, he pushed open the door and went in.

Violet was sitting in the bathtub fully clothed. A bathtub full of pink water. Her handcuffed wrists were resting on her knees and she was hunched over, a thin stream of blood oozing from a nasty, ragged-looking cut across her left wrist. A pair of tiny nail scissors were lying on the floor.

Holy fuck. What the hell had she done? No, scratch that. It was completely obvious what she'd done. She'd tried to slit her wrists.

A surge of some emotion he couldn't immediately identify went through him, but he ignored it, going instantly into cold, calm crisis mode.

He didn't speak, moving quickly across the bathroom, pausing only to grab a hand towel from the rail. She turned her head, her face almost dead white, her eyes heavy lidded.

"Hey," she said in a thick voice. "Was wondering when you'd get here."

Ignoring her, Elijah took his keys from his pocket and unlocked the cuffs around her wrists, getting rid of all her bracelets as well as the cuffs. There were marks on her skin, prompting another odd surge of that emotion he couldn't quite figure out, but he ignored that too. Wrapping the hand towel around her cut wrist, he pulled it tight. She gave a small groan. Bending, he reached into the lukewarm water of the bath and scooped her out of it. Her clothes were dripping wet, bloody water everywhere, and she was starting to shiver.

With ruthless efficiency and without hesitation, Elijah stripped her of her bloody, wet clothing, then wrapped her in one of the big black bath towels. She didn't protest, just let him do what he wanted, her dreadlocks hanging wetly down her back, her skin so white her face looked like a Kabuki mask.

Leaving her sitting on the side of the tub wrapped in the towel, he hunted for the medical kit and found it lying on the floor, all its contents strewn around. So that's where she'd found the scissors. He'd forgotten they were there. Stupid.

Gathering up the medical kit contents, he packed everything back in the box before going back over to Violet. Then he lifted her into his arms, grabbed the box with one hand, and carried both of them out into the lounge area.

She was warm in his arms, resting against him limply, all the fight gone out of her.

Sitting down on the couch with her in his lap, he put the medical kit down beside him, then carefully grabbed her cut wrist. The blood had clotted nicely, but he could see she'd cut quite a hole in it. No tendon damage from the looks of things and she'd also managed to miss the vein.

Christ, she was lucky.

"Are you going to take me to the hospital?" she asked, slurring a little.

He glanced at her. Her eyes had half closed, turquoise blue framed by pale golden lashes, watching him.

Ah. So that's what she'd been trying to do.

The odd emotion inside him shifted, making his chest tighten. Couldn't be respect, surely. Why the hell would he respect a silly little girl who'd slit her wrists in an effort to get away from him?

She's a fighter, that's why.

"No," he said flatly, dismissing both the thought and the emotion.

Instead he reached for the medical kit and got out some Vicodin. "Here, take these." Pressing a couple of tablets into her good hand, he leaned forward and picked up the glass of water left over from her breakfast.

She took the tablets without a protest and swallowed them down, watching him as he took out the other things he was going to need. A needle and some surgical thread.

"Oh," she said.

He really should wait until the drugs had kicked in, but he didn't like the look of that wound and she couldn't afford to lose any more blood otherwise he really would have to take her to the hospital.

With a series of quick, precise movements, he cleaned the wound, ignoring her gasp of pain. Then he threaded the needle. "This might hurt," he said and gripped her wrist hard.

Violet took an audible breath, but said nothing.

Elijah pushed the needle into her skin. Her wrist tensed, her muscles locking, another soft gasp escaping her. But after that she made no other sound.

It didn't take long to get the wound closed up, Violet silent throughout. Then he bandaged it quickly. She'd started to shiver again and he realized that not only was the towel covering her damp, but his own T-shirt was wet through and she'd been resting against him.

He couldn't have said why he did what he did next, especially since there was no reason at all for it. Physical discomfort had never bothered him that much after all. Yet he pulled his wet and bloody T-shirt off over his head anyway and threw it on the floor. Then he unwrapped her from the towel and reached for the soft, dark blue blanket he'd given her the night before, tucking it firmly around her and covering up all her pale, golden skin.

Then for another seemingly inexplicable reason, he pulled her into his lap again, letting her rest warmly against his bare chest.

Shock must have kicked in, either that or the painkillers were starting to work, since she turned into him and curled up against him like a kitten.

It was the strangest thing. He'd captured her, shot at her, kept her handcuffed nearly a whole day, threatened her with being locked in a dark room with no light and with starvation, and yet here she was, nestling into him like he was her protector or something.

Had to be the drugs. Had to be.

Her lashes were lowered, her gaze on his chest, and she was so fucking warm. It had been a long, long time since he'd just held a woman like this. A long time since he'd held a woman, period. Not since Marie.

That goddamn stupid feeling in his chest shifted again, tightening.

The light from the windows glinted in her golden lashes, in her damp hair. Such a pretty color, more silver gold than deep yellow, a kind of gilt. Her skin was very smooth and still way too pale. But it made her mouth look very full and very red. Like Snow White.

Jesus. Why the fuck are you thinking about Snow White? What the hell is wrong with you?

"I wanted you to take me to the hospital," she said after a moment, her voice all sleepy and thick. "At least, that's what you were supposed to do."

"You really thought that would work?" Christ, his own voice was sounding a bit too rough for his liking. "You're lucky you didn't cut a tendon."

"The nail scissors weren't sharp enough." She wrinkled her nose. "But they were all I could find."

"You're a silly little girl." He tried to make it cold. "You don't know what the hell you're doing."

"I didn't need to know. I just wanted to make it bad enough that you'd have to take me to the hospital."

"And you'd escape from there? Was that the idea?"

"Yep." Her mouth curved. "Really screwed that one up, didn't I?" She sighed, her body all warm and relaxed and heavy on him. "You're hot. It's nice."

Definitely the drugs.

"You're a fool," he said roughly.

"Yeah, I know. But the pain's gone, it's all good." Violet raised her uninjured hand and before he realized what she was going to do, she touched the eagle on his chest, the stupid cliché of a tattoo he'd gotten in the dark weeks after he'd found out about Marie's death.

He went utterly still, shock ricocheting through him.

Her hands were very gentle, her fingers tracing the lines of the eagle's wings up to where it disappeared under the dressings of his gunshot wound, then down to the heart it held in its talons, then the few drops of blood dripping down his right pec. "This is interesting," she murmured. "What does it mean?"

And he found he couldn't speak. Because it had been years, nearly an entire decade, since anyone had touched him like this. So lightly, gently. Sending shivers of . . . *fuck* . . . was that heat chasing over his skin?

Every muscle locked, his body going tight.

No. Hell no. Where had this reaction come from? He'd stripped himself of every physical need, every soft emotion. The only things he had to have were food and drink and ice-cold anger. That was all that sustained him, that was all he needed until the day came to claim his revenge.

After that he didn't give a shit what happened to him. He didn't give a shit about anything.

And yet now, suddenly, Violet fucking Fitzgerald was running soft fingers over his tattoo and although he knew he should brush her hand away, shove her off his lap, he couldn't seem to move.

"It doesn't mean anything," he heard himself lie. "I got it years ago."

"Hmmm." Her fingers smoothed over him. "You've never really liked me, have you? Why not? What did I ever do to you?"

He blinked, the question unexpected and taking him completely off guard. Just like everything else about this situation.

Why was he sitting here, letting her touch him? He should move, he really should.

Yet he didn't. He just sat there, holding her wrapped up in the blanket as she ran her fingers idly over his chest. Those pretty gilt lashes of hers had fallen closed and somehow she'd nestled herself even closer to him. "Answer the question," she said sleepily, dragging her nails lightly over him.

Sensation caught him by the throat, an electric shock of it. Like her nails had caught an exposed nerve.

He hadn't wanted a woman for years. At first grief had done its work nicely and he'd had a good two years of not even seeing women as sexual creatures. But then his libido had started firing up, grief or not, and he'd had to take himself in hand both literally and figuratively. Even the shit he'd seen working for Fitzgerald, the trafficking shit he'd had to involve himself in, hadn't managed to cool his stubborn libido. Not that he'd availed himself of any of the women on offer. He didn't want to be with anyone other than Marie. Not ever. All he wanted was to take his revenge and then let whatever happened to him afterward happen. Live, die, he didn't much care which.

Over time, he'd gained a reputation for being ice cold, a reputation he cultivated since it suited him. Plenty of Fitzgerald's associates had tried to bribe him with women or money or drugs, but none of that ever worked with him. He'd stripped himself of everything for precisely that reason. Because if you didn't want something, no one could use it against you.

That was what Fitzgerald had found so valuable about Elijah. He was incorruptible. Loyal. And he was ruthless.

He'd descended into the pit with Fitzgerald and made himself into a monster.

He was okay with that.

But what he was *not* okay with was being touched as if he were . . . some kind of fucking animal. Petted like a cat or a dog. As if he were harmless. And there was no way in this fucking world that he was harmless—there were plenty of people now dead who could attest to that.

Yet still Violet Fitzgerald snuggled herself up against him as if he were safe, as if she trusted him. Touching him like she had the perfect right to do so, as if he was hers.

Like Marie did.

His throat had gone dry and that tight, shifting thing in his chest wouldn't budge; that she was high as a kite on Vicodin made not the slightest bit of difference.

He found himself looking down at her, studying her face the way he had the day before, when she was curled up asleep on his bed. She'd made him feel strange then too, and he hadn't been able to work it out. Because what was she to him? A stupid little innocent who hadn't even realized a monster had fathered her. He'd spent years protecting her and that cold bitch of a mother, and he'd never found her particularly interesting. Just your typical rich girl, spoiled and entitled and doing her teenage rebel thing about ten years too late, wafting around and relying on Daddy's dirty money to do exactly what she pleased.

Yet hadn't he thought only yesterday that probably wasn't her? Certainly the woman he'd captured hadn't turned into the crying, desperate mess he'd expected.

She'd been prepared to slit her wrists in order to escape, and he didn't know whether that made her stupid or whether that made her brave.

The blue sapphire in her nose glittered, the finely drawn lines of her face relaxed. Her lashes had fanned out across her cheeks and finally there was a bit of color in them. Her fingers had stopped stroking him, thank fuck, and now they were just resting there.

She looked like she'd fallen asleep.

And he realized something.

One edge of the blue blanket had fallen away, revealing the pale curve of one breast and the soft shell pink of her nipple.

His breath locked and he stared, transfixed.

He'd seen plenty of naked female breasts in the course of his employ with Fitzgerald. On strippers and hookers and the poor trafficked women Fitzgerald used like currency. They had never moved him, never made him want. Pretty easy when they were attached to women who were desperate with fear or desperate for drugs, or money, or any one of a thousand things that Fitzgerald could give them.

But this was different. Violet wasn't desperate or afraid—at least not right now. She was relaxed and warm in his arms, her fingers lying still on his skin. And he could feel the heat radiating out from them, curling through him in a way a woman's touch had never done so before, not since his wife's death.

The curve of her breast was perfect, the pink of her nipple so delicate.

He couldn't look away. And he found himself breathing out, gently, a soft stream of air over her skin, watching as her nipple hardened in response.

A surge of intense heat went through him, something rough and primitive grabbing him by the throat.

He shifted his hold on her, the blanket falling away further, revealing more of her breast. It was beautifully shaped, small and high, her nipple now flushed a deeper pink.

She sighed, arching a little in his arms, sensual as a cat.

Let her go. Move the fuck away from her.

Yet he couldn't seem to do it. He could feel the softness of her ass and thighs across his lap, the weight of her pressing down against his groin. Jesus Christ, he was actually getting hard.

When was the last time he'd gotten a hard-on in response to a woman? Not since Marie. For the last seven years he'd gotten erections in his sleep in response to dreams, and that had been fine. His hand had been the only release he'd needed.

But fuck, this was a flesh-and-blood woman. His little insurance policy. His bait. Evelyn Fitzgerald's goddamn daughter and he was getting hard for her, which was wrong on just about every level there was.

Still he didn't move. His hand came up as if of its own accord, his fingers lightly tracing that tantalizing curve. She felt so fucking soft, so fucking warm, his heart just about stopped. A line of goose bumps rose over her skin as she gave another sigh. Lifting her arm, she put it over her head, half turning on his lap as if seeking the touch of his hand.

Holy Christ.

Let her the fuck go. This is wrong and you know it.

It was and yet he found himself reaching out to touch her all the same. How long had it been since he'd felt something this soft? This smooth? How long had it been since he'd touched something purely because he liked the sensation against his fingers?

He traced the curve of her breast again and her skin felt like silk, like satin. Expensive, luxurious. Her nipple had gone even harder and he couldn't resist circling it with his thumb.

Violet made a soft sound in her throat and her back arched like a cat's.

He dragged his thumb lightly over her nipple and the little peak hardened further beneath his touch. So he did it again. And again. Dragging his thumb back and forth in a slow, easy motion.

Her skin flushed and he watched, mesmerized, as the flush crept down her neck and over that beautiful breast, and he wanted to fling back the blanket, watch it spread all over her body.

She made another one of those sounds, a sigh of pleasure, of approval. As if she liked what he was doing to her. And her hips shifted, her butt pressing harder against his rapidly stiffening cock.

Hunger pulsed through him, a dark, desperate kind of hunger. Unfamiliar. Wrong. And he found himself panting like a dog.

Jesus Christ. He had to stop this. Now. Get himself under control, make himself cold. Remember who he was supposed to be.

Without any ceremony at all, Elijah shoved her out of his lap, heading straight for the bathroom.

He didn't look back.

He needed a cold shower and he needed it now.

CHAPTER FIVE

Violet came to consciousness slowly, aware of a crashing sound coming from somewhere. Cautiously she opened her eyes. The living room area was empty; the sounds were coming from the kitchen area.

Her wrist ached and she felt dry-mouthed, like she had a hangover.

She was also distressingly naked.

Shit. What had happened? How long had she been out?

Moving slowly, she sat up, a wave of dizziness making her shut her eyes for a second. When it had passed, she opened her eyes again then reached for the glass of water on the coffee table in front of her and took a couple of swallows.

It made her feel marginally better.

Sitting back on the couch, she clutched the blue blanket around herself and extended her left wrist. There was a white bandage around it.

She pulled a face, wincing slightly at the ache.

Okay, so she'd screwed up majorly. The scissors had been too blunt to cut cleanly, the blood making her fingers slippery and unable to get a good grip, so she'd ended up dropping them on the floor. Then the pain had nearly knocked her out. She didn't remember how long she'd sat in that bath, slowly bleeding. She only knew she hadn't wanted to get out and grab the scissors to try and cut her other wrist.

She'd tried to force herself to finish the job despite her own reluctance, only to find that she hadn't moved, that she was still sitting there in rapidly cooling water, pain beating in her head like a drum.

Then the door had suddenly crashed open and Elijah had been there.

She'd never thought she'd be actually glad to see him, but right in that moment she had been. She wasn't even conscious of how badly she'd failed, only that now that he was here, everything would be okay.

He'd been so utterly expressionless, so utterly cold, and yet when he'd scooped her up out of the water and stripped off her wet, bloody clothes, his hands had been very gentle. And when he'd wrapped her in a towel and taken her out into the lounge, all she'd wanted to do was lie against the warmth of his big, muscular body and just rest.

Her mind had been hazy with shock and pain, and yeah, the stitches had hurt like a bitch. But the matter-of-fact way he'd cleaned up the mess she'd made of her wrist then stitched it up, had been oddly reassuring. The drugs had helped too.

Violet swallowed, more hazy memories crowding her brain. Of the heat of his body beneath her. The hard, muscular wall of his chest. His skin, smooth as oiled silk under her fingers. The lines of a tattoo. And a half-waking dream of him returning the favor, the gentle movement of his thumb on her breast . . . then his hands shoving her unceremoniously away.

A prickling wave of heat rushed over her skin, her nipples hardening right on cue.

Shit. That had definitely *not* been a dream.

She took a shaky breath, wrapping the blanket more tightly around her.

Had she really let him do that? Let him touch her? And why? What on earth had possessed her?

She could still feel the texture of his skin beneath her fingers, the flex and release of his muscles as she'd touched him. She'd asked him some questions—she didn't remember what they were—yet he hadn't answered. Only sat there and held her as his warmth seeped into her shaking body, making her relax and fly a little with the effects of the Vicodin.

And then he'd touched her. So gentle. And it had felt . . . so good. Oh, God, so very good.

Jesus Christ, she must be crazy. The last thing she needed right now was an inappropriate response to her captor. Did that make her kind of sick that she'd responded to it? Or was it just Stockholm Syndrome? Maybe it was.

She swallowed, her mouth dry all over again.

Her father had always been very strict when she'd been younger, vetting her boyfriends and making sure she knew that if she slept with anyone before marriage, there would be severe consequences. As she'd gotten older, she'd found his boundaries infuriating, kicking against them whenever she could, but the prohibitions on sex hadn't been one of them.

Because she knew her own hunger. The dark, deep yearning. There was a hole inside her. An emptiness that desperately wanted something to fill it, and it scared her, it always had.

The first time her high school boyfriend had kissed her, she'd felt it. The need to be touched, to be held. The need to feel wanted. It had been so strong, she'd pulled away, terrified that if she gave into it, he'd somehow see how desperate she was. How completely she wanted to lose herself.

She didn't know why she felt that way or why she was so hungry for touch. But she'd used the excuse of her father's wrath to avoid sex long after she was too old for it to be convincing. And after that, she'd cultivated the image of the sexually experienced free spirit, which intimidated some men and put off others. And for those who weren't either intimidated or put off, she acted the part of the clingy girl desperate for commitment, and that soon frightened off the rest.

God. Somehow with the drugs and the shock, she'd forgotten her own rules. She'd let Elijah hold her. Touch her. She'd let herself touch him and it had been . . .

She put her hands over her face, feeling the yearning inside her twist and shift, wanting something she was never going to let it have. Because out of all the men in all the world, Elijah Hunt was the very last one she'd give herself to.

Footsteps sounded, and she quickly dropped her hands. Elijah was coming toward her holding a plate of food, eggs and bacon and toast, and her starved body suddenly started clamoring for sustenance. And not just for the food either.

There was a pulse, right down low inside her, that made her take note of the white cotton of his T-shirt stretching over his muscular chest. And the way the worn pair of dark denim jeans he wore sat low on his hips. He was built like a gladiator, strong and hard all over. As she had good reason to know.

He stopped all of a sudden, and she dragged her gaze from his body up to his face. And met his black eyes, sharp and cold as obsidian. There was nothing warm in those eyes, nothing of the heat she'd felt in his touch. And yet still she could feel herself blush like a fool, a wave of it rushing over her skin, inexorable as the tide.

He must have seen it too because his gaze abruptly became darker, colder. Then he took another few steps over to the coffee table and dumped the plate of food down on it. "Eat," he said curtly. "You lost quite a bit of blood yesterday."

She thought about protesting just for the hell of it, but then that would be asking for trouble. Making sure the blue blanket was tucked firmly around her, she leaned forward and picked up the cutlery. "How long was I asleep?"

"Over twelve hours."

She blinked. "I was out for that long?"

He stared at her, eyes glittering. And it struck her that although his scarred face was completely expressionless, he was actually in a towering rage. It was there in his eyes, an icy black flame leaping high, radiating menace.

For some completely insane reason, a small, electric thrill went through her. Half excitement, half delicious fear.

Oh Jesus. Was she crazy? Sick? Perhaps this whole abstinence thing had been a huge mistake. Perhaps it was now coming back to bite her on the ass. Because attraction to Elijah was the very last thing she should be feeling. Especially after yesterday.

She'd completely screwed up her plan and now not only had she gone through all that pain for nothing, but she was possibly also looking at him being mad enough to make good his threats from the day before, of putting her down in the dark room.

Violet looked away, down at the plate of food, trying to calm her frantically beating heart. "So I guess this means I get the room in your basement then?"

"You could have killed yourself." His voice was hard. "Did you have any idea what you were doing?"

"Well obviously not, otherwise I'd be in a hospital bed right now and this would be shitty hospital food." She didn't look at him. No, she wasn't going to justify or explain herself. Her plan hadn't worked and now she was stuck here. With him.

Fuck, she was an idiot.

"Now I guess I'll have to put up with your bullshit instead." Picking up the fork, she jabbed it viciously into the scrambled eggs. "On the bright side, there's always the chance for septicemia to set in."

There was a heavy, tense silence.

She tried to ignore him, taking a bite out of her eggs. They were annoyingly delicious.

"I should put you down in the basement," he muttered. "Lock the fucking door and throw away the key."

Violet flashed him a belligerent glance. "Oh come on. What would you have done in my place? If some asshole took you hostage and told you that he was going to give you to some douche-bag crime boss? I'm sure you'd just sit around on your hands whining."

Elijah said nothing, standing there tall and dark and dangerous as hell.

Another of those shivers went through her, the feel of his hand on her breast lingering on her skin like an echo. And for a second she couldn't look away from him. Held completely by his cold, furious, magnetic black gaze.

The silence between them deepened, lengthened.

Tension pulled tight.

And then she saw it, the briefest flicker of something that wasn't ice or fury in his eyes. Something hot.

Her breath caught.

She hadn't thought once about why he'd touched her or about why he might have wanted to, especially when everything about him radiated ice and snow and granite. As if nothing touched him, nothing affected him.

Except for the small fact that she had.

A memory came back to her, of the hard length of his cock pressing against her as she'd lain in his lap. Oh, yeah. He'd been affected all right, and judging from that brief glimpse of heat in his eyes, he wanted her still.

Was that why he was so angry?

Sure, it is. He wants you and he doesn't like it.

He certainly didn't like it, especially judging by the way he'd shoved her away the night before, despite the massive hard-on in his jeans. She'd been so out of it, all she'd noticed was the fact that he was no longer touching her and that she had been disappointed, before passing out completely on the couch.

She took another bite of egg, chewed thoughtfully, then swallowed, her gaze still on his. "You're really pissed at me, aren't you? So why aren't I all locked up in the basement yet?"

He was silent, the look on his face impenetrable. Then after another moment, he turned around abruptly and stalked back into the kitchen.

Okay then. So he wasn't going to answer her. Well, since she wasn't locked up in his basement, it probably meant he either didn't want to or wasn't going to do it any time soon.

Finding that vaguely reassuring, Violet continued to eat the rest of the food while she turned over in her head what her next move was. Her wrist was beginning to throb, but the food made her stomach feel less unsettled, so that was something. She was still a prisoner though, and obviously that wasn't going be changing any time soon, not unless she could think of another way to get out. Tricky when she considered her limited options.

Then again, what else was she going to do? Just sit here and wait to be given to Jericho? Wait for someone to rescue her?

You'll be waiting forever. Mom isn't coming for you.

Violet put down her fork, trying to ignore the small, sharp pain that slid through her. She'd been trying to tell herself that her mother would come, but the reality was that Violet wasn't certain. Hilary Fitzgerald had her own agenda that she didn't share with anyone close to her—if there was anyone who was actually close to her—and Violet was pretty sure her own daughter didn't rate on that agenda. Or if she did, it wasn't high up.

The pain tightened, but she fought it down. No use getting emotional—that wouldn't help. She had to think clearly here, and it was better not to count on her mother. But Honor she could count on, couldn't she? Her friend would want to find her. The only problem with that was waiting until Honor realized she was missing, and who knew how long that would take? Her father's death had to have made the news by now though, so surely Honor would be trying to get in touch with her.

That didn't help her right at this moment of course. And there was still the info she had about Theo.

The sound of heavy footsteps came again, a mug of coffee appearing beside her empty plate.

"Coffee," Violet said, blinking at the mug. "You bought me coffee. What the hell kind of hostage taker are you?"

"I told you I wasn't interested in hurting you."

"Yeah, but making me breakfast and bringing me caffeine?" She picked up her coffee and sat back on the couch, wrapping her fingers around the warm mug. "That's above and beyond, Eli."

The expression on his face didn't even flicker. "You need clothing and since I'm not leaving you here by yourself anymore, you're going to have to come with me."

Hope flickered inside her. So maybe yesterday hadn't been such a total loss after all. It was true, she did need clothes since she'd conveniently gotten blood all over the ones she had, and since those were the *only* ones she had, it was either she get more or walk around naked.

That's one way of managing the situation.

She stared at him, the thought sitting in her head. What would he do if she just threw off the blanket? She affected him, she knew that now, and as her brain so helpfully supplied, using her female charms would be one way to get what she wanted. It wouldn't be the first time she'd used a bit of flirtation on a man—she might be a virgin but she wasn't innocent, that was for sure.

Only, she wasn't sure if a "bit of flirtation" would have any effect whatsoever on Elijah.

Sex would though. Definitely.

"A shopping trip?" She took a sip of her coffee, watching him from over the rim of her mug as she let her blanket slip a little. "How exciting."

And Elijah's gaze slipped with it, the darkness in his eyes deepening.

Her heartbeat sped up, the flicker of hope becoming a steady flame. He wanted her, which was excellent, because once you knew what someone else wanted, you could use that to get what *you* wanted. Hadn't her father told her that?

Your father. The monster.

Violet pushed the snide voice in her head away. Yes, her father *had* been a monster, but shit, did that make every lesson he'd ever taught her a lie? And what else was she supposed to do? Sit there helplessly and wait for rescue?

No freaking way.

Ostentatiously she hiked up the blanket, taking a silent breath as Elijah lifted his gaze back to hers. There were flames in his eyes and they burned.

Her heart beat faster and she became very, very aware of her nakedness, her skin going all tight and sensitive beneath the blanket.

This is not *a good idea.*

She ignored that thought too. "Or"—her voice sounded a little husky, which didn't hurt—"I guess the alternative being I could just walk around naked."

The rough lines of his face hardened, the scar twisting his mouth whitening. The bruises he'd been sporting the previous day had deepened, and now he didn't look just dangerous. He looked lethal. Not an elegant blade but a club. Heavy and brutal, ready to smash anything he didn't like right out of existence.

He moved in that sudden way he had, the way that took her by surprise since a man that big shouldn't be able to move that quickly, coming toward her, inexorable as the tide. And a wild kind of panic wrapped long fingers around her throat, her earlier confidence crumbling utterly.

But she wasn't going to give him the satisfaction of letting him see her fear, so she remained where she was, clutching her pathetic blanket around her as he came right up to the couch and stood in front of her, bending down and putting his hands on the couch back, one on either side of her head.

There was nothing hot about him now as he leaned over her. He was black ice. "You think you can play me, princess?" he demanded, his voice a low, rough growl. "You think I'm going to follow you around like a puppy dog with my tongue hanging out? I'm not one of those little rich boys you can manipulate and toy with just by flashing your tits."

Oh no, she'd never make that mistake. She had an idea about what he was, about what kind of man she was dealing with. But she wasn't going to let him intimidate her, no matter what he threatened her with.

So she didn't look away, letting him see her own determination as he bent over her. "You didn't seem to mind those tits yesterday, as I recall. In fact, you seemed to quite like them." And he had. Right up until the moment he'd suddenly pushed her off him as though she'd burned him, oh yes, not forgetting that. "In fact"—she lifted her chin—"maybe you even took advantage of them later? After I passed out?"

Something changed in his eyes, she didn't know quite

what, but suddenly the space between them was full of pressure, like a storm front approaching. A dark, leashed violence that made her breathing shorten and her heart race wildly. Terrifying. Exhilarating.

This man was a force of nature and a deep, secret part of her wanted to throw herself into the hurricane.

Little bitch. There she sat, all naked and wrapped only in a blanket. With her goddamn dreadlocks and vivid eyes, thinking she could manipulate him with a glimpse of her body. Thinking she could use sex to play with him. Thinking he was weak enough to fall for it.

Well, aren't you? You were last night.

The thought made him even more furious with her than he was already. And he was pretty fucking furious.

The cold shower he'd had last night had dealt with the hard-on in his jeans, but it hadn't made the slightest bit of difference to the hunger that burned in his blood. He'd had to work himself into exhaustion with the punching bag for hours to stop himself from going over to where she lay on the couch and doing exactly what she'd just accused him of.

Then he'd stormed off to the bedroom to try and get some sleep, but the feel of her skin was on his fingertips and he couldn't get the sound of her sighs out of his head. And it wasn't until he'd taken himself in hand that he'd been able to get a bit of relief.

Even so, he hadn't slept much after that. He could usually operate as normal on little or no sleep, but this morning he'd felt like shit. And when he'd stalked out of the bedroom and into the living room, there she'd been on the couch, still asleep. The blanket had slipped down revealing one smooth shoulder and the curve of her breast, and he'd felt the fucking hunger pour through him like a tide.

It was like she'd flipped a switch on inside him and he had no idea how to turn it off.

But one thing was for sure. For seven years he'd kept himself cold and focused and set on his goal. He wouldn't allow himself to be distracted from it by one little rich girl now, no matter how goddamn sexy she was.

"Listen to me," he murmured, staring down at her. "I could care less about your fucking tits. Yesterday was an aberration and it won't happen again, no matter how often you keep flashing them around."

She'd pressed herself back into the couch, a flicker of what looked like fear crossing her face, and that was good. That was how it should be. He needed her afraid and obedient because he was getting pretty damn sick of her fighting him all the time.

"So here's what we're going to do," he went on, not waiting for a response. "I have a few things I have to do this morning and because of your little performance yesterday, I can't leave you alone. Now, I don't give a shit about whether you wear your filthy, wet clothes or whether you go naked, but unfortunately either of those options will draw attention. And I can't have attention. So we're going to have to get you something else to wear."

Her jaw had gone tight, and behind the fear in her eyes, a spark of determination glowed. "Fine," she said. "Then we'll go out. God knows, I could use some fresh air."

Jesus, even now, the damn woman was refusing to be cowed.

It only added to his fury, though he wasn't even sure why. She was so pretty and delicate, like a china figurine he could crush with one hand. Covered in only a blanket while he was fully clothed. She was vulnerable. She should be trembling with fear. Yet she wasn't.

Why the hell did some part of him, something deep in the recesses of his black heart, like that?

In fact it only made the hunger in him worse. Made him want to rip aside the blanket that covered her so he could see all of her. He was pretty certain she didn't dye her blonde hair, but he very much wanted to see if he was right.

You shouldn't have gotten close to her.

Yeah, that had been a mistake. But backing away now would be to admit that this damn hunger was stronger than he was, and there was fuck-all chance of him doing that.

Driven by some need he didn't really understand, perhaps only the need to test himself, he lifted one hand and took one of her dreadlocks between his fingers. It was much softer than he'd expected, like raw silk. With a certain amount of deliberation, he began to wind it around his hand, staring down at her all the while.

She'd gone completely still, her eyes widening slightly. Watching him like a deer watches a lion stalking toward it. "What are you doing?"

You bastard. What would Marie think of you now?

Marie wouldn't have thought of anything. Marie was dead.

"Like I said, I don't want attention. Which means these"—he tugged on the dreadlocks wrapped around his hand—"are going to have to go."

Violet blinked. "What do you mean these will have to go?"

He stared back, unyielding. "I mean you're going to have to cut them off."

"Are you kidding me?" A green spark of anger flared in her eyes.

"Do I look like I'm kidding? Everyone knows what you look like, princess. Especially with those fucking things on your head."

"So I'll wear a hat!"

"No." He couldn't leave her here by herself, yet having her with him while those very noticeable and distinctive dreadlocks were on her head was absolutely not happening. "I'm not leaving anything to chance this time."

Fury burned in Violet's gaze. "You asshole. It took me years to grow—"

"You only grew them to annoy your goddamn mother so don't start pretending they're holy fucking relics." Slowly he unwound the dread from his hand, ignoring the strange reluctance that went through him as he did so. "You have two choices, princess. Either you cut them yourself or I cut them off for you."

If looks could kill, he'd be carried home in a bucket. "You're a prick."

"So I've heard." He made himself push away from her, and it absolutely wasn't to do with the fact that if he spent another moment bent over her, feeling her warmth and breathing in the very faint scent of sandalwood, he'd rip that blanket away and—

What? Put your hands on her? Fuck her?

Hell no. He wasn't going to end seven years of celibacy with Violet Fitzgerald. He wasn't going to end it at all—at least not until he'd avenged Marie's death. And that wasn't going to happen until Jericho and maybe his whole fucking operation was burned to the ground.

But he wouldn't think beyond that now. Because thinking beyond that opened the door to needs and desires and expectations. And those would kill his determination to do what he had to do stone dead.

Violet sat up, glaring at him. "You can't make me do it."

"You think?"

"You're not going to shoot me, and if you were going to put me down in that basement, I would be there right now." Her chin lifted. "So really, what else have you got left to threaten me with?"

Of course. This was Violet. And she never did what she was told.

Reaching down, Elijah took out the knife he kept in his boot and held it loosely in one hand. "Sounds to me like you want me to give you a haircut."

Her face went pale, but he suspected that was from rage not fear. "You wouldn't dare."

"You're seriously asking me that question?" He lifted the knife, letting the light glitter along its razor-sharp edge. "I wouldn't advise struggling against a man armed with a blade."

Abruptly she pushed herself to her feet. She was inches away from him, the blanket held firmly under her arms, her shoulders bare, golden dreadlocks falling down in a shower around her head. Her eyes were bright with anger, vivid against her pale skin. "You wouldn't hurt me," she said, like she knew it for fact. "You just told me you weren't interested in doing so. Plus you stitched me up last night and cooked me food."

"Don't mistake that for anything but what it is. I want you in one piece for Jericho, that's all." He flipped the knife in his hand, an easy demonstration of skill that he hoped would make her think twice about any more arguments. "Last chance, princess. Are you cutting your hair or am I going to have to tie you up and cut it myself?"

Something in her gaze flared. "I hate you."

"Hate all you want." He stepped closer to her. "I don't give a shit." And it wasn't a lie. He *didn't* give a shit. The only thing he cared about was taking down the man who had killed Marie. And Violet was the means to that end. That was all.

Yet the fury in her eyes didn't let up and she didn't look away as he reached out for her dreads for the second time, almost as if she was trying to stare him down.

Well, she could try. But if she thought his conscience was going to kick in, she was shit out of luck. He didn't have a conscience. He couldn't afford one.

Taking a bunch of dreadlocks in his fist, Elijah pulled them tight. Her hair must have grown some because there were at least a couple of inches growing out from her scalp. She wouldn't be completely bald at least.

Weren't you supposed to not care about that?

Violet had gone completely still, her posture rigid. She didn't struggle. She only kept staring at him as if she could burn a hole right through his forehead.

Ignoring her, he raised the knife and sliced through the gilt strands. The blade was sharp, cutting effortlessly, barely tugging on her scalp at all.

She didn't protest or try to pull away. She only stood there with her arms folded, the expression on her face one of complete and utter fury.

But he didn't stop. He continued to reach for those long silver-gold tails, cutting them off one by one, until he was standing in a circle of raw, golden silk with Violet in the center.

As he'd cut, the glow of fury in her eyes had grown brighter and brighter, so that by now she was virtually incandescent with rage.

With only three inches of hair on her head, she should have looked smaller and more vulnerable but for some reason she didn't. Her eyes were electric, her features seeming stronger and more clearly defined, no longer overpowered by the wealth of hair. There was a proud slant to her jaw, an elegance to the shape of her head and neck.

Christ. She wasn't merely pretty any longer. She was stunning.

Elijah let the last lock of hair fall to the floor, unable to drag his gaze from her face. Because for all that burning fury in her eyes, she was also trembling.

Something in his chest locked, which was goddamn stupid since he hadn't hurt her, merely cut off her fucking hair. Yet the sight of her trembling made that strange, tight feeling get even tighter.

Then she blinked hard, a small tear escaping to slide down the curve of one pale cheek.

And he couldn't help himself. His hand lifted as if of its own volition to cup that proud jaw of hers, his thumb sweeping across her soft skin to brush away the moisture.

She shivered.

Then she went for the knife.

CHAPTER SIX

It was his hand against her skin that did it, the touch gentle yet searing her like a streak of fire. And it broke the strange, furious paralysis that had gripped her. The one that had her wanting to scream and struggle against what he was doing and yet stand very, very still.

Because there was another feeling that had her in its claws. As if with each cut of the knife, a small part of her was being cut away. A part she didn't want and didn't need. Sloughed away like dead skin from a scar.

She didn't know where the feeling had come from or why, but it held her motionless. Torn between the part of her that raged against what he was doing and the still, quiet part that wanted to know why she felt different as each lock of hair fell to the floor. Why she felt she was changing with each pass of the knife.

So that at last she stood there, her head feeling so light she thought it might float away, and as the last lock fell, his eyes went wide, something unreadable flickering in the lightless depths.

A surge of emotion went through her, rage and fear and loss all combining together into one overwhelming wave, making her have to clench her jaw hard and blink to stop stupid tears from falling. But one escaped anyway. Which was when he'd touched her, warm fingers sliding over her jaw, his thumb moving over her cheek.

She moved before he could, reaching for the knife held loosely in his other hand. Not to attack him, since even in the grip of this weird emotional storm she knew she couldn't win against him. But maybe just because she could, because it gave her some power.

He didn't move as she snatched it from him, his fingers falling away from her jaw, that strange expression flickering across his face.

The hilt felt warm against her palm and she held onto it tightly, her breathing coming fast and hard. Her scalp prickled as the air moved over it, no longer protected by the heavy weight of her hair, and she was suddenly conscious all over again that not only was she completely naked except for the blanket, she'd also been completely shorn.

You've got nothing to hide behind now.

She remained motionless as the realization struck her, a great wave of fear making her feel so vulnerable and exposed, she wanted to run away and hide.

Turning abruptly, one hand clutching her blanket while the other clutched the knife, she went quickly toward the hallway, moving in the direction of the bathroom.

"Where are you going?" he demanded.

She didn't stop and she didn't turn around. "I want to see what you've done to my head, you bastard." Well, that too, but mainly all she wanted was to get away from those sharp black eyes and the terrible vulnerable feeling that had gripped her.

In the bathroom, she cautiously approached the mirror, dreading what she'd see.

Then she stopped. And stared.

The young woman in the mirror stared back, spikes of

blonde hair sticking up all over her head, making her look a little like an outraged dandelion. Her eyes were very blue and the shape of her face seemed . . . different. Sharper. More angular.

Violet swallowed, unable to drag her gaze away.

She'd had her dreads for nearly five years and Elijah hadn't been wrong—she'd had them put in to annoy her mother. Hilary had been trying for years to turn her daughter into what Violet could only assume was a younger version of herself. A perfect Upper East Side society wife-in-training. And Violet had just gotten sick of it.

Her mother had refused to speak to her for days afterward and Violet had told herself that was exactly what she'd wanted, thrilled she'd gotten some kind of reaction out of ice-cold Hilary.

But over the years, her hair had started to become something more than merely a subtle dig. It had started to become part of her persona, part of a mask she hadn't even realized she'd been wearing.

Until Elijah had ripped it away.

She tilted her head, not looking at her butchered locks, but at her face. Yes, she looked even more naked without her hair. Yes, she looked vulnerable. But also . . . there was a strength to her features she'd never seen before.

Who was this woman? This woman who'd been kidnapped and shot at. Who'd sat in that bath and sliced her wrists. Who'd had her hair cut off with a knife.

She was different. Stronger. A woman who didn't need to hide.

What was she hiding from in the first place?

Interesting thought, because Violet herself had no idea.

A movement caught her eye and the sound of boots scuffing on the tiles of the bathroom.

She didn't turn because of course it was Elijah. She

could see him rest an arm against the door frame and lean on it, his attention on her.

"If you're worried I'm going to slit my wrists again, you don't need to." Even her voice sounded different. Firmer somehow and more certain.

He didn't reply, watching her.

Fine. If he wasn't going to talk, then she wouldn't.

She glanced down to see the nail scissors sitting on the vanity so she picked them up and glanced back into the mirror. Then she began to calmly tidy up the ragged ends of her hair.

Elijah kept watching her, not saying a word or making a move toward the knife she'd put down on the vanity. He didn't need to though, because she wasn't going to use it. She was through with desperate measures. It was time for a plan with a little more thought behind it.

The silence was thick and tense, but Violet ignored it as she made a few last cuts before placing the scissors back down on the vanity again then tilting her head in the mirror.

She'd aimed for more of a pixieish look instead of the dandelion thing, and she had to admit, it wasn't a half-bad job. Her head still felt weirdly light, and it was strange to feel air moving over her neck and shoulders, but now that the anger and the fear had subsided, she was left with a weird feeling of . . . actually, she didn't know what.

Her father was dead. Her brother was presumed dead. Her mother was on some other planet that didn't include her and had always been.

She was alone. And yet . . .

You can be whoever you want to be now.

Violet turned from the mirror and met Elijah's piercing dark gaze. Held it. "Are we going out or what?"

He didn't even blink at the hard demand in her tone. "You need something to wear."

“What did you do with my clothes?”

“They were covered in blood so I got rid of them.”

She refused to feel the slight pang of regret that went through her. Those clothes were part of the old her. She didn’t need them now. “So what am I going to wear while we get more?”

His gaze narrowed. “Wait there.”

With an abrupt movement, he turned away and went off down the hallway. A couple of minutes later, he was back, a long-sleeved T-shirt in his hand. “Here.” He held it out to her. “You can wear this.”

Violet took it from him and examined it. The faded black cotton was soft, and it must have been one of his because it was very long. It was going to swamp her, but considering she didn’t have anything else to wear, perhaps that was a good thing.

“No pants?” she asked.

“I don’t have any that will fit you.”

She glanced at him. “But it’s cold out.” She didn’t have any underwear either, but she’d be damned if she mentioned that.

His dark eyes were unblinking. “I have a jacket you can wear.”

“Okay fine. And then what?”

“What are you talking about?”

“After we’ve gotten me clothes. Then what?”

The expression on his face closed down. “Then you stop asking me fucking questions. Get dressed. You have five minutes.”

She was ready in two. After he’d mercifully left her some privacy, all it took was to drop the blanket and pull the T-shirt down over her head. The cotton felt soft against her skin and as it fell around her, she was engulfed in the dark, spicy scent of a forest, with the cleaner, sharper scent of new snow. Him . . .

God, that smell. It made her shiver. Made her heart beat fast and that was just so wrong given everything he'd done to her. But it was also a weapon, wasn't it? A weapon she hadn't discarded yet, no matter what he'd said about manipulating him.

Turning, she looked at herself in the mirror once again. Sure enough, it did swamp her, the hem reaching mid-thigh and the neckline half falling off her shoulder. Jesus, she looked like a little girl playing dress-up with her daddy's shirt.

No, you don't. You're wearing his *shirt. And you look sexy.*

She frowned, staring at herself again. Her shoulder was pale against the black cotton of the loose neckline, and it was painfully obvious she wasn't wearing a bra.

You can use that. There's more than one way to overpower a man after all.

Yeah, but that worked better when the man in question wasn't looming over her and telling her not to play with him. Except . . . he hadn't looked like he'd minded when his hands were on her the night before. When he'd caressed her breast, his fingers on her nipple gentle yet firm.

Violet caught her breath as her body tightened at the memory. Okay, so she was a little sick for liking that, but she remembered the look on his face as he'd watched her, hunger stark in his black eyes.

You made him drop his guard. You made him want. That's why he's so pissy with you.

Slowly she let out a breath. Oh yeah, he wanted her all right. But he didn't want to want her—that was the issue. He had a weakness and he knew it. A weakness she could exploit if she went about it in the right way.

Yes, that was how to do it. Fuck grabbing his gun or his knife and trying to overpower him physically—that would never work. And she'd blown her one chance with hurting herself, which left using her femininity as the only option. So why the hell not? It wasn't exactly as if she had a lot of other options, and God, he had no qualms about using his superior strength against her. This was *her* advantage, so why not use it? After all, she'd done it before on occasion, with her professors at college—male and female—flirting a little to get extensions on her essays and lecture notes ahead of the class. Sometimes it worked and sometimes it didn't, but she'd had a pretty good track record.

Elijah wasn't any different.

You might even quite like it yourself.

Violet shoved that particular thought way. No, this was only about getting away and getting free, nothing more. She shouldn't think about it in any other way, especially not *that* way. Elijah wasn't one of her professors, or a fresh-faced college boy. He was a killer and simply far too dangerous for her not to be fully focused on what she needed to do.

If this was the approach she was going to take, she'd have to be very careful about it indeed.

Giving her hair another quick tousle—finding the shortness of it weird all over again—she turned from the mirror and went back out into the living area.

Elijah was standing near the front door, his phone in his hand. He turned as she came out of the hallway, his gaze running expressionlessly over her, betraying nothing.

He was good, she had to give him that. She might as well have been a block of wood judging from his reaction.

"It's a little short," she said, tugging at the T-shirt, and sure enough, his gaze dropped to the length of her legs revealed beneath it.

Again though, there was no discernible reaction. "It'll do," he replied. "Put your boots on, then this." He reached for a long black coat hanging from a peg next to the door then tossed it in her direction.

She caught it, the soft weight of quality cashmere heavy in her hands. It was beautifully tailored and expensive, and would cover up most of what his long-sleeved shirt left bare. Just as well really, since the weather outside the apartment's windows was looking dire.

Going over to the couch, she sat down to put on her boots, noticing as she did so that her cut hair had all been cleaned away. And weirdly there was no pang of regret or even of anger at the thought, as if those emotions had been cleared away along with her hair. Just as well. She had no time for those kinds of feelings, just steely determination. That was the only thing that was going to get her out of this.

After she'd put her boots on, she picked up the coat and slid her arms into it. As she'd expected, it was deliciously warm, the by-now familiar scent of snow-clad forests filling her senses. His coat. For some reason she had a ridiculous urge to wrap it around her and snuggle into it.

Instead she rolled up the too-long sleeves and buttoned it up, and then, spying what looked like a scarf hanging from another peg by the door, she went over and grabbed it, tying that around her waist to keep it belted tight.

Elijah watched her expressionlessly. Then he raised his phone and took a couple of photos of her.

She frowned. "Hey, what's that for?"

He didn't respond, putting away his phone in his jeans pocket. "Couple of things before we go," he said flatly. "You stay close to me and you don't pull away. I have my gun and I *will* shoot you if you try anything. It has a silencer on it so no one will hear if I pull that trigger."

Violet pushed her hands into the pockets of the coat. "Oh sure, and no one's going to notice if I suddenly start bleeding from a surprise gunshot wound either."

"Are you willing to risk that?"

She didn't look away. "I slit my wrists yesterday. You tell me."

"You have no money, no ID. How far do you think you'll get if you somehow manage to slip away?"

"I can find a cop. It won't be that difficult."

He studied her for a long moment, his gaze opaque. "You can run, princess. But I will find you." His voice was soft but as cold as the sleet against the window outside. "I will hunt you and hunt you, and I will never stop until I have you. I'm not the kind of guy who gives up, understand?"

An icy shiver went down her spine, part fear, part that strange excitement. She ignored both sensations. "Sure. I understand." *I don't give up either, asshole.*

But she didn't say that last part aloud.

Elijah gripped Violet's upper arm and drew her in close as they stepped out of the building and onto the sidewalk. She gave a little shiver, but didn't try to pull away. He'd given her a black beanie to wear, both as a disguise over what remained of her hair and for warmth, yet even despite the hat and his coat, she must have been freezing because the wind cut like a knife.

Or maybe the shiver was because of you.

He frowned. Why the hell was he thinking about that? And why the hell did it matter to him why she shivered?

Dismissing his thoughts, he tugged her harder against him, one hand wrapped around her arm, the other in the pocket of his leather jacket, fingers curling around the grip of his gun. Ready to pull it out if she ran.

She hadn't been wrong up in the apartment. If she tried to run, shooting her would only draw unwanted attention so if he was prepared to do that, he'd have to pull the trigger while she was still standing next to him, so he could pick her up and take her back to the apartment to treat her with a minimum of fuss. In other words, not particularly practical.

Which left only the hunting-down option.

She hadn't liked that, but then that was the general idea, especially since he was running out of ways to keep her in line. She was turning out to be a far trickier prospect than he'd anticipated. Shit, even cutting her hair off hadn't quelled her. In fact, as she'd come out of the hallway, wearing his shirt, her hair all in short, soft golden spikes around her head, she'd looked tough, meeting his gaze as though he was an opponent she was taking on.

He'd had to fight with himself not to react to the hard kick of possessiveness at the sight of her in his shirt, to the surge of desire as his gaze had traced the soft curve of her bare shoulder, the press of her hard nipples against the cotton, the long length of her bare legs.

It was madness, especially the possessive part. There should be no reason for that, none at all, because he hadn't gotten possessive with Marie, and she'd been his goddamn wife. Then again, he'd been a different man back then. An easier, more laid-back man.

You were soft. If you'd been who you are now, she'd never have been taken.

His fingers dug into Violet's upper arm in unconscious reaction, and she made a little sound. But he eased off only slightly. At least this one wasn't getting away. Not today. Not if he could help it.

The sleet had stopped by the time they'd gotten outside and it was mainly the wind that blew around them as they began walking. He'd debated about where to take her since he wanted to stay away from the subway and any surveillance cameras. Luckily while he'd been out on his various different reconnaissance missions, he knew there was a women's clothing store a couple of blocks away from the apartment building. It was situated on a particularly busy street, but he hoped that might work in their favor and make them more easily lost in the crowd than if they were by themselves.

"So," Violet said conversationally, "are you going to tell me anything about this Jericho guy and why he wants me?"

"No." Elijah kept his reply curt as he studied the street, keeping an eye out for any potential threats. So far there was nothing overtly suspicious, but then it paid to never be too cautious about such things.

"Do you even know why he wants me?"

His jaw tightened. How did she manage to ask the questions he didn't have the answers to? Because no, he had no idea why Jericho wanted Violet. Fitzgerald had never mentioned it and it hadn't seemed important enough for Elijah to find out. Even now, he didn't really care why. All that mattered was that Jericho wanted her and would hopefully make a personal appearance when it came to retrieving her.

"Why is not important," he said as he guided them around a group of tourists standing in the middle of the sidewalk, looking at a map and gesticulating. "And no, you don't need to know anything about him."

"I hate to disagree with you, but considering I'm the one who's going to be given to him, it's kind of important to me."

He didn't reply. This conversation was futile and he saw no point in continuing it.

But Violet clearly hadn't finished.

"He might want to kill me," she said. "Have you thought of that? You might be giving me to him so he can torture and kill me. Does that mean anything to you?"

Wasn't that what happened to Marie? She was taken, tortured, then killed.

A needle slid beneath his skin, and he had to clench his teeth against the sensation. No, fuck that. He couldn't let himself be concerned for Violet, not after he'd spent so many years turning himself into the kind of monster that could take down other monsters. Not after sacrificing the man he'd once been on the altar of his vengeance. He was too far down the path and couldn't turn back, not now. Not for one particular woman. He had no conscience. No scruples. No mercy. Not anymore.

"That," he said coldly, "is no concern of mine. You can stop talking now."

She didn't reply, her attention focused ahead of her. He was walking quite quickly and she had to trot to keep up with him, her breath fogging in the cold air around them. Her body was warm next to his and he could smell that tantalizing sandalwood scent beneath the smells of the outside world, the wet asphalt and exhaust, the trash and the drifting perfume of freshly ground coffee from a café.

It is a concern of yours. Wasn't that the whole point of this? Avenge Marie, take him down so no other woman gets hurt?

The needle slid deeper.

Elijah gripped her harder, and ignored the slight pain. He couldn't afford to care. Violet was a sacrifice for the greater good, and that's all that mattered. That's all that could be allowed to matter.

They continued on down the street in silence for a couple of blocks, the wind whipping Violet's coat around her legs and sending cold tendrils beneath the hem of his leather jacket.

Christ, she must be freezing and yet she hadn't said a word, her gaze steadfastly ahead.

Music drifted on the icy air, hard and fast, a driving beat coming from one of the stores on the corner of the block. It was the one he was heading for, the one that sold women's clothing.

He did another quick scan of the surroundings, but again there were no threats so he headed straight for the store entry.

"Here?" Violet muttered as they stepped inside.

"If you were expecting Fifth Avenue, you're shit out of luck. You get something here or you stay in my shirt." He glanced down at his watch. "You have ten minutes." He didn't want to stay out longer than strictly necessary, since the longer she was out of the apartment, the greater the risk of discovery.

Violet threw him an enigmatic look before moving over to a rack of what appeared to be pants. He followed her, keeping hold of her, his attention on the rest of the store.

There were a few other customers, none of them looking in Violet's direction, and a sales assistant behind the counter wearing black ripped jeans and a lot of silver jewelry, talking animatedly on her phone.

Violet's attention was on the rack of clothes, but he could feel the tension in her arm beneath his fingers.

"Do you have to loom over me like that?" she murmured, pushing aside a hanger. "Give me some space for God's sake."

Was she serious? Give her some space so she could take off? "No. Choose something quickly. This isn't a fashion show."

She didn't reply, shoving aside another hanger.

His phone vibrated and he let her go momentarily to reach for it, keeping one hand on the gun in his other pocket. There was a text from the number he was using for Jericho, the one he'd sent the photos he'd taken earlier to.

What do you want?

Short and to the point. Nice. He liked dealing with people who didn't beat about the bush. Quickly, he texted a response.

To talk. Fitzgerald is dead. I want in.

There was no immediate reply for a couple of moments. Then suddenly the phone began to ring.

Violet glanced at him, her eyes narrowing. He gripped her hard, hauling her back out of the store and onto the sidewalk, away from the store's loud house music, ignoring her startled protest. Then he hit the accept button.

"You are not the one to be making demands," a male voice said in French. "You will have the girl at—"

"Shut the fuck up and listen," he interrupted harshly. "I want to talk to Jericho. In person. That's the only way he'll get the girl, understand?"

"You cannot—"

"If I don't get what I want, then he won't." Not waiting for a response, Elijah hit the end button and pocketed the phone. Ball was in Jericho's court now, let him deal with it.

Violet was staring at him, her eyes vivid in her pale face. "Why do you want to talk to him?"

Elijah bared his teeth. "None of your fucking business. Now let's go get these goddamn clothes." He curled his fingers tighter into her arm, making a move toward the store again.

But she stood firm. "If he doesn't agree, are you going to kill me?"

For some reason, the starkness of the question felt like a small electric shock, jolting him. He'd killed before, many times in the course of seven years, and he'd gotten to the point where it no longer concerned him. Everything he did had been for Marie, for the greater good of taking down Fitzgerald, and if that meant killing a few people who deserved it, then he was okay with that.

But he never killed women—that was his line in the sand. And the thought of killing Violet . . .

That fucking needle slid all the way through him. Yet he couldn't betray any softness, give away any sign that the thought bothered him, because he needed her compliant. And fear was the best way to get compliance.

So he said nothing, jerking her with more force toward the store.

She must have realized she wasn't going to get anything from him, because she didn't say another word, going with him as they stepped back inside. And when he went over to the rack she'd been looking at earlier, she went without protest.

She seemed more focused this time around, grabbing some black pants off the rack almost straightaway, then a green top from somewhere else and a black leather jacket from yet another rack as she moved deeper into the store.

Then she stopped and looked around, searching for something. He was about to ask what it was, when she abruptly headed to a corner down the back where there was a small rack of what looked like women's underwear, except they weren't pretty and lacy, more black and slick, with lots of straps and buckles.

Of course. He'd thrown out her underwear along with the rest of her bloodstained clothes.

And almost as soon as the thought had occurred to him, he found his gaze following down the length of her body as she leafed through the bras. Fucking hell. She was naked under that shirt of his. No bra. No panties. And if he was to reach out and run his hand up the back of her thigh right now, there would be nothing in his way . . .

That predatory thing inside him growled, starving suddenly. For soft, smooth skin and heat, for rounded curves that gave under his hand, for the warm pressure of a body on his, and for husky, needy cries in response to his touch.

Violet reached for a bra that seemed to be an arrangement of black straps more than anything else and a pair of matching black panties, and although she was swamped by that coat, he found himself staring at her as if he could see right through the wool to her naked body beneath.

Because of course he remembered what she looked like,

even though at the time he'd made himself ignore her nudity as he'd stripped the wet bloodstained clothes from her shivering body, wrapping her up in a towel.

Yet he wasn't thinking of that, but of her in his lap, arching into his hand . . .

Fuck. He was getting hard. Definitely time to get out of here.

Digging his fingers into her arm, he tugged her away. "Time to go, princess."

Again she resisted. "Let me try these on."

"You can back at the apartment."

"Yeah, and I'll freeze to death before I get back there." That steely determination was back in her eyes again. "It'll only take me a couple of minutes, I promise. I'll put the clothes on, then we can leave."

He shouldn't care, he really shouldn't.

Outside the wind had picked up and, judging by the temperature, there was probably going to be another late-winter fall of snow.

She's cold. One minute won't make much difference.

Elijah cursed under his breath. "One minute."

She blinked a little and her mouth opened, as if she hadn't been expecting him to capitulate and wanted to say something. Then, clearly thinking better of it, she shut it again and turned away, heading toward the fitting rooms without another word.

If he hadn't been watching her carefully, he might have missed the spark of what looked like triumph in her gaze.

Clever little bitch. Well, whatever it was she was planning—and she was obviously planning something—she wasn't going to get far, not if he could help it.

He followed her to the fitting rooms down the back of the store and when she went into one, he stepped inside it with her.

She whirled around, holding the clothes she'd taken

against her chest. "What the hell are you doing? Ever heard of privacy?"

"After what happened the last time I left you alone? I don't think so." He closed the door firmly behind them then leaned back against it, folding his arms. "Now put those clothes on."

"Are you kidding?" Temper glowed in her eyes. "Not with you standing there."

"Too bad. You've got one minute to change and if not, then I guess getting warm isn't so very important to you after all."

CHAPTER SEVEN

Prick. The fucking prick. Then again, did she really expect anything different? She could even understand his reasons, considering the last time he'd left her on her own, she'd ended up in a tub full of bloody bathwater.

Still, she didn't want him staring at her while she got changed. Unfortunately it seemed as if he had other ideas.

This could be good, though. Remember what you wanted to do?

Violet narrowed her eyes at him. She probably could have gotten away while walking down the street to get here. All it would have taken would have been a quick jerk to pull out of his grip, or maybe a scream to draw attention. He would have to let her go if he didn't want people looking at him or calling the cops. But then she'd have him on her tail like the freaking Terminator, and she had no doubt at all he'd be ruthless in getting her back. Not to mention that other people might get hurt were he do to so.

So she had to find another way. A way to make him *want* to let her go. If she could get him to lower his guard, see her as a person, a woman espeically, that might generate some sympathy in him for her. Get him to empathize with her.

A pretty tall order for a man who seemed entirely carved out of black ice.

Then again, he'd touched her. Had run his fingers over her with gentleness. He'd even taken care of her too, all of which made her believe that there *was* an actual human being underneath all that ice.

She just had to find him, release him. Psychology 101.

"Fine," she said crisply as she shoved the hangers full of clothing at him. "Hold these."

It was only an instinctive reaction that had him grabbing the hangers before they fell to the ground, she was sure. But grab them he did and because she was watching, she didn't miss the flicker of surprise on his face.

Excellent. Surprise was good. Surprise meant he was off guard.

She stepped back, bending to take off her boots. Then, barefoot, she straightened, her hands falling to the scarf she had wrapped around her waist. It didn't take much to undo it, a small tug, her gaze holding his.

Another flicker of reaction moved through those black eyes, though what it was, she couldn't tell.

The scarf dropped to the floor and she let it, her fingers moving to the buttons on the coat, undoing them one by one. Then she shrugged out of it, letting that drop to the floor as well so she stood in front of him wearing the long-sleeved T-shirt he'd given her and nothing else.

The store's music blared, that hard, driving beat making her feel like she was part of some kind of strip show. Which oddly enough helped, because that's exactly what this was.

If he was so determined to stay here and watch, then she was going to make sure he got his money's worth. Anything to get under that icy exterior of his.

She reached for the hem of the shirt, her fingers curling underneath it, her heart starting to beat faster and faster. If she took this off, she'd be naked. Right in front of him.

He's seen it before.

Yeah, he had, when he'd taken her from the bath and stripped all her clothes off. But somehow that was different. She'd been in pain and shock, and he'd been very matter-of-fact. He hadn't lingered and most importantly, he hadn't stared at her the way he was now. Because that stare made it different. Made her nervous. And yet . . . it made her excited too.

Jesus. She was getting off on this, no doubt about it, which either made her sick or desperate, or possibly both.

Stop procrastinating and do it.

Violet gripped the hem of the T-shirt and jerked it up and over her head before she could think more. Then she flung that down on the floor too, lifting her chin and meeting his gaze.

A wave of goose bumps washed over her and it had nothing to do with the chill.

Because there was something in his eyes, the same thing that had been there when he'd held her in his arms and touched her. A dark, relentless kind of hunger that seemed to be fixed on her and her alone.

His gaze raked down her body in a slow, deliberate way before rising back to her face again, and she couldn't seem to look away. There was the faintest wash of color on his high cheekbones, his beautiful, scarred mouth hard. His jaw had gone tight, his whole posture still and vibrating with tension.

His eyes glittered, black and hot as tar as they stared into hers.

Oh yeah, he wanted her alright, she could see it plain as day.

The goose bumps washing over her became prickles of heat, the nervousness sitting in her gut shifting, changing.

And for the first time since he'd taken her, Violet felt the balance of power tilt in her favor.

She almost smiled. Who knew getting naked could actually make her feel like she was in charge of things?

Holding his gaze, she took a couple of steps toward him, coming closer. Watching as the expression on his face became more intense, the flame in his eyes burning hotter. His knuckles were white on the hangers of clothes, the plastic creaking under the pressure of his grip as she approached.

Even better. This was working far more effectively than she'd thought. Shit, if she'd known he'd react like this, she needn't have carved that hole in her arm at all. She should have just taken her clothes off first up.

She stopped in front of him, only inches away, her pulse loud in her head, triumph and exhilaration threading through her. "You can hand me those panties if you like," she murmured. "Because as you can see, I don't have any."

He didn't look down, kept that intense black stare on hers. "What did I say about playing me, princess?" There was a rough edge in his voice, a dark heat that made something inside her shiver.

"I'm not playing you," she said calmly. "Obviously if I'm going to put on those clothes, I have to take off the ones I'm wearing. And since you refused to leave . . ." She let that hang there, raising a brow at him. "I didn't think you'd have such a problem with me being naked."

Abruptly the plastic hangers and clothes fell to the floor and warm, astonishingly strong fingers wrapped themselves around her throat.

Her heart just about stopped beating.

And then she was being turned, swung around so it was she who was standing with her back pressed to the fitting room door, Elijah standing in front of her with one hot palm resting on her throat, the other flat on the door beside her head.

Her pulse rate rocketed, panic flaring inside her. And yet along with it, an intense awareness of his hand on her skin. Of her own nakedness. Of the cool wooden door at her back.

Of the darkness of his eyes as they stared down at her. Of the heat in them . . .

A heat totally at odds with the ice in his voice as he said, "You're manipulating me, Violet. Don't think I don't know what you're doing."

A tremor shook her that had nothing to do with the fact that he saw right through her, that he knew exactly what she'd intended, and everything to do with the feel of his hand on her, a heat that burned right through her skin, down through muscle and bone, leaving an imprint on the very fabric of her being. A scar she'd never get rid of.

She stared up at him, searching his face, forgetting utterly what she was supposed to be doing, yet not really knowing what she was looking for. Only that what she wanted to see wasn't there.

You wanted him to drop his guard, remember?

Struggling to breathe—and not because his grip was cutting off her airway, but because his touch had somehow emptied her lungs of oxygen—she tried to focus on his rough, scarred features. Tried to see past the blank walls behind his eyes.

Hunger glittered there, a raw, unguarded desperation that had nothing to do with the chill in his voice or the hard expression on his face. A hunger that for some reason he was keeping leashed tight. Because why wouldn't he take her if he wanted her? He could, she would be powerless to stop him.

Rape is for cowards and animals.

"You want me." The words came out of her in a husky whisper. "Don't think I don't see it."

The hunger in his eyes flared. "Pushing me is a bad fucking idea."

"Why?" The hand on her throat was so hot. God, *he* was so hot. His body was like a goddamn furnace she wanted to warm herself against, because she was cold. So very, very cold. "You keep saying that, but really, I don't know why you keep warning me. You can't kill me and you don't seem to want to hurt me. So why shouldn't I push you? You've taken me hostage, shot at me, kept me prisoner in that stupid apartment of yours. Don't you think I deserve a little payback?"

His gaze had dropped to her mouth, the hand around her throat lying heavy on her skin. His thumb was pressing over one collarbone and there was a slight movement to it, almost as if he was caressing her.

Violet's mouth dried, the touch igniting something inside her. The realization of how hungry she was herself, how she was starving for something though she didn't know what.

Yes, you do. You're starving for him.

No, she couldn't afford that. If she let that hunger rule her, there was no telling when she'd be able to stop. It seemed inconceivable anyway. This man was holding her captive in order to give her to some crime boss, for God's sake. Why on earth would she want him?

And yet the way he'd touched her yesterday. There had been gentleness in him, and heat, and desperation too. Everything she'd been craving for herself . . .

Dangerous. You're not supposed to go down this path.

"No," he said in a cold, flat voice. "I don't think you deserve anything at all."

His thumb pressed gently against the ridge of her collarbone, almost yet not quite moving. His body was so close to hers, the heat of him warming her bare skin. Her nipples had gone tight and hard, and she could feel his breath against her neck.

Another shiver wracked her.

"I wouldn't mind, you know." The words came out hoarse and she hadn't meant to say them, more spilling out before she could help herself. "If you wanted to have me, I . . . I wouldn't mind."

Elijah's big body was motionless and she thought she saw shock in his gaze. Then his expression closed down. His hand dropped away from her throat and he took a step back, the look on his face impenetrable, the dark flames in his eyes vanishing.

"Get dressed," he said curtly.

Then he pushed her gently to the side, pulled open the fitting room door, and walked out.

Elijah waited by the store counter, his hands in the pockets of his leather bike jacket. One hand curling around his gun because shit, he had to hold onto something that reminded him of his goddamn purpose. Especially when he was also trying to quell the intense hard-on in his jeans.

He couldn't get the sight of Violet out of his head. The way she'd pulled off his shirt and dropped it on the ground, then stared at him, her eyes full of challenge as she'd stood there completely naked.

Of course he'd known what he was in for when he'd joined her in the fitting room. And he'd known she wouldn't be happy about it. But he hadn't wanted to leave her there by herself because who knew what she'd manage to get up to if he couldn't keep an eye on her? He couldn't afford any surprises like the one she'd sprung on him in the bathtub the day before. Especially not in public.

He'd thought he could handle her. He'd thought he had

himself under control enough that her taking off her clothes wouldn't affect him in the slightest.

But he'd been wrong.

She'd walked toward him, her body smooth and golden and lushly curved, and he'd felt the weight of every single day of the past seven years of abstinence pressing down on him. Crushing him. Those small, high breasts he'd touched, stroked. The graceful indent of her waist and the swell of her hips. The soft thatch of golden curls between her thighs.

He'd gotten hard, so hard, almost instantly. And she'd been all determination, showing him she wasn't afraid, getting right up close. He'd seen the triumph in those beautiful turquoise eyes of hers, had known he hadn't hidden his desire from her as well as he'd thought.

So he'd had to assert himself somehow, show her he was still in control.

That didn't work out so well, did it?

He could feel the heat of her skin against his palm even now. Smell the scent of her body, musk and sandalwood. He'd frightened her, and yet it hadn't only been fear in her eyes; there had been heat there too.

All he'd been able to think about then was the way she'd been in his lap the day before, the way she'd arched into his hand, wanting more. A little cat wanting to be stroked.

Fuck, he'd wanted her. And that had made him so goddamn angry, because he knew that she was also playing him. That she was using the strange chemistry between them to get to him, probably using sex to change his mind about giving her to Jericho.

You should have just taken her.

His fingers curled on the gun, the metal warming beneath his palm. The fucking sales assistant was still talking on the phone, oblivious.

Perhaps he should have. He could have lifted her up

against the door of the fitting room and unzipped his jeans, let her sink down on his cock, holding her there while he emptied himself of this ridiculous craving.

"I wouldn't mind . . ."

Christ, that husky voice, the spark of pure blue in her eyes as she'd stared at him. . . . She'd wanted him too. But he'd known in that instant he couldn't do it. It was hard enough managing his own hunger let alone hers, and bringing them together would be madness.

It would negate the whole of the last seven years.

Movement near the fitting rooms caught his attention, and he turned to see Violet coming toward him, holding the empty hangers in her hands.

She wore a pair of tight-fitting black leather pants, a silky-looking green top, and a black leather bike jacket. It was such a change from her normal hippie-looking outfits that he couldn't help staring at her. Gone was the free spirit in the chiming jewelry and brightly colored silk skirts. In her place was a tough biker chick with a guarded, wary expression.

He wasn't sure if that was an improvement or not.

Stopping by the counter, she handed him the hangers and the tags she'd obviously removed from the clothes. "Here. You'll need these."

He took them from her and pulled out his wallet, adding up the prices then extracting some cash and dumping it on the counter. The sales assistant clearly had the phone attached to her ear because she didn't stop talking, but he wasn't waiting. He didn't need the change anyway.

Grabbing Violet's arm again, he tucked her in close as they headed out of the store.

The walk back to the apartment was far more tense and she made no effort to talk to him, which he appreciated. It was hard enough trying to keep his mind on what he was supposed to be doing and not on the way the smell of her leather jacket combined with her own scent to make something new and utterly sensual.

Fuck, this was ridiculous. With any luck Jericho would be getting in contact real soon and then she wouldn't be his problem anymore.

They came to a stop at an intersection, waiting for the signal. His building was just up ahead and he was running over in his head his plans for when Jericho got in contact, where he was going to get the man to meet him, and how that was all going to play out.

Then Violet jerked suddenly away from him.

Because he was a little distracted, his reaction wasn't quite what it should have been, his fingers closing around her arm just a fraction too late.

He cursed viciously, but she was already running, flinging herself across the street heedless of the traffic, ignoring the sounds of car horns as she dodged them. And for a second he found himself watching in amazement, because shit, the gall of the woman. She just never gave up, did she?

Then he was running himself, plunging into the crowded mass of vehicles after her. Tires squealed, more horns sounding, the shouts of drivers echoing as he slid over the hood of one car then dodged a motorcycle. He ignored all of them, his attention fixed on a small figure in black running for her life down the sidewalk.

She hadn't a chance of course. He was stronger and faster, and although fear must have given her wings, his anger was rocket fuel. She was his only chance to get to Jericho, and he was not letting her get away.

The distance between them decreased by the second, and when she turned her head to look behind her it decreased even more as she slowed. She whipped her head back around and tried to put on a burst of speed, but even that wasn't going to save her.

He wasn't even near to being winded.

There weren't a lot of people around, but even so he had to catch her quickly in case someone decided to take action and call the cops. Which would be the last fucking thing he needed.

He ran faster, closing the distance.

Violet was heading toward a group of people standing on the sidewalk up ahead chatting, but she must have realized she wasn't going to reach them in time, because she suddenly changed direction, darting down what looked like an alley way between two buildings.

Bad idea.

He reached the alley seconds later, racing after the dark figure fleeing down it.

Catching her at the halfway point, Elijah reached out and grabbed her, hauling her around then pushing her up against the rough brick of one of the buildings bordering the alley.

She struggled at first, pushing against him, and then, when he didn't move, she went still, lifting her chin and staring up at him. She was panting, her skin flushed pink with exertion, her blue-green eyes glittering. Fear flickered there, unmistakable. Yet not as much as he'd thought. In fact, she looked more angry than anything else.

Christ. This woman.

"What the fuck was that?" He put a hand on her shoulder and pinned her against the wall. "You do that again and I'll make you wish you'd never been born."

She stared at him, the fear disappearing, replaced by a kind of determined defiance. Then, shockingly, her mouth curved and she gave a breathless laugh. "Oh, come on. I had to try, right?"

And for some reason he couldn't possibly fathom, her laughter made a surge of intense rage go through him. He was sick of her bravado. Sick of her defiance. This determination to push him, test him. This complete refusal to be cowed.

She had to stop. She had to learn he was somone to be feared. Not some weak little fuck in a suit who could be manipulated into doing whatever she wanted.

She wanted to push him? Consider him pushed.

"You think this is a game?" He leaned in, so close they were almost nose to nose. "Well, do you, Violet? You think that when I catch you, it's your turn to chase me?"

Her smile became twisted and he could see the rage begin to flicker again in the turquoise depths of her eyes. Rage and fear, they always went hand in hand. So she was scared and she hated it, and she didn't want him to see it. Well, fuck, he could work with that.

"Of course this is a game," she said, a sneer in her voice. "It's called outwit the big dumb criminal." Her breath was coming in rushing bursts—he could hear it despite the noise of the traffic coming from the street. "Am I winning yet?"

"No." He stepped closer, forcing her harder against the wall with his body, physically intimidating her. "You don't get to win. You don't get to do anything but shut the fuck up and do as you're told."

Even now, even when he was looming over her and his anger had to be scaring her, she had that little chin of hers lifted. And there was something other than anger gleaming in her eyes. A spark of . . . Jesus. Was that excitement?

"Or what?" Violet demanded. "You keep telling me about all this stuff you're going to do—"

He reached out with his other hand, took her jaw in a hard grip, cutting off the stream of words. "I keep telling you that you should be afraid," he said, coating each word with ice. "But you don't listen. Perhaps you'll listen now."

Her eyes had gone wide and for some reason her gaze had dropped to his mouth. An unwanted physical awareness began to seep through him. Of how soft her skin felt against his fingers and how red her lips were. How she'd trembled when he'd put a hand to her throat back in the store. . . . She'd wanted him. Except she had no idea what she was asking for.

So? Show her. Scare the shit out of her.

Elijah tightened his grip on her jaw just a little, tilting her head back.

Then he covered her mouth with his.

She'd known it was going to happen. From the moment he'd taken her jaw in his hand, his fingers pressing against her skin, she'd known. Something about the fury in his eyes, about the way he'd looked at her. Intense, focused. As if she was the only thing in the world he was aware of.

Her heart was slamming hard against her ribs, her breathing out of control and not just from her desperate getaway sprint. She didn't understand why running from him had had wild sparks of excitement scattering through her, not when logic told her she should be terrified.

Sure, she had been scared and yes, angry too, especially when he'd caught her.

But a deep part of her had known she'd never be able to escape him. And that same deep part had wanted her to run anyway, to have him chase her.

So he had. He'd taken off after her in a wild hunt, just as his surname promised.

She hadn't known till he'd caught her how much she'd wanted to be caught, and she'd known that was wrong. How weird it was to feel thrilled that someone had come after her, had chased her, run her down, because they didn't want her to get away from them.

No one in her life had ever come after her. No one had ever chased her.

Which probably only went to show how fucked up she

was. Because it wasn't as if Elijah wanted her for anything more than bait.

But right in this moment, Violet didn't care. His mouth was on hers and he was kissing her, and it was raw and passionate and so hot she was going to go up in flames.

She wanted this. Despite everything she knew about herself, despite everything she was afraid of, she wanted this so badly. And she wanted him to take it so she didn't have to make the decision herself.

He kissed her the way he'd run her down, conquering her, taking her. His tongue pushed deep into her mouth, tipping her head back against the brick wall behind her, allowing her no space to pull away or deny him. And then there was nothing but heat, the taste of him, earthy and dark, with a kick of alcohol like black coffee laced with scotch.

She groaned, unable to help herself, hunger flooding through her. There was just something about the ice in his voice and the heat of his mouth, with the way he was holding her jaw, not painfully tight yet firm. Keeping her in place as he devoured her.

The contrasts of him made her shiver with delight. Because *something* was shattering that cold, merciless exterior of his, and letting the heat of the man beneath it show through. Something was getting to him, changing him, and she thought that something might be her.

It was thrilling. Powerful. Finally, after all these years, she actually reached someone.

Her fingers pressed up against the granite-hard wall of his chest, the cotton of his long-sleeved shirt so warm. She loved the feel of him, the leashed strength and power beneath her palms. The flex and release of hard muscle. And she loved, too, how helpless she felt next to him, even though she had no idea why that was. Probably something to do with control, but she couldn't really think about that right now. Not when he released her jaw, running his hands behind her head to curl into the short spikes of her hair, holding onto them tight, pulling her head back even further.

Kissing her harder.

Her hands slipped down his chest, finding their way underneath the hem of his shirt and finding smooth, fever-hot skin beneath it.

Elijah made a sound in his throat, harsh and raw, and suddenly she was pinned to the wall by the length of his body, one powerful thigh thrust between hers, pressing the seam of her pants hard against the most sensitive part of her.

She shuddered, her hips flexing helplessly against him as he tore his mouth from hers and kissed along her jaw and down her throat. There were teeth against her skin, grazing, a sharp pain as he nipped her. But that didn't matter. The pain was all part of it. A great, dark bonfire of sensation that she wanted to burn in.

This is a really bad idea. You weren't supposed to let yourself go like this.

No, she wasn't, and yet she couldn't remember why.

Was it so wrong to want to be touched? To be kissed? Was it so wrong to be wanted by someone, even if it was by the man who'd captured her at gunpoint?

No one had come after her but him. No one had wanted her but him.

She wasn't going to give that up, not yet.

"You should be afraid of me, princess." His voice, rough and gritty near her ear, his breath warm against the side of her neck. "Why aren't you afraid?"

Her hands slid up over the hard surface of his stomach, feeling every dip, every hollow. Reading the sharp definition of his muscles like a blind woman reading Braille. "Because you want me," she murmured thickly.

"Because you won't hurt me. You talk big, Elijah, but you're not as cold as you like to make out."

The fingers curled in her hair tightened, his mouth nuzzling her throat. "You shouldn't say those things. Don't you know that only makes me want to show you why you're wrong?"

"Do it." She was panting because the pressure of his thigh between hers was driving her insane. She couldn't stop herself from rocking against it, seeking more friction, more pressure. "I told you before I wanted it."

"Fuck." The word sighed against her skin and she shivered as his free hand slid down over the front of her top, cupping her breast, his thumb brushing over the hard outline of her nipple. "You've got no idea what you're even asking for."

Well, maybe she didn't. Then again she wasn't stupid. "Perhaps I'm not the one who's afraid. Perhaps it's you."

His hand on her breast shifted, her nipple caught between his thumb and forefinger. And a gasp tore from her throat as he pinched her. Hard.

"And what would you know about me, you delicious little bitch?"

Such icy words said in a cold, cold voice. They made her shiver with delight. Because threading each of those words was a heat that gleamed like a strand of gold through a coal seam.

He was trying to distance her with them, maybe. Yet when she looked up into his face and met his dark eyes, it wasn't distance she saw there. Or snow and ice. She could have burst into flame from one look alone.

"Show me then," she whispered, unable to look away. "Show me what I should be afraid of."

He stared at her, his gaze sharp and bright as obsidian, and a fleeting doubt streaked through her mind. Perhaps she shouldn't have said that after all.

But it was too late. Because suddenly he bent and his mouth was on hers again, ravaging, taking. A hard, desperate kiss that had her hands sliding around his waist and up his back, her fingers digging into all that hot skin and hard muscle, holding on tight as he devoured her like a starving man devouring the first meal he'd had in years.

Then he lifted his head again, letting go of her hair and her breast, his fingers moving to the waistband of her pants and pushing them down with a short, sharp movement, taking her panties with them.

You're really going to let him do this? Screw you in an alleyway in the middle of the day? This is what your desperation will lead you to do . . .

God, who the hell cared about her desperation and what she was doing? Did it really matter? She was twenty-six and she'd been alone a long time, starved for contact, for touch. For a connection in some way to one other person. Her father was a monster, her mother a society ice queen, and her beloved brother, the only deep connection she'd ever had, was gone, disappeared.

Now this was all she had. And she didn't care whether that made her so desperate she'd let this man screw her up against a wall in the middle of the day. She didn't care about any of it.

So she ignored the voice in her head. She ignored everything. The people moving past the entrance to the alley, the music coming from one of the windows above her head, the sirens and car horns. The roar of the city.

There was only one thing that mattered and that was him and what he was going to do.

The cold air on her skin raised goose bumps everywhere and she was shaking as he put his hands on her waist and turned her around so her back was to him.

"Hands on the wall," he ordered.

She didn't even think about not obeying, the brick rough

beneath her palms as she did as she was told. She couldn't get a breath, her heartbeat roaring in her head like a hurricane.

His arm slid around her waist, holding her, and there was heat against her back. Her breath sawed in and out, little chills running up and down her spine.

She could hear the sound of a zipper and she had to close her eyes, bite down hard on her lip because she didn't know what sounds were going to come out of her mouth and she was half afraid of begging or pleading, or moaning with hunger. She might even cry, because for some reason this was agony. The combination of visceral need and anticipation, of not being able to see what he was doing. Not being able to know . . .

"Elijah." His name was a raw whisper as she turned her head, her cheek against the brick. "I—"

His free hand slid down her stomach, his fingers pushing through the damp curls between her thighs, finding and circling her clit, cutting her words off dead. The breath left her in a sharp exhalation and her hips jerked, pleasure streaking through her like lightning. "Oh . . . God . . ."

She'd used her own hand like this some nights, when she'd been lonely and craving something she didn't have a name for, bringing herself some pleasure. But her own touch had never been this hard, this ruthless. His thumb pressed down hard on her clit while he slid a finger inside her, tearing a groan from her and making her legs tremble. This pleasure wasn't the slow build she was used to. This was sudden and raw, an electric shock from a hundred-volt cable.

Barely able to process that touch, she nearly groaned again when heat burned along the length of her spine as he pressed her against the wall, his fingers suddenly spreading her sex wide, the head of his cock pushing against her entrance. Then he flexed his hips, thrusting hard and deep without any kind of hesitation at all, impaling her.

A hoarse little scream tore from her throat, because although she'd been expecting pain, she hadn't expected that raw pleasure to get even sharper. Or that the combination of both should be so intense, so vicious. That he'd feel so big and that he didn't stop. He drew back, then thrust again, pushing deep, shoving her against the bricks in front of her. One arm was still curled around her waist, his other hand between her thighs, his fingers circling and stroking her clit with merciless expertise, intensifying the pleasure with every stroke.

Words came out of her mouth, words she barely heard, and she didn't know whether it was a plea to stop or a plea to continue. "Elijah . . . please . . . Oh God . . . please . . ."

His teeth were at the side of her neck, and he was moving inside her even deeper, even harder, each thrust pushing her into the wall, and her legs were shaking, the maddening circling of his fingers relentless. She could hardly breathe through the sharp edge of pleasure.

This was way more than she'd thought. Way more than she'd ever imagined.

He bit her in the sensitive place between shoulder and neck, the pain only adding to all the sensations, the stretching of her sex around his cock and the merciless friction as he drove himself into her. The brick scraping at her palms, scratching her cheek. The iron weight of his arm around her, the slide of his fingers on her clit. Ruthless, searching.

A rough, cold wall at her front, a hot, hard wall at her back. And she was crushed between.

God, she loved it. Perversely it made her feel safe, protected. All those hard surfaces containing all the wildness inside of her. A wildness gathering tighter and tighter, a wave about to break. A bomb about to explode. She squeezed her eyes shut tighter, her whole body beginning to shake, sounds she had no control over starting to come out of her mouth.

She wanted to turn, to see his face, see if he was feeling this like she was, but she couldn't. And a nameless panic gripped her, as if she was on a roller coaster moving faster and faster, and she couldn't stop it or slow it down. Because nothing would. She was going to come and come hard, right here in this alleyway, with a man who she'd repeatedly tried to tell herself wasn't dangerous.

But he was. Of course he was. She just hadn't realized where the danger was coming from.

He was right, she should have listened.

Then his thumb pressed down on her clit as he thrust high and hard, and the wave broke, the bomb exploded, her scream bouncing off the buildings on either side of them.

And she came and came and came.

CHAPTER EIGHT

Honor paced back and forward in front of the tall windows of Gabriel Woolf's Tribeca apartment, watching as the sleet hit the glass. Crap weather for a really crap day.

"Eva'll be here in five," Gabriel's deep voice rumbled from behind her. "She's got a lead."

Honor stopped and turned to stare at the man she'd fallen so unexpectedly and so deeply in love with.

He was coming across the apartment toward her, tucking his phone away into the pocket of his jeans, all contained power and leashed menace. God, so sexy. Construction magnate and ex–motorcycle club president, he was the ultimate bad boy.

She'd never get tired of watching him.

Gabriel reached her, his long-fingered hands settling on her waist, pulling her close. His dark eyes were fierce, searching. "You okay?"

Honor swallowed, letting herself lean against him, content to absorb his heat and strength for a moment. "No, not really." Because she wasn't. The last few weeks had been hell. First Alex had been shot and almost killed, then the real identity of Gabriel's father had come out. Evelyn Fitzgerald, pillar of New York society, also rapist, murderer, drug lord and pimp.

And now that the man was dead, she couldn't get ahold of Violet, his daughter and her best friend.

She was worried, terribly worried, and no amount of pretending otherwise was going to work. Before all the crap had gone down with Fitzgerald, Violet had sent a text telling Honor she wanted to see her. Honor hadn't replied immediately, too caught up with the discovery that it was Fitzgerald who'd been behind many of the awful things that had happened to her friends. But after he'd subsequently been shot and the truth about him being Gabriel's father had come out, she immediately picked up her cell and tried to call her friend.

Except Violet hadn't answered. She hadn't texted either.

Which made Honor worried, because there had been something urgent in the first text Violet had sent. *I need to tell you something.*

And now she'd seemingly disappeared.

At first Honor had wondered if it was shock at Violet's father's murder—security expert Zac Rutherford's cleanup crew had removed all evidence of the real cause of Fitzgerald's death, courtesy of Eva and point-blank range, planting evidence that would lead police to the assumption of a professional hit. But as the hours had ticked by and there was no contact from Violet, Honor had begun to wonder if something more sinister had happened.

Fitzgerald had a lot of enemies and now that he was gone, there were probably many people who'd want to take advantage of that. People who might find his daughter fair game. His unsuspecting daughter.

Honor had tried getting in contact with Hilary Fitzgerald, Evelyn's wife, but the woman was refusing all calls and Honor wasn't able to get any information about Violet from her secretary who'd obviously been tasked with fielding all the attention.

Going around to Violet's Upper West Side apartment

had drawn a blank too. There had been no answer to her knocks, the apartment remaining silent.

It was then that Honor had become officially worried and gone to Gabriel.

They really didn't need another problem, because although Fitzgerald was now dead, the remains of his empire were still very much alive and someone would want to know who'd taken it out. Someone would want payback. Then there was the fact that the man's drug and human trafficking businesses seriously needed taking down, and if anyone could do that, it was the Nine Circles. Eva King, CEO of Void Angel, one of the country's biggest tech companies, and tech head extraordinaire, had already begun putting together evidence for an anonymous tip-off to the CIA and Interpol, since getting the authorities involved was the next step.

Yet Gabriel had been insistent that tracking down Violet was a priority. Not that any of the others had protested. Violet was now his half-sister, and that made her one of theirs.

His hands tightened on Honor's waist. "We'll find her," he said with his characteristic certainty. "Don't worry, baby."

She rested her palms on his chest, loving the hard warmth beneath the dark blue cotton of his T-shirt. "Thank you. I know there's not a lot of time, what with—"

"Hey," he interrupted gently but firmly. "Violet's your friend and she's my fucking half sister. You really think I'd just let her disappear?"

Honor sighed. "No, of course not. We've just got a lot of other things to think about. And . . . well, I don't even know if she *is* missing."

"She's not answering your calls or your texts, and she's not at her apartment. That's enough for me to start getting worried, especially after what happened to Fitzgerald."

Honor stared at the material of his shirt. "She's not involved in any of what went on with her father, Gabe. I know she's not."

A gentle finger caught her beneath her chin, tilting her head up so she met his dark brown eyes. "I know she's not. Believe me. But that shithead's got lots of enemies around, and now that he's gone, she's a sitting duck."

Anxiety twisted inside Honor's chest. "What if she's dead already? What if someone got rid of her?"

Gabriel's thumb and forefinger gripped her chin a little harder. "Hey, we don't know what's happened and wild guesses won't help. She's a valuable hostage. Which means if she's been taken, someone's gonna want to keep her alive."

He wasn't wrong. She just had to keep hold of that hope. "Okay, you're right." Honor let out a shaky breath. "It's just going to come as a huge shock to her. God, she'll be so scared."

One corner of Gabriel's mouth turned up a little. "I don't know her like you do, but if she's related to me in any way, she's not gonna be scared. She's gonna be pissed."

Honor thought about it for a moment. Violet was laid-back, a perpetual student, always giving the impression that she was flitting through life and never settling. But there had been moments when Honor had wondered if that was the real Violet. Whether there was something more behind the dreads and the silvery jewelry and hippie clothes. At college Violet had hung out with the arty, alternative crowd, and Honor had heard the stories of their wild parties and even wilder sexual exploits. Her friend gave off the impression of a free spirit who did what she wanted and didn't care what anyone thought of her. Yet she'd been very caring about other people. Certainly she'd always been very supportive of Honor.

Sometimes though, Honor got the feeling that all of it

was an act, a mask Violet hid behind. That her concern for other people was merely a way of distracting from her own issues, a method to keep everyone at a distance. Honor had never pushed it with her friend, since at the time she'd been running from things herself. But now she wondered about it.

Maybe Gabriel was right. Maybe Violet was stronger than Honor thought.

At that moment, there was a buzz from Gabriel's security system, heralding Eva's arrival no doubt.

Sure enough, a minute or two later, a small woman in black jeans, an Iron Maiden T-shirt, black leather jacket, and steel-toed Doc Marten boots stalked in. Her silver hair was in a long ponytail down her back and she carried a small laptop with her.

There was something different about her today that had Honor frowning. Then she realized. Eva didn't have Zac with her.

"Hey." Eva greeted Honor shortly as she headed toward Gabriel's heavy wooden dining table. "You're going to want to see this."

Typical Eva. She wasn't very demonstrative and didn't mess around with small talk, but once she gave her loyalty, it was to the death.

"Eva," Honor began as she followed the other woman over to the table, "I can't thank you enough for—"

"It's okay," Eva interrupted, putting the laptop down on the table. "Violet needs to be found, that's all there is to it."

Gabriel, who'd gone to open the door, now emerged from the hallway, his phone in his hand. "How did you get over here, Eva? Zac just called to ask whether you got here safely."

Eva gave a snort as she pulled out a chair and sat down, reaching out to push a button on the computer. "Asshole.

I already texted him to tell him I was here." Despite her obvious annoyance, there was a thread of something that Honor thought was probably affection in her voice.

The past couple of weeks had changed things for all of them, and while some of those things hadn't been good, some of them were. Like Zac and Eva finally getting together.

Honor had been surprised to learn they hadn't been an item before, considering the way Zac stood guard over her like Cerberus before the gates of Hell. But given Eva's traumatic background, it wasn't any wonder.

"He said you came by yourself. On the subway." Gabriel's disbelief was palpable. Before a couple of days ago, Eva never went anywhere by herself.

Now, the small silver-haired woman only lifted a shoulder "What can I say? I'm a badass motherfucker."

"You can say that again." Gabriel came to stand behind her chair. "What made you want to go and attempt something like that?"

"Zac likes the subway. I wanted to see it from his point of view."

"Cute. But Zac wasn't happy about it."

"Zac can stick it up his butt." Eva sounded completely unconcerned. "Do you want to see this lead or not?"

"Yes, we most certainly do," Honor said crisply, giving Gabriel a quelling look. "What have you got?"

Gabriel gave her a wolfish grin, but stepped back, giving her some room to see the screen from behind Eva's chair.

The other woman's fingers moved quickly over the keyboard. "Okay, so I ran that facial recognition software I've been playing with through a couple of databases. And it came up with a hit." She pressed a button and a picture abruptly came up on the screen.

It looked like it was a still from a security camera, given the angle. A shot of a subway car full of people.

Eva's fingers moved on the track pad, and the picture zoomed in on a woman sitting with her hands folded in her lap. The magnification made everything a little blurry, but there was no mistaking the long dreadlocks hanging down the woman's back. Or the little stud in her nose. The finely drawn lines of her pretty face.

Violet.

Honor let out a shaky breath. There was a time stamp on the image. Yesterday afternoon, at least an hour or so after everything had gone down with Fitzgerald. "That's her. So she was on the subway."

"Yeah, but wait. There's more." Eva pressed another button and another series of shots came up. Pictures of Violet sitting there, then standing up as everybody in the car started to do the same, moving toward the doors. Must have been slowing for an approach into a station.

"Look," Eva said softly. And the last picture came up. Of Violet waiting to get out, standing among the crowd of people.

At first Honor couldn't see what the big deal was, and then Eva slowly magnified the image. Behind Violet, standing very, very close, was a tall, massively built man in a long, black overcoat. Again, his features were blurry, but nevertheless she recognized him. The scarred face, the dark, cold, empty eyes. Elijah.

"Fuck," said Gabriel.

His arm had come around Honor's waist and for a moment she could only lean against his big, warm body and stare at the image on the screen.

"Yeah," Eva muttered. "And that's not all."

Another series of images popped up on the screen, all taken from what looked like more security cameras. Of

Violet walking out of the subway station with Elijah. He was standing very close and had one hand on her arm, the other lowered and hidden in the folds of his coat.

"He's got a gun on her," Gabriel murmured.

"That's what I thought too." Eva touched the track pad again, bringing up another image. This time it was the outside of the subway station and it was possible to see Violet and Elijah standing on the sidewalk with a cab drawn up beside them.

Honor didn't know what to feel. Relieved that Violet wasn't dead—or at least she hadn't been yesterday—or even more worried considering who'd taken her. "God, so what does that mean? That she's been kidnapped by this Elijah guy? But . . . I mean why?"

"Elijah's an asshole, no doubt about it," Eva said quietly. "But Zac and I had dealings with him. Up in Fitzgerald's office, he was supposed to have a gun on me the whole time and yet at the crucial point, he let me go. I don't know why. I do know he wanted to kill Fitzgerald himself and he was really pissed when I pulled the trigger."

"Not forgetting what happened in Monte Carlo with Alex," Gabriel added. "He tipped Alex and Katya off about Fitzgerald's interest."

Honor shook her head, glancing back to the image on the screen. Violet's face was curiously blank, but Honor recognized that look. Shock. Fear. Whatever Elijah wanted her for, it wasn't good.

"He was going to kill Zac though, wasn't he?" she asked Eva.

Eva nodded. "Yeah, but like I said, he was pretty fucking pissed. He wanted Fitzgerald's head."

"So he's gone after his daughter instead," Gabriel murmured. "He wants her for something. Revenge maybe."

"It doesn't matter why." Honor looked at him. "What matters is that we find her."

Gabriel didn't reply, but then he didn't have to. She could see nothing but fierce agreement in his eyes.

"Funny you should mention that," Eva said. "Because I got the name of the cab company from the taxi in that security camera shot. Managed to hack into their databases too. You can see all the fares and where they went, it's very handy."

Honor glanced at Eva. "Please tell me you—"

"Way ahead of you." Eva gave her a smug grin. "They were dropped off at a West Village address. I checked the street and it's a park, nothing much there unfortunately. But they would have had to walk to wherever they're going, which means we can narrow down their destination pretty significantly."

Honor frowned. "But they could have gotten another taxi, couldn't they?"

Gabriel released her to lean over Eva's shoulder and study the laptop screen closely. "No," he said. "I don't think Elijah would have wanted to risk too many people seeing him. Didn't Zac get a shot off at him? "

"Yeah, he did. But the bastard ran before Zac could take him down." Eva did something with the track pad and another program came up, a map with lines going everywhere. "I'm trying to predict directions they might have taken at the moment and am running that facial recognition stuff through security-camera footage from the area. There aren't many cameras unfortunately, but with any luck, something will turn up."

Honor tried to pull herself together. God, she'd been through worse. She just had to hope Gabriel was right and Elijah wanted Violet for something specific. Something he wanted to keep her alive for.

"Well," she said firmly. "If he's got a gunshot wound, he can't have gotten far."

"He better not have." Gabriel's smile had turned razor

sharp. "No one fucks with my family and gets away with it."

"Shit." Eva sat forward all of a sudden, staring at her laptop. "Looks like we've got him nailed down." She typed something and another picture popped up. A street view this time, of a couple waiting for a crossing signal. And if Honor hadn't already known Elijah, she would have had to look twice at the woman standing next to him in order to recognize Violet.

Because all her hair was cut off.

"Oh my God," Honor murmured, shocked. "What happened to her?" Violet had had dreadlocks for years, and Honor had gotten used to the long golden tails of her friend's hair. Now Violet looked almost . . . naked without them. Small and vulnerable.

"This is today," Eva said. "A couple of hours ago from the looks of things."

"We got an address?" Gabriel was all business.

"Yeah, totally." She called up another program and typed something into it. "Just sent it to your phone."

"Good." Gabriel stepped away. "Time to go see a man about my fucking sister."

Oh really. So he was going without her? No damn way.

Honor reached out and caught his arm. "I'm coming."

But he had that look on his face she recognized, the one there was no arguing with. "Not this time, baby."

"She's my friend, Gabe."

"And like I said, she's my fucking sister."

Eva rolled her eyes. "Jesus, so much testosterone. I can't handle it."

Gabriel ignored her, his dark eyes squarely on Honor. "Let me do this, baby. Let me help Violet. I didn't get the chance to take on Fitzgerald, and fuck, I've got to do something."

It was as close to pleading as he ever got, and she knew

the need he had to take care of what was his. He hadn't told her anything of what had happened when he'd gone up to Fitzgerald's apartment to take one last look at the body of the man who'd fathered him, and she hadn't asked. He'd tell her when he was ready, and perhaps this was part of it.

She sighed. "Okay. But promise me you'll be careful."

"I promise." He reached out and drew her in for a swift, hard kiss. "And I'll bring her back, Honor. I'll promise you that too."

Elijah turned his head into the thick, short silk of Violet's hair, panting like a dog, the blood roaring in his ears from the aftereffects of the first orgasm he'd had with another person in seven years.

He couldn't seem to get a proper breath. His senses swam, full of the scents of sandalwood and musk, the sound of the music pouring from a window above them ringing in his head. And the softness of the woman between him and the wall.

What the actual fuck had he done?

He was still buried balls deep inside her, the tight heat of her pussy clenching hard around his cock, the sound of her scream echoing around him. And he knew he'd screwed up, that somehow he'd made a mistake. Because why else would the years of iron control have deserted him, leaving him fucking Violet Fitzgerald of all people, his goddamn prisoner, in a dank alleyway?

He didn't even know how it had happened. All he'd wanted was to scare her, make her see what a bad idea it was to push him. Show her the reality of what she wanted, the reality of him.

But she hadn't protested. She hadn't been scared. She'd reached for him and touched him instead.

Marie would be appalled.

And she would. He'd never done anything like this with her.

Fuck. Fuck. *Fuck.*

Shoving himself from the wall, he jerked his jeans back up then tucked himself away, trying not to see how his hands shook. Violet was still leaning against the brick, her head turned to one side, her eyes closed, her leather pants pulled down to her knees.

His chest felt tight. She looked like a fragile piece of porcelain that had cracked and then been badly glued back together. A tear gleamed on her cheek, and there was something desperately vulnerable about her bare skin, pale in the cold light of the alleyway. Her neck, left bare by the haircut he'd given her. The even paler curves of her ass and the swell of her thighs . . .

He couldn't take it. Tugging up her panties and pants, he smoothed them into place then pulled down her silky green top, covering up all that painfully bared skin.

He couldn't understand why this mattered to him. Why the sight of her shattered like that made him feel weak. It disturbed him on a deep level he wasn't aware he still felt these days. Because surely he'd smashed that part of himself into oblivion? Apparently not.

She didn't move as he touched her, standing there as if she needed the wall for support. And then as he stepped back, she swayed and he realized that shit, she *did* need that fucking wall.

He caught her before she slid down the rough brick and into a heap at his feet, his arm around her waist, drawing her into his body. She was so warm, and her feminine scent hit him again like a rock to the back of the head.

Jesus fucking Christ, he had to get himself together.

And then she turned her head into his chest, as if she was seeking comfort and reassurance.

This time it didn't feel like a rock to his head but a knife between his ribs.

What a fucking joke. Doesn't she know what you are? What a monster you've turned yourself into?

He wanted to push her away, finish the lesson he'd been trying to teach her, but for some reason he just couldn't bring himself to do so. And then he caught a glimpse of blood on her cheek, a scrape from where he'd shoved her against the wall. The tightness in his chest clenched even harder and he found himself wanting to touch that scrape, wipe the blood away.

"We have to go." He forced the words out, rough and sharp as broken glass, keeping his hand exactly where it was.

She was leaning against him, her eyes shut. "Gimme a minute." Her voice didn't sound any better than his.

But he didn't want to wait another minute, not with her standing close to him. Not with her scent everywhere and her heat right up against him. So he moved, bending to scoop her up into his arms, then turning and striding forward to the alleyway entrance.

She weighed almost nothing, so slight and insubstantial.

"Don't." She made a cursory protest, wriggling and pushing at his chest. But he ignored her, holding her tighter as he stepped onto the sidewalk, continuing on to the apartment just up ahead.

There was no one around, and the few people that were didn't even turn to look at them.

One good thing about New York. Nothing much drew people's attention.

Violet had stopped protesting, lying still in his arms as he got to his building and stepped inside. She had her face turned away and her eyes were resolutely shut. She kept them that way as he took her upstairs and into the apartment, kicking the door shut behind him.

And only once it was closed did she twist out of his arms. He let her go, not knowing what the hell else to do. His wound ached, probably due to that sprint after her and yet, despite that, his cock was semi-hard because apparently once wasn't nearly enough.

No fucking way. Not again. He wouldn't lose it like that a second time. He'd be goddamn ice.

Violet didn't turn to look at him, starting in the direction of the hallway.

No wonder. She probably wanted to wash him off her.

Let's not forget the fact you had unprotected sex too.

Fuck. This wasn't getting any better, was it?

"I'm clean," he said, his voice harsh in the silence of the apartment.

She stopped, but didn't turn around. "What?"

"I said I'm clean. We had unprotected sex, Violet."

"Oh. That." She sounded curiously blank. "Well, I'm clean too."

Her acceptance and complete lack of inflection made him angry for some obscure reason. "If you want proof though, you're shit out of luck."

She was silent a moment. Then she turned, her face white, the blood on her cheek like a desecration. "I don't want proof. But if you need it from me, you should know that I haven't had sex before. So you got lucky. You screwed a virgin."

It shouldn't have made any difference. It should have meant nothing.

But it didn't.

Elijah's hands curled into fists, an intense, hot feeling beating behind his ribs. He had to get out of here. He had to get away from her. Just for a bit. Just to calm himself the fuck down and figure out what the hell he was doing with his goddamn hostage.

"I'm going out," he snapped, ignoring her little confession, because if he made it into a big deal, it would be. "Am I going to come back and find you bleeding out in the fucking bathtub again?"

Her jaw looked tight and there was something glittering in her eyes. Something he didn't want to see. "Oh, what? So you trust me enough to leave me alone now?"

"Answer the fucking question."

"No, I am not going to slit my wrists in the bathtub again."

"Good." He turned without another word and went to the door, stepping out and locking it behind him.

Out on the sidewalk, the sleet had started up again, the wind blowing biting pieces of ice that stung against his cheeks. It was cold, but at least it blew out all the remaining sandalwood and musk scent clouding his brain.

He took off in the opposite direction from where they'd come, heading for a park a couple of blocks down. He didn't let himself think about Violet. Pretending that moment in the alleyway had never happened was the only way to deal with it. The only way to get rid of that crushing feeling in his chest. The feeling he'd made a mistake that there was no coming back from.

Fuck. He was thinking about it again. That was *not* happening.

He dug into his jeans pocket for his phone and checked it. Still nothing from Jericho. For a second he debated sending the man a text telling him time was ticking down. But again, that would be giving too much away and he didn't want to appear desperate. He'd made the move, it was now Jericho's turn.

Passing by a newsstand, he bought a paper and took a

look through it quickly. There wasn't much in it this time about Fitzgerald, only a few passing mentions of stocks falling and boards in uproars following his murder. Nothing about the apparent disappearance of his daughter.

Excellent. There was no heat on his tail, which gave him plenty of time to come up with something if Jericho didn't show.

Approaching the park, he ditched the paper in a nearby trash can. He was just about to walk on when the back of his neck prickled.

He looked up sharply. Ahead of him, parked against the curb was a huge black motorcycle, a tall, golden-haired man in sunglasses, jeans, and leather jacket leaning against it.

Ah, fuck. He knew that prick. Had spent weeks gaining intel on him and the rest of his buddies. Gabriel Woolf, construction magnate and ex–outlaw biker. And clearly the guy was not here by coincidence, because even real life, as fucked up as it could be sometimes, wasn't that random.

How the hell had the guy found him?

Elijah curled his fingers around the Colt in his pocket. He kept his stance loose, ready to move in case the guy did something stupid like pull a gun. Thoughts of Violet fell away, the heat replaced instantly by cold, hard ice.

Woolf took his sunglasses off, holding them negligently in one hand. His dark eyes were absolutely expressionless as they met Elijah's.

"Woolf," Elijah said flatly. "What the fuck do you want?"

The other man held his gaze. "You got something of mine. I want it back."

"What the . . ." He stopped. Violet. Woolf was talking about Violet, he had to be. Which meant that he knew Elijah had her. Fucking wonderful. So how had that happened? And how the hell had Woolf tracked him down?

Briefly Elijah debated denying the fact he had Violet, but there didn't seem to be much point. She was a useful bargaining chip anyway, especially if Woolf and his friends wanted her too. He could use that, he definitely could.

"The Fitzgerald princess?" He clicked off the safety of the Colt in his pocket. "That's not going to be happening."

"Yeah, see, that's a problem." Woolf's voice was rough, but still casual. Like this was no big deal. "My woman's her best friend and pretty cut up about the fact that Violet just up and disappeared. And I don't like to see her upset. Which makes getting Violet back pretty fucking important to me."

"I don't care what's important to you," Elijah said coldly. "Your friends took something of mine, and if that means I have to take something of yours to get what I want, then I'm fucking doing it."

The expression on Woolf's face gave nothing away. "You wanted Fitzgerald's head, didn't you?"

Elijah wasn't surprised the other man knew. He'd been very clear about what he'd wanted to Zac Rutherford and Eva King. "I did," he snapped. "And I helped your so-called friends so they could help me get it. And then they took it from me."

Woolf stared at him for a long moment. "So what do you need Violet for?"

"None of your fucking business." As if he'd reveal any of his plans to this man.

"Like I said." Gabriel shifted on his feet, but he kept his hands where Elijah could see them, not obviously going for any weapon. "That's a problem for me."

"Too bad. I'm not interested in your problems."

"You might be more interested if I told you that you have a target on your back right now."

Elijah didn't bother looking around. If Woolf had him

covered, it wan't going to be obvious. Instead he made an effort to look relaxed. "You really think I'd go out without a backup plan? I've got someone on Violet. If I don't come back, then she won't either." A total fucking lie, but that didn't matter. He'd organize it as soon as he got back to the apartment.

Jesus, he wasn't on his game right now. He'd let her distract him, turn him from his purpose, and that couldn't happen again. He'd call some of his contacts, get something in place to make sure Violet stayed guarded. Then he'd put the pressure on Jericho, get this thing fucking done.

Woolf didn't say anything immediately, but there was something going on behind those hard, dark eyes. The man hadn't gotten where he was today by being stupid. "What was so important to you about Fitzgerald?" he asked after a moment.

"Why the hell should I tell you?"

Another moment of tense silence.

"Violet's my half sister," Woolf said. "Which makes her family. And you don't fuck with my family, understand?"

The words were hostile, no mistake about that. But Elijah also understood he'd just been given something important.

Violet was Woolf's half sister? How the hell did that work?

"Why would you tell me that?" he asked, ignoring his own curiosity.

"I give you something, you give me something." Woolf folded his arms. "Now's your chance, fucker."

"I don't have to give you a thing. Not when I have what you want."

"True. I could just have you shot right now and Violet'll have to take her chances."

"If Violet dies, your woman will be upset." Honor

St. James, of course. Violet's best friend and sister of Alex, the man he'd warned off back in Monte Carlo. The man who hadn't listened.

He didn't give a shit about either of them.

Woolf's features hardened. "Sacrifices. We all have to make them."

Of course they did. And hadn't Elijah sacrificed everything to get where he was now? To be within striking distance at last of what he wanted?

He stared at the other man. He knew about Woolf. Knew about the man's friends. Knew that revenge was what had motivated them.

Once, many years ago, he'd actually met Alex St. James. Back in another life, when he'd had Marie at his side, he'd been a member of Alex's exclusive Second Circle club. Privately Elijah had despised the man, thinking him a shallow, arrogant playboy who used his money and popularity to make himself feel important.

Now though, it was different. A man with demons was easy to recognize when you had a legion of your own following you.

St. James, Woolf . . . they're like you in many ways.

The Colt was warm against his palm. So easy to pull the trigger now, shoot this bastard in the chest. Except of course that would draw attention.

Gabriel Woolf's dark eyes held his without flinching, and Elijah was sure the bastard knew exactly how close to death he was. And didn't seem to give a shit. It was . . . impressive.

"You wanted Fitzgerald's head?" Woolf said in a low, hard voice. "Well, so did the rest of us. We wanted him dead, just like you. And now he is, yet you've got Violet. Which says to me that you're planning something more. Something bigger. Something that involves her." He paused, his gaze sharp. "Revenge. That's what you want, isn't it?"

Well, shit. The guy was guessing clearly, but they were pretty well-educated guesses. Still, that wasn't any surprise, not when it had been Woolf's own quest for revenge that had ended with Fitzgerald dead on the floor by Eva King's hand. In fact, if he hadn't been so set on revenge himself, he wouldn't have begrudged the tech CEO her own little piece of it. But unfortunately, she'd taken what he'd been waiting for and working toward almost an entire decade.

"Revenge," Elijah spat. "If it was as simple as that, I would have killed that motherfucker years ago. But it's not, and you've got no fucking idea what I want. So keep your guesswork and your speculation to yourself."

Woolf ignored him. "I know revenge. I know exactly how simple it is."

But Elijah hadn't trusted another soul for years. He wasn't about to start now. Easing off his finger on the Colt, he said flatly, "This conversation is over. I'm going to turn around and walk away, and if you don't want Violet Fitzgerald dead, you'll let me. I suggest following me is also a pretty bad fucking idea."

The other man's jaw tightened. "She's still alive then?"

"Yeah." Elijah gave him one last cold look. "She is. So far."

Then without waiting for him to respond, he turned around and began to walk away.

Woolf didn't call after him and no shots were fired.

And no one followed him.

CHAPTER NINE

Violet turned the shower mixer straight to hot, as hot as she could stand, then she pulled off all her clothes and got underneath the stinging spray, flinching only slightly as it hit her still-sensitive skin. She shivered, feeling weirdly hot all over, like she was burning and yet there was a piece of ice sitting in the middle of her soul.

No wonder. You screwed your captor. Just how fucked up are you?

Losing her virginity up against a wall in an alley to the man who'd kidnapped her . . . Yeah, that ranked pretty highly on the fucked-up scale. It should have felt sleazy and wrong, but it hadn't. It had been painful and raw and . . . God, amazing. Addicting. Feeling connected like that to someone else, for the first time her in life . . . She didn't know quite how to describe it. As if there had been a hole in her soul and he'd filled it.

There was no use pretending she didn't know how it had happened this time. She knew, oh yes, she did. She'd wanted him. She'd been desperate for him. For his heat and his hard, rough touch. Loving the fact that she was the absolute focus of that intense, cold black gaze. That he'd come after her, chased her down like a deer in the forest.

Shit, she was so screwed up. Was she really that desperate for attention she found it thrilling to be chased by her captor? Did she really want to feel wanted that much?

It's not surprising when you consider your parents.

No, she wasn't going to think about her parents. Not now. There were too many skeletons in that particular closet and she didn't particularly want to go digging through them.

Violet grabbed a cake of soap and began washing herself with deliberation, shivering a little at the slickness of her hand on her own skin. He hadn't hurt her and yet she felt raw, like the top layer of her skin had been taken off, leaving the rest of her flesh achingly sensitive to any touch. And the soap and water seemed to make no difference to the feeling. If anything, they only made it worse.

God, she had to stop this. She'd just had unprotected sex with the man who'd kidnapped her at gunpoint, and who knew what was going to happen because of that? Encouraging the feeling was only going to make it worse not better.

She sighed and put the soap back, shutting off the water firmly, then she stepped out of the shower stall and grabbed a towel, drying herself off before pulling on her clothes again. Wiping away the steam from the mirror, she examined the graze on her cheek from where she'd turned it against the brick wall as Elijah slammed himself into her.

Definitely insane. How could she have let that happen? The chances of her getting pregnant were slim since she'd just had her period, but the chance was still there. And as for anything else, she'd believed him when he'd told her he was clean. He didn't have any reason to lie and given how icy and remote he was, she couldn't see him being a dirty manwhore with tons of other women.

Not that appearances were anything to go by clearly, her father being a case in point.

And speaking of . . .

Yeah, that whole mess hadn't gone away. She might have made a very poor decision to finally have sex and had her mind completely blown, but she remained Elijah's hostage and that hadn't changed. And if she didn't figure out a way to escape, he was going to use her as bait to draw out a major crime boss whom he was then going to kill. What would happen to her after that was anyone's guess, but she didn't want to find out.

What she wanted was to follow up the lead she had on Theo, because God knew she wouldn't ever be able to come to terms with anything until the mystery of her brother's disappearance was solved. And in order to do that, she had to escape.

Perhaps there's a better way. Perhaps you can work with Elijah on that.

She frowned at herself in the mirror, her brain turning over the thought.

Okay, so Elijah wasn't going to kill her and he clearly wasn't going to hurt her either. But he wanted this Jericho guy, and she was apparently the key to drawing Jericho out. Maybe if she told Elijah that she was willing to help him get Jericho, he'd help her follow up her Theo lead?

There was, of course, no reason for him to do so. Then again, she could make life difficult for him.

Not forgetting the fact that now you know he has a weakness.

Her.

Violet smiled at herself, trying to ignore the stupid leap of excitement inside her at the thought of tangling again with Mr. Tall, Dark, and Scarred. She'd have to be careful, obviously, if she was going to exploit that particular vulnerability, especially when it was likely to get her caught up in it too. But if she knew the danger, she'd keep her head.

Make sure she stayed in charge of anything that went down. It was certainly worth a try, wasn't it?

The sound of the apartment door slamming shut echoed down the hallway, sending a shiver of ridiculous anticipation rolling through her.

She dismissed the feeling, lifting her hands to her short damp hair and running her fingers through it. It had started to curl, which was annoying, but there was nothing to be done about that. She was going to have to live with it.

Bracing herself with a deep breath, Violet was just about to go out into the main apartment living area, when Elijah strode past her down the hallway without a second glance. He disappeared into the bedroom and slammed the door after him.

She blinked at the closed door. Okay then. So he clearly wasn't in any mood to talk.

For a second she debated following him, but then dismissed the idea. She wasn't going to go running after him and begging him to listen to her idea. She had to start off strong and confident, as if she had power in this, because anything else would only end up ceding it to him, and he *really* didn't need any more power.

So she went back down the hallway and out into the apartment living area, automatically heading for the bookshelves again, if only because they gave her something interesting to look at while she waited.

But she didn't end up having to wait long.

She'd just bent to try to read the spine of a particularly old-looking book, when Elijah's footsteps came from behind her. She turned. And her mouth dried.

He'd changed from his jeans into a pair of loose black shorts that sat low on his hips and a fitted gray tank top. The tank left a lot of bronzed skin on show, revealing the hard-packed muscle of his shoulders, upper arms, and biceps. His legs were powerful and strong, with long, lean calves, and really, it wasn't any wonder he'd run her down earlier. Against a man with so much physical strength at his command, she hadn't a chance.

He went straight over to the gym area of the apartment and picked up the pair of boxing gloves that were on the floor by the punching bag. With a series of sharp, practiced movements, he pulled them on and tied them. Then, without glancing in her direction once, he began to attack the punching bag like it was his own personal enemy.

Violet could only stare, watching as his fists came out with frightening speed, the sounds of impact echoing through the apartment like pistol shots. And her breath caught because although she'd known how dangerous he was, the danger had always come from the gun he'd held pointed at her. She'd never seen him actually fight. But now he was definitely fighting, without qualm and without holding back, and quite frankly it was a little terrifying.

The power in those fists as they hit the bag was lethal, the muscles in his shoulders and upper arms flexing and releasing as he rained a hail of blows onto the bag. But even more frightening was the fury in his coal-black eyes, as if he wanted to tear something, or someone, apart.

Held motionless partly through fear and partly through that humming, tingling excitement she was beginning to recognize, Violet let herself watch him. He was like a machine, the bag swinging as he struck it again and again, the hard thumping sounds filling the apartment like blows from a jackhammer. Then he stopped for a moment, his attention on the bag as if he was checking to make sure it was still whole. He wasn't breathing hard, but a fine sheen of sweat gleamed on his skin.

Desire gripped her, because really, he was mesmerizing. Hard and raw and primal. Brutal too, yet beautiful for all of that. There was something about his strength, about his power, that attracted her on the most basic level. A cavewoman response no doubt, but there was no denying it.

She'd never thought she'd be the type to be attracted to that kind of masculinity, and yet here she was, unable to tear her gaze away from him.

Bastard. He'd screwed her up against a wall and then left. And now he was back, he was swinging at that bag like she wasn't even here. What the hell was his problem?

She wandered over to where he continued to rain punches down onto the bag, stopping a little distance away. He clearly wasn't going to talk, which meant she was going to have to.

"What happened?" she asked after a moment.

He didn't look at her. "None of your fucking business."

"So you're sulking?"

That got her a blazing glance from those dark eyes, sweeping over her like a flame from a blowtorch. But only for a moment, before he directed his attention back to the punching bag.

All right, so no talking about where he'd gone.

"Tell me about Jericho," she tried again. "Tell me what's going on with him."

Once again, he said nothing, his right fist snapping out and sending the bag twisting and turning on the rope it was suspended from.

Oh, fuck this.

Violet stepped forward and grabbed the bag, holding it steady. It was very heavy and she'd only just grasped it when he sent another punch to it, the impact vibrating through her body like she'd been hit by a bus.

He stopped immediately, fury crossing his scarred features as he straightened. "What the fuck are you doing?"

She caught her breath, holding on tightly to the bag, meeting his dark gaze head-on. "I'm trying to get some information, asshole. But you're too busy sulking about something to talk to me. I have to get your attention somehow."

He swiped the back of his hand across his forehead, wiping away the sweat. "Information? Why the hell would you think I'd give you information?"

"Because I asked for it."

His mouth twisted. "That's not how it works, princess."

"Then how does it work?" She let go of the bag and, before he could launch another punch at it, moved between him and it, the heavy canvas at her back. "I'm not going to cower at your feet or collapse in a puddle of fear. You can't threaten or intimidate me, Elijah. Not anymore."

Something in his eyes burned. "I can put you in the room downstairs."

"Yeah, you could. But you haven't yet, have you?"

"There's still time."

"That won't benefit you, though."

"It'll give me some fucking peace and quiet."

Violet straightened, squaring her shoulders, fully prepared to bluff him if need be. "Don't you want to hear my alternative plan?"

His dark brows drew down, the scar that ran through one of them white. "What plan?"

She held his gaze. "A little give and take. You give me something, I give you something."

"Why the fuck would I do that? You haven't got anything I want."

"Oh really?" She reached out, her hand shaking only a little, trailing her fingers over the damp cotton of the tank that stuck to his body, down over his chest and the hard corrugations of his abs. God, he felt so hot, so good. "I can think of something."

A muscle flexed in his jaw, but he didn't move. "I thought I told you about the dangers of playing me."

There was fury in his gaze, yet whether that was

directed at her in particular she didn't know. "I'm not playing you." She made herself hold his intense dark gaze. "I'm only telling you that I want information and I'm prepared to pay for it."

"Pay? With what?"

"Isn't it obvious?" She spread her hand out where it rested on his flat stomach, feeling the contraction of taut muscle beneath her palm. He was as unyielding as that damn brick wall. She swallowed, her mouth dry, hoping this wasn't as much of a gamble as she feared. "Me."

The look in his eyes flared, but the line of his jaw got even tighter. "You? But I don't want you, princess." He lifted one gloved fist and knocked her hand away. "I already had you, remember?"

It hurt, no pretending it didn't. Which was stupid because in order for it to hurt, she had to care and she'd thought she didn't care. Yet his utter dismissal slid under her skin like a thin sliver of glass.

Seriously. What did you expect? Hearts and flowers? Him getting down on his knees and declaring his undying love? You stupid little virgin.

Violet pushed the thoughts away hard. Getting hurt over this made no sense at all, and what's more, she couldn't afford to. She needed information. She needed him on her side and getting all teenaged-girl about it wasn't going to help.

"Of course I remember." She made no move to touch him again, keeping her hands in fists at her sides, staring up into his hard, scarred face. "I was there too, if you recall."

He took a breath, the cotton of his tank stretching over his broad chest, the tip of the eagle's wing of his tattoo showing beneath the material. "And it won't happen again." His voice was utterly certain.

Shit. There went that idea. What the hell did she do now?

Frustration began to rise, bringing with it her own anger. "Look, you bastard, hasn't it crossed your mind that telling me why you want to kill Jericho so badly might be a good thing? I mean, maybe I'll even be able to help."

He gave a harsh laugh. "Help? You? I don't think so, princess. All you need to do is be alive when he comes for you."

"And then what'll happen? You'll kill him? Is that before or after he kills me or whatever the hell he wants to do with me?"

Elijah lifted his hands, ripping off the gloves. "You keep making the same mistake, Violet. You keep thinking I give a shit about what happens to you. And I don't. All that matters, all that has *ever* mattered, is putting a bullet through that motherfucker's brain." Fury poured off him, the emotion almost palpable as he threw the gloves carelessly onto the floor.

"Why?" She couldn't stop the question from tumbling out. "What the hell did he do to you?"

Elijah looked at her, and the fury in his black eyes hit her like a blow. "Oh, he didn't do anything. It was your father who destroyed everything." He took a sudden step toward her, the movement unexpected enough that she backed away, only to be brought up short by the heavy punching bag against her spine. "It was fucking Fitzgerald who took *everything* I cared about away." He closed what little distance between them there was, his heat and fury pressing down on her like a blast wave from an explosion, his voice low and rough and vicious. "But he's dead and so I have to find some other way to do what needs to be done."

She found she was pressing herself hard into the unsteady weight of the punching bag, staring up into his eyes. Half of her going still like prey before a relentless hunter, the other half mesmerized by the sheer intensity of him.

Struggling to ignore the heat of his body only inches away, she tried to concentrate on what he was saying. "Dad did this? Did what? I don't understand what—"

His hand flashed out and she flinched, only to feel his fingers grip her jaw tight, tilting her head back. Then he bent, his midnight eyes so close and so dark. "Your father destroyed my life." Fury roughened the edges of the words. "So I spent the past seven years working my way to destroying his. But now he's dead and the only way to ensure all that work hasn't been a complete fucking waste of time is to take out Jericho." He paused, staring down into her face. "And if that means using you to do it, then that's what I'll do. It'll be poetic fucking justice. "

A shiver went down her spine, fear curling through her. Okay, so maybe her protestations that she wasn't afraid of him were a bit premature. Because there was no mercy in his expression. No softness at all. Only a hard, burning rage like a perpetual flame inside him.

But there was something else behind it too. Something bleak. Desolate. Lonely.

It pierced her fear, slid through her own anger, and struck deep in her soul. Because it felt familiar. As if she too had that kind of emptiness deep inside her. An emptiness that only wanted to be filled.

She didn't quite know what impulse it was that had her raising her hand and cupping the side of his face. Only that she hated that bleakness, that emptiness. And she wanted to do something about it, ease it somehow. Show him that she understood, that he wasn't alone.

He froze, his eyes going wide at the touch.

Rough stubble lined his jaw, scraping against her palm while the skin of his cheek was smooth and warm. And before she could stop herself, she traced the scar that twisted his mouth with her thumb, shifting her fingers to follow its path up across his cheek, narrowly missing his eye before slashing through one dark brow.

He didn't move and the grip on her jaw didn't lessen. But his eyes glittered, a hurricane in them. "Don't touch me." There was a raw sound running through the flat command in his words, undermining them like rust through an iron bar. "Don't you dare fucking touch me."

But he was touching her and that didn't seem fair, so she kept her hand right where it was, stroking her thumb across his mouth again, feeling the softness there. The only thing soft about him.

He made a sound in his throat and suddenly his grip on her jaw tightened even more. Then he closed the distance between them and took her mouth with his.

He hated the way she touched him. Hated how the gentleness of it contrasted so much with the rough way he was holding her. Hated how she was looking at him as if she saw something in him. Something that wasn't there.

Because there *was* nothing there. Nothing but anger and the grief he'd buried so far down he'd forgotten it still existed.

Fuck her and the way she managed to unlock those emotions purely with the touch of her hand. Fuck the way she made him so hungry, when he'd spent so many years excising those hungers from his life completely.

Fuck the way she'd just made him confess how his life had been destroyed, how she'd made him reveal it, because of who she was, because she was Fitzgerald's daughter.

That prick was dead, Elijah couldn't hurt him anymore, but he had Violet. He could take out his rage on her.

Monster. Marie would have gotten out that pearl-handled gun you gave her for Christmas and shot you.

She would. But Marie was dead and so was the man who'd given her that gun.

He was Elijah now. That was the path he'd chosen and he had to walk it to the end.

Violet's hand was gentle on his face, so he gripped her wrist and pulled it away, twisting her arm up behind her back, forcing her up against him. Keeping his grip on her jaw, he pushed his tongue into her mouth, into all that heat and softness, wanting her to protest, to push against him, to fight.

To stop him.

But she didn't. She melted against him instead, her body pressing itself to his, her mouth opening, letting him in, kissing him back just as hot and hungry as he was.

He sunk his teeth into her bottom lip, punishing her for accepting him like this. For not fighting, for wanting it when, if she'd had any sense at all, she should be pushing him away and running from him.

She only shuddered, a low moan coming from her throat. Then she angled her head and bit him back. And he didn't know quite what happened, but something inside him snapped as the sweet, sharp pain of her teeth shot straight to his already hard cock.

He didn't pull away, accepting her nip as he gripped her jaw tightly, exploring deep into her mouth. Sliding his tongue along hers, pouring all his hunger and his anger into her, ravaging her, devouring her.

Years since he'd kissed anyone, years since he'd even wanted to. But this . . . She tasted so hot, with flavors of mint and coffee, and something sweet that was all Violet. It made him furious because he liked it. Because he wanted more. Because she was drinking him down as if she was desperately thirsty, accepting all his anger, embracing it.

She shouldn't. She really shouldn't.

He jerked his head away from her, looking down into her face. Her eyes were glittering, her pupils dilated. Christ they were the most beautiful color. "You know why I'm doing this, don't you?" he said, not caring how harsh his voice sounded. "It's not because I want you. It's because you're that motherfucker's daughter and since he's dead, taking it out on you is the next best thing."

He'd said it to hurt her, but it wasn't hurt that crossed her face, but defiance. "Right, so you're taking it out on me with sex. Like I'm going to complain about that."

His grip on her jaw tightened, and he felt her tremble. "You want me to hurt you? Is that what you want?"

"You won't hurt me." She was so calm, staring at him as if she could see behind his anger. As if she could see all the dark space inside him. The dark space where everything that made him human had once been.

Since the moment he'd taken her all she'd been doing was pushing his boundaries and taunting him. Provoking him.

And you let her. Because you like it.

"You've got no fucking idea," he growled, tugging her arm up higher behind her back, forcing her body harder against his.

"Do it then." Challenge burned in her eyes. "Hurt me, Elijah. Hurt me the way you wanted to hurt my father. I dare you to."

He should. Because he could break that slender arm of hers, crush that delicate jaw. Make her scream in agony. Make her hurt the way Fitzgerald had made Marie hurt.

But he couldn't do it, he just couldn't bring himself to take that step. Even the thought of it made his skin crawl, made his chest so tight he could barely draw in a breath. And he didn't know what she'd done to him, because conscience was another thing he'd gotten rid of. Another useless part of himself that got in the way of his plans.

How was she doing it? How was she uncovering all these things inside him he was sure he'd cut out long ago?

He had no idea, it didn't make sense, and he was still so fucking angry. But he couldn't hurt her and because he couldn't hurt her, there was only one thing he could do.

He kissed her smart, stubborn mouth again. Harder, deeper. Pouring all his anger into her, all his grief, making her take it. And she didn't flinch. Her lips parted and let him in, her mouth hot and soft and generous, accepting everything he gave her. Taking all that rage and turning it into something else, heat and hunger and need.

She was an alchemist. A witch. She worked magic and he should have been hurling her from him, but all he wanted was to pull her close. Lose himself in her the way he'd been denying himself for so many years.

So he did.

Breaking the kiss, he released her so he could drag that silky green top of hers up and over her head. Violet didn't protest, and she didn't say a word when he reached around her to jerk open the catch of the complicated arrangement of straps and black lace that was her bra. Then that fell away and those small, perfect tits with the pretty pink nipples he'd traced with his thumb were bare before his gaze.

But he didn't stop to look because that wasn't all he wanted.

With a sharp movement, he jerked the expensive leather pants she'd made him buy down her legs, taking the lacy black panties with it. Then he dropped to his knees in front of her, pulling them all the way down and helping her step out of them.

She was naked now, nothing between him and all that silky, bare skin, and he couldn't tear his gaze away. Pretty ankles and long, elegant calves. Soft thighs perfectly framing the golden curls between them. The curve of her hips and the graceful indentation of her waist . . . so utterly feminine. Reminding him of everything he'd been missing for such a long time.

She stood there motionless, and he could hear the sound of her quickened breathing, watching as goose bumps rose all over that golden skin. He leaned forward and placed his hands behind her ankles, running his palms up the backs of her calves to her knees, then up to her thighs, spreading his fingers out to touch as much as he could of all that warm, smooth bare flesh.

She trembled, her breath catching sharply.

He looked up at her, his palms resting on the swell of her buttocks, the heat of her soaking into his palms, turquoise eyes meeting his, dark with the same hunger that burned inside of him.

"See?" Her voice was roughened and hoarse. "You can't do it, can you? I told you so." She sounded so confident. Like she knew him. Yet another fucking challenge.

She doesn't know you. She would run from you if she did.

Hell, she'd already done that, hadn't she? She'd run from him just before, only to let herself be taken by him when he'd caught her.

Gently he squeezed the soft flesh in his hands, watching as her pupils dilated, lips parting in a soundless gasp. The heat of her pussy was right there and he could smell her arousal, the musky spicy scent making his mouth water. Christ, he was so hungry. It had been a long, long time since he'd tasted a woman.

He couldn't hurt her, she was right about that. But it didn't mean he couldn't make her scream.

"You don't know me, princess," he said, low and hard. "You know nothing at all." And he squeezed those soft buttocks, sinking his fingers into her flesh, drawing a shuddering sound from her as he pulled her in close.

Then he bent his head, nuzzling between her thighs, inhaling the scent of musk and woman, feeling another tremble go through her. Yeah, he was going to make her scream, make her understand that she couldn't fuck with him. That her touch didn't make him feel things he'd thought long dead. That she didn't get to him the way she did, not at all.

He was the one who had the power here. He was the one in charge.

His hands tightened on her butt and he covered that pretty little pussy of hers with his mouth.

Violet went stiff in his hands, a raw sound escaping from her.

Fuck, yes. That's what he wanted to hear.

He licked her, running his tongue up the entire length of her sex then circling her clit in a light, easy stroke, feeling her shudder. God, the taste of her, salty and sweet at the same time, and so fucking delicious. It had been so long since he'd had this. So goddamn long.

He circled her hard little clit with his tongue again, teasing her, listening for that raw sound again and hearing it like a reward, all low and hoarse and desperate. So he did it once more, flicking with his tongue before running it back down the silky, wet folds of her pussy, finding the entrance to her body and pushing deep inside.

She gave a choked cry, her hands landing on his shoulders as if for balance, the weight of her body suddenly sagging against him. "Elijah . . . God . . ."

He pushed his tongue deeper, moving one hand from her butt around to stroke her clit with his thumb before parting her wet flesh with his fingers, allowing him greater access.

She began to tremble, the sound of her ragged breathing echoing in the apartment, her fingers digging into his shoulders. "Oh . . . I can't . . . slow down . . ."

But he didn't, because he wasn't going to do what she said. She was the one who'd pushed him into this, which meant she had to deal with the consequences.

He was going to make her wish she'd let him stay with the punching bag.

Spreading her with his fingers, he licked her, using his tongue to fuck her while his fingers stroked and teased the tender nub of flesh between her thighs, pinching it hard, making her give hoarse little sobs in his ear. Her body tensed, her hips trembling between his hands, and he kept going, kept pushing her because she never stopped pushing him.

"Elijah, please . . . I can't . . ."

The desperation in her husky voice only goaded him on, because, yes, he wanted her begging. He wanted her at his mercy, and if he couldn't get it through fear, he'd get it through pleasure. She'd been going to use sex to get what she wanted from him after all.

"You're not doing this to me again, princess," he growled against her wet, salty flesh. "You're not manipulating any more fucking confessions out of me. I keep telling you I'm not a toy you can play with. It's about time you learned exactly who you're taking on."

Lifting his head, he shifted his grip on her, sliding two fingers into all that tight, wet heat. Then he leaned in again, running his tongue in slow, deliberate circles around the hard bud of her clit.

Violet gave a low moan. "Oh . . . fuck . . ." Her nails were almost drawing blood on his shoulders, her inner muscles tight around his fingers as he slid them slowly in and out of her. "I don't . . . Elijah . . ."

"I want you to scream," he murmured. "I want you to scream and scream hard." And he pushed his fingers deep, licking her over and over, relentless. Showing her no mercy. Until she gave him the ragged scream he'd wanted, and her whole body shook, her pussy clenching hard around his fingers.

The scent of sex filled his nostrils, the taste of her in his mouth. She was panting, leaning against him as if she'd collapse if he wasn't there. And it should have made him satisfied that he'd gotten that from her, a surrender of sorts. Yet he wasn't satisfied. He felt just as hungry and desperate and angry as he had when she'd first touched his face.

Easing her away from him, he straightened and rose to his feet. Then he picked her up in his arms. She'd gone all soft and relaxed, her face flushed, her expression dazed, one hand rising to touch his chest. And he didn't know why he wanted to hold her, not when he was still so furious.

Turning, he carried her over to the sofa and laid her down on it, but instead of walking away, he found himself spreading her thighs and settling himself between them, the heat of her pussy pressed against his hard, aching cock. Then he put his palms down on either side of her head, bracing himself so his full weight wasn't resting on her, looking down into her face.

It felt good to have her naked and exposed and vulnerable while he was fully clothed, good to have her under him, smooth and warm just waiting for the touch of his hand. At his mercy completely.

Desire gripped him tight, like it had earlier that day in the alleyway, his dick in no way satisfied by that brief encounter. Fuck, she was so soft, her body giving beneath his, accommodating him, making him so very aware of everything he'd been missing.

He bent his head to her neck, turning his face against

her throat and inhaling the musky, feminine scent of aroused woman. Then he licked her, the salty-sweet taste of her skin going straight to his head.

She shivered in response, her body shifting under his, her hips moving, rubbing that hot little pussy of hers against his jeans, leaving him in no doubt that despite what he'd just done to her, she was as hungry as he was.

Ravenous, he opened his mouth on her shoulder, biting her.

"Eli . . ." There was no sarcasm in the name now, only a husky heat that moved through him, unstoppable, inescapable. Making him want, making him even more desperate.

So he bit her again, harder.

Her hands were on his back, sliding down to the waistband of the shorts he'd put on for his workout, moving under the cotton of his tank to touch his bare skin and much to his horror, he felt himself shiver in response.

Jesus, what the fuck was happening to him? This woman was dangerous and in ways he'd never expected.

He jerked his head up, shifting to grab those wandering hands of hers and lifting them above her head, pinning them there against the arm of the sofa. He was careful with her injured wrist, making sure the pressure was on the one that hadn't been cut.

She blinked, looking up into his face. "I want to touch you."

"No." His voice sounded rough and unsteady, not like him at all.

"Why not?"

"Because I fucking said so, that's why."

She stared at him and for a moment there was only a thick, heavy silence between them.

Her eyes were so dark, all that vivid color a thin band

surrounding the black of her pupils all full of arousal and heat. And he wanted to look away because she was staring at him like she could see everything there was to see about him. But that was a weakness he wouldn't concede, so he just stared back, letting her look.

Then she said suddenly, huskily, "I don't know what it was that Dad did to you, and I know that I can't make it any better. But"—she took a breath—"I'm sorry for whatever it was."

The statement was so out of left field that it took him a second to fully process what she'd said. And then, when he did, it was like she'd lit the fuse on his anger all over again, because what the fuck was she thinking? That offering him an apology would make any difference?

It didn't change things. It didn't make what her father had done to Marie any less than the horrific crime it was and it sure as hell didn't make Marie any less dead.

He opened his mouth to tell her exactly what he thought of that fucking apology, but she hadn't finished, because she added, still husky and soft. "And I want you know that you can have anything from me. Anything at all, it's yours."

Anything . . .

Heat flooded through him, because, Christ, he could think of exactly what he wanted from her. All the things he wanted to do to her. All the time he had to make up, all the cold, empty years he could fuck away the memory of. Payment for Marie's death.

It was wrong and it should only add to the anger since there was nothing, *nothing*, that could make up for what Evelyn Fitzgerald had taken from him. Not money, not power, and most especially not the warm, willing body of this young woman.

Yet he didn't move away or release her.

He only looked down into those beautiful eyes of hers,

slowly darkening with a terrible sympathy he wanted to destroy completely.

"I don't just want anything," he said, not caring how harsh he sounded, not caring how rough. And then he leaned down so his face was inches from hers. "I want *everything*."

CHAPTER TEN

The intensity in Elijah's black gaze was inescapable, leaving her in no doubt that he meant exactly what he'd said. And he would take everything, because she would let him.

It was a terrifying thing to realize and if it had been any other man, she would have shoved him off her and run from the room.

But he wasn't any other man. There was that bleak emptiness behind his eyes and the words that echoed in her brain, fury vibrating in every syllable.

Your father destroyed my life.

She hadn't fully taken on board that comment earlier, too caught in the fury and heat of him to understand, but now, looking up into his fierce, intent face, she began to understand that something truly terrible had happened to this man. Something her father was responsible for. And now Elijah was taking that out on her.

The weight of him pressed down her, and he was so damn hot. But there was nothing she didn't like about it, nothing she didn't want. She had to make up for her father's sins somehow and if that involved letting this man do whatever he wanted to her then she'd do it.

She hated that look in his eyes. Hated the bleakness. It

felt familiar to her, as if she'd felt it herself, and all she wanted to do was take it away.

"Do it then," she said hoarsely. "You can take it all."

And she didn't expect for a moment that he wouldn't. He wasn't a man who hesitated about anything, let alone took half measures.

Sure enough, as soon as she'd said the words, black heat flared in his eyes and his head dipped again, his mouth burning against her throat.

Violet closed her eyes, shivering as his teeth nipped the fragile cords of her neck, his fingers tight around her wrists held above her head. She could feel the hard length of his cock pressing against her sex and she couldn't stop herself from rocking against it, trying to get more friction, more pressure.

But he wouldn't let her, the heavy weight of his muscular body crushing her into the sofa cushions, pinning her down so she couldn't move. Then his free hand was on her, moving from her shoulder down to her left breast, cupping it in his palm, squeezing, his thumb circling her hardening nipple. She tried shifting again, restless and wanting, arching into that teasing hand, gasping as he pinched her hard. Pleasure shot through her, a streak of it arrowing straight between her thighs, and then he did it again and she groaned, moving helplessly, unable to keep still.

His head dropped further, his mouth moving down her body. He cupped her breast in his palm, his tongue finding her nipple and circling, licking. Then he sucked it into his hot mouth, drawing hard on her, sparks scattering behind her closed lids as the pleasure wound tighter and tighter.

Oh, God, this was so good. She was going to drown in this if she let herself. And why not? It was better than slitting her wrists in a bath or running down a cold and icy street. Better than a gunshot ricocheting behind her. Holding back was overrated, clearly. Perhaps giving everything was the way to go, especially when he was going to take it anyway.

Elijah bit gently on her nipple and she gave a long, low moan of frustration, her hips shifting, trying to ease the intolerable ache that was building and building.

But he released her all of a sudden, sitting up and back, leaving her lying there on the sofa with her arms above her head, her legs apart, still trembling. Completely naked and exposed.

She took a breath, starting to bring her hands down.

"Don't move," he ordered roughly. "Stay exactly like that."

Slowly she put her hands back where they were, shivering under the intensity of his black gaze. Because he kept on looking at her as if he couldn't get enough of the sight, focusing particularly on her throat, then her breasts, then finally her sex. Hunger glittered in his eyes and she got the feeling he was testing himself. Perhaps even testing her too.

She tried to calm her breathing, but that didn't work with him watching the rise and fall of her breasts. Making her so aware of her hardened, sensitized nipples and the pulsing ache in her sex.

Elijah got off the sofa, reaching over to a brown paper bag that was sitting on the coffee table. He picked it up and took out whatever was inside it, crumpling and discarding the bag carelessly back onto the table. In his hand was a box of condoms.

Violet stared at it. "When did you get that?" Her voice sounded cracked and dry.

He didn't reply, taking out a condom packet and ripping it open, his movements unhurried and very deliberate, full of intent. With one hand he pushed down his shorts and his boxers, exposing the long, thick length of his erection. Then he rolled the condom down over it in one easy motion.

She couldn't stop staring. At the movement of his hand, at all that hot skin, at the size of that hard cock as he eased the latex down. There was something so unbearably sexy about the way he did it that she found her own fingers curling, wanting to touch him the way he was touching himself.

He turned back to her, the lines of his face drawn tight with the vicious hunger that was starting to sink its claws in her too.

God, she wanted him to take off his clothes. Wanted the oiled silk of his bare skin against hers. She wanted to run her fingers all over those hard, tight muscles, learn the shape of him.

She wanted too much. But then that had always been her problem, hadn't it?

He didn't take off his clothes.

Instead he knelt between her spread thighs, looking down at her, making her feel so very vulnerable and completely at his mercy. Which in turn only seemed to feed into the desire that was shortening her breath and sending her heartbeat out of control.

He reached out, his fingers trailing down her stomach to tangle in the curls between her thighs, then going lower, finding her clit, stroking and circling.

Violet trembled, a soft whimper escaping her, the arrow of pleasure becoming sharper, heavier.

"Look at me," he demanded, low and rough.

And she couldn't help but obey, meeting his obsidian gaze, falling into it, drowning as his finger moved over her tight, aching flesh. Then his touch moved lower, sliding over her slick folds to the entrance of her body and pushing in, testing her.

Sensation rippled through her and she gasped, shuddering as his finger slid in deep then out again, pinned by the look in his eyes as he watched her.

It should have made her feel even more vulnerable, even more exposed to have him look at her like this, as he systematically tore apart all her walls and barriers with the touch of his hand. And she kind of did. But she also felt a certain sense of power. Because she wasn't the only one affected, he was too. It was there in the heat in his eyes, in the hard line of his jaw, in the tightness in his shoulders and neck. In the stain of color on his high cheekbones.

She affected him as badly as he affected her. And it came as a shock to realize she'd never been fully conscious of having that power before. Had never really felt she'd had much affect on anyone in her life. Sure, she'd gone out of her way to make her mother angry with her, but that hadn't changed her mother's behavior. Hadn't made Hilary pay any more attention to her. Her father too, had always seemed to be focused on something else, not her. Especially after Theo had disappeared.

She wanted to affect people. She wanted to feel connected. She wanted to make a difference. And she was definitely making a difference to Elijah.

He eased his fingers out of her and positioned himself between her thighs. Then he spread her open, impaling her with his cock in one deep, hard push.

Violet gasped, arching up, shuddering, her sensitive flesh burning at the stretch of him inside her. It had hurt the first time and although it wasn't nearly as sharp now, she still wasn't used to it, and he hadn't held back.

Staying buried inside her, he ran his hands up the backs of her calves and her knees, lifting them then pulling her legs up high around his waist, allowing him to slide even deeper.

A ragged, desperate sound escaped her, becoming even

more desperate as he leaned forward pressing her against the arm of the sofa while he placed his hands on it, gripping tight. Then he lowered his head, his gaze inches from hers, and he kept looking at her as he drew back his hips and thrust. Hard.

She gave a hoarse cry, the angle grinding her clit against his cock, and the spear of pleasure grew edges so sharp they began to cut. He thrust again, hard and deep and ruthless, before drawing back and shoving inside her once more, pinning her between the arm of the sofa and his thighs.

Violet began to pant, her breathing ragged and broken. With each flex of his hips, with each slide of his cock, she felt herself slowly torn apart by sensation. The heat of him all around her, the heavy weight of his body pressing down on her, the feeling of him inside her, was intoxicating. Overwhelming.

His biceps flexed as he thrust, shoving himself into her, his own breathing harsh. And those inky eyes of his were so close, staring down into hers, so deep and dark that they were all she could see. The whole world was nothing but that dark, velvety blackness, the thrust of his cock, the furnace of his body, and the endless stretch of pleasure drawn so tight it was going to snap at any second.

Then it did, a hoarse scream breaking from her as he brought her to climax with another thrust, the pleasure a shock wave moving through her, bright as a bomb blast. But he didn't stop, he kept going, a driving rhythm that had her aching body gathering itself yet again.

"Eli . . ." His name sounded raw and desperate, and she didn't really know why she was saying it. Maybe to stop this because she couldn't take it anymore. Couldn't handle the sheer intensity of him. "Please . . ."

He ignored that too. Driving into her body, his gaze never leaving hers, his breathing becoming ragged and harsh.

Another climax began to build and she felt herself rushing toward it, falling like she'd just jumped out of a plane with no parachute, hurtling to the earth with no way to slow herself or stop. With no chance of rescue. Turning over and over, the ground rushing up.

"Elijah!" She screamed his name this time, her body arching beneath his as he ground his pelvis against her aching clit. As the push of his cock inside her became too much, too intense.

Screaming again, wordlessly, as the earth rushed up to meet her and she hit it, shattering beneath him like a piece of fine china. Becoming nothing but a thousand glittering shards as he moved faster and faster, his hoarse cry echoing in her ears as he followed her over the edge and into oblivion.

Elijah wasn't conscious of much but the blood roaring in his veins and the sound of his own heartbeat, loud as a drum in his head. The aftereffects of the pleasure that had just annihilated him still had him in its grip, moving through his body like small, sharp electric shocks.

He could barely breathe.

He felt like he was coming apart at the seams, disintegrating. Which was just not fucking acceptable. At all. He'd already disintegrated once in his life and that had been when Marie had died. He'd put himself back together, but he couldn't do it a second time. Not when there was so little of him left.

Pressure came against his chest, Violet's hands pushing, and he realized he'd fallen forward on her, his weight pinning her to the arm of the sofa at her back. Fuck, she was so soft under him, the warmth of her body surrounding him. He was still deep inside her and he could feel her pussy clenching him tightly, holding on like she didn't want to let him go. If he wasn't careful he was going to get hard again.

Easing out of her, he shifted back so he wasn't crushing her, giving her some room. The pressure against his chest lessened, but she kept her hands right where they were, just above his pecs, her fingers spreading out over his skin, splaying like starfish. Her lips were red and swollen from those hard kisses he'd given her and her face was pink, a flush that spread all the way down her throat and breasts, right down to her stomach where the indentations of the waistband of his shorts had been impressed into her flesh. She was pink below that too. And wet . . .

"You've ripped a stitch," she said, frowning, her attention on the bandages wrapping his shoulder, her fingers gently moving to touch.

And, fuck, it hadn't even been a minute since the last climax and already he *was* hard again, wanting again. Christ, he had to get some space, some air. Get where he couldn't see the marks he'd left on her skin or smell the musky scent of sex. Where he couldn't see her taut, high breasts or the slick folds of her pussy, or feel her hands on his skin.

Elijah pulled away, ignoring the confusion in her eyes, and got off the sofa, heading toward the bathroom. He didn't look behind him and she didn't say a word.

In the bathroom, he got rid of the condom then leaned on the vanity a moment, trying to get his head around what had just happened.

Sex. That's what fucking happened. That's all that fucking happened. What the hell is wrong with you?

Yeah, shit, he had to pull himself together. Had to stop letting her and whatever this insane chemistry was between them get to him. So he'd broken his pussy drought. So what? It didn't mean anything. He couldn't let it, not when he was going to be handing her over to Jericho. And as for all this "you help me, I help you" bullshit . . . . She was going to have to get over that right now.

She was his hostage. That was the beginning and the end of it.

Yet for some reason he couldn't seem to get his head around that thought. As if there was a part of him that wanted her to be more than that. As if there were shards of the man he'd once been still alive inside him. Shards of his forgotten humanity . . .

No. Fuck, no. He didn't want to be that man again. Never, ever. That man had allowed Marie to be taken. That man hadn't been able to protect her right when she'd needed it most.

That man had to die and stay dead.

He straightened, staring at himself in the mirror, his gaze catching on the stain of red on his tank. Blood. She was right, he *had* pulled a stitch.

Tugging off the stained cotton, he let it drop on the floor, examining the bandages on his shoulder. Blood had started to seep through, flowers of red against the white, an echo of the rose the eagle on his chest grasped.

There's always blood. No matter what you do, there's always blood . . .

"I was right."

He looked sharply in the direction of the doorway and there she was, standing with her arms crossed over her bare chest. Why the fuck had she followed?

She didn't look at him, her attention on the wound on his shoulder, blonde brows drawing down. Then, to his surprise, she moved into the bathroom, coming over to him. "Sit," she murmured. "I'll do this."

And his surprise deepened into shock as he found himself doing exactly what she said without a word, sitting on the edge of the bathtub and spreading his knees so she could stand between them.

She didn't seem to care that she was naked, that the rosy tips of her breasts were almost brushing his chest, or that he could see that pretty little thatch of curls between her thighs. Once again her attention was on his shoulder, her brow wrinkling in concentration.

He was supposed to be getting away from her, not sitting here letting her get close. And yet he couldn't seem to bring himself to move as she lifted her hands to the bandages, beginning to undo them. Her touch was so gentle and somehow the fact that she wasn't looking at him while she did it made it easier. She stood so near too, the warmth of her body somehow familiar, easing something inside him he hadn't realized was drawn tight.

She didn't speak as she unwound the bandages, and he wasn't conscious of the fact he'd put his hands on her hips until he felt the heat of her skin seeping through his palms.

How the fuck had that happened? Touching her wasn't what he was supposed to be doing either.

Yet he didn't take his hands away. It had been too long since he'd touched anything so soft, so smooth. Like warm satin. Too long since he'd allowed himself anything even remotely sensual, and he couldn't bring himself to stop. Something inside him was starving, desperate to be fed.

Slowly he let his hands stroke down the sides of her hips, trailing his fingertips over the curve of her buttocks, down to her thighs then back up again. Holy fuck, she felt so good. He let one hand rest on her hip, turning the other over and stroking the backs of his fingers across her stomach. Goose bumps raised in his wake and he stared, mesmerized by the movement of his hand and by the little obvious shivers that went through her as he stroked her.

"You should probably not do that," she murmured. "At least not until I'm finished."

Yeah, he probably shouldn't. But suddenly he didn't

give a shit. Ignoring her, he tugged her in closer, spreading his hands out on her hips so he could feel warm skin against his own. She smelled of sex and sandalwood and Violet, and he was fucking hard again.

Jesus Christ, he was a mess.

She made a soft, disapproving sound in her throat, but didn't try to pull away from him. Instead, she tugged the mess of bandages off his shoulder, examining the wound with a critical eye. "You've only pulled one stitch and it doesn't look bad." Her mouth quirked. "Not that I'd know of course."

That slight curl to her mouth was mesmerizing. He'd done so many hard, violent things to her and yet here she was, standing naked in front of him, tending his wounds and nearly smiling just after having let him fuck her senseless. He didn't understand it.

Her bright, blue-green gaze found his. "You want me to clean it up?"

"Yes." His voice sounded strange, all rusty and broken.

Some expression he didn't recognize crossed her face. But all she said was, "Okay then."

He had to let her go so she could get what she needed out of his box of medical supplies, suggesting a few of the items since he knew more about dressing wounds than she did. But then she was back, standing in front of him as he let her clean the wound, murmuring a few instructions as she got out some clean bandages to bind it all back up again.

As she wrapped the last piece of gauze around his shoulder and tied it off, he reached for her again, unable to help himself, his hands on her hips, pulling her in close. Then he leaned in closer still, so his forehead pressed against her chest, and shut his eyes, inhaling all that sweet scent, feeling that tightness inside him uncurl even more.

He didn't know what he was so hungry for, but for

some reason she seemed to be what he needed right now and he'd be fucked if he wouldn't take it. Ignoring it hadn't worked and continuing to pretend he didn't feel it hadn't worked either.

But he remembered what it was like to want, just as he remembered the pain when you couldn't have what you wanted.

It wasn't until now that he realized he'd been in pain for a very long time.

Violet's hands rested on his shoulders a moment then he felt them move to trace the muscles of his upper back, up and down in a gentle motion, as if she was trying to soothe a wild animal. And this time he didn't pull away, letting her touch him. Letting himself have this moment.

He'd probably end up regretting it, but right now he didn't much care.

Sliding his hands around, he eased them down over the curve of her buttocks, warm, giving flesh filling his palms. She gave a sigh, her fingers stroking the back of his neck then moving up into his hair.

"You're not the only one who wants something, you know," she said after a long moment of silence. "You want revenge. I want the truth about my brother."

Her brother? Where the hell had that come from? Not that he wanted to know.

Yes, you do.

He did.

Elijah had come to work for Fitzgerald years after his son Theodore had committed suicide jumping off a bridge. He hadn't ever met the young man, but whatever had happened to him, hadn't interested Elijah in the slightest. He'd been in the middle of enacting his own tragedy and hadn't wanted to involve himself in other people's.

"You never met him," Violet continued softly, not waiting for him to respond. "But he was . . . such a good guy.

Such a great older brother. He taught me to ride a bike, balance on a skateboard, played me all the cool music . . ." She paused. "He taught me to question. To never take anything at face value. So when he died"—another pause, but those fingers in his hair didn't stop stroking—"I didn't believe it. They never found his body, you see, and I just couldn't figure out why he'd do something like that. He was near to completing his law degree at Harvard, was engaged to a really wonderful woman, had a fantastic career lined up with one of the really big firms. It just didn't make any sense."

Elijah didn't want to know, didn't want this window into her life, and yet he kept silent, pressed against her warm, naked flesh, as she went on, talking as if to herself.

"I know it looks like the classic success on the outside and impossible personal standards he couldn't live up to bullshit on the inside, but taking his own life like that wasn't Theo. He didn't run away from his responsibilities and he . . . would have said something to me if he was struggling, I know he would."

Her voice had gotten a little thicker, echoes of loss running through it, and he wanted to tell her to stop because he could feel those echoes pulling at the ones inside himself, reminding him of his own loss, his own pain. But still he stayed quiet, letting her speak.

"Anyway, he left me a note. I found it in my bedroom in the middle of a book he'd loaned me. It said *Be careful.* I didn't know what it meant and was going to ask him about it. And then he disappeared." Violet's fingers moved in his hair, her fingertips gentle on the back of his neck. His cock was hard and he wanted to pull her down on him because that was better than hearing the pain in her voice, yet something inside him held him back.

"He's not dead, Elijah," she said quietly. "In fact, I have evidence he's alive." Abruptly her fingers tightened in his hair. "That's why I need to get out of here. Why you need to let me go. I have to find him."

It wasn't loss in her voice now but desperation, and he didn't like what that did to him. Didn't like the way it made his chest tight and his own determination waver for just a second.

He jerked his head up and looked into her blue-green eyes, keeping his hands right where they were, hard on her hips. And there it was in her face, that desperation stamped all over it. And pain. And grief.

"Please don't leave me to Jericho." The raw honesty in her tone lined his ribs with barbed wire. "Please. I'll be your bait if you need it, but please don't leave me with him, not when I'm so close to finding my brother."

He hadn't thought about what would happen to her after he used her to lure Jericho out, because her well-being or otherwise hadn't concerned him. But as he stared up into her eyes, into her flushed and lovely face, he realized that had changed and no matter how much he didn't want it to, her well-being concerned him now.

How had that even fucking happened? And what the fuck was he supposed to do now? Growing his conscience back again wasn't supposed to happen, especially not when he was so close to his own goal.

Her hands shifted, holding onto his shoulders, and she didn't look away from him. And he was struck by the fact that although he was dangerous to her and she should be protecting herself against him, she was doing the opposite. Making herself vulnerable all over again by revealing these truths to him, by begging him.

"Why are you telling me these things?" he demanded, his voice sounding strange and somehow wrong in the hard, tiled space of the bathroom. "Why the fuck do you think I care what you want?"

"Because you're sitting here letting me clean up your

wound. Letting me touch you. Letting me talk about Theo. Because everything I've just given you, you could have taken for yourself and you didn't." Her throat moved, the look in her eyes unflinching. "I don't know why, whether it's a weird, fucked-up case of Stockholm Syndrome or what, but . . . I trust you, Elijah."

He felt the words slide through him like a sharp, heavy blade, transfixing him.

Trust. Holy fuck. Was she insane? Why the hell would she trust a monster like him?

"You shouldn't." His hands tightened on her hips. "Trusting me is the last thing you should do."

"I know that. Intellectually that's obvious. But whether I should or not, the truth is that I do."

The barbed wire inside his chest was painful, cutting him to ribbons.

You aren't worthy of anyone's trust . . .

"It changes nothing." He kept his tone harsh.

Her mouth was so soft-looking, so red. He wanted to tug her head down and taste it.

"Perhaps not. But . . . I've never told anyone about Theo before. You're the only one who knows."

The wire pulled tight, digging in, and he opened his mouth to say something else, some lie about how he didn't give a shit. But that wasn't what came out.

"He killed Marie." The words were out before he had a chance to take them back. "Your father and Jericho, they killed my wife."

CHAPTER ELEVEN

Gabriel poured scotch into one of the Second Circle's fine crystal tumblers then carried it over to the woman who sat on the couch, her black hair glossy in the firelight coming from the hearth in front of her.

His beautiful Honor, who was looking pale and worried. Well, fuck, he could relate. He was feeling a bit pale and worried himself.

They were in the Nine Circle's favorite meeting place, a room in Alex St. James's club, the Second Circle. With wood-paneled walls, tall library bookshelves, wingback chairs and a long leather sofa, the space was reminiscent of a Victorian gentleman's study rather than one of the most modern and exclusive private members' clubs in New York.

Alex himself, Honor's brother and Gabriel's best friend, stood in front of the fire, his arms folded, watching his sister. He didn't look so worried, but Alex always hid his feelings well. Then again, Gabriel recognized the gleam in the other man's too-blue eyes. Whether he hid it or not, Alex was concerned for his sister.

Sister . . .

The word echoed weirdly inside him. He was still getting used to the thought of a sibling, had barely had much time to process it at all what with everything that had been going on. But now, after meeting with that prick Elijah, the fact that he had a half sister was smacking him full in the face.

A sister who was currently being held captive by a cold-eyed asshole who was using her for some kind of revenge plan.

Gabriel knew revenge, had spent a good portion of his fucked-up life pursuing it himself, so he understood where the guy was coming from. But the fact that he was using Gabriel's newly discovered half sibling to get it had destroyed every bit of sympathy Gabriel had for him, not that there was much to start with anyway.

Elijah Hunt had nearly gotten two of Gabriel's friends killed, and now he had Gabriel's sister. That made Gabriel more than pissed. That made him fucking enraged.

"Are you sure she was okay?" Honor took the tumbler from him, staring up at him as she did so.

"He said she was alive." Gabriel sat down next her, sliding an arm around her waist and drawing her close. He fucking hated seeing her so unhappy. It made him want to kill someone. "I believed him."

"But he wouldn't say where she was or why he had her?"

"No. I was going to shoot the bastard right then and there, but he said he had Violet under guard."

"And you believed him?" Alex asked.

Gabriel flicked his friend a glance. "I could have bluffed him out, but I didn't want to do that without more information. Anyway, we know the area she's in and Eva's trying to see if we can pinpoint it further by using Violet's cell phone signal."

"I thought we couldn't find that anymore?"

"Yeah, but Eva thinks she can pick up its last known position. She's working on it now."

By the fire, Alex was standing very still. "You know, I've been trying to figure out why that asshole was so familiar," he murmured. "Even back in Monte Carlo I was certain I'd seen him before."

Gabriel raised a brow. "So?"

"So, I did some searches of my own. Through the Second Circle membership records on the off chance it might throw up something." Alex had the fucking smuggest look on his face.

"What?" Gabriel demanded. "You found something?"

Honor's attention had shifted from the fire to her brother, her body tensing against Gabriel's.

Alex's blue gaze gleamed. "Yeah, actually, I did. When the club first opened ten years ago, we did a massive publicity drive and pretty much had thousands of membership applications even before the doors opened. I went through each and every application because I wanted to vet them personally. Hell, I even interviewed some of the applicants before I granted approval."

Gabriel watched his friend's face. "Don't tell me he was one of them?"

"He wasn't," Alex said softly. "But his wife was."

"What?" Honor was frowning at her brother. "Stop being cryptic, Alex."

"I was looking back at some old pictures of the opening party we had, and he's there in the crowd with his arm around this tall brunette. And it wasn't until I saw that picture that I remembered that the reason he's so familiar is because I used to see him around here in the early Second Circle days."

"But you said he wasn't a member," Gabriel murmured.

"No, he wasn't. I tried doing a search on his name, but turned up nothing. He wasn't a member. Which means that the only way he could have been at that party was if he was someone's guest."

"So, the brunette . . . ?" Honor took another sip of her scotch.

"I went through the names and photos of the first lot I granted membership status to. She was there. Marie Archer. A high-up in one of the big investment banks. She had a guest signed up on a permanent basis, her husband. A guy called Kane Archer." Alex paused, the firelight leaping across his face. "Kane Laurent Elijah Archer."

Gabriel narrowed his gaze at the other man. "Shit. So maybe that's why we haven't been able to turn up anything on him? We're looking at the wrong name?"

"That was always the risk. Zac certainly thought that was a possibility."

Honor leaned forward and put her scotch down on the coffee table in front of her. "Did you find anything on him then?"

"Yes. Kane Archer was into venture capital. Started out young from what I could find on him and was doing extremely well with a firm he started up himself." Alex dropped his arms and began to pace in front of the fire. "He used to come here a lot with his wife, judging from the records. I remember him, but my memories are a little fuzzy." He flashed a brief, self-deprecating smile. "I was going through an . . . experimental phase at the time so pretty much *all* my memories are fuzzy."

Honor rolled her eyes. "Thanks for sharing, Alex. Okay, so what happened to him then? How did he get from Kane Archer, venture capitalist to Elijah Hunt, mercenary?"

Alex stopped pacing. "That is the sixty-four-million-dollar question."

"Did you give the name to Zac?" Gabriel leaned back against the couch, still holding onto Honor. They needed to get on top of this because the more they knew about this asshole, the quicker they could find some way of getting Violet away from him.

Alex gave him a long-suffering look. "Of course I gave the name to Zac."

"What about his wife?" Honor asked quietly. "What happened to her?"

"I gave her name to Zac too and—" A chiming sound came from Alex's pocket. "And that should be him right now." Pulling his phone out, he hit the answer button. "Yo, Zac. You got anything? Yeah, okay. Putting you on speaker now." Moving over to the coffee table, he put the phone down.

"Okay, so here's what Eva and I found." Zac's deep voice with its clipped, English accent filled the room. "Kane Archer apparently died in a car accident seven years ago. The police found his car overturned and ablaze in a quiet backstreet. They determined he'd crashed it while drunk and probably grief-stricken after the disappearance of his wife. Archer reported her missing two months prior to his death. She vanishes while at dinner with Elijah present."

Interesting. Very interesting indeed.

"Was she ever found?" Gabriel asked.

"The missing person's file has remained open," Zac replied. "Though police turned up no trace of her. After her husband died there was little impetus to keep searching."

"Wonderful," Honor said dryly. "What about her family?"

"She had none. In fact . . . where was it . . ." The sound of papers being shuffled came down the line. "Ah, yes. She was an only child and her parents died when she was in her teens. Same with Archer. His parents died soon after he was killed in the car accident."

"Grim." Alex folded his arms again. "So basically his wife disappeared and then from the looks of it, he faked his own death."

Gabriel released Honor and sat forward, going back

over his meeting with the cold-eyed, scarred man once more. "Revenge," he said slowly. "He's after revenge."

Honor turned to him. "He said that specifically?"

They'd already talked about it after he'd gotten back from the meeting, but it was worth repeating for the others. "No. He wouldn't admit to anything. Like a fucking locked box. But I know when a man's looking to kill and Elijah Hunt sure wanted to kill someone."

"He wanted Fitzgerald's head." Zac's voice was flat, certain. "And he was pretty fucking upset when Eva shot him instead. It sounds to me as if he's still on the revenge track, he's just had to change his target."

"To who?" Honor's blue gaze moved from Gabriel to Alex then back again. "And why?"

"I know why." Gabriel glanced at his friend standing near the fire, because he suspected Alex knew why too. And sure enough, there was understanding in the other man's eyes.

"His wife," Zac said, confirming it. "He wants revenge for something that happened to his wife."

"Fucking love," Alex muttered. "Gets you every goddamn time." He looked impatiently down at his watch then let out a breath.

Gabriel didn't need to ask what he was checking for. Katya was out on a fact-finding mission about Eva's traitorous driver, Temple, who'd disappeared after they'd come back from confronting Fitzgerald. And clearly, judging from Alex's restlessness, she was late getting back.

"I don't give a shit why he wants revenge," Gabriel growled, Alex's impatience suddenly getting to him. "I want know to who the fuck his target is. And why he needs Violet for it."

Sounds came from the phone on the table. A door closing and footsteps, Zac murmuring something.

"I have an idea why." It was Eva. "A woman mysteriously vanishes and then her husband turns up working for Fitzgerald and wanting revenge? I'm sure you can work it out yourselves too."

"Ah, fuck." Alex's voice was full of disgust.

"Yeah," Eva said. "Fitzgerald took her for his little business."

"Oh God." Honor shook her head and reached for the tumbler on the table.

It made sense, that was for sure. Gabriel felt an unwanted sympathy for the man turn over inside him, which was just fucking annoying. Because regardless of the whys, Elijah or Kane or whatever the hell his name was still had Violet.

"We need to know who he's after," he said flatly. "He said it was more complicated than revenge, that if it was as simple as that, he'd have have killed Fitzgerald years ago. But he didn't."

The fire leapt in the grate, a shower of sparks erupting from it.

"If his wife was taken by Fitzgerald, then I know what he wants," Eva said.

But Gabriel had already worked it out for himself. "He doesn't just want the guy dead, he wants to take down the whole fucking empire too."

A small silence fell, the implications of that slowly sinking in. Because they all knew how twisted that empire was, how complicated. And that was only what they'd seen of it in the States. Evelyn Fitzgerald's little crime industry went beyond this country, had tendrils that snaked into other parts of the world, linking to other crime syndicates in China, the Middle East, and Europe just for a start. Who knew how deep it went? How far?

"He can't do it alone," Eva said finally. "He'll need help."

Gabriel glared at the phone. "What the fuck? Getting

Violet away does *not* involve helping the prick who took her. We leave that shit to the authorities."

"Seriously?" Eva sounded annoyed. "Since when did you ever want to involve the authorities, Gabe?"

Unfortunately, Eva had a point. He must be getting soft in his old age. "Okay," he said reluctantly. "No authorities. But I'm not helping that motherfucker. He's lucky I didn't shoot him when I had the chance."

"If he's bent on taking down Fitzgerald's human trafficking ring then I don't give a shit what you want." Eva's voice was hard. "I'm going to give him any help he needs."

Of course she would, and he'd probably do the same if he had Eva's history. Still, there was a life at stake here. "And if taking that down means Violet gets hurt?" he asked harshly.

There was a silence this time.

"We need more information," Honor said, her voice abrupt. "We don't know anything about Elijah Hunt or his motives, and what we have now is just guesswork. Eva, have you made any progress with Violet's cell phone signal?"

"It's not broadcasting now so it's either off or destroyed, but yeah, I have a last known position for it," Eva answered. "It's in the West Village, where Gabe met Elijah, so that kind of confirms where she might be. Whether she's still there or not is another thing."

Impatient, Gabriel rose to his feet. "Give me the address, Eva. I'll get over there now."

"Wait." Zac this time, his tone flat with command. "We need a plan, Gabe."

But Gabriel was done waiting. This shit—*all* of this shit—had been going on for far too long and he was sick of it. He wanted Honor happy, wanted his family safe, and if that meant taking out one bastard who kept getting in the way, then he was all for it.

Reaching over to the phone, Gabriel picked it up. "I go get Violet and maybe I'll let Hunt live. That's the motherfucking plan, asshole." Then he ended the call and tossed the phone to Alex, who caught it, the look on his face enigmatic.

Honor had risen to her feet, turning to face him. "Are you sure this is a good idea? I think Zac might have a point. Sitting down and working out a plan isn't wrong."

"No, but the longer we chat about plans and shit, the longer that gives Hunt to go find somewhere else to keep Violet. We need to move now before he moves her." He reached out, settling his hands on her hips and tugging her close, looking down into her pale, pretty face. "It'll be okay, baby. I'll get her back."

Honor's dark brows pulled down. "Be careful, Gabe."

"Always." He bent and kissed her. Hard.

Violet stared down into Elijah's dark gaze and felt something inside her crack apart. Her mouth opened and she started to say something, though she wasn't really conscious of what it was—probably something trite and ridiculous since her brain was still reeling from what he'd just revealed.

But before she could get the words out, the sound of his phone ringing came from out in the lounge.

Abruptly, he pushed her away and got to his feet, striding out of the bathroom without a word.

Violet just stood there, staring down at the white porcelain of the bath where he'd been sitting only seconds before. Broad shouldered and massive, all that bare tanned skin smooth and hot to the touch.

He'd had a wife. A wife her father had killed.

She had no doubt he was telling her the truth—he had no reason to lie.

Her vision wavered, tears filling her eyes. Which was

stupid and wrong, because what right had she to cry for a woman she didn't even know? And why did she feel so responsible? She hadn't been the one to kill her after all.

Nevertheless, she felt the weight of it rest on her chest like a boulder, heavy and inescapable.

Now she knew why he wanted to use her. Why he looked at her with such fury.

He must see his wife's killer every time he looked at her.

We're all monsters, Violet. Even you . . .

Violet wiped the back of her hand over her face, scrubbing away the ridiculous tears, a cold hard splinter of ice settling deep into her soul. No, that wasn't right. It was her father who'd done it, not her. But maybe what had happened to her was a kind of karma. Perhaps she shouldn't fight him, let him use her however he wanted, make up for what her father had taken from him. Because how else could she make it better?

Why do you want to? After what he's done to you?

So he was a killer, a criminal. But he was also . . . grieving. She'd sensed the pain of his loss even though she hadn't quite known it for what it was or why. She knew now though. He was a man with a wound that went deeper than the one on his shoulder. A wound that still ached and bled and hurt. He had a hole inside him, just as she did. Except the hole inside Elijah could never be filled, because the woman he needed to fill it with was dead.

At least she had evidence that Theo was still alive, that she still had someone.

She turned, moving out of the bathroom and going down the hallway.

"About fucking time." Elijah's voice drifted from the lounge area. "What can you give me?"

She paused in the hall doorway, leaning against the frame.

He was standing with his back to her, half naked, his wide, powerful shoulders tapering down to a narrow waist, the shorts sitting low on his hips. She itched to touch him again, to run her fingers across those powerful muscles, feel them bunch and flex under her hands. To hear his breath catch and his deep, harsh voice whisper her name.

She wanted him. Wanted to take him in her arms and soothe him, heal him. Wanted to take that bleak, cold look away from his black eyes and give him something warm to hold onto instead.

Can anyone say Stockholm Syndrome?

Oh yeah, and she had all the symptoms loud and clear. But she didn't give a shit. Her father had taken something from him and it was now her job to give it back.

He turned all of a sudden, as if he'd sensed her standing there, his gaze sweeping over her, now absolutely expressionless. Making her feel vulnerable for some reason, aware of her nakedness in a way she hadn't been before. Then, still talking to whoever was on the phone, he turned back again, walking away from her toward the kitchen area and disappearing through the doorway.

Clearly he wanted privacy. Did that mean he was talking about her? To Jericho? Were they arranging a meeting right now?

I'm going to put a bullet in his brain.

Well, at least that made sense now too. Why he took her, why he wanted to kill Jericho. Why he was so set on it.

Revenge.

Violet swallowed. She could understand it. When someone you loved was taken from you, after the shock and the grief, anger was the next emotion to hit and for some people it hit hard. In fact, some people never got past it. Looked like Elijah was one of those people.

She went over to the punching bag where her clothes

were lying strewn on the floor and picked them up, starting to dress. Staying naked made her feel too exposed, and she was feeling exposed enough as it was.

When she'd finished she looked toward the kitchen area. Elijah still hadn't come out, but she could hear the low rumble of his voice, the words indistinct.

Deciding her fate maybe?

A little uprush of panic went through her and she had to turn and pace to the windows and back to get rid of it.

No, panicking was not helpful and after all she'd been through already, it seemed ridiculous to start now. What she needed to do was think of her next move. Initially it had been to help him lure out Jericho, but now? She wasn't sure.

Elijah knew more about Jericho than she did obviously, but she was betting the man was possibly even more dangerous than Elijah himself was. Killing him would certainly be an in-your-face kind of move. Surely Elijah would be aware that there would be reprisals for that kind of thing?

Violet stared sightlessly at the sky beyond the high windows.

Oh yeah, he was aware. The bleakness behind his eyes, the emptiness . . . He wasn't expecting to survive his revenge.

The thought made her heart squeeze tight and hard inside her chest.

She didn't want him to die. Sure, he was cold and he'd been rough with her. He hadn't been kind to her in any way, shape, or form, and really, losing his wife wasn't an excuse. And yet . . . There had been glimpses behind that emptiness in his eyes, glimpses of a man who wasn't all black ice. Who was passionate and demanding, certainly. But not only that.

He hadn't hurt her. He'd given her antinausea pills for Christ's sake. He'd lifted her out of that bathtub full of bloody water and wrapped her in a blanket. Bound the cuts. Given her painkillers.

Yes, he needed to keep her alive for Jericho, but he hadn't needed to do any of those things for her. Things that were aimed precisely at making her comfortable. At easing her pain.

We are all monsters, Violet.

He might be on the outside, but inside, somewhere under all that hard, cold ice he surrounded himself with, there was also a man.

A man she wanted to know more about. A man she wanted to heal.

Are you crazy? You've only known him two fucking days.

Yeah, well, in that case she was crazy. And she didn't care how long she'd known him. After a couple of years studying psychology she knew her own feelings well enough.

What about what Theo said? Always question.

She had questioned. She'd been constantly questioning herself since Elijah had brought her here and right now, she was fucking sick of it.

Turning away from the window, she paced over to the sofa, glancing toward the kitchen again. Still no sign of him. She turned back, went over to the bookcase and stood in front of it, searching through the spines of the books as if they could tell her the truths about him she so desperately wanted to know.

An older book in among all the paperbacks caught her eye and she reached out, pulling it off the shelf. It was a hardback, with an early sixties–looking cover. A first edition of Robert Heinlein's *Stranger in a Strange Land.* Vintage sci-fi and probably worth a bit of money by now.

Were these his books?

She opened the cover and leafed through the first few pages until she caught sight of the scrolling, cursive writing on the title page, boldly ignoring the fact that writing on a first edition would lower its value.

Kane, I told you I'd get you paper. Happy anniversary, darling husband. I love you. Marie.

Violet frowned. Who the hell was Kane?

"Get the fuck away from there." Elijah's voice was flat and hard with command.

Violet turned, still holding the book, meeting his gaze and seeing nothing at all in his black eyes. Nothing but darkness. As if his earlier confession hadn't happened.

As if he hadn't just told her that her father had killed his wife. *He killed Marie . . .*

Oh God. *He* was Kane.

She blinked, realization spearing her like a blade as she took in the rest of the apartment. At the strange little lounge setting in front of her that had seemed so out of place when she'd first come here. The bright rag-rolled rug. The sofa. The coffee table. The romance in the shelves behind her . . .

They were furniture from another time and another place. A time when he'd been married. When he hadn't been Elijah Hunt, but another man.

"Tell me about Marie, Elijah." she said abruptly, her voice cutting through the heavy silence. "Tell me about Kane."

The darkness in his eyes was suddenly full of flames, fierce, hot. Burning high. And she braced herself for whatever was going to come next.

But then his head snapped around, that fierce gaze locking onto the front door of the apartment. And for a second she couldn't work out what the hell had drawn his attention.

Then she saw that the steadily blinking lights of the security pad by the front door had gone dark.

He was already moving toward the door when it was kicked in, banging open so hard it bounced off its hinges, admitting three figures all with their arms outstretched, weapons in their hands.

Shock froze Violet where she stood and for a second she could only stand there, watching as the violence unfurled in front of her.

Elijah hadn't stopped moving, in fact, he'd accelerated, running toward one of the figures while someone else shouted. A gun went off, the sound exploding through the apartment followed by the shatter of glass.

And Violet found that she was moving too, but not away from what was happening. She was running toward it, her heart thumping loud in her ears, fear gripping her. Fear for him.

Elijah was grappling with another man, while a second man, tall, lean and black-haired, familiar-looking, trained a gun on them. The third figure, a woman with long blonde hair and dressed in a black suit, who looked as lethal as the gun she held, also trained a gun on the pair on the ground.

These people, they were going to kill Elijah. And she couldn't let that happen.

"Stop!" She screamed the word, launching herself at the man who'd just aimed a vicious punch at the bandage on Elijah's shoulder. As the blow landed, Elijah went white, stumbling a couple steps, his lips pulling back in a grimace of pain. Red bloomed against the new bandages she'd only just bound around him.

"Stop it, you prick!" Violet shouted again, and before

she could think twice about what she was doing, she stepped between the man and Elijah.

He was familiar. Wide shouldered and tall, built along the same massive lines as Elijah. Dark eyes, blonde hair. Brutally handsome features. It was Gabriel Woolf.

Which means this is a rescue.

Violet shoved the thought aside. She didn't care what it was right now, not when all that mattered was that they stopped hitting Elijah.

Gabriel's dark eyes settled on her, an expression she didn't quite understand in his gaze. "Are you okay?" he asked harshly. "Did he hurt you?"

There was movement behind Gabriel and the black-haired man, who Violet could now see was Alex St. James, Honor's long-lost brother, said in a low, dangerous voice to Elijah, "Don't you fucking move, asshole."

"Violet." Elijah completely ignored him. "Step away."

"No." She didn't bother looking behind her, keeping her gaze trained on Gabriel. "Not until I get a promise that they won't hurt you."

Gabriel's dark brows drew down. "What the fuck? You know we're here to rescue you, right?"

"Princess," Elijah's voice was softer this time. "Get the hell out of the way."

She was shaking for some reason—probably shock—and she had the most ridiculous urge to burst into tears. Either that or to turn around and walk straight into Elijah's arms.

You fucking idiot. They came for you. Someone actually came for you.

She should be thrilled. She should be running toward the door, getting out and never looking back.

But all she could do was stand there, staring at the three people training guns on the man behind her, murder in their eyes.

"I'm not moving," she said thickly, focusing on Gabriel. "Promise me. Promise me, he won't get hurt."

"Any particular reason you're defending him, Violet?" This from Alex, whose blue eyes never left Elijah.

She didn't know Honor's brother. Had never met him. But Honor had told her all about their reconciliation after she'd gotten together with Gabriel. Her friend was happy, but that hadn't changed Violet's opinion of Alex. Which was poor.

Violet opened her mouth to reply when Gabriel took a sudden step forward and reached out to take her bandaged wrist in his hand. "What the fuck is this?" he demanded. "Did he do this to you?"

She jerked her hand out of his grip. "It's not what it looks like, okay?"

"Touch her and I'll kill you, prick." Elijah's voice came from behind her, cold as ice.

Gabriel's attention flicked to him. "Oh no, I've had enough of this bullshit. Come with me, Violet, we're—"

At that moment Elijah's hands were around her waist, pulling her back against the heat of his body and holding her there. "*We* are going nowhere," he said flatly. "You and your friends can fuck off out of my apartment."

The guns trained on Elijah had now moved. To her.

Violet swallowed. She was okay with being his shield, especially with him half naked and his bare skin pressed up against her back, a reassurance rather than anything more sinister. It made her feel weirdly powerful.

She relaxed against him, hoping he'd understand it meant she trusted him.

Gabriel looked furious, while Alex's blue eyes glittered coldly. The blonde woman hadn't moved, but there was a frown on her face, her green gaze looking from Violet to Elijah then back again.

Then she said, her accent clipped and Russian sounding, "Why are we doing this? We are all on the same side." She lowered her gun, her attention focusing on Elijah. "Nice to see you again, Mr. Hunt."

Elijah slid an arm around Violet's waist, heavy as an iron bar. " 'Nice' is a relative term, Ms. Ivanova," he said coldly. "Why is it you people are always involving yourselves in other people's fucking business?"

"We involve ourselves when you take something that's ours." Somehow there was a gun in Gabriel's hand and he was pointing it straight at Violet.

"I'm not going to kill her," Elijah said. "If that's what you're worried about."

"And yet you're quite happy to use her as a human shield." Alex's voice was full of disgust. "Fucking coward."

Violet felt Elijah's muscles tense, the arm around her waist tightening. And it was instinct to lay her hands gently over his forearm, using touch to soothe him like she would a wounded animal.

She felt his breath across the back of her neck, a soft, inaudible exhale, and the hard, bunched muscles underneath her fingers gradually eased.

"He's not using me," she said firmly. "I'm protecting him."

All three sets of eyes focused on her once more.

She lifted her chin and met them each in turn.

"You heard what the lady said." Elijah pulled her closer. "Now make like the good soldiers you are and fuck off."

"Why?" Gabriel demanded, looking at Violet and ignoring Elijah. "We know he kidnapped you at fucking gunpoint, we have the security camera footage to prove it."

So they had been looking for her. That must have been Honor's doing.

"She doesn't have to explain herself to you," Elijah said icily. "Now, I'm not going to—"

"We know about your wife." It was Alex who cut in, keeping his gun exactly where it was. "And we know what you want."

Behind Violet, Elijah had gone very still.

"You want revenge," Alex continued. "And you would have had it, if Eva hadn't pulled that trigger."

Violet didn't dare take a breath, knowing something was happening but not sure what or even what Alex was talking about. It was important though, that much she was certain of.

"Yes," Elijah agreed, a harsh edge to his voice. "I would. I told you to keep out of it. I told you to stay the fuck away. But you didn't listen, did you? You just had to keep searching."

"We had our goddamn reasons." Alex's tone was hard. "And if you know who I am, then you'll know what those reasons are."

Elijah had begun to back away slowly, imperceptibly, taking her with him. And she went, not even understanding why, only knowing she had to go with him because if she didn't, something terrible was going to happen. "Oh, I know your reasons," Elijah was saying. "I know who the Seven Devils are. I already destroyed two of them."

The other three looked at one another, glances Violet couldn't interpret.

Who the hell were the Seven Devils? And what did he mean by destroying them?

Gabriel's expression was like iron. "Fuck this bullshit," he said coldly. "This ends now."

Violet didn't understand quite how it happened, because neither Gabriel or Alex moved. But somewhere a gun went off and she was suddenly thrown violently to the side. Biting off a scream, she threw her arms over her head as she crashed to the floor.

The wood beneath her vibrated with a heavy impact, the sounds of shouting filling the room.

Wild with inexplicable fear, she was already on her feet again, turning around in time to see Gabriel lift a hand, a wicked-looking gun held tightly in his fist.

Only to bring it down hard across Elijah's face.

CHAPTER TWELVE

Elijah came to, his vision blurry, his cheekbone hurting like fuck and his shoulder wound feeling like someone had kicked the shit out of it with steel-capped boots.

Jesus, what the hell had happened? Last thing he remembered, he'd finally gotten the phone call he'd been hoping for, the one from one Jericho's flunkies naming a time and place for a meeting. Then after he'd ended the call, he'd come out of the kitchen area to find Violet standing there with the Heinlein Marie had given him for their first wedding anniversary.

And she'd asked him . . . what? Something important. Something that had hollowed him out like she'd reached inside him with a melon-baller and scooped out his heart.

After that . . . Shit, that's right. The front door of his apartment had flown open—God knew how, since his security system was state of the art and no one should have been able to get past it—and Gabriel Woolf and his merry band of assholes had burst in.

Mother *fuck* . . . What had he missed? What had he done that had given his position away?

He blinked hard, trying to get his eyesight working, taking a scan around at where he was.

Bare room. Concrete floor and gray brick walls. No

windows. Lit with a harsh, white fluorescent light. Your standard torture room in other words.

He was sitting in a chair, unbound, which was a mercy. But not, apparently, unguarded.

In front of him stood four people. Woolf. Rutherford. King. And Alex St. James. They were all looking at him, their expressions ranging from completely blank to ice cold to furious. None of them had guns but he felt the prickle at the back of his neck that told him someone somewhere had a weapon trained on him.

A slight turn of his head and he spotted a fifth person. The bodyguard, Ivanova. She was the one with the weapon and it was pointed directly at his head.

Okay then.

He said nothing, shifting slightly in the chair, staring back at them expressionlessly because he'd be fucked if he gave them anything. Their insistence on sticking their noses where they didn't belong had ended up destroying years of planning. They were no friends of his.

"Good afternoon, Mr. Hunt." Rutherford was the one who broke the silence, his cut-glass British accent sharp. "I have to commend your ingenuity. You've proven to be a bit of a bastard to track down."

Elijah shrugged, fighting down the urge to wince as the movement aggravated his shoulder wound. "I'm hardly likely to make it easy for you."

Rutherford's amber gaze dropped to Elijah's shoulder. He was still bare-chested and wearing the shorts he'd put on to take out his rage on the punching bag. Felt like years ago. The bandages were bloody again and he had a sudden flashback, of Violet's hands on him, wrapping the gauze around his shoulder, her fingers gentle . . .

"Is your wound troubling you?" Rutherford murmured. "I apologize. It's not like me to miss."

Elijah ignored the dig. "Mind hurrying this Q&A session, or whatever the fuck this is, along? I have things I need to do."

"Things such as using Fitzgerald's daughter for some kind of glorified revenge plan?"

The words were mild enough, but it prompted another rush of memory about the confrontation in his apartment. St. James telling him they knew about what had happened to Marie. That they knew what he wanted. At least they *thought* they knew what he wanted.

"Yeah," he said flatly. "That."

Woolf's expression hardened, the glitter in his dark eyes furious. "Over my dead fucking body."

Elijah met the other man's gaze. "That can be arranged."

"Fuck's sake," Eva King said disgustedly. "Can we stop it with the dick measurements? I'm kind of over it." She stepped forward, a small, delicate woman in black jeans, heavy boots, and an AC/DC T-shirt, her long white-blonde hair in a ponytail down her back. "I've got some questions that are actually relevant."

This was the woman who'd taken Elijah's revenge from him and all because he'd made one stupid fucking mistake. Yeah, she was brave, he'd give her that. He'd been impressed with her fighting spirit when he'd brought her to Fitzgerald, but that didn't mean he'd forgiven what she'd done.

Elijah glowered at her, unable to stop the uprush of sudden anger that twisted in his veins. "What makes you think I'm going to tell you anything?"

He noticed Rutherford had taken a small step so he was right behind her, his posture tense. Clearly he didn't like his little girl being threatened.

Another memory flashed behind Elijah's eyes, of Violet pressed against him. Of his arm around her, holding her close. Of the strange feeling of wanting to take her and hide her away. Protect her from all those guns trained on her.

They thought he'd been using her as a shield to protect himself. Hell, that's exactly what he'd told himself he was doing, because there was no way they were going to take him. No way they were going to take her either. He needed her, after all. Yet that hadn't explained the fury that roared through him when St. James had pointed it out. Or why he'd felt himself relaxing when her fingers had rested on his arm. Or even the inexplicable need he had to turn them both around so that his back was facing all those guns.

But he hadn't done that. He'd seen the almost imperceptible move that Alex's beautiful bodyguard had made, a shift in posture that told him she was going to fire, and he'd shoved Violet aside to get her out of the way instead.

He didn't know why he'd done that since it was obvious Woolf and his friends wouldn't hurt Violet. That it wasn't her they were aiming at, but himself. And yet all he'd thought about was making sure Violet was well out of the line of fire.

Because you want her alive and whole for Jericho. Right?

Yes. Of course. That was it.

And yet all the same, he couldn't seem to take his eyes off the expression on Rutherford's face. A glittering, dangerous look that promised death to anyone who touched what was his.

Fuck. Pull yourself together.

Eva thrust her hands into her pockets, her head tilting, giving him a steady, sharp look. "I get it, you're pissed with me 'cause I shot that prick. But if you think I'm going to apologize for it, you're shit out of luck." It was true. She didn't look in the least apologetic. "Anyway, if you wanted his head so badly, why did you let me go?"

Up in Fitzgerald's office, Elijah had stood there with his gun held to Eva's head, a hostage for Rutherford's good behavior. Doing his good soldier act. It had taken him at least five years to get it right, but by the time Fitzgerald finally made him his right-hand man, he'd perfected it.

No one, least of all Fitzgerald, had ever suspected him of any ulterior motive, any secret plan.

He'd become one of Fitzgerald's men so thoroughly that sometimes he'd forget that there had ever been another way to be.

He'd almost forgotten up in that office.

"Because it looked like that guard dog behind you was going to shoot him," he said at last, because really, there wasn't any reason *not* to tell her. "And I wanted that honor for myself." He paused, giving her back a cold stare. "Except then you picked up the fucking gun and did it instead."

Eva was silent a moment. "You want to know why?"

"No."

"Because what happened to your wife nearly happened to me." The words were hard and cold, falling into the room like bits of ice.

Ah, so that was the answer. Another small piece of the puzzle falling into place.

He'd never asked his boss why Fitzgerald had wanted him to get Eva, since asking questions was never a prudent move. But that didn't mean he hadn't tried to find out. Over the years he'd built up a pretty good network of contacts who fed him all sorts of information about Fitzgerald's operations, and yet that particular piece of information had eluded him.

"What?" she said, correctly interpreting the look on his face. "You didn't know?"

"No. I didn't."

"Please. You can't tell me you were his favorite pet, following his orders so faithfully, and yet you didn't know why he wanted me so badly?"

Elijah gave her a silent scan that had Rutherford behind her tensing even more. Yes, she was just the sort of woman

Fitzgerald liked. Small and delicate, beautiful and strong. So he could break them.

Like Marie.

He forced the thought of Marie away. He didn't want to feel sympathy for this woman, for any of them. Sympathy was just another emotion that got in the way of what he needed to do.

Ignoring the reference to his wife, he said, "I've only been his 'favorite pet,' as you put it, for five years. If he'd had you in that time, I would have known about it."

Eva stared at him. "It was seven years ago."

"Then that's why I didn't know."

Her brows twitched. "You don't think there's anything wrong with that? With him keeping me like an animal in a cage?"

A silence fell, as if this was a very important question and the answer mattered. Of course they'd think that. What they failed to understand was that it didn't. His opinions, his feelings, made no difference, only what he did.

That's a fucking lie and you know it.

No, it wasn't. It was a necessary truth. A truth he had to believe, because if he didn't, if he thought feelings actually made any difference at all, he was fucked. They were a weakness, and he couldn't be weak. Not again.

"What I think is irrelevant," he said coldly. "The facts are that you fucking killed him and destroyed seven years of planning."

She frowned at him. "What planning? I hate to say it, but seven years seems pretty fucking long to plan for killing that asshole. Only took me two seconds to pull that trigger."

Elijah sat back in the chair, flicking a glance at the others. They were all silent, all watching him.

Well, why not give them the truth? He certainly wasn't going to be getting out of here without a fight and he needed to. He had a meeting with Jericho scheduled, a meeting that required Violet. Perhaps telling the truth would move things along.

"You think I only ever wanted Fitzgerald's head?" he said. "Yes, I wanted to kill him, but that's not all. I wanted to take down his whole fucking empire too."

Eva's brows twitched again, while Woolf's dark eyes narrowed. St. James's expression was completely enigmatic, while the massive man standing behind Eva stared at Elijah as if he was waiting for someone to give the word to launch an all-out attack.

The gun trained on him didn't move an inch.

"For your wife?"

Eva's voice was flat, and despite the leash he had on himself, Elijah felt his anger twist, pulling at it. "This has got nothing to do with her." He tried to make it sound icy, but for some reason it didn't. It sounded angry. Furious.

"Marie," St. James said, as if he was tasting the name. "Her name was Marie. I remember her. I remember you too, Kane."

Anger burst in his brain, a bright, white explosion.

Those nights he'd tagged along with Marie to the Second Circle, hating the place but going anyway because she always got such a kick out of being a member of such an exclusive club. Where they'd met some people who'd then introduced then to Fitzgerald. Even then he hadn't liked the guy, some instinct telling him there was something 'off' about him. An instinct he'd ignored because Marie had liked him, had thought he'd be useful to them and their respective businesses.

Fuck, he'd been a fool. Weak minded with love, never realizing the wolf his sheep of a wife was lying down with. He'd ignored the warning signs, and now Marie was dead.

Kane Archer should have been put down before he'd ever allowed her to set foot in that place.

Elijah stared into Alex St. James's blue eyes. "You do not say her name, not now, not ever. And as for Kane . . . He's dead and has been for seven years."

Alex said nothing, only continued to stare expressionlessly at him, but Elijah didn't make the mistake of thinking the guy had nothing to say. There was something sharp and frighteningly perceptive behind that blue gaze.

"Okay, well, I for one don't give a shit who you were or why you're doing what you're doing," Woolf said suddenly, sounding impatient. "All I want to know is who you've got in your sights now that Fitzgerald's dead and why you needed Violet."

"As I said," a light, accented voice off to the side added, "I think you want the same thing we do."

The bodyguard.

Slowly Elijah turned. She'd shot at him in the apartment and missed, possibly deliberately. Her eyes were very green and very cool, and not at all uncertain.

"If you want the same thing I do," he said, "then why the fuck do you keep getting in my way?"

"Because you involved my goddamn sister," Woolf growled.

Elijah turned back to the other man, who'd stepped forward, his hands loose at his sides, no doubt ready to deal out more damage if he didn't get the right answer.

More pain didn't bother Elijah, but unwillingly a small thread of respect wound through him. At least Woolf knew the right questions to ask. Knew what didn't matter and what did.

"I involved your fucking sister because Ms. King here shot the man I've been trying to take down and I needed a backup plan. She was it."

"Why? What do you need her for?"

They didn't know. They didn't know about Jericho.

Then again, why would they? He was a shadowy figure, his identity a closely guarded secret. No one had met him, no one knew who he really was, not even Fitzgerald. And the only reason Elijah even knew was because Fitzgerald had been wanting in on the guy's territory and needed all his men behind him.

You should tell them.

Ah, but why? This was his battle, his war. He didn't want anyone else fighting it for him, taking away the victory that was rightfully his, because shit, they'd already done it once before. Telling them now would only make them involve themselves again, and that was the last thing he wanted.

So he said nothing.

Woolf's lip curled. "Hate to break it to you, but Fitzgerald's fucking little empire is still going strong. Which means you've done sweet fuck all to take it down."

"Not quite fuck all. If you know Fitzgerald then you know about the Seven Devils. And if you know about the Seven Devils, you'll know that three of them, other than South and Fitzgerald, are dead." The Devils had been part of Fitzgerald's group of college friends, young men who'd been hungry for more money and power than they already had, and been drawn to get it illegally under Fitzgerald's influence.

"You killed them?" St. James asked sharply.

"Not personally, but I engineered their deaths." He'd worked hard at that too, to make sure they went down and yet to hide his own involvement. Fitzgerald had never guessed. "As for the other two who are still alive . . . it would have been only a matter of time."

"There's someone else." Rutherford spoke unexpectedly. His amber eyes hadn't moved from Elijah, not once. "You're going after someone else."

Elijah gave him back a cold smile. "Is that right?"

Rutherford's gaze intensified. "Someone who wants Violet."

Fuck.

Oh come on. Did you really think they wouldn't guess at some point?

Well, he'd hoped. They'd been so interested in other facts, they hadn't seemed interested in working anything else out. Turned out he was wrong.

He leaned back in the chair, letting his hands rest loosely on the arms of it. "Congratulations. You've worked out something very simple."

"Who?" Rutherford's voice virtually cracked with command, hard as a whip snapping. "Who wants her?"

The authority in his voice had no effect on Elijah whatsoever. He stared at Rutherford instead, turning something over in his head.

Maybe he should tell them, or at least use the information as a way of getting Violet and getting out of here.

"I'll tell you," he said slowly. "On one condition."

"Fuck no," Woolf spat. "You're not making any fucking conditions."

But Rutherford ignored the other man. "What condition?"

"Zac." Woolf's voice was a growl. "We can find this shit out ourselves, we don't need this prick. Hell, maybe he told Violet? She'll tell us."

Of course they could get a name out of Violet. But what they couldn't get was Jericho's contact details. Only he had that.

"No." It was Eva who spoke, her silver eyes glittering. "That'll take time, and I'm sick of this cagey bullshit. I want it to be over. Like now."

"You heard the woman," Rutherford murmured. "What's your condition?"

Woolf muttered something vicious, but the others ignored him.

A dumb move. Especially because they sure as shit weren't going to like that condition.

"It's not difficult. You let me go unharmed."

There was a silence.

"But that's not all. Is it?" This from St. James, his blue gaze narrowing.

Elijah allowed himself another smile. "Of course not. I want Violet too."

Violet sat on the massive black leather couch in Gabriel Woolf's Tribeca apartment with her hands clasped together, feeling a little dazed and oddly disconnected from things.

Maybe it was shock. At least, that's what Honor kept calling it. Because surely what she should be feeling was enormous relief at finally being out of Elijah's apartment. And gladness that her friend had come through and that she'd been rescued.

But she didn't. Instead, along with the weird disconnectedness she felt . . . worried. Unsure. Bizarrely she kept glancing around for Elijah and being disappointed that he wasn't here.

After she'd seen Gabriel deliver that knockout blow, he and Alex and the blonde bodyguard had bundled her up into a large black truck. They'd thrown an unconscious Elijah in the back and then they'd taken her here. Elijah they'd taken . . . somewhere else. To Zac's place apparently, according to Honor.

Violet did not find that in the least bit reassuring. And then reflected on the fuckedupedness of worrying about her captor and being concerned for his welfare.

Jesus Christ. Two days she'd been in that apartment—hardly enough time to get to know someone let alone feel what she felt for Elijah. Which meant she *really* was screwed up beyond all recognition.

Honor came back out of the kitchen with a mug of extremely hot, strong coffee, putting it on the low table near the couch. Then she sat down beside Violet, a concerned look on her face.

It was strange. Her friend looked just like she always did. Same smooth, black bobbed hair and delicate feline features. Same deep blue eyes. Same taste in beautifully tailored, professional-looking outfits. And Violet couldn't quite understand how her friend could be just the same, when it felt to Violet like her whole world had shattered.

Shouldn't the earth have moved? And why the hell was New York still even standing?

But of course the world and everything in it was the same. It was she who'd changed.

"Are you sure you're okay?" Honor asked after a moment. "You don't want me to call a doctor or anything?"

For a second Violet didn't understand what her friend was talking about. And then she realized. Her wrist. "No, I'm fine," she said, resisting the urge to pull down the sleeves of her top to cover the bandage.

"Not for . . ." Honor paused. "Anything else?"

Violet frowned at her. "What else?"

Her friend's blue eyes were very direct. "Did he hurt you, Violet?"

"No." A flash of something that felt very much like anger went through her. "No," she repeated sharply. "Of course he didn't hurt me. And if you're asking whether he raped me, then no, he didn't fucking do that either."

Honor didn't seem to take offense at her tone, only gave a nod. "Well, okay then. I had to check. I mean there's your wrist and," she gestured at Violet's shorn head, "the fact that you've had your hair all cut off. I just wanted to make sure you were okay."

Violet reached for her coffee, anger still twisting inside her and not really wanting to show it. Because her friend was only trying to help. Honor didn't know what had happened between her and Elijah, and if she did . . . Well, shit, she'd probably be appalled. Or maybe not. Maybe she'd be expecting something like that to happen, because God knew Violet had been hiding behind the façade of the sexual free-spirit for years.

She sipped her coffee, holding onto the mug with both hands, the hot liquid warming her.

Honor said nothing, letting the silence sit between them, though Violet knew her friend must have had a thousand questions all waiting to be asked.

Eventually, she said, "I'm fine, Honor. Really."

The other woman scanned her face as if she was checking her over. "Can I ask what happened?"

Violet took another sip of the coffee. "You don't know?"

"Eva managed to track you via security camera footage on the subway, so we saw Elijah kidnap you at gunpoint. Then Gabriel found him and tried to convince him to let you go. We got to the apartment eventually by picking up the last known signal from your phone."

Another jolt went through her at the realization that a day ago this would have meant so much to know her friend was tracking her, had been trying to find her. But now she just felt . . . empty.

"Yeah," she sighed. "That's pretty much what happened." Because what else could she say? Honor didn't need to know all the details.

Another silence fell.

"What happened to your hair?" Honor asked eventually.

"Elijah didn't like the dreads," Violet said. "So he cut them off."

An expression of concern crossed her friend's face. "Oh, Vi . . ."

"It's fine. I was getting sick of them anyway." Weird how little she felt about that now. How pathetic her attempt at rebellion had seemed and how stupid getting angry when Elijah had cut them had been. It was just hair, after all.

"Sick of them?" Honor echoed, the crease deepening between her brows. "But you—"

"I didn't want them," she interrupted. "Like I said, it's fine."

The other woman stared at her. "You're in shock, aren't you?"

Violet blinked, realizing abruptly how she'd sounded. "Maybe. I mean, I guess it's not every day you get kidnapped by some freaky-ass dude and then get told your father was murdered."

Honor sat back. "Oh. So you know."

"Yeah, I know." Violet gripped her coffee mug tighter. "Elijah told me some . . . other things as well."

"Ah." There was sympathy on Honor's face, but also a kind of unflinching honesty that made Violet want to turn away and pretend none of this ever happened. Because there was a part of her that had secretly hoped what Elijah had told her wasn't true. That he'd been lying to her. That her father wasn't dead and wasn't the Godfather of some evil empire of crime.

But one look in Honor's blue eyes told her that was a vain hope.

All of it was true.

Violet made herself hold her friend's gaze. "Tell me, Honor. Tell me about Dad."

Honor's brow creased. "Perhaps now's not the best—"

"Tell me." Holy shit, was that her voice? Since when had she sounded so hard?

Honor gave her a measuring look, as if she was checking to make sure Violet was still Violet. "Okay then," she said. "So what do you know about him so far?"

"That he ran a drug operation. That he was into sex trafficking. That he had some kind of underground casino thing going on right here in New York." Saying it all out loud, to another person, felt wrong. Felt on some level like a betrayal.

Honor let out a breath. "Unfortunately, yes, he was doing all those things."

Violet swallowed, the last shred of hope vanishing. "I see."

"You should also know that . . . what he did affected some of Gabriel's friends."

You don't want *to know.*

No, she really didn't. But she couldn't ignore it, couldn't run away from it. The time for pretending ignorance, the time for running away was past. Her father was dead, which meant she had to deal with this herself.

She gripped her mug hard, feeling the hot burn of the china under her fingers. "What did he do?"

"He kept Eva King as his personal sex slave for at least two years." Honor's voice was so very calm. So very level. "And . . . I'm so sorry, Vi, but he had my father killed."

Didn't seem to matter how hard she gripped the mug, it slipped from Violet's fingers anyway and smashed onto the hardwood floor. Hot coffee went everywhere, soaking into the leather of the couch, into her trousers, splashing the silky green fabric of her top.

Honor exclaimed softly, moving to help clean it up, murmuring about burns or some such crap.

But Violet didn't hear her. Because coffee spillage was the least of her worries.

She got up from the couch, feeling like she was freezing solid. As if she were *already* frozen and one hard blow would shatter her into a thousand pieces.

She didn't know Eva King, but there was one salient fact about the woman she was aware of, the fact that was often trumpeted in the media. Eva was young, younger than Violet was. Which meant that her father had . . .

A wave of nausea went through her, so strong it was all she could do not to be sick on the floor right then and there.

And Honor's father, Daniel . . .

Violet walked to the windows of the apartment and stood there, waiting for the nausea to pass, for the cold brick that was sitting in her stomach to melt. Waiting to feel normal again.

What the hell? After this? You'll never be normal again.

The truth of it was a punch to the face, a blade straight through the heart. Because no, she never would be, not after this. Not now that she knew what her father was. Not now that she knew what he'd done.

Her eyes felt dry and gritty, and she was surprised that outside the windows of Gabriel's apartment the world was going about its business as if nothing had ever happened.

Jesus. And she'd been reflecting on how her life had blown apart not ten minutes ago. That was nothing compared to this.

There was a pressure in the back of her throat, like she was going to cry, and yet her eyes remained stubbornly dry. Because no, she wasn't going to cry. That would be indulgent and it did sweet fuck-all to help the people her father had hurt.

She felt a sudden, violent need to look into Elijah's bleak, black eyes. To have his voice telling her these hard, rough truths. Because he knew what it was like to live with a monster. He understood. He'd been living in that pit for seven years himself.

Violet found she'd curled her hands into fists at her sides. "I need to talk to Elijah," she said in a rough, croaky voice.

"The others have him." Honor's voice came from beside her. "They've got questions."

Violet didn't look around. "I don't give a shit what they have. *I* need him, Honor. I need him now."

Her friend remained silent, didn't ask why Violet needed him, why the hell she wanted to be with the man who'd held her hostage for two days. And just as well, because how did you explain that kind of thing? How did you explain the feeling of having more in common with a hardened criminal than you did with your best friend?

"That's not all, Vi," Honor said, quiet and steady.

Oh God. There was more?

"Your father . . . raped Gabriel's mother."

Violet's hearing felt dull, as if she'd been hit over the head with something heavy.

"Gabriel is your half brother."

The ground shifted beneath her feet, the world turning in dizzy circles around her. Everything had changed, everything was different. So different she didn't even recognize where she was anymore.

She wanted familiarity, understanding. And there was only one person in the world who could give her that right now.

"Elijah," she whispered.

CHAPTER THIRTEEN

They finally let him out of the bare concrete room an hour later, shutting him in another room that looked like an old-fashioned gentleman's study. They locked the door and left some asshole standing outside it as a guard.

Elijah could have escaped easily enough if he'd set his mind to it, but he wasn't going anywhere without Violet. They hadn't given him an answer about whether they were going to let him take her, but he could wait. Not for too long, though, especially since he would be meeting Jericho in just a few days.

He'd give them another couple of hours and if they were still screwing around, he'd get out of here and go find Violet himself.

Rutherford had given him a T-shirt to put on, which he supposed was polite. But they didn't do anything about the bloody bandages wrapping around his shoulder. Luckily the wound had stopped bleeding, so that was something. Still hurt like a bastard though.

Waiting was always a mindfuck, so Elijah began to pace around the room, giving his body and mind something to do instead of dwelling on pointless questions such as what they were going to do with him and where the hell Violet was.

This had to be Rutherford's place, what with all the dark

wooden library shelves and cabinetry, the leather sofa and high wingback chairs. There was just something intrinsically very English and particular about the decor that reminded him of Marie's London-born parents.

"I remember you too, Kane."

Yeah and he remembered Alex St. James. The arrogant little shit who'd flirted with his wife. Who'd made his club so exclusive, so damn attractive that Marie hadn't been able to resist wanting to be part of it since she'd always loved feeling special.

She'd made him feel special too.

Grief hit him in the chest, so strong he stopped dead in the center of the room. A grief he thought he'd fought and killed and buried. Grief for his wife. For what he'd lost when she died and for all the years of bearing that loss since.

No. Fuck no.

Forcing the emotion away though sheer bloody-minded will, Elijah made himself move again, over to the windows, to the bookshelf, the chair by the fireplace, to the sofa, and back once more.

He couldn't be thinking this shit. There were people he had to call, some stuff he had to set up. He didn't want to go into a meeting with Jericho blind, especially given the man's reputation. And there was also the fact that his flunky had agreed to everything Elijah had said without arguing. Battery Park. The Esplanade. 3 p.m. Come alone.

No argument always meant something was up. He just had to find out what.

Then there was the other thing that he'd had to put on hold while he'd been holed up with Violet. What to do with the remains of the Fitzgerald empire.

His goal had always been to take it down, and gradually over the years he'd been undermining it from the inside, eroding it away piece by piece and in such a way that

Fitzgerald had never noticed. Right up until Eva King had put a bullet through his brain, he'd still believed that the deaths of two members of his little coterie, the Seven Devils, had been due to a car accident and a mugging, respectively. As Elijah had intended when he'd taken them down.

However, now that Fitzgerald was dead, that goal was a little more difficult. Especially if he was going to take out Jericho. Especially if he didn't survive the attempt. Then again, perhaps he could leave that to Gabriel Woolf and his friends. They certainly seemed keen. Hell, if Jericho was dead, he didn't care what they did with whatever was left. As long as they destroyed it, of course.

From the hallway outside the study came the sound of voices.

Elijah froze, staring at the closed door. Because he was damn sure those voices were feminine. Which meant . . . Violet.

A weird adrenaline rush had the blood pumping hard in his veins, and he was moving to the door before he'd had a chance to think about why he was doing so.

It opened while he was still halfway across the room, and sure enough, Violet came in, followed by a dark-haired woman with familiar blue eyes. Honor, Woolf's lover. Behind her was the guard, who gave Elijah a warning look.

Like that would ever be enough to stop him if he wanted to get out.

Then again, Violet was finally here and he didn't want to make things difficult for her with her friend so he stopped where he was, waiting. Deliberately not thinking about why not making things difficult for Violet was quite so important.

And then he got a good look at her face and everything ceased to matter.

She looked broken, like a piece of china smashed into pieces and poorly put together again. Her face was white and there were circles under her eyes. She wasn't wearing the clothing he'd bought her, but a pair of dark blue skinny jeans and a soft sweater the same deep turquoise of her eyes. Expensive, low-key clothes that somehow made her look even more vulnerable than she did already.

He began to move toward her and to hell with the asshole standing guard behind them, but then she said, "Elijah, stop."

And he did, because the same expression of desolation in her face was in her voice too, and he found he couldn't ignore it.

Violet turned her head a little toward her friend. "I need to speak with him alone, Honor."

Honor St. James flicked a glance at Elijah. "I'm not sure I can—"

"Please." Violet never took her gaze from him, as if he were a lifeline and she was drowning.

Something heavy and unwelcome shifted in his chest.

Honor sighed. "Okay." She gestured to the guard. "Come on, let's give them a few minutes."

A few seconds later, the door closed behind them, leaving Violet and him alone in the room.

He took a step toward her, but she held up a hand. "No. Wait. I have to ask you some questions."

Again, he stopped, held by the awful note in her voice. The one that seemed to reach inside him, looping wire around his heart and pulling tight.

"What questions?" he demanded. "What's happened, princess? Are you okay?"

"No. I'm not okay." Her voice had thickened, and she stood there with that terrible look on her face. He wanted very badly to do something, but he didn't quite know what that something should be. Perhaps something violent, that would involve pain and preferably to the person who'd put that expression on her face.

"What happened?" he asked again. "What did they do to you? Because if they did something, I swear to Christ—"

"They didn't do anything. They told me about Dad."

Ah. Well, that was never going to be easy for her, was it? "About how he died?"

"Among other things." She stopped. "He hurt people, Elijah. He hurt them. Gabriel's mother. Eva King. Honor's Dad. God, so many people." Her pale throat moved, and he could almost see the shattered pieces she was holding together break again, into smaller pieces, all jagged and sharp. "I need to know something. I need to know whether you were a part of it. Whether you knew about it." Another pause. "What did you do for him, Elijah?"

He'd never hidden what he was, what he'd done. Not from himself and not from anyone else. He'd embraced the identity he'd created for himself, the mercenary Elijah Hunt, ruthless and dark and absolutely as cold as ice. Taking down Fitzgerald had required it.

He hadn't made any excuses for his behavior and he'd never regretted it. Regrets would kill him.

Except now, staring into Violet's eyes, he thought that perhaps he might have regrets after all, because he wanted to tell her that no, he hadn't done anything bad. That he hadn't been a part of those things she'd mentioned. That he wasn't the monster she so clearly feared he would be.

But he had and he was. And he couldn't lie to her.

So he said, "What he did to Woolf's mother was before my time and no, I had no idea about that. Same with Daniel St. James. But yes, I shot Honor's stepfather. I was supposed to kill him, but I missed the shot. The man wasn't like the others and his death would have been pointless. As to Eva King . . . Again, that was before my time. But he had other girls that I knew about."

Violet's face was still deathly pale. "What happened to them?"

"Some of them I managed to get out. Others I couldn't without blowing my cover."

"You kidnapped Eva. Honor told me."

"Yes. I did. Fitzgerald wanted her and I couldn't stop him. I did what I could to give both her and Rutherford the opportunity to escape." He held her gaze. "I did what I could to help *all* of them get out before anyone else got hurt."

"Oh." She fell silent for a long moment, staring at him, and he hated that look on her face. Hated it for reasons he couldn't have explained even to himself. "Why? Why did you work for him? And what were you hoping to achieve?"

"His death. And the death of that fucking empire he built up."

"Because of your wife?"

"Yes." There was no other answer.

Violet stayed where she was, her blue-green eyes burning into his, and he didn't look away. He had no idea why she wanted to know these things, or whether it would change things between them, but he was what he was and there was no changing what he'd done. He couldn't pretend otherwise. Anyway, she should know what he was by now. He hadn't held himself back when it came to dealing with her.

"I'm sorry," she said suddenly, thickly. "I'm so sorry, Elijah." Suddenly she was walking toward him, closing the distance between them, coming right up to where he stood, and then putting her arms around him.

Shock held him frozen to the spot. The heat of her body was right up against him, and part of him—the raw, desperate, grief-stricken part—wanted to shove her away. And yet he couldn't. Her arms were slim and they held him so lightly, yet they felt like iron bands around his waist. Chains holding him fast.

She bent, her forehead resting against his chest. And then she began to cry.

The band looped around his heart pulled even tighter. So tight it was painful.

He'd watched plenty of people cry over the years, both men and women. Tears of sorrow, of anger, of pain. Of fear and desperation. But none of them had ever moved him. His heart had been long hardened against anything as weak as pity or mercy.

But now . . . The sounds of Violet's sobs were doing something to him. Breaking him in ways he couldn't describe. She'd come to give him comfort, the first person to do so in years, and yet now she was the one who was crying. Holding onto him as if a storm was tearing at her and she was terrified of being blown away.

Why? Did she expect him to give her comfort in return? Didn't she know that he wasn't the kind of man who did that? He hadn't been that kind of man for years.

And yet despite that, he found himself lifting his arms and putting them around her slender figure, gathering her in close. Holding her like she was holding him.

The tension in her body abruptly relaxed and she cried harder, deep, gut wrenching sobs that had him holding her even tighter, as if she were coming apart at the seams and only he could keep her together. He found himself whispering inanities he didn't even realize he was capable of, his mouth against the short, soft spikes of her hair. "Hush, princess. It's okay. Everything will be fine, I promise."

He didn't know how long he stood there holding her, but after a while her sobs eventually quieted into soft hitched breaths before dying away completely. Then they both just stood there for a good couple of minutes until, abruptly, Violet pulled away.

He almost reached to haul her back but sensed she needed a moment, so he let her go, watching as she turned away from him, dragging an arm over her eyes.

If anyone had come into the room right at this moment, he would have killed them.

Violet's arm dropped, her cheeks shiny with tears, her eyes red. "All I wanted was to find my brother," she said in a thick voice. "That's all that mattered to me. But now? Fuck. After hearing about everything my father has done? It's selfish. Theo's probably really dead and I've been wasting years—*fucking years*—chasing a ghost." She took a small, ragged breath. "But you know who's not dead? Jericho. And he should be, Elijah. He fucking should be. So if you want to use me to take him down, then from now on I'm all yours."

She had thought she'd be the one to comfort him. She hadn't realized that the moment she put her arms around him, she'd be the one needing comfort. Absorbing his strength like a flower deprived of sun absorbs light. She even half expected him to pull away the way he'd done a number of times before, but he didn't. He just stood there, so hot and strong and immovable. Like granite. And then he'd put his arms around her in turn, and because it had been so long since someone had just held her while she cried, she didn't question it. She just took it.

It was kind of a relief to cry, because she hadn't done so since the apartment and there had been so much building up inside her. Grief and shock and the terrible bleakness that had settled on her soul as Honor had named her father's crimes.

A bleakness she'd never be able to escape.

But she could have this, a moment or two to cry and to take some comfort. God knew, she didn't deserve it, not after what her father had done to her friend, to all these other people too, but she'd allowed herself to take a couple of minutes.

And then she'd forced herself away, because for two days she'd managed to bear the fear and the uncertainty of being held captive and hadn't broken. She wouldn't break now. Especially not now that she had a new purpose.

She would make things right. She would help Elijah take down Jericho if it was the last thing she did.

Elijah didn't say anything, which was unexpected. She'd hoped he'd look at least a little bit pleased, but he didn't. If anything he looked more . . . concerned. Except that wasn't an expression she associated with him, so it couldn't be, right?

He was standing in front of her, still in his exercise shorts; and someone must have given him a T-shirt because last time she remembered, he hadn't been wearing one. In fact, last time she remembered, he'd been on the ground having been hit in the face by Gabriel. Who'd also gone for the wound on his shoulder.

Oh shit. She'd been so lost in the horror of what Honor had told her about her father, she hadn't even stopped to think about what had happened to Elijah. What Gabriel and his friends had done to him. Perhaps they'd hurt him. Perhaps that was why he was looking at her like that.

Wiping her face to get rid of the last of her tears, she scanned his scarred, brutal face. There had already been bruises on it when he'd kidnapped her, now there were more. One darkening on his cheekbone and around his eye socket, making the scar that ran across his face seem like a stark white line. His lower lip was bloody too.

"Are you okay?" She took a step toward him, closing the distance once more. "What did they do to you? I saw Gabriel punch you in your shoulder—"

The words died in her throat as Elijah's big, warm hands suddenly reached out, cupping her face. She stared at him in surprise. Because the touch was gentle, and the look in his eyes . . .

"You had a lead," he said. "You said you had a lead on your brother."

She blinked, not understanding where he was going with this. "Well, yeah, but that's not important anymore—"

"It's important to you?"

Violet stared at him. There was a fierce gleam in his eyes now and although the words had sounded like a question, she got the impression that they weren't. Like he knew already. "It was important before," she said slowly. "But now . . ."

"Why not?"

"Why do you think? God, after everything Dad did, me trying to find a dead man seems a little dumb. Especially when I can help you take Jericho down."

But he was frowning now, his gaze moving over her face as if she was a difficult book he was trying to read. "Why are you doing this, Violet? This . . . concern over me. Binding up my gunshot wound. Throwing yourself between me and Woolf. Telling them not to hurt me. And now . . ." His thumbs moved almost absently along the line of her jaw, a soft caress that seem to wake every single nerve ending into full awareness of him. Of the heat of his palms cupping her cheeks, the hard warmth of his body inches from hers. "You're giving up what's important to you in order to help me kill a man. Why?"

Good question. And one she had yet to come to a decision about. Because fundamentally, she had no idea why. Oh, she knew the answer with regard to Jericho, that was clear to her at least. But the rest?

You're falling for him, dickhead.

No. No way. Falling for him would be . . . all kinds of wrong. Really, what kind of idiot would she be to fall for her kidnapper? Yeah, she'd had sex with him, but she wasn't one of those girls who fell for the first man she had sex with.

How would you know? You've never had sex or fallen for anyone before.

Violet swallowed. "I'm helping you because I need to fix what my dad did. Not for any other reason."

He didn't let her go, those thumbs moving back and forth along her jawline, making her shiver. "And throwing yourself between me and Woolf's gun?"

"I'd do that for anyone." And that wasn't a lie. She would. *That's not the whole truth though, is it?* "Anyway," she went on, trying to drown the voice in her head because it felt too raw and exposing, "what's it to you?"

He didn't reply, staring at her in that intense, sharp way he had. As if he could see the secrets of her soul, the secrets she didn't even know she had. And then just as suddenly as he'd held her, he released her, turning toward the door. "If you want to help me then we need to get out of here." His voice had turned cold. "There are some people I need to contact, things that need to get set up."

The imprint of his palms still burned like fire against her cheeks, the gentle motion of his thumbs on her jaw a featherlight, ghostly memory. He'd always been hard and rough with her, never gentle. Never . . . tender.

Something that felt awfully like disappointment twisted in her chest, as if she'd said the wrong thing or made a mistake in some way. Except she couldn't think of what mistake she'd made. Or why it even mattered to her.

No, that was another lie. She knew why it mattered.

"Elijah," she said before she could second-guess herself.

He turned back, the look on his face impenetrable. "What?"

"I lied. I wouldn't put myself in front of Gabriel's gun for anyone."

"But you did for me?"

"Yes. I did for you."

His dark brows drew down, and for a long moment he only looked at her, black eyes enigmatic. But all he said was, "Come on. We have to go."

What she was expecting she didn't know, but that wasn't quite it.

You hurt him.

The words echoed in her brain. Unbelievable. Ridiculous. How could she hurt a man like him? He was so strong, like a mountain—he didn't bend and he didn't break. Besides, in order to hurt him, he'd have to care about what she'd said, and he didn't. Did he?

He'd turned back, striding to the door. Honor had warned her that Gabriel and the others were clear that they'd wanted Elijah to stay at Zac's place while they decided what the hell to do with him. And she didn't think that Elijah just walking out of here was going to work.

Then again, he wasn't a man who let people stop him when he wanted to do something.

Pushing away all the other disturbing thoughts, Violet followed him to the door. "I'm not sure they're going to let us go," she said as he reached for the handle. Because together they were "us" now, right? "Honor told me they didn't want you getting out."

"Then they should have put a better guard on the door." Elijah didn't even hesitate, pulling open the door.

Honor was waiting outside in the hallway, talking to someone on the phone. But as soon as the door opened and she noticed them, she ended the call, sliding the phone into the pocket of her tailored, black suit jacket. Her blue eyes went straight to Violet, as if checking to make sure she was okay.

And then the guard stepped into the doorway, blocking it.

Honor opened her mouth to say something, but Elijah's

hand shot up and, before anyone could move, he took the guard by the throat and slammed him into the hallway wall opposite the door. The guy began to raise his hands, trying for some kind of last-minute defense, but by then it was too late. Elijah's fist caught him full in the face and he dropped like a stone.

"Are you coming, princess?" Elijah didn't look in Violet's direction, his attention firmly on Honor.

Violet's heartbeat had begun to speed up. She'd been planning on convincing Honor to let them go without a fuss, but Elijah had pretty much killed that plan.

"That was unnecessary, Mr. Hunt," Honor said in a cool voice, completely unfazed by the sudden explosion of violence.

"Really? And I suppose you would have let me just walk out of here, Ms. St. James?"

Honor's gaze flicked to Violet. "Well, that depends on what you're about to do. Such as grabbing my friend here and trying to kidnap her again."

"He's not trying to kidnap me." Violet stepped into the hallway, coming up beside Elijah. And then, very deliberately meeting her friend's eyes, she reached out and took Elijah's hand, twining her fingers through his. "I'm coming with him because I want to help."

Perhaps it was a risk taking his hand and revealing herself like this. And not only to Honor, but to Elijah as well. But hell, why not? The battle was coming and she'd picked a side. She wasn't ashamed of that.

Elijah didn't look at her, but he didn't pull away either, his hand still and warm in hers.

Honor's gaze fell to their entwined fingers, then rose to look back up at them. "I see," she said softly. "Gabe is going to *hate* that."

"I don't give a fuck whether he hates it or not." Elijah's voice was flat. "I'm taking Violet with me and that's final."

"You want to go, Vi?" The question sounded casual, but Violet knew it wasn't. She could hear the subtext. *If he's forcing you, let me know. I'll help you.*

"It's okay, Honor," she said steadily. "I need to go with him."

"You know what he's going to do, don't you? What he wants you for?"

"She's not stupid," Elijah said, his tone icy. "Of course she does. That was the first thing I told her."

Honor flicked him a glance that was strangely measuring. "We need the name, Mr. Hunt."

"No, you don't. I'm sure Ms. King can find out for you. If she can break my security system, she can find out that minor detail."

Honor pursed her lips. "How did you know it was Eva?"

"There's only one way to open that door without the combination code and that's to reset it. It's a top-end Void Angel system and there's only one person who could possibly have hacked into it so quickly."

So that's how they'd gotten into Elijah's apartment. She still didn't know whether she was pleased about that or not.

"You know Gabriel and the others are in the next room right now." Honor's gaze was level. "All I have to do is call out. And we know where you live. We can stop you."

"You could. But you won't. Because the person I'm going to kill is exactly the same person you want dead too." He smiled one of his terrifying smiles. "Ask Ms. King. She'll be in agreement I'm sure."

"But we don't even know who that person is."

"Then you'll just have to trust me."

Honor snorted, clearly disbelieving.

"You can," Violet said quietly as she tightened her fingers around Elijah's. "And if you don't trust him, you can trust me. I know what I'm doing."

But her friend didn't look convinced. "He captured you, Vi. You're a psychology major. You must know—"

"Yes, I know. Stockholm Syndrome, et cetera, blah, blah." She held Honor's gaze. "You can believe what you like about that, but you have to know I'm also doing this for the people Dad wronged. To make up for all the pain he's caused. You have to let me, Honor. You have to."

She could feel Elijah's impatience. She knew he wanted to go and go now, and to hell with Honor and the rest of them. But she didn't want to leave with a fight, because that, in the end, wouldn't help anyone.

Honor stared at her. "You know who he's going after?"

For a second she struggled with her conscience, with her loyalties. Elijah hadn't told them, which meant he must not want them involved and she could see why. He wanted this to be his fight, not theirs.

She could feel his dark gaze on her, fierce and cold, but he didn't say anything. As if he was waiting for her to make the choice.

So she made it.

"No," she lied. "I don't. He wouldn't tell me."

Honor's gaze flickered as if she knew Violet was lying. "But you trust him anyway? Really?"

"Yes." The word wasn't hard to say, mainly because it wasn't a lie. "I do."

The other woman looked at her for a long moment. Then suddenly, she let out a breath. "Go, then. I'll make sure the others don't come after you." Her gaze flicked back to Elijah. "But I can't guarantee they won't. They have their own reasons for wanting to follow up on this."

"Then they'll have to bear the consequences," Elijah said shortly. "Consider yourself warned, Ms. St. James." And without another word, he turned toward the front door.

"Vi," Honor murmured as Violet slipped past her. "Be careful."

"I will." She forced a smile on her face even though smiling was the last thing she felt like doing. "And thanks."

But Honor didn't smile back, and the worry in her blue eyes stayed with Violet for a long time after they'd gone.

CHAPTER FOURTEEN

Honor waited for Gabriel and the others in Zac's study, her hands clasped on her lap.

None of them were going to be terribly happy with her about letting Elijah go, but really, what did they expect? Zac had left one guard. One. Hardly a match for Elijah, and it wasn't as if Honor could stop him if he'd tried to leave.

Still, she probably should have told them that Elijah and Violet had gone. Yet she hadn't and she hadn't worked out why that was yet.

She hadn't expected her friend to want to go back to him and the fact that Violet had was a worry. Yet . . . Honor suspected there was something deep and complicated going on between Elijah and Violet. She'd seen it in the glances they'd given each other, in the way Violet had reached for his hand, had told Honor she'd trusted him.

For some reason it reminded her a little of her and Gabriel. So no, she hadn't warned the others or tried to stop Violet from leaving. She'd let them both go because fundamentally they wanted the same things that she and the rest of her friends wanted. And because Violet had held his hand and he hadn't pulled away.

Maybe she'd regret it. Maybe she'd made the incorrect

choice. But she had an instinct about those two and she didn't think it was wrong.

One thing she was sure of though. Gabriel was going to be pissed.

Luckily she could handle him when he was.

She waited a while, to give Elijah and Violet some time to get well away, and soon enough, the door to the study opened and her lover came in, closely followed by all the rest.

Gabriel's dark eyes scanned the room quickly then came to rest on her. "Where is he, baby?"

Honor lifted her chin. "I let him go."

Oddly, he didn't seem too upset by this. "And Violet?"

She pushed herself out of the chair and walked slowly over to where he stood. His temper didn't frighten her, never had. She knew how to deal with it. "She went with him."

Something dark flashed in his eyes. "What do you mean 'she went with him'?"

"Where's my guard?" Zac was standing behind Gabriel, his amber eyes fixed on her. "He wasn't outside?"

"No," Honor said, not looking at him, keeping her gaze on Gabriel. "Elijah took him out. I had to send him to the emergency department to get his broken nose checked." They all seemed pretty calm about this. Too calm. What the hell was going on?

"Explain, baby," Gabriel demanded. "Because 'she went with him' sounds like it was voluntary. And I have to say, I'm real unhappy about that."

And here it came, his temper.

Honor placed a palm in the center of his broad chest and looked up at him. "It's okay. She's your sister and you want to protect her. But yes, it was voluntary."

"Fucking sisters," Alex muttered. "Can't live with 'em, can't live without 'em."

"So let me get this straight. It was her choice?" Gabriel looked in no way appeased. "You told her about me, right? About everything?"

Honor met his gaze, unflinching. "Yes. It was a lot to take in and I think . . . Look, I don't know what went on with her and Elijah, but things are a lot more complicated there than we thought."

The silence in the room suddenly became deafening.

" 'Complicated'?" Gabriel's voice was deceptively mild. "What kind of 'complicated'?"

He *really* wasn't going to like this.

Briefly Honor debated not telling him because it was sure as hell going to sign Elijah's death warrant. Then again, Elijah could handle himself, clearly.

"The usual kind," she said at last.

Alex sighed and walked over to one of the chairs near the fireplace, throwing himself down on it. "Just let me get comfortable before you go postal, Gabe. I wouldn't mind watching the boot being on the other foot for a change."

Gabriel ignored him. "Fuck that. I'm going to get her back. Now."

"No," Honor said firmly and closed her fist in the fabric of his T-shirt, holding him still. "Violet wants to help Elijah. She wants whoever he's going after dead as well, and you need to let her do it." She held Gabriel's dark eyes with her own. "This is her recompense for everything her father did. You have to let her have that."

Gabriel's expression twisted and he abruptly pulled away from her, turning and stalking toward the closed door of the study.

Honor watched him, knowing him. Knowing he wasn't going to walk through it.

And sure enough he came to a stop in front of it, staring at the dark wood. Then he lifted a fist and slammed it into the paneling. "*Fuck*," he said viciously.

"We were always going to let him go, Gabe," Alex commented from his position on the chair. "This is what we planned, remember?"

Ah, so there was something going on. "What plan?" Honor glanced around at the others, then narrowed her gaze at Gabriel. "What are you talking about?"

"We wanted to let him escape on his own," Gabriel said roughly after a moment. "Zac put his least-experienced guy on the door for form's sake, but basically we needed him to leave."

"Why?"

It was Zac who spoke. "Because we think he's already organized a meeting with whoever it is he's after. Eva can find out the name we need, but obviously the details of this meeting—if there is one—are trickier to discover. So our plan was to let you bring Violet here and he'd take her—"

"That was *your* plan," Gabriel interrupted curtly.

"And it's a fucking good one, you agreed," Zac continued, all calm. "Anyway, I put a tracking device in the hem of the sweater you loaned her. We can track her, which means we can track this meeting Hunt's organized."

Honor blinked, trying to take it all in. "When did you do that to my sweater?"

"Still means Hunt's got her." Gabriel said to Zac, ignoring her question. The expression on his face had cleared, but there was anger burning in his dark eyes.

"She is a strong woman." Katya, over by the fireplace near Alex's chair, sounded decisive. "Don't underestimate her."

Gabriel threw her a scowl. "You don't know her."

"Neither do you," Alex reminded him. "You saw the way she leaped in front of him in spite of all the hardware pointing in her direction. That wasn't what we'd expected."

Gabriel straightened out the fingers of the hand he'd

punched the door with and gave them a shake. "He probably brainwashed her."

Honor sighed. "That's what I thought too, but I don't think it's like that. Actually, reminds me a bit of you and me."

Gabriel scowl deepened. "In that case, he's a dead man."

"Oh quit with the macho bullshit," Eva muttered. "Point is, Elijah did what he was supposed to do and escaped. Violet's with him of her own choice, and if Honor thinks that's legit then so do I. He'd not going to hurt her, right?"

Honor gave the other woman an approving look. She'd come to respect the hell out of Eva King. "Uh no. I definitely think that's not in the cards. But I wouldn't have minded a heads-up about the plan though."

"Gabe thought it best if you didn't know," Eva said. "Elijah's a smart bastard, and we didn't want him picking up on things he wasn't supposed to."

Well, that was true. Remembering that sharp black gaze that seemed to see right inside her, Honor could see the wisdom of their decision. Even thinking about it made her shiver. Made her also wonder just what the hell Violet thought she was doing.

"Okay, fair enough," Honor said aloud. "But you realize that tracker will only work if she keeps the sweater."

Zac folded his arms. "Oh, I think she'll keep the sweater. She didn't have any other clothes, did she?"

"No," Honor admitted, thinking about the coffee-stained clothing she'd left in Gabriel's laundry. "She didn't."

Gabriel thrust his hands into the pockets of his jeans. "Okay, so now we're all caught up, the plan is to find the name of the asshole Elijah is trying to take down. And we track Violet, see what's up with this meeting. Then we go get her. Agreed?"

"What about Elijah?" Honor looked up into his dark eyes, knowing the answer already.

Gabriel smiled. "Then I fucking kill him."

Elijah pushed open the door of the apartment, resetting the code on the security system even though it was pointless. If Eva King could hack into it at a moment's notice then there wasn't much point even having a coded lock. Then again, the imperative to keep the place locked down had gone now that Violet was here of her own free will.

Coming back to the apartment was probably a stupid idea, especially now that Woolf and his friends knew the location. He had a few other bolt-holes scattered around Manhattan he could fall back on, but none of them had the remains of the life he'd had with Marie stored there and he couldn't just abandon that. He may have gotten rid of the grief, but the same urge that had made him gather that small store of belongings after she'd died and keep them safe had him heading back to it now.

He closed the door after Violet and locked it reflexively.

She stared at him as he did so, making him pause. Did she think he was going to keep her captive again? "You made your choice," he said flatly. "Are you regretting it?"

"No."

"So what's the problem?"

She studied him for a long moment. "Are you going to give me the code?"

A simple question with a not so simple answer.

Part of him wanted to say no, she couldn't have it because he just couldn't risk her leaving, not now, not at this stage. And yet, another part of him wanted to give it to her because back there, in Zac Rutherford's hallway, she'd taken his hand. She'd told Honor she'd trusted him.

Of course, her trust or otherwise was irrelevant to him . . . wasn't it?

Bullshit. You liked that she trusted you. You wanted her to. And now you want to give her something in return.

The space between them suddenly shimmered, becoming thick with something he didn't quite understand. But he could still feel the warmth of her fingers twined with his, her grip firm, certain. And he could still see the desolation in her blue-green eyes. She was hiding it, but it was there. She'd been dealt a blow and if he wasn't careful, it could be mortal.

"Yes," he heard himself say. "I'll write it down for you." He turned to the console table beside the door, grabbed a pen and paper from a small drawer at the side of it, and quickly scribbled down the code.

Then he held it out.

Violet's gaze flickered to the paper then back up again, and then one corner of her lovely mouth curved in a small, but unmistakable, smile.

And that tight feeling was back in his chest again, like he'd been given a gift he hadn't realized was precious until now.

She took the paper and folded it up without looking at it, tucking it into the pocket of her jeans, and he abruptly turned away, because he had shit to do right now and watching Violet Fitzgerald smile was not part of that.

His cheek ached as did the gunshot wound in his shoulder, but he ignored both injuries like he ignored that tightness in his chest. He'd get painkillers for the first two and as for the last . . . well, that wasn't anything a bit of refocusing on his goal wouldn't cure.

Turning in the direction of the dining table, he spotted his phone sitting on top of it and went over to get it. He had a couple of overdue calls to make.

"Elijah."

He paused, glancing back at her. "Yes?"

"Have you got a phone I could borrow?" She had her arms crossed over her chest, her hands tucked beneath her armpits as if she was cold. "I need to call my mom."

There wasn't any reason not to let her use one now, and he had the burner phone he'd bought earlier, the one he'd been contacting Jericho on. It was sitting next to his own personal phone on the table, so he picked it up and held it out to her. "Use this. And if you're cold, I can put the heat up."

A look of surprise crossed her face as she came over to take the phone. "Oh . . . uh . . . no, it's okay. I'm fine." Another of those tiny smiles. "But thanks for the offer."

Christ, why had he said that? It only made that fucking feeling in his chest get worse.

He turned away without speaking again, grabbing his phone and punching in the number of the first of the contacts he had to call, pushing all thoughts of Violet from his head.

Fifteen minutes and four calls later, he'd managed to get a good idea of how the land lay after Fitzgerald's sudden death. Several factions within his little empire were now jockeying for position to take over where he'd left off, and some of them were throwing around accusations that Elijah had killed Fitzgerald and was hoping to take over himself. A number of people thought this was a great idea, and he'd already had one contact offer to back him should he want to make a move. And the rest? Well, they just wanted him dead.

After he'd ended the last call, he leaned back against the kitchen counter, where he'd gone to keep his conversation private, and stared at the floor, turning things over in his head.

Jesus Christ, fucking Gabriel Woolf and his friends had a lot to answer for. It wasn't only that they'd killed Fitzgerald and ruined Elijah's revenge plans, they'd also cut the head off a hydra. A hydra that was now in the process of growing new heads, probably more than one.

That was the problem when you got rid of one fucking dictator; there were always plenty more who rushed to fill the power vacuum.

Elijah let out a breath. If he wasn't careful, he'd was going to end up with an even bigger mess than he first started with, not to mention the fact that he'd have to ingratiate himself with yet another power-hungry prick who wanted in on all that money. Plus there were all those international connections that Fitzgerald's death had left hanging, not only Jericho but the links to the Triads and the Russians.

You still want to take that shit down, you know what you have to do.

Yeah. He'd have to take over. Make sure the whole network was destroyed properly. Because the authorities could only do so much, while he could move outside the bounds of the law if he had to.

Something in him staggered at the thought, burdened by the sheer weight of it. But he'd been doing this for seven years already, a few more wouldn't hurt.

Guess that means taking down Jericho isn't a kamikaze mission after all?

He shifted against the cupboard at his back, the edge of the counter digging in.

He'd thought it was. He'd thought taking Jericho down trumped everything, even his own life. But . . . if he wanted to take down the guy's empire and Fitzgerald's as well, dying wasn't exactly the way to achieve it.

What about Violet?

He'd been resting back on the counter with the heels of his hands and now he found he'd curled his fingers under the edge of it, gripping on tightly as if to stop himself from doing something violent.

You can't let Jericho have her.

He hadn't given any thought to what would happen to her after he'd brought her to the meeting with Jericho. All he'd imagined was gunning down that bastard and finally bringing all that time in his own personal hell to a close. But now . . . he wanted to think about what would happen to her. He wanted . . . shit. He wanted to make sure she was safe.

A strange, foreign realization, since caring what happened to someone hadn't exactly been high on his list of priorities, not for a long time.

Straightening, Elijah walked to the kitchen doorway, looking out into the cavernous apartment space. Violet was standing by the windows, talking on the phone, her back to him. The fading evening light touched the tips of her hair in rose gold and turned the exposed skin on the back of her neck the same color. She looked small against the high windows. A brave woman and strong, yet vulnerable too.

A certainty he couldn't remember feeling before settled down through him, and ignoring it seemed wrong.

No. He couldn't let anything happen to her. He wouldn't. He would find a way to make sure she stayed safe, and fuck whether that mattered or not. Because the fact was that it did.

She mattered. To him.

The thought sat in his head, and by rights he should have shoved it away since feeling anything at all for anyone wasn't allowed. But he didn't. He let it sit there, the dark, hunger inside him rousing in response. Wanting. Wanting her.

Over by the windows, Violet must have ended her phone call because she lowered the phone slowly, her head bending. Her shoulders slumped, as if something heavy had just fallen on them, and he didn't like that, didn't like it at all. She had enough to bear as it was.

Pushing himself away from the door frame, he began to walk over to her.

She must have heard him approach because she turned suddenly. Her face had that white look again, the same one she'd had earlier in Zac's study, and her mouth was a hard, straight line. "Oh hey," she said flatly. "You finished your calls?"

He ignored the question, moving over to her, closing the space between them. "What's wrong?"

She lifted a shoulder. "Oh nothing. Just . . ." She stopped and tossed the phone negligently down onto the couch cushions. "It doesn't matter."

He didn't stop to think why he wanted to push her to tell him, or even why he wanted to know. Maybe it had something to do with what he'd just realized himself. Whatever it was, he responded without thinking, reaching out to her and taking her chin in his hand, turning her back to face him.

"Tell me," he demanded, knowing he sounded rough and demanding and not giving a shit. Because her eyes had that bleakness in them again, the one she was trying to hide, and he didn't like it. Not one fucking bit.

Her gaze flicked away from his, but she remained still, and for a terrible minute he thought she might cry again. And he couldn't have that, not when her earlier tears had almost torn him open.

"It's my mom," she said eventually, her eyes at last meeting his. "Remember what you told me a couple of days ago? That no one was coming for me? Well, looks like you were right."

He frowned. "No, I wasn't. Your friends came for you."

"My friends. But not my family."

"What are you talking about?" For reasons he couldn't have explained, he released her chin and opened his hand, letting his palm slide down the column of her neck to rest on her throat, gripping it lightly. Gently. A possessive hold.

Her eyelashes fluttered, lowering, and he felt her lean into his palm as she drew comfort from the touch.

Oh Jesus . . . this woman. What the fuck was she doing to him?

"Mom didn't want to speak to me. Her secretary tried to fob me off, but I made her put me through. And . . . she hadn't realized I was missing. Dad's been dead for two days and she didn't even know I was gone. She hadn't even bothered to ring me to tell me he was dead." Violet's voice was flat, but he heard the raw undercurrent beneath. "I know we never got on well, but this . . . She didn't want to talk about it, didn't want to see me. I told her I'd come home, but she wasn't interested." Another pause and then her lashes lifted, her blue-green eyes staring straight up into his, and he could see her pain. Unhidden. The look of a woman who'd lost everything. "First Theo. Then Dad. And now my mom. Is it me, Eli? Is it something I did? What's wrong with me?"

It felt like a hook caught in his chest, tugging hard, tearing painfully at him, and this time he couldn't tell himself he didn't know why it hurt. He knew. It was because of her. Because he wanted to make it better for her, wanted to take that pain away.

He tightened his grip on her throat, keeping it gentle yet firm, so she felt the pressure instead of that pain. "There's nothing wrong with you," he said roughly. "You just had shitty luck with your family."

Her jaw was tight, her mouth whitening. "Yeah, really shitty luck. And now I don't even have that. I've lost them all. Every single one of them."

"No. Not all of them. You had a lead about your brother."

"Yeah, a lead. Great. It's probably nothing."

"What is it?"

"It's stupid. And doesn't mean—"

"Tell me, Violet." He applied a little bit more pressure, letting her know this wasn't a request, her pulse beating fast beneath his palm.

Her eyes widened, a flare of heat leaping high.

Ah, fuck, yes. That's what he could do for her. That's how he could make it better. Give her pleasure, make her feel good. And maybe this time he wouldn't take anything for himself. He'd just do it for her, because she needed it.

But first, he wanted answers about her brother.

She took a small, sharp breath. "I lived in Paris for a while, came back earlier this year. But while I was there, I did a little bit of asking around about Theo. He used to love the city, always wanted to go. We used to talk about going there one day together . . . Anyway, I left my number in various places, plus a picture of him, and a little while afterward someone rang me to tell me to go talk to this café owner in Montmartre. So I did and I showed her the picture and she told me that yes, she'd seen him. About six months ago he used to come in every day. Then one day he vanished and she never saw him again. She couldn't tell me anything more so I let it go." She swallowed, and Elijah felt the movement of her throat against his palm, making him spread his fingers out over her skin, soaking up the warmth of her.

"I came back to New York pretty quickly after that," she went on. "And I tried to do some more looking around, but I came up with nothing. And then a couple of days ago, the facility storing Theo's stuff got in touch. They told me someone had accessed his storage locker." She looked at him. "There's only one person who could have done that, Eli, and it's not me. Or any of our family. I already tried to get access to his stuff, but the staff at the facility wouldn't let me. Only Theo has authorization."

Curious in spite of himself, Elijah studied her face. "Tell

me more about this locker. Do you know what he had in there?"

"No, not a clue. But . . . I don't think anyone else knows he has it."

"Then how did you find out about it?"

"Remember I told you he left me a note? It was on the back of an advertisement for the storage company. He'd written a number on it too."

"The locker number?"

"Yes. Like I said, I tried accessing it myself, but they wouldn't let me. So I paid them a bribe and told them to let me know if anyone else tried to. I was hoping to see if anyone else knew about it. And I heard nothing at all for years." She looked up at him. "Until a couple of days ago. The day you kidnapped me in fact. I was on the subway going to meet Honor to tell her that the storage facility had contacted me. That someone had accessed his locker."

"Him?"

"Well, I thought so." Her gaze flicked away. "Maybe it's nothing though. Maybe it's a mistake. I probably need to accept the fact that Theo's dead." She didn't add anything more, but that raw undercurrent was still there, a grief he was intimately acquainted with.

"No," he said forcefully. "No you don't need to accept it. Not until you've seen a body. Not until you know for certain."

She stared at him again, the look in her eyes almost fearful, though he wasn't sure why. "Do you know how long I've been thinking that very thing? Years, Elijah. Fucking years. And yet every time I think I've found something, I come up with nothing."

He held her and stepped right up close, looking down into her face. "My wife disappeared and for two whole years I had no idea where she was, or even if she'd died. But I didn't stop searching for her, not once. Jesus, if I'd had that kind of lead, I wouldn't have let anything stop me from finding her."

She shivered and he felt it, saw fear shift across her face. But this time he understood it.

Hope was terrible and fearful, one more thing he'd excised from his life.

So he shouldn't be encouraging it in her, yet he couldn't seem to stop himself. Family meant something to her, he could see that, and he hated the thought of her having lost all of hers. And if there was any way he could help her, he would.

Then the expression on her face changed, the look in her eyes becoming searching. "What happened to her, Eli? You never told me."

But he didn't want to talk about Marie and he didn't want her to ask. So he did the only thing he could think of to shut her up.

He tightened his grip upon her throat, bent his head, and stopped her from speaking with his mouth.

His kiss was a lit match to dry tinder and Violet felt her whole body go up in flames, a roaring conflagration that had her struggling. The phone call with her mother had been so damn painful, and she just wanted to forget about it, to let go and burn.

But she was getting to know Elijah, and this kiss was a distraction technique if ever there was one. He didn't want to talk about his wife, and she was betting he didn't want to talk about his previous existence as Kane either. So did she take his kiss and lose herself? Or did she push for more?

She had no right to push for more of course, no right at all to demand explanations. But he was hurting, grieving. A man who still hadn't recovered from the death of his wife. Why else would he spend all those years working on a complicated revenge plan?

It made her hurt for him. Made her wonder what kind of man he'd been before his wife's death had twisted him. What kind of man he'd been when he'd been Kane.

The black-eyed mercenary Elijah gave away nothing, left no clues. He was all fierce, focused intensity, cold as an ice storm. And maybe that should have warned her that in fact there *was* nothing left of the man he'd been before. This man before her was all that remained.

But she didn't believe it. The mercenary in him wouldn't have taken care of her, wouldn't have put his arms around her and held her when she cried, wouldn't have given her the code for the door. And he certainly wouldn't have gripped her chin and made her tell him about her brother, encouraging her to hold onto that lead, hold onto hope.

Kane was still there inside him, somewhere. The memory of a kinder, caring man. A man held prisoner by grief and the consuming need for revenge.

She had to let him out. Set him free.

Violet raised her hands and pushed against his rock-hard chest, pulling her mouth away from his.

Elijah lifted his head, his inky gaze blazing. Both with dark heat and a warning. *Don't ask. Don't come any closer.*

Fuck that.

"Tell me about her, Kane," she said, very deliberately. "Tell me what you lost."

His head jerked back at the sound of the name, shadows moving in his eyes. But his hand remained heavy and hot at her throat, a subtle reminder of his strength. And her own susceptibility.

"Don't call me that." Ice seemed to crystallize around the edges of each word. "Kane is dead."

"No, he's not." She kept her palm where it was, over his heart, pressing harder. "He's right here."

The flame in his eyes burned cold. His other hand gripped the back of her neck then slid higher, into her short hair, pulling her head back. "He's dead," Elijah repeated. "And so is she. And I'm not fucking talking about them."

This was a dumb move. A really dumb move. But she couldn't seem to shut herself up. "Why not? I've told you all about my dysfunctional family. You know all about my asshole dad. You've just seen how important I am to my mother."

"So? This isn't sharing time, princess. I don't have to tell you a fucking thing."

She was prodding a sleeping tiger and she knew it. Yet she kept going. He was in pain, she could almost feel it. "I know. I get it. You don't want to talk. But you're hurting, Elijah. You're grieving. And it helps to—"

"I said no." His hands tightened in her hair, exposing her throat. "Shut the fuck up. You know nothing about it."

"I don't know about what? I don't know about grief? About loss?" She moved the hand on his chest, slid it up to touch his face, the bruise on his cheek, the cut on his lip. "How dare you. How dare you say that to me when I've just lost everyone I've ever loved."

But there was anger in his eyes, and as he jerked his head away from her touch, she knew if she kept going, kept pushing, he wasn't going to give her anything but rage. A small thrill went down her spine at the thought, a primitive, atavistic part of her wanting the storm. Yet she suspected that, in the end, that wouldn't get her what she wanted.

There were other, better, gentler ways.

This was a man who'd been fighting a long time. Fighting his grief and his anger. Fighting for his position. Fighting to take the revenge that had ultimately been denied him. So how could she make him fight her? And what would he do if he didn't have to? What if she just gave him everything he wanted?

Violet dropped her hand and let it rest against his chest. He had her head drawn so far back it was nearly uncomfortable, his fingers pulling her hair painfully. His other hand, the one around her throat, was heavy, the pressure he was exerting enough to make her not want him to grip her any tighter. The tension in him was palpable, a dark, slowly gathering wave.

His lips were drawn back from his teeth in a snarl and he looked like he was debating either kissing her or strangling her, and hadn't decided which.

God, he was so angry. Perhaps it was time to give him one less thing to fight.

"It's okay," she whispered, before he could say anything he might regret. "You don't have to tell me if you don't want to. Just know that I understand."

His eyes glittered, a midnight sky covered with stars. "No, you don't." The hoarse growl of his voice rumbled through her like a caress. "Nobody fucking understands."

And his grip tightened like a vice and his head came down and he was kissing her, his mouth savage. It was a punishment, a warning. It was hot, brutal, his tongue pushing into her mouth, his hand a fist in her hair, holding her still as he deepened the kiss, taking whatever he wanted, his body hard as a wall of granite against her.

But she didn't fight him. Instead she relaxed into his hold, melting into him, letting herself go soft in his arms, letting him take whatever he wanted from her. She closed her eyes, keeping her hands unresisting on his chest, her mouth open to his kiss as he ravaged and devoured, anger pouring off him like a waterfall over the edge of a chasm.

And slowly, so very slowly, she felt the tension in him began to ease. The tight grip of his fingers in her hair loosened, the pressure of his hand on her throat lightened. The savage, brutal kiss gentled, becoming not so much a forced domination as a sensual seduction, his tongue exploring, tasting.

She shivered all over in response, because although she loved the roughness and the hunger, this too was intoxicating.

His hands moved, shifting to cup her face between his palms, exploring her deeper as his thumbs stroked the underside of her jaw and the sides of her neck, up and down in a caressing movement.

Violet spread her fingers out on his chest, pressing herself against him, absorbing all that heat then giving it back to him. She could feel the hard length of his cock against her stomach, so she shifted her hips, teasing him a little.

He growled, his mouth leaving hers to move over her jaw and down her neck, kissing her, nipping her. His tongue on her skin, tasting her.

She let him take whatever he wanted, sliding her hands up to his shoulders and stroking him, caressing the back of his neck, loving the power of the muscles there and the smooth hot skin that covered them. God, she could touch him all day and never get tired of it. Never.

"You need to be naked," he said roughly against her neck. "Now."

He didn't wait for an answer, merely tugged her borrowed sweater up and over her head, getting rid of the rest of her clothes with the same ruthless efficiency. Again, she let him do whatever he wanted, raising her arms so he could get the sweater off easily and lifting her feet so he could get her jeans and panties off too.

And when she finally stood there naked, he put his hands on her hips and pulled her hard up against his body, sliding his palms over the bare skin of her buttocks and squeezing, holding her there, flexing his hips so his cock rubbed up against her clit. Making her shiver and tremble. Making her want to move herself, chasing the friction.

But she didn't, keeping herself still. "What do you want, Eli?" Her voice was all husky and smoky with desire. "Anything at all. I'll give it to you."

He was staring at her, his gaze intense as he flexed his hips again, the ridge of his hard cock grinding over her clit. A soft gasp escaped her, a knife-edge of sharp pleasure sliding through her.

"What do I want?" he echoed harshly. " I want to take you apart."

She met his gaze, shivering as he moved against her, each shift of his hips giving her that tantalizing, teasing friction. There was something so erotic about being naked with him like this, vulnerable and at his mercy while he was fully clothed. Vulnerable and yet powerful too.

"You don't have to do that," she said softly. "I'll do whatever you want me to do. Be whoever you want me to be." She took a ragged breath. "I know there are many things you have to fight, Eli, but I'm not one of them. Not tonight."

He said nothing, his fingers pressing hard into the soft flesh of her buttocks, circling his hips in a slow grind against her clit that had her panting and trembling even harder.

"L-Let me take care of you." She stared into his face, into his eyes. "Let me make you feel good."

Again there was nothing but silence. Silence and those black intense eyes that could be so cold and yet burn so hot. He didn't look away, staring into her, and he didn't stop that insane shift of his hips, holding her tight and close, moving her so that she began to pant harder, her breathing spiraling out of control.

That hard ridge pressing against her, the material rubbing and teasing, sending intense little electric shocks through her entire body. Tearing gasps from her throat. Her nipples were aching, stiff points, and each movement he made shifted her breasts against his chest, sliding the cotton of his T-shirt against her sensitized flesh, heightening everything.

The tension inside her began to gather into a tight, hard knot, and she began to feel desperate because this wasn't supposed to be what happened. She was supposed to give him pleasure, not the other way around. Yet she'd told him he didn't have to fight her, that she'd give him whatever he wanted, and if what he wanted was to drive her insane then so be it.

Instead she clung to his shoulders, digging her fingers in to steady herself. Holding on for dear life as he ground harder against her. And in spite of herself, she couldn't stop from moving her hips against his in response, seeking that friction, wanting more of it, even harder, even faster.

"You're wet," Elijah growled, his voice ragged and gritty. "So fucking wet."

The muscles of his shoulders flexed and released under her fingers, and she dug in harder, the pleasure gathering ever tighter inside her. She shifted restlessly, moving, seeking, becoming increasingly desperate as a sharp intense climax neared. "I d-didn't want . . . Eli . . . this w-was supposed to be for you . . ."

"This *is* for me." He slid one hand further over the curve of her buttock, reaching down between her thighs, and she groaned as his fingers stroked the exquisitely sensitive flesh at the entrance to her body. "All of this is for me. And now you're going to scream for me because that's what I want too."

And she understood at last. This was a test and he wasn't going to drop his guard until she'd passed it. But then that made sense, didn't it? Especially when he'd spent so long defending himself, keeping himself protected. He wasn't going to be vulnerable for her just because she'd asked. His trust had to be earned.

She blinked as another thing occurred to her. Was there anyone else he trusted since his wife had died? Oh, but she knew the answer to that. No, there was no one.

No one except you.

Violet took a shuddering breath as his fingers moved suddenly, sliding deep into her sex, bowing her spine, her body arching, bringing her clit hard against the agonizing ridge of his cock. And the tight little knot inside her released in a white-hot wave.

She screamed like he'd told her to and when his mouth covered hers, she screamed again, her whole body convulsing as the orgasm ripped through her, making her shake and tremble in his arms.

Elijah's hold tightened as the intensity began to fade, leaving her knees weak and her heartbeat racing out of control. She could barely stand and her ears were ringing.

Jesus, she really should have foreseen he'd take control like this because that's the kind of man he was. After so many years spent looking after no one but himself, he wasn't going to leave himself open to just anyone, still less a woman he'd taken captive and only known a couple of days.

Still, she'd desperately wanted to look after him. Give him something to take the pain away, if only for a little bit. Was it too much to hope for that after he'd let her take care of that gunshot wound, given her the code for the door, and let her call her mom, he'd let her give him pleasure too?

Did you really expect he would?

She had. Kind of.

Elijah's hold on her shifted, the hand between her thighs moving up to rest on her lower back, his arm tight around her. He lifted his other hand, running the pad of his thumb along her lower lip.

She gave another helpless shiver at the touch, the after-shocks of her orgasm sparking like cut electrical wires, and tipped her head back slightly, meeting that enigmatic black gaze.

He was a beast of a man, that's what he was. Dangerous. Merciless. Wholly unpredictable. But she knew why that was now. He was wounded inside, hurting from a blow that had never healed, a loss he'd never come to terms with.

Because he doesn't want to heal it or come to terms with it.

As Violet looked up into his face, she knew the truth. Of course he would never want the wound to heal, because he needed the pain. It fueled his anger, and without his anger he wouldn't have his revenge.

Which means he'll never let you get near. He'll never let you help him.

His physical wounds maybe. But his emotional ones? No.

She swallowed against the lump in her throat, a bleak certainty filling her. And she didn't try this time to ask herself why that thought made her so upset because she knew.

She'd fallen for him and she had fallen hard.

CHAPTER FIFTEEN

Elijah kept a tight grip on the woman in his arms. She swayed against him, all soft skin and naked heat, her vivid eyes clouded with pleasure. But there was something else in her expression too, and he thought it looked like bitter disappointment.

Of course it's disappointment, you fucking prick. She wanted to give you something and you wouldn't let her.

But what the fuck else could he do? Marie and what had happened to her, how he'd failed her, were out of bounds. He wouldn't ever tell anyone, a secret he would keep until he died. And if that caused Violet some disappointment, then so be it.

He just hadn't expected that it would cause him pain too.

She turned her head away, resting her forehead against his shoulder. He could see the curve of her cheek flushed pink from the orgasm he'd given her, her lashes a small thick fan of gold against her skin.

He ached. Not just his cock, but his chest too, like someone was pressing down hard on it.

"I know there are many things you have to fight, Eli, but I'm not one of them."

But he'd wanted to fight her, that was the problem. That's all he'd been doing for seven fucking years, and he'd had to because how else was he going to do what he had to do? Keep fighting and trust no one, those were the lessons that working for Fitzgerald had taught him. Those were the only lessons that mattered. And he couldn't stop now just because some lovely girl seemed to have the ability to reach right inside his chest and put her hand around his heart.

No, fuck that, it wasn't his heart she had her hands around.

She'd wanted to take care of him, make him feel good, but he couldn't let her in, not even a little bit. Because he had a feeling that once he did, he'd never want to let her go.

Would that be so very bad?

Elijah pushed the insidious thought away. He shouldn't even be thinking shit like this, not when he had Jericho to meet and a plan to work out. A plan for how to protect the lovely girl in question.

He looked down at her, all soft golden spikes of hair and creamy, satin skin. The sandalwood scent he associated with her had faded over the past couple of days, and now she smelled faintly of flowers and the musky scent of sex.

Christ, he wanted to eat her alive.

He took a step back in the direction of the couch, holding her in his arms, taking her with him as he sat down so she ended up in his lap. Her head turned, her cheek against his chest, and then she stilled.

His heart was beating fast, and he was so fucking hard. Her butt was pressed to his groin, the heat of her pussy soaking through the fabric of his shorts, and suddenly he wanted to be naked, to feel her against his bare skin.

He reached for that stubborn little chin of hers and tipped her head back so he could look down into her face. She didn't resist—which surprised him—staring back at him with a wary expression. She seemed more guarded now, as if she was hiding something, and he knew she didn't want him to see her disappointment. Too late.

He ran the pad of his thumb across her bottom lip, enjoying the warm, giving softness of it. "I know what you want," he said after a moment. "You want to make it all better."

"Is that so bad?" She had crossed her arms, covering her breasts in a protective gesture that annoyed him, even if he understood it.

Resisting the urge to pull her arms away, he satisfied himself by continuing to stroke his thumb back and forth on her lip, keeping it gentle even though he felt anything but. "It's not bad, it's just not going to happen."

Violet met his gaze silently, her jaw tight. Then she said, "I know why you need it, Eli. All that anger and pain . . . It's fuel, isn't it?"

He wanted to deny it. Wanted to deny that he even felt either of those emotions, but he couldn't. It would be a lie. They were there no matter how hard he'd tried to get rid of them, lingering like ghosts in his mind, in his heart. And she was right. He did need them. Because without them . . .

You'd be useless, soft Kane Archer. The man who let his wife die.

Fucking hell, this conversation needed to end. She seemed to be able to see below the surface of him in a way that nobody else could, and that was unacceptable. Yet another reason he had to keep her out any way he could.

"This isn't amateur psychology hour, princess." He slowed the movement of his thumb, tracing up to include the delicate curves of her upper lip too. "And I'm not your fucking patient."

Temper flashed across her face. "You think I don't know that?"

"Then stop trying to psychoanalyze me." He dropped

his hand from her mouth, holding her gaze. "I don't need it. I don't want it."

Her jaw jutted mutinously, a green spark of anger glowing in the blue depths of her eyes. "I'm just trying—"

"I don't care what you're just trying to do." He leaned forward to the box of condoms sitting on the coffee table in front of him and took one out, leaning back against the couch again. "You can't save me. Not if I don't want to be saved."

She looked away, down to the condom in his hands. Then she grabbed it from him and tore open the packet, turning to face him, sitting up and straddling him with her knees on either side of his thighs. "Fine," she said tightly. "I'll just fuck you instead."

It was the response he wanted and yet it made him angry. Because he didn't like that she wouldn't look at him. Didn't like the disappointment in her voice that laced each word.

Didn't like that he cared.

But he didn't know what else to say. This was the way it had to be and he had nothing else to offer her.

The anger stirred inside him, thick and hot, threaded through with a frustration he didn't understand. Jesus Christ, what the hell did she expect? For him to get all emotional and pour out his heart to her like a goddamn teenage girl?

Okay, so maybe the grief and the pain and the anger hadn't entirely gone like he'd thought, but that didn't mean he had to share them with her or anyone else for that matter.

He grieved his wife. He was angry that she'd died. No, not angry, fucking *furious*.

And yeah, that was fuel. Seven years was a long time to pursue revenge, but he'd always understood it was a long game. And he had to have something to keep the engine running hot.

Violet was reaching for his shorts, all business now. The expression on her face was shuttered, her jaw full of tension. There was no softness there anymore, none of that terrible understanding that had the ability to crack him apart. It was the way it should be.

Yet he hated it.

Fucking hell. You liar. You do want her to save you.

Elijah pushed her off him all of a sudden as if he could push away that thought too. Because it wasn't happening. It was too late for him, had been too late the moment Marie died. The day he'd finally realized the depth of his failure and what he'd have to do to make amends. Nothing could change that. Nothing could change what he'd had to do over the course of seven years either.

There was no saving him.

Violet's eyes were wide and wary. "What did I do now?"

He couldn't explain, not when he was barely able to even admit it to himself, so he ignored her. Standing, he pulled off his T-shirt and dropped it on the floor, doing the same to his shorts and boxers, until he was finally naked.

Then he turned back to her.

She was sitting on the couch, the condom clutched in her hand, staring at him. Flushed and golden and bare.

Christ, he'd had enough of this emotional shit. Enough of talking. Maybe once he'd been able to do that, share his feelings, let someone in, but that had been a long time ago, before Marie had died. Now the ability had been burned right out of him. And the sooner Violet learned that, the sooner she understood that he had nothing to give her, the better.

He reached out and grabbed the condom from her, rolling it quickly down his achingly hard cock. "Turn over." He made the order hard and cold.

She frowned. "What do you mean?"

He could have told her that he wanted her on her

stomach so he didn't have to look at her face or see the disappointment in her eyes, but he didn't. Instead he moved over to her and without a word, flipped her over so she was facedown. Instantly she put her hands on the couch cushions, levering herself up a little. "Eli, I—"

"Stay like that. Don't fucking move."

Her mouth became a hard line, but she did what she was told, turning her head to watch him as he got onto the couch behind her. He knelt and put his hands on her hips, lifting them up and back. Her skin felt so good under his fingers, soft and satiny smooth.

He looked down, unable to help himself, following the elegant curve of her spine, the indent of her hips, the swell of her buttocks, the sweet vulnerability of her bare neck. And fury and hunger twined suddenly inside him, making his heart race, making him pant like a fucking dog.

Why did he always feel this way around her? Why could he never make sense of it?

Because you don't want to make sense of it. Just like you don't want to admit that you want her to save you.

The truth stared him in the face, inevitable. Irrevocable. It had been a long, long time since he'd had an emotional response to anything and he was out of practice. Self-analysis had never been his thing anyway, and besides, while he'd been with Fitzgerald, he simply couldn't let himself think too deeply about anything.

She mattered, he'd already decided that. But he'd thought that had been an intellectual decision, a clear, logical choice.

Yet something inside him wanted more than that. That darkness, that hunger, the yearning he couldn't ever admit that he felt, it wanted so much more. To consume her, devour her, make her his in every way possible. Hold her tight. Keep her safe. Never let her go.

It rose up inside him, inevitable as the pull of the tide,

shattering the hard, cold shell he'd tried to surround himself with. He found himself gripping her hips as he positioned himself, holding on tight as if he was afraid she was going to get away, before pushing hard and deep inside her, the wet heat of her pussy clenching around his cock like a vise, a choked cry coming from her.

And he couldn't stop. He pulled out then flexed his hips, slamming back inside her. She made another soft, desperate sound, her body trembling, but even then he didn't pause, didn't take a breath. He did it again and again, watching her body move restlessly beneath him, her head turning to the side, her lush mouth open, panting like he was.

Pleasure and that primitive, savage need began to unfurl inside him on great, black wings, making him grab the back of her neck to hold her still as he drove himself inside her. Violet jerked, her spine bowing, a long, low moan breaking from her. He could feel her pussy squeezing him tightly as the orgasm gripped her, and he felt the satisfaction of it rip through him like a hit of Columbia's finest.

Oh fuck, yes. He couldn't resist this. He'd been too long without it, without warmth and softness and the smooth skin of a woman under him. He'd been too long without Violet. And hell, maybe he didn't need to go without anymore. She wasn't going anywhere in any hurry and he could gorge himself on her while he had the chance. He didn't have to let her in, he didn't have to open himself up. But he could give her this. That would be enough wouldn't it? He wasn't the only one who'd gone without.

He slid his free hand down her back, feeling her muscles shift and flex as he thrust into her, listening to her hoarse cries. She shivered under his touch, the cries turning into little sobs.

"Again, Violet," he murmured roughly.

She shook her head, but he reached for one of her hands, gripping her wrist and pulling it down, guiding her fingers between her thighs to her clit. "Touch yourself," he ordered. "Again, princess. Again." And he covered her hand with his, moving her finger on her own slick flesh.

"Eli . . ." His name was a broken sound. "Please . . ."

He slowed his thrusts right down, easing in and out, watching her shift and tremble beneath him. She'd told him she wouldn't fight him, and she wasn't. She was all soft and pliable, like prey in the jaws of a wolf.

She had surrendered.

Yours now.

Satisfaction spread through him, the hunger coming with it, and there was no thinking anymore. Only the raw, savage desire that gripped him tight whenever she was around.

Elijah held his hand over hers, guiding her finger in tight, slick circles around and around her clit, stroking his cock in and out of her, not stopping, not pausing. Driving her closer and closer to the edge. She sobbed then gave a sudden hoarse scream, her whole body shaking as she came.

Then he pushed her down flat and leaned forward, right over her, his hands on either side of her head, covering her with his body. And he began to fuck her hard, deep, fast. Giving into the savagery inside him, so that the sounds of flesh hitting flesh echoed in the room, along with the hoarse gasp of his breathing and her sharp cries.

He lowered his head as the pleasure began to tear into him, sinking his teeth into her shoulder, wanting the salty taste of her skin on his tongue as he came. And when the orgasm finally detonated, blowing his mind completely, he came down on her, pressing her softness into the couch.

"You're mine, princess," he whispered as it began to hit. "You're fucking mine."

Violet kept her eyes shut tight, her brain cloudy with the effects of two intense climaxes in a row, fighting to breathe. Because he was all around her, the heat of his body, the scent of forests and snow and sex, and Jesus, she could even hear the strong, steady beat of his heart.

It should have been suffocating, she should have felt crushed. But she didn't. In fact, there was a part of her that wanted to lie here forever and never move. There was something comforting about the weight of all that muscle, all that contained power. She felt safe tucked beneath him, anchored. No longer alone, but protected.

You're mine, princess. You're fucking mine.

The words echoed and reechoed inside her head, and the warm, safe feeling began to dissipate. What the hell did he mean by that? He'd been very clear that he wasn't going to let her in, so why was he getting all possessive of her?

She swallowed, her throat dry, the aching, lonely thing inside of her shivering with pleasure at the thought of such possessiveness. At the raw heat in his voice as he'd said it. No one had ever gotten possessive of her. No one had wanted her enough, and even thinking about it made her feel desperate. And also afraid. She'd lost so much already—did she really want to let herself think she could have this?

The weight on her eased, and she had to bite her lip to keep from protesting, wanting it back. He slid from her body, shifting away from her, and then there was cold air at her back, the couch dipping then rising up again as he got off it.

She kept her eyes closed, listening to his footsteps

recede, then she curled up tight, folding herself around the ache in her chest.

How had it come to this? That she'd fallen for the man who'd kidnapped her at gunpoint? A hard, cold man, twisted by grief and the need for revenge. A man who wouldn't ever let her help or heal him. A man who wouldn't ever trust her.

She'd hoped that by not fighting, that by surrendering to him completely, she'd get him to drop his guard. Yet he hadn't, not even a little bit.

How naive of her. How stupid. Perhaps she should have used that damn code when he'd given it to her and just gotten out.

Footsteps sounded again, coming closer and closer. He moved quietly for such a big guy, but she could hear the sound of his breathing as he paused beside the couch. She could feel the heat of his bare skin too. He was close.

She didn't move, keeping herself curled up tight. With any luck he'd just leave her alone, which would be good, because right now she had nothing left, feeling bruised and hard, used both physically and emotionally.

Pathetic. He won't give you what you want and now you're sulking like a little bitch.

Well, okay, yeah, it was pathetic. But shit, she'd had a hell of a day. All her fears about her father had not only been confirmed, they'd ended up being worse than anything she could possibly imagine. Her mother had basically told her not to call her. And now she'd ended up having feelings for a guy who shot at her.

How fucked up was that?

You really are your father's daughter.

The thought was like a knife sliding beneath her skin, cold and sharp. Perhaps she should never have let herself believe it when he'd told her there was nothing wrong with her. After all, there had to be a reason why her brother had disappeared. Why her mother had always been distant. Why her father and ended up being such a monster.

No, she was being ridiculous, wasn't she?

She curled up tighter, only to feel a pair of powerful arms slide beneath her, lifting her, gathering her up against the hard, hot wall of his chest. She opened her eyes, finding his inky stare looking down at her.

"I don't want to talk," he said in a soft, rough voice. "And I'm not going to give you my life story. But if you need someone to make you forget for a while, I will."

The dryness in her throat intensified. It wasn't the capitulation she'd wanted and she was starting to think he just wasn't the kind of man who'd bend, not even a little. But it was an olive branch of sorts. "And if I don't?"

"Then you don't, and you sleep on the couch."

Violet swallowed. What a bitch of a choice. Part of her wanted to tell him to fuck off, that she'd take the couch and to hell with him. But she was too raw and too lonely, and the feel of his arms around her was far too good.

"I don't want to sleep on the couch," she said thickly.

He stared at her for a second, his gaze merciless. Then he turned and headed toward the hall doorway with her held tight in his arms.

"I couldn't save her," he said, short and abrupt.

She glanced up at him in surprise. "Couldn't save who?"

"My wife." He wasn't looking at her, his attention on where he was going, so she took a minute to study the forceful lines of his face, all hard planes and harsh angles. Not daring to breathe in case he stopped speaking.

"Fitzgerald befriended her. Promised to help her with her career. I told her it was too good to be true, but she told me not to worry. That this would be great for her. I shouldn't have listened."

Her throat was tight, her heart heavy and hurting. So

he *was* giving her something of himself, even though he said he wouldn't. Yet it made her ache even more. "That wasn't your fault," she murmured.

A flash of darkness as he glanced down at her. "No. It wasn't. It was Kane's."

She swallowed past the tightness. "It wasn't his either."

"Bullshit." Elijah's voice was flat with certainty. "He made a mistake. He should have been harder with her. Should have protected her more. But he didn't. He loved her too much instead."

Violet felt something curl up tight in her chest as they made their way down the hallway to the bedroom, felt her eyes get dry and sore. Of course he'd loved his wife. Where else had all this rage come from? Love. Love was *always* the problem.

"I thought you said you didn't want to talk," she said hoarsely.

"I don't."

He carried her into the bedroom without another word, going over to the big bed with the black velvet quilt on top. The big wide bed he'd ordered her not to go anywhere near two days ago.

She was tempted to say something about that as he put her down on it, the velvet quilt soft and sensual against her bare skin. But he didn't give her a chance to either speak or think about what that meant. Instead he followed her down, pushing her beneath him, his mouth finding hers, hard and demanding.

And there was no talking at all after that.

"Okay," Eva said from her chair beside the fire, her attention on the laptop balanced on her knees. "I've finally managed to track down some info. It's not much, but it's something."

Gabriel thrust his hands into the pockets of his jeans,

trying to keep his impatience in check. "Well don't keep us in suspense," he said acidly. "Fucking spit it out."

Eva raised an eyebrow at his tone but let it pass without comment. Looked like his extremely bad mood was obvious. "The name we're looking for is Jericho," she said.

The Second Circle meeting room was silent for a long moment.

Alex, sitting on the couch with Katya and Honor, frowned. "Never heard of him."

"Not many people have." Zac was standing beside Eva's chair, looking down at her laptop screen. "He's a fairly shadowy figure from the looks of things, and what little information we have about him is sketchy."

Fucking wonderful. Yet another criminal asshole to track down.

Gabriel clenched his fists in his pockets. Opposite him on the couch, Honor gave him a level, blue glance. A sudden uprush of intense desire caught him by the throat and it was all he could do not to leap over the damn coffee table, pick her up in his arms, and take her somewhere quiet where he could forget all about this fucking mess for a while. Forget about the fact he had a sister. A sister who was in deep shit.

But of course he couldn't do that with Honor. At least not yet.

"That's it?" he demanded, getting himself the fuck together. "That's all we know?"

Eva eyed him. "This guy's gone to a lot of trouble to hide himself, so you're going to have to give me more than just a couple of hours if you want more info." She looked down at her screen again. "But what I did find out was that he—or at least businesses he's associated with—have a lot of fingers in a lot of different pies. Trafficking, drugs, weapons. A whole lot of bad shit basically."

"What's his association with Fitzgerald then?" Gabriel

tried to make it sound less like a demand, but failed miserably.

"I think that's obvious," Zac said in his usual calm way. "They're both in the same business. I'd say Fitzgerald was angling to grow his little empire and wanted Jericho's European connections."

"Shit." Alex sighed and looked at Katya. "Should have kept Conrad alive, sweetheart. He might have come in handy right about now."

Katya snorted. "I have no regrets about South, and I'm sure we can find the information we need our ourselves." She glanced around. "What about the remaining members of the Seven Devils? Perhaps they know something?"

The Russian woman had a point. There were two Devils still alive, and one was Honor's stepfather. The Circles club hadn't bothered with them, since Guy Tremain was still recovering from a gunshot wound to the head and was having memory problems. The other, Mantel, Zac was keeping under surveillance just in case he decided to make a move toward taking control of Fitzgerald's empire. So far he hadn't, though maybe he was just biding his time.

"Good idea," Zac said. "Perhaps I should pay Mr. Mantel a visit. I've been meaning to have a chat with him anyway."

"You know how much I enjoy your little chats, Zac," Alex commented lazily, leaning back on the couch and sliding an arm around Katya's waist, "but do we really want to upset people right now? After Fitzgerald's very public death?"

Zac lifted a shoulder. "I'll be discreet. From what we've managed to discover, Mantel hasn't been active in Fitzgerald's empire for years, though given these men's ability to hide their nasty little secrets, who knows?" He smiled and it wasn't pleasant. "I'm sure he'll be willing to talk if offered the right incentive."

Gabriel shifted on his feet, angry and restless. "He needs to know he's a dead man if he tries to take on any of Fitzgerald's shit, understand?"

"Of course. Don't worry, Gabe, I'll make sure he knows his position."

"Okay, so what other options do we have for finding this Jericho motherfucker?" Gabriel paced down to the end of the fireplace before turning back. "I want to know why he's after Violet. What he wants her for."

Eva pushed the laptop shut. "Could be Fitzgerald was hoping for an alliance. These criminal factions are like medieval kingships in a lot of ways. Marriage and shit like that tying people together."

"But Fitzgerald is dead," Honor pointed out. "So why does Jericho, or whoever this man is, want her now?"

"Good fucking point." Gabriel paced back toward Eva, fists clenched tight. Christ, not being able to do anything sucked balls. "If it's an alliance he wanted, then he's shit out of luck now."

"Unless he wants to take over Fitzgerald's operation," Eva said. "Then again, why would he need Violet? From what I can gather about this dude, he's pretty goddamn powerful. He could just waltz in and take it if he wanted to."

"So there's absolutely nothing about this guy anywhere?" Alex asked, black brows drawn together.

"Nope." Eva pulled a face. "All I managed to find were mentions of him. And from the sounds of it, even the people who work for him don't know who he is."

"Excellent. Another shadowy underworld figure." Alex's tone was acidic. "Just what we need."

Gabriel stopped pacing, abruptly sick of all the talking. He wanted to act. The longer they pissed about trying to figure things out, the longer it was going to take to get Violet back. And he *really* wanted to get Violet back.

Fitzgerald had screwed enough with his family. This shit was going to end.

"What's happening with Violet?" He looked at Zac. "Any movement on that little tracking device?"

The big mercenary shook his head. "No. Looks like she's back at Hunt's apartment."

"At least my sweater is," Honor murmured.

Not appreciating the reminder, Gabriel shot her a narrow glance. "Yeah, well, that's all we got, so we'll assume that she's there." He glanced once more back at Zac. "Shall we go pay Mantel a little visit then?"

"I can do this on my own, Gabe."

"I know you can, but I gotta do something." He only just refrained from kicking the coffee table. "Waiting around like this is driving me fucking insane."

"Yes," Honor said, pushing herself up from the couch. "Please take him with you, Zac. He's driving me insane too."

"I'll join you," Alex offered. "I could do with some fresh air."

"With your shoulder like that?" Zac nodded toward the shoulder in question. "I don't think so."

Alex raised a brow. "And here was I thinking you were actually going to chat."

"I could go," Katya offered. "I am quite skilled at negotiations."

"Oh I know how skilled you are, Katya mine." Alex was grinning. "Believe me, I know."

Katya gave him a disdainful look, yet the corner of her mouth had turned up.

"Are we done here?" Gabriel growled, in no mood to watch Alex and Katya flirt with each other. "Because if you hadn't noticed, there's some important shit going down that's gotta be handled."

"Hey Gabe. Chill out." Eva put her laptop in the battered black messenger back that sat beside her chair then got to her feet. "Okay, if you guys are going to have a Zac chat with that bastard, I'll get back home and do some more digging about this Jericho guy."

Gabriel refrained from telling her his opinions about the idea of "chilling out." How the fuck was he supposed to do that when his half sister was about to be used as bait to lure out some major goddamn crime lord? It didn't matter that he barely knew her, that he'd only had a few days to get used to the idea of having a sister at all. She was the only family he had and he wasn't going to let anything happen to her.

Zac, however, caught his eye, and Gabriel knew the other man understood. Zac had had a sister once too.

"Actually," Alex said. "I think I will come with you two. I remember Mantel from the good old days back at the Lucky Seven. Might be able to think of some good leverage."

Gabriel glanced at Alex and saw the same look he'd seen in Zac's eyes.

"Welcome to the club, Gabe," his friend said dryly. "Isn't it wonderful having a sister?"

Violet woke with something large, hot, and extremely heavy lying on top of her. It certainly wasn't the quilt, though that was pretty heavy. The quilt wasn't breathing for one thing.

Sleepily, she opened her eyes. It took her brain a couple of seconds to catch up with the fact that she wasn't in her own bed, though she felt comfortable enough to be. And that she wasn't alone.

A thrill of fear went though her before she remembered. Elijah.

She blinked and reoriented. She was in his room. In his bed. Which meant that the heavy thing lying on top of her was likely to be six feet, four inches of muscle-packed male. And sure enough, when she looked down, a powerful arm was wrapped possessively around her waist, as weighty and strong as iron chains.

It made her feel good, despite the near suffocation factor. As if he didn't want to let her go. A dangerous thing to think about a man like him, especially when he'd been very clear about what he was and was not going to give her.

Ignoring the feeling, Violet twisted so she faced him and saw that he was asleep, thick black lashes lying still on his sharp cheekbones, his breathing slow and regular. He looked so much younger, his face relaxed in sleep, all that seething, dark, cold menace hidden. Even . . . vulnerable, a word she'd never thought could be applied to a man as hard as he was.

Except he hadn't always been Elijah Hunt. He'd once been a man called Kane, who'd been in love with his wife. Who'd lost her.

Violet followed the path of the scar on his face, her fingers itching to trace it for some inexplicable reason. Maybe this man here, fast asleep with his arm around her, was that Kane. A kinder, gentler man. A more vulnerable man.

A scarred man.

She studied his face, fascinated all of a sudden. Where had he gotten that scar? And the other ones, because there were lots of other ones. She'd seen them last night as he'd kept her beneath him, or above him, or in front of him, surrounding her with that hot hard body of his, that equally hot, hard cock buried deep inside her. He hadn't let her touch him though, no matter how much she'd begged. And she had begged, pathetic damn woman that she was.

Her gaze dropped to the tattoo of the eagle on his chest, carrying the heart dripping blood. And she couldn't help it this time, she got one arm free and put her fingers on it. His skin was so smooth and hot, the muscle beneath it hard.

She thought she knew what that tattoo meant. It was for his wife, wasn't it?

He loved her too much. Elijah's voice last night, blaming Kane. Blaming himself. Which was stupid because, God, he hadn't known then what her father was. How could he? Not even she'd known, and she'd been his daughter.

Violet spread her hand out on his chest. He hadn't wanted to talk, yet he'd given her that little piece of his own tragedy nevertheless. He'd trusted her with it.

His heart beat heavy and strong beneath her palm and suddenly her breath shivered in her throat, desire catching her like thorns in a bramble bush. She wanted to touch him, taste his skin, have him moan in her ear the way she'd moaned in his. Drive him as crazy as he'd driven her the night before. Make her mark on him somehow before he let her go.

The thought made her glance away, down at her own body pressed hard and tight against his. Examining the marks he'd left on her. The bruises from his kisses and his teeth on her breasts and down further, on her inner thighs. He'd probably left them on her throat too since that, apparently, was a major erogenous zone for her, and he'd seemed to have made it his mission to find out all those little places on her body that made her gasp and burn.

Pity vice versa was a no go.

She let her fingers run down over the tattoo and further, across the hard, sculpted muscle of his abs. He felt so good. Powerful and strong, and yet so warm. This man wasn't cold, he was a goddamn bonfire.

Her fingers brushed lower and she felt his abdominal muscles tense beneath her fingertips. Okay, so did that mean he was awake now? But he didn't move and he didn't speak, so she kept touching him, moving even lower to the trail of hair that led down between his powerful thighs. And lower still, her fingers moving over the smooth, hot skin of a very impressive morning erection.

A shudder went through him as she curved her fingers around him, but still he didn't speak. Nor did he pull away.

She didn't look at him, sensing somehow that eye contact would break the spell. That he'd end up pulling away or turning it back on her, and she would have lost this chance. So carefully she kept her gaze on the tanned skin of his chest, letting her fingers measure the length and girth of him, stroking up and down his shaft then lightly circling the sensitive skin around the head.

His breathing changed, becoming harsher, his body tensing against hers.

Violet circled his cock with her hand and squeezed lightly. She'd only touched a man like this once before, and that had been Aaron, her one and only boyfriend. They'd never slept together, though she'd gone down on him a couple of times, a process that hadn't been all that successful since Aaron had been so nervous of her father finding out, he'd found it difficult to keep it up.

He'd been afraid with good reason as it turned out.

Elijah was different though. He'd never been afraid of her father and he was a damn sight tougher, harder and more powerful than Aaron had ever been. God, why did she find that so helplessly attractive?

Whatever the reasons, it was majorly hot and so was he. And she wanted to taste him. Right now.

Slowly, holding him tight in her hand, Violet bent to press her mouth to his chest. The salty flavor of his skin made her shiver with delight and she couldn't resist touching him with her tongue, licking him like a cat.

Then before she knew quite what was happening, one large, warm hand came to settle on the back of her head, his fingers curling into her short hair, and he shoved her down.

Oh, so he *was* awake. Very awake.

His body shifted and she found herself lying between his thighs as he sat up, his dick still held tight in her fist. Once again he didn't speak, putting his other hand on her head, moving his grip until she was held firmly between his hands, and there was pressure as he urged her head down even further.

Her throat was dry and her heartbeat was speeding up, the ache of desire suddenly as sharp as her hunger.

It was very clear what he wanted her to do.

Obeying without thought, Violet gripped him tighter and opened her mouth, circling the satiny skin of his cock head with her tongue. The sharp hiss of his indrawn breath sounded in the quiet of the bedroom, his hand moving again, fingers curling even tighter in her hair.

And oh Jesus, he tasted so good. Salty and musky and male. She closed her eyes and began to explore him in earnest, licking his hard shaft then circling once again the slick head.

He made a growling sound, deep in his throat, his hips flexing, pressing his cock insistently against her lips so that she had no choice but to open her mouth and let him inside. She shivered helplessly as he slid in deep, pressing against the back of her throat. But she took him, because this was what she'd been wanting to do since last night. Make him feel good, take the pain away. And finally he was letting her.

It would have been better if he hadn't been the one in charge, but she had a feeling that would always be the case with Elijah. He wasn't a man who handed control to others, not even a little bit. So she'd have to work with what she had and that, as it turned out, was quite a lot.

As he began to thrust into her mouth, she sucked him,

licked him. Squeezed him with her hand. And with her other hand, she began to stroke him. His stomach, his thighs, and further, sliding to cup his balls, then feeling them begin to tighten in her hand.

He made another deep, growling sound as she stroked them too, squeezing the base of his cock, increasing the suction. His grip on her had tightened, his breathing ragged and harsh.

"Fuck," he said finally, the word almost sounding like a prayer. "Fuck, princess."

And then he was thrusting harder, faster, and making short, rough sounds as he fucked her mouth. Until he fell out of rhythm, his body abruptly drawing so tight she thought he might break. Then he let out a low, guttural roar as he came, his hips jerking, his fingers so tight in her hair it was painful. She kept her eyes closed, her heart thundering as she swallowed him down, feeling weirdly as though she'd won a victory of some kind.

A strange, tense moment passed, his hands on her head, his cock still semihard in her mouth, his body shuddering. Then he pulled her head away from him and rolled to the side, putting his feet on the floor and getting out of the bed.

She blinked as he walked from the room without a backward glance.

Great. What had she done now? Had the blowjob been that crap?

But no, she knew it wasn't that. He was so guarded, so wary, and maybe she'd managed to crack his defenses just then. And perhaps he'd walked away so he could get them back up again.

Yeah, probably a little too much amateur psychology, but at least that was a better reason than because he'd hated having her mouth on him.

The only problem was that the whole thing had left her

aching and restless, need pulsing hot and heavy between her thighs. She could taste him on her tongue and, God help her, that only made her hotter.

Slowly, she sat up, debating whether or not to follow him, maybe entice him back to bed. And then he appeared in the doorway again, her clothes in his hands.

The expression on his face was impenetrable as he came over to the bed and tossed the clothes down on it. "Get dressed," he said shortly. "I'll get us some breakfast and then we're going out."

Violet opened her mouth to suggest that maybe breakfast could wait for a moment, but he was already going over to the dresser near the windows and taking out some clothes for himself. His movements were short and sharp, and he was radiating tension like a fire radiates heat.

She didn't understand what she'd done, but clearly more sex was out of the question.

Swallowing back the real questions she wanted to ask, she made do with, "Going out where?"

"I'll tell you over breakfast." He pulled on boxers, jeans, and a dark, charcoal gray long-sleeved T-shirt. Then he took out a pair of socks and once more walked from the room without another word.

Violet sat on the bed staring after him, trying to get her stupid emotions back under control. Patience was clearly the key with Elijah, so she'd have to try a little harder to cultivate that patience and not push too hard.

Why are you the one having to do all the work? Why can't he be the one to come to you?

She pulled a face at the snide voice in her head and how it made it sound as if this was a relationship she and Elijah were having, and not just two people having sex. There was no relationship. And she was the one doing the work because she was the one who wanted more. All he wanted from her was the sex.

Slowly Violet got out of bed and grabbed her clothes, heading for the shower. A bit pointless to wash herself clean when all she had to put on were already-worn clothes, but she suddenly felt the need to have a bit of space away from him.

She took her time in the shower, washing her hair and soaping herself down, letting her hands linger on her own skin, unassuaged desire echoing through her. It made her shiver, and briefly she toyed with the idea of getting herself off just to ease it. She glanced toward the door, a sudden fantasy of him throwing it open to find her with her hands between her thighs, then storming over and getting into the shower with her, pinning her to the walls, and taking control.

But the door remained stubbornly closed.

Violet sighed, her own touch abruptly unsatisfying. Shutting off the water, she got out, dried herself, and dressed. Pausing in front of the mirror, she pulled a face at her spiky hair, wishing for a hairdryer to get at least some semblance of a proper hairstyle, but there was nothing like that in Elijah's bathroom. Instead she made do with running her hands through it a couple of times, before making her way down the hallway and out into the main room of the apartment.

The smell of coffee drew her to the kitchen, where she found Elijah briskly making toast and bacon and eggs. She stopped in the doorway, staring at him. He looked so domestic standing there at the stove, turning over the eggs with slick economy.

"Go sit at the table," he ordered without looking at her. "I'll bring it out to you."

The protest was there, ready on her tongue, but she pressed her lips hard against it. Patience and no pushing, right?

She turned and went out again, going over to sit at the

dining table like a good girl. It had a glass top, the surface absolutely spotless, the dining chairs surrounding it works of minimalist art in white steel.

Was this another remnant of his life with Marie? And had she chosen it or had it been his decision?

She gave another look around the apartment, at the bits and pieces of his earlier life, at the way they'd been arranged so carefully. The bed had been one of those bits and pieces, she was sure of it, but she had the feeling this apartment hadn't been theirs. This was all his, and yet he'd furnished it like his old life. So careful, so deliberate. Why? A reminder of what he'd lost?

Grief stuck in her chest like a sharp stone. After Theo had disappeared, she used to go into his old room and just hang out there. Sit on his bed and look around at his things as if they could somehow conjure up his absent spirit. It had been a comfort and yet at the same time, it had made things worse. Because Theo was gone and all those things of his couldn't bring him back. They only served to make the pain sharper.

Violet looked down at the cool surface of the table, unshed tears clogging her throat. Jesus Christ, she was a mess. Pretty much the story of her goddamn life.

The sound of plates on the glass of the table jolted her and she looked up to see Elijah pushing a load of eggs and bacon and toast in front of her, following it up with a mug of coffee.

"Thanks," she muttered, grabbing the cutlery he'd also put down beside the plate and hoping he hadn't seen her blinking back tears. "You'd make someone a lovely wife."

He ignored that, sitting down opposite her and digging into his own breakfast.

Typical Elijah. His refusal to engage was so fucking annoying.

There was a brief silence as they ate, and then he asked shortly, "Where's your brother's storage facility?"

Violet stared at him, the question so unexpected she wasn't sure what he was talking about. "Storage facility?"

"The one you told me about. The place you said was accessed recently. Where is it?"

Carefully, she put down her knife. "Why do you want to know that?"

"Because that's where we're going."

She blinked. "What do you mean that's 'where we're going'?"

Elijah's black brows drew down. "Are you having problems with comprehension this morning, Violet? We are going to go take a look in your brother's storage locker. It's a relatively simple concept to grasp."

Her heartbeat had stilled, and there was a strange clog of emotion in her throat. "Why?" she asked bluntly. "What's Theo to you?"

"Theo is nothing to me. You, on the other hand, are." His black eyes didn't waver from hers. "Your brother is a loose end you need to tie up. And once you have, we can concentrate on Jericho."

What was he saying? For a second she forgot completely about Theo, too busy thinking about what Elijah meant. Did he mean that she *was* something to him? Or only in relation to Jericho?

Wow, desperate much?

She swallowed, trying to get rid of the emotion sitting there. Okay, she could drive herself mad trying to guess his motives. Hell, he was a straight-up guy, maybe she should just ask him.

Violet reached out for her coffee mug and wrapped her fingers around it, letting its warmth heat her chilled hands. "What do you mean I'm something to you?"

Something in his eyes flickered, but he didn't look away.

"You're my means to an end." His voice was cold. "And I can't have you distracted thinking about other things, not when we need Jericho thinking this meeting is entirely legit."

He was lying. She was't sure how she knew or what had given it away, but something deep inside told her that not only was he lying to convince her, he was lying to convince himself.

Perhaps he knew that too, because he went on quickly, without waiting for her to respond. "Jericho has to believe you're going to go with him, and that what I want are the business links he promised your father. That I'm going to take over your father's empire."

She sipped her coffee, studying him, the emotion making its way down her throat to sit in her chest. "And what happens to me?"

"I'll make sure you're safe." No hesitation this time and no flicker either. He totally believed it. "You won't be going anywhere with him."

She wanted to ask what was with the sudden urge to protect her, especially when he'd never been concerned about what happened to her after he'd given her to Jericho before. But she stayed quiet. God knew, she shouldn't be thinking about this anyway, not when he'd offered to help her follow up on her lead on Theo.

Haven't you given up on that?

Well, yeah, she had yesterday. It had seemed selfish and wrong to keep looking for a dead man when compared to putting right the crimes her father had committed.

She took another sip of her coffee. "Theo doesn't matter. I told you yesterday that—"

"I know what you told me. But it'll cost us nothing to go have a look."

Another complex mix of emotions shifted in her chest. Hope and fear. Hope that she'd at last find out the truth about her brother. Fear that what had happened to him *was* the only truth.

"It might cost *me*," she murmured under her breath.

Elijah's midnight gaze held hers, uncompromising, ruthless. "You're strong enough," he said, and this time there was not even a hint of a lie in his voice. "Believe me, Violet. If there is a cost, you're strong enough to pay it."

CHAPTER SIXTEEN

The storage facility was situated in what used to be a parking garage near Hell's Kitchen, a slick and shiny operation manned by a self-important fuck with an oily smile who made it very clear that if Violet wasn't authorized to have access to the storage locker then access she wasn't going to get.

The guy was only doing his job, but Elijah didn't give a shit whether Violet was authorized or not. She needed to follow up that lead on her brother, and he was going to help her.

Yeah, he'd told her it was because he didn't want her distracted when they went to meet Jericho, but that was bullshit. And he knew she hadn't believed him. Yet he couldn't tell her the truth, not when he could barely admit it to himself.

This mattered to her, and so it mattered to him. Because he couldn't get out of his head the look on her face the day before after she'd ended the call with her mother, the bleakness in her eyes. It hurt him, made him feel like shit, brought back all the terrible memories of how Marie had disappeared, how he'd searched and searched for her and hadn't been able to find her.

Not knowing what had happened to a person drove you insane, and he didn't want that for Violet.

So when the prick behind the counter shook his head dismissively at Violet, Elijah gave him one of his terrifying smiles, the one that was usually a warning to anyone with any sense of self-preservation. "I suggest you give Miss Fitzgerald the key to the locker," he said, letting menace drip from each word. "Unless you like dealing with very difficult customers."

The man squinted at him and then, obviously seeing the violence in his eyes, paled. "I'm sorry, sir. I can't. It's against company policy."

Elijah had his Colt in the waistband of his jeans, but he wouldn't need it. A bit of friendly persuasion should do the trick. He moved, lightning fast, reaching out and grabbing the guy's shirt, hauling him half over the counter. The man made a strangled sound, fear moving across his face.

Elijah gripped him tightly, keeping that cold smile on his face. "May I suggest you make an exception?"

The guy, proving he had shit for brains, tried to struggle. "I'll call the police!"

But it was Violet who answered, her voice full of scorn. "Call away. The police chief is a friend of my father's, and I'm not sure he'll be too happy when I tell him I was only trying to retrieve something from my brother's locker. Especially seeing as how he's a real family-oriented kind of guy."

The man panted, looking from Elijah to Violet, then back again.

"Make a decision, prick," Elijah said coldly. "Miss Fitzgerald's a busy woman."

In answer, the man fumbled around with something behind the counter, which he eventually pushed across toward them. "Here's the key. Now let me go."

Violet picked it up, giving the man a disdainful look. "Excellent. If you're lucky you might get to keep your job. You can let him go now, Mr. Hunt."

Clearly she was playing up her princess role.

Elijah released the man, but gave him a hard, narrow look. "You call anyone, anyone at all, and I'll have your hide. Understand me?"

The guy gave a jerky nod, looking like he was going to piss himself.

Violet was already walking in the direction of the lockers so, dismissing the front-desk guy, Elijah turned and followed her.

There were surveillance cameras everywhere, and no doubt their altercation with the front-desk guy was caught on tape, but Elijah wasn't concerned. He had a hacker contact who could probably get in and erase anything that needed to be erased.

He texted the contact as they moved down the narrow corridor, windows onto the city on one side, the small numbered doors of the storage lockers on the other.

Eventually Violet slowed and came to a stop in front of one. She didn't do anything for a moment, staring at the number on the front. Her face had gone pale and there were dark rings under her eyes.

No big surprise given everything that had happened the day before. Not to mention the fact that he hadn't let her sleep much the night before.

His cock, the inappropriate fuck, hardened at the memory of smooth, satiny skin and musky, feminine heat. The sounds of her cries in his ears. Oh yeah, and not forgetting the blowjob she'd given him that morning. Been a long, long time since he'd gotten one of those.

His instinct had been to push her away the moment she'd started touching him, but he just hadn't been able to make himself do it. His body had wanted the pleasure, had craved the touch, and especially given everything they'd done the night before, holding back had seemed ridiculous.

So he'd let her. And the feeling of her mouth around his

dick had been . . . fucking heaven. Hot and wet and, Jesus, so good. Too good. He'd sat there, looking down at her, the orgasm resounding in his skull, his brain furiously trying to make plans for how he could keep her after the whole Jericho thing had been resolved.

Which was crazy. Because he didn't want to keep her. What he wanted was to grab the reins of her father's empire and take it apart piece by piece. And if he needed sex, he could have it from any woman, he didn't actually have to have it from Violet.

Pushing away the desire and the tight, uncomfortable feeling in his chest as he watched Violet look at the storage-locker door, he said, "Do you want me to open it?"

Slowly, she shook her head. "No. I have to do this."

"Don't be afraid." The words came out of him before he knew he'd meant to speak. And he really didn't know why he'd said them, because there wasn't anything to be afraid of. Yet he could sense her fear and knew what it was. The fear of hope. The fear of pain.

Her head turned, her vivid eyes meeting his. She didn't speak, but there was something wordlessly grateful in her gaze that had him moving closer to her, unconsciously thinking to add his strength to hers. Not that she needed it. This woman could probably take on the world if she had to.

Violet looked away and approached the door, grasping the padlock and unlocking it with a sharp, definite movement. Then she pulled it open.

A soft sound escaped her.

Elijah frowned, staring into the locker. It wasn't very big and what was there seemed to be pretty standard stuff: some clothes, an electric guitar in a case, a football, some books, and a whole stack of what looked like vintage vinyl. The guy must have liked his music.

Violet had moved closer, pushing a few things aside,

sorting through the clothes then sliding aside the big stack of vinyl. The look on her face was closed, her mouth in a hard line.

Was this difficult for her? Going through her brother's things? It had to be, surely, even after he'd been gone so long. He remembered suddenly the sight of Violet holding the book Marie had given him for their first wedding anniversary, how the pain had caught at him like a blow, shocking and somehow even more painful because he hadn't been expecting it.

He remembered opening the present and seeing Marie's face watching him, alight with anticipation and pleasure. She knew he'd liked old science fiction and the first-edition Heinlein had been perfect. Paper, she'd said. For our first anniversary.

Grief shifted inside him again and he found himself reaching for Violet, needing to touch her, to have her soft, cool fingers on him. He stopped himself at the last minute. He didn't need *anything* from her, and now was certainly not the time.

"Are you okay?" he asked instead, keeping his tone flat and uninflected.

She didn't look at him. "Yeah, I'm fine. It's just . . . memories."

He wanted to say he understood, but he didn't. That way lay a slippery slope and he wasn't going to fall down it. "See anything that might be of interest?"

"No. Not really. I thought that maybe—" She stopped all of a sudden. "Wait a second." Reaching past a stack of books, she pulled out an envelope. Her name was written on it.

Her hand was shaking and she stared at it like it contained her death warrant, and this time he couldn't stop himself. He closed the distance between them, wrapping his fingers around her wrist to stop the shakes.

Her gaze snapped to his, eyes wide.

"It's okay," he said, lying through his teeth, because obviously this was very far from okay, but wanting to reassure her nevertheless. "Open the envelope, princess."

She looked back down at the manila envelope in her hand, her name scrawled across it in a bold, flowing script, and swallowed. Then she gently pulled away from him, the shakes now gone. With a quick motion she ripped it open and looked inside, frowning. Tipping it up, she held out her hand and caught the small USB memory stick that slid out into her palm.

Well, that settled it. Whether her brother was alive or not, he was trying to tell his sister something. And whatever it was, the answer was on that memory stick.

"He knew," Violet whispered, staring down at the small piece of electronics in her hand. "I think he knew."

Elijah didn't ask what she meant. The same thing had occurred to him too. "You think he found out what your father was?"

Violet nodded. "I just don't know what else this could mean. My name is on the front of it, for God's sake. And that note he left . . ." She trailed off then looked up at Elijah. "He wrote 'Be careful.' " Her eyes had gone very wide, her skin the color of the snow outside. "He found out about Dad. Theo knew what he was doing." It wasn't possible for her to get any whiter, but somehow she did. "And he d-disappeared. They never found his body, Elijah, but it was determined to be suicide. What if Dad—"

"No." Elijah cut her off before she could finish. "Your father wouldn't have arranged for his son's death. He wouldn't." And this too wasn't a lie as far as Elijah knew. Fitzgerald had always been an old-fashioned empire builder, and his children would have been part of those ambitions. His son would have been his heir. Though perhaps if that son had wanted nothing to do with his father's empire, Fitzgerald might have turned nasty. The man had been of the opinion that anyone not for him was against him.

"How do you know?" There was a strange look in her eyes, a suspicion that hadn't been there before. "You don't know why Jericho wants me so badly. How do you know Dad wouldn't murder his own son?"

He wished he could be more certain, take that burden at least from her. But he couldn't. What had happened to Theodore Fitzgerald had occurred before Elijah had come on the scene, and his boss had never spoken about it. "I can't be sure," he admitted, hating that he couldn't give her the confirmation she was obviously desperate for. "He was ruthless when people wouldn't do what he wanted them to do."

Violet looked away from him, her luscious mouth white around the edges. "Dad was distraught when Theo disappeared." The words sounded like she was talking half to herself. "He had the entire New York police department searching for him. And I can't believe that was an act. I just . . . can't."

What could he say? Nothing. Because he knew what he did about Evelyn Fitzgerald, and the man was an actor of Oscar-worthy proportions. The role of distraught father would have been just another part he'd played. But he couldn't tell Violet that. Not now.

"You have no proof your brother is dead though." He made his voice hard and sharp to cut through that horrible, shuttered look on her face. To give her at least one fact that wasn't bad. "Did you ever think he might have faked his own death?"

Violet blinked, her throat moving as she swallowed, visibly trying to pull herself together. And it was instinct that had him reaching for her before he even realized what he was doing, sliding his arm around her waist and drawing her in so her soft heat rested against him.

She looked up sharply, staring at him, surprise in her eyes. Then, after a moment, she put one hand on his chest, her fingers splaying out. There was something about the way she did it, something about the heat from her palm seeping into him, like a connection was being forged between them.

It made part of him want to pull away, deny it, because a connection with her was the last thing he wanted. And yet he couldn't bear to move. It would hurt her, and hurting her, as he was beginning to find out, was something he just wasn't prepared to do.

"I guess he could've," she murmured. "I mean, I never believed the suicide verdict. I just wasn't ever clear on why he would do something like that. He had nothing to escape, or so I thought."

She had started to relax against him, as if she'd done this thousands of times before, absorbing his strength and his warmth, taking comfort from him like this was the most natural thing on earth for her to do. And he felt satisfaction uncurl inside him, lazy as a cat stirring in the sun.

It was good to provide her with comfort. Good to be there for her. And *damn* good for her to take it from him without question, without protest. As if she never expected him to do anything else.

"Looked like he had plenty to escape." Elijah's voice was all rough around the edges and threaded through with heat, and he couldn't seemed to adjust it, make it as hard and cold as it had been before. Instead he tightened his arm around her, holding her close. "The real question is if he did fake his own death, what's he doing now?"

She had relaxed totally now, leaning into him. "Maybe the answer is on that memory stick?"

"Possibly. We need to get home, have a look at it." Pity he would have to move to get there. Because right now, he was perfectly happy standing in the corridor of a storage facility with Violet in his arms.

At that moment, his phone buzzed.

Fucking wonderful timing.

He shifted his hold on Violet, reaching into his back pocket and taking it out. Then, as he looked down at the screen, cold began to spread out inside him. He knew the number. Jericho.

Without a word he let Violet go and turned, taking a few steps away as he hit the accept button. "What?"

"Change of plan, Mr. Hunt." The voice on the other end of the phone was male, slightly nasal, and spoke in French. "You and Miss Fitzgerald will meet Jericho at the designated place in half an hour."

A burst of adrenaline flooded through him. "We agreed tomorrow," he said in the same language, trying to keep himself cold and focused. "That was the plan."

"And I am changing it." The voice sounded completely calm.

Elijah glanced toward Violet, who was looking back at him, her expression wary. "You can't change it, you prick. I have what you want."

"Perhaps he doesn't want it as much as you think he does."

Jesus. Elijah turned his back on Violet. "Does he want her dead?"

"Half an hour, Mr. Hunt. Don't be late." There was a click and the line went dead.

Elijah gave a savage curse, anger licking up inside him.

Half an hour was no time to get to Battery Park let alone contact the people he needed to be in place too. Which meant his plan for keeping Violet safe was in severe jeopardy.

Rage seethed inside him, seeded through with sharp bits of icy fear.

No, *fuck*, he could not allow either emotion any control in this situation. He had to be sharp, and cold, and ruthless.

"Elijah?" Violet's voice from behind him, concern edging her tone.

Struggling to get himself in hand, he turned back around and met her gaze. There was concern in the depths of her eyes, and a trepidation that began to turn into fear. Clearly she'd seen the black rage on his face.

"Jericho," he said flatly. "He's changed the meeting time. We have to go now."

Her eyes went wide. "Now?"

"He gave me half an hour."

"But I'm not—"

Elijah walked back to her and took her upper arm in a hard grip, cutting off her words. He had no time for reassurance now. No time for comfort. This was what he'd worked toward all those years and he was not letting it slip through his fingers.

But he wouldn't let her get hurt. He just had to come up with some way to get his revenge and to keep her safe in the next half hour. Easy.

"We have to go, princess." He paused and even though he had no time for any of that, he added. "Don't worry. I'll make sure you're okay."

Then he turned and began to walk fast toward the exit, pulling her with him.

Violet didn't think she could take much more. She'd had enough of secrets. Of hidden pasts. Of her family virtually disintegrating in front of her eyes. Of being kidnapped and threatened. And now she had to deal with this. As if having to go through Theo's things and finding that memory stick he'd clearly left for her wasn't bad enough, she was now on her way to a meeting with a crime lord called

Jericho. Where she would be the bait that would enable Elijah to finally kill him.

Not that that wasn't what she wanted as well, she'd just thought she'd have a little more time to build up to it. At least time to process what she'd discovered at the storage facility and see what message Theo had left for her.

But apparently not. Apparently fate had other ideas.

Elijah's grip was tight on her arm as they exited the building and he started scanning up and down the street, looking for a cab. At first she'd thought it was because he was afraid she would run, especially after they'd gotten outside and he'd pulled her in close to him. But then he'd released her for a second before sliding an arm around her waist and pulling her in even closer. And that didn't feel like he was afraid she'd get away. That felt like he was holding her because he wanted to touch her, because he wanted to protect her.

He'd already told her that morning he was going to make sure she was safe, but even though he'd just reiterated that, she didn't feel safe. She felt like she was walking into a bear trap.

Amazingly, a taxi pulled up almost as soon as Elijah had stuck out his hand, and he wasted no time, pulling open the door and bundling her into it. Then he slid in beside her, closing the door and giving the address to the cabbie.

"What do you want me to do?" she asked him, trying to force away the growing sense of fear that was carving a nice little home for itself in her gut. "When we get there, I mean."

Elijah had taken his phone out and was busy typing something into it. He didn't look up, but again that muscular arm slid around her waist and she was hauled against his body, his hand resting flat on her stomach, heavy with possession. "Just stay close and let me do the talking."

She took a deep, steadying breath. Okay, so she could do this. She'd faced down this man at gunpoint and she'd managed to bear the truth about her father. She'd emerged from both of those trials by fire still standing. Unbroken. And there was no fucking way in hell she'd break now.

One hand curled around the memory stick in her palm while the other reached for the man beside her, coming to rest on one powerful denim-clad thigh. He was so strong. She could feel that strength running through him like electricity through high-tension wires. And he had a lot of it to spare. Enough for her too.

He glanced at her, his eyes intense, full of storms and darkness. "Do you trust me, Violet?"

"Yes." She didn't even have to think about her response. It was automatic.

If he found this gratifying he gave no sign, though the arm around her tightened fractionally. "Then you have to do what I tell you to when I tell you to, understand?"

"Yes, okay."

He paused, his attention wholly focused on her. Staring at her as if he was seeing her for the very first time. "I had a plan," he said quietly. "To keep you safe. But Jericho's changed the fucking rules on me and there's no time to put that plan in place."

A shiver of fear ghosted over her skin, but she refused to let it get to her. She could do this, and she was going to. Helping Elijah put Jericho in the ground would be worth it. "I'll be okay," she said firmly, as if saying it would make it so. "We're going to get this sonofabitch."

His harsh, handsome face looked carved from stone, the scar bisecting it gone white. His eyes glittered like obsidian, sharp and hard. And she thought, just for a second, that she saw something softer in them. As if her words had touched something inside him.

Then unexpectedly he reached up, took her face between his large, warm palms and held her an instant, staring down at her. "I *will* keep you safe, princess." The words were heavy, weighted like a vow. "I promise you this." And before she could respond, he bent his head and kissed her.

Violet went still, waiting for the hard, hot demand of his mouth on hers.

But it didn't come. Instead he was gentle, his lips brushing hers before his tongue dipped inside to taste her, a delicate sip rather than a deep swallow. It was tantalizing, sweet, unlike any of the others he'd given her. She shuddered, opening her mouth to him, letting him take it if he wanted. But again, he didn't. He explored slowly, savoring her taste, learning her contours. His fingers were gentle, his thumbs stroking back and forth along her cheekbones. The gentleness of him made her chest ache and her throat tighten. He was so big, so strong, and so cold. And yet his touch on her was light as a butterfly's wing.

Her senses reeled, the prick of unexpected tears sharp behind her closed lids. How could he make her weep like this with just one kiss?

His hands slid over her jaw and down her neck, his thumbs now brushing the underside of her jawline. The kiss gentled even more before he lifted his mouth from hers. She was shaking, a strange, constant vibration that went deeper than an unsteady hand or wobbly legs. It felt like her entire soul was trembling. She didn't want this to end, and words of protest nearly came out. But she kept quiet at the last minute because they were in a taxi going to meet Jericho and there was no time.

The look on Elijah's face was unreadable and he didn't say a word. He kept his hands where they were for one long minute, his fingers pressing lightly against her neck as if he was memorizing its shape.

Then he took them away and turned, reaching for his phone again and looking down at the screen. As if the moment had never happened.

She leaned back against the seat, wanting to fold her arms around herself because she was pretty sure her heart was going to come out of her chest if it beat any harder. Her lips tingled, and she could taste him on her tongue. And she wished suddenly, passionately, that they were back at his apartment where she could reach out to him and pull him close again. Kiss him again. Fall back into that wide bed of his and forget the rest of the world existed.

But unfortunately it did. A brutal, harsh world, the reality of which was going to hit hard in about twenty minutes.

Elijah muttered curses beside her, then leaned forward to urge the cabbie to drive faster.

"We should have taken the subway," she murmured, unable to think of anything else to say.

"Too late now," he said shortly.

The rest of the trip was silent, the cabdriver doing his level best to speed up the journey.

They got there with minutes to spare.

Elijah tossed the driver some cash while Violet got out, looking around nervously. He joined her a second or two later, once again putting his arm around her as if he couldn't bear not to touch her.

"Remember." His voice was quiet. "Do what I say, okay?"

"I remember." She swallowed, forcing down her fear.

They crossed the street and headed into the park, joining the crowds of people taking advantage of the nice, late-winter weather to enjoy the sun and sparkling blue of the river. Tourists and sightseers of all nationalities, joggers, people out walking their dogs, and office workers on a break having a stroll or heading somewhere.

All the people around calmed Violet somewhat, which was stupid. Just because there were a lot of people around didn't make this whole thing any less dangerous.

"Why here?" she murmured as she and Elijah walked toward the Esplanade. "It's very public."

"That was the point." He wasn't looking at her, his gaze focused on where they were going, his whole posture radiating leashed tension, as if ready to explode into movement at the slightest provocation. "We're less likely to get shot in a crowd."

"But that makes killing him slightly problematic, don't you think?"

"Yes. But I wasn't really concerned about that."

Violet glanced at him. His face was set, hard, menace radiating from him like heat from a desert road. "What do you mean you weren't concerned about that? Shooting a person in broad daylight usually results in a murder charge."

He lifted his shoulder. "Like I said, that didn't concern me."

Shock coursed down her spine. "What? You'd go to jail?"

"Killing Jericho may mean I end up with a death sentence anyway. Jail or death, either doesn't worry me. Or at least, it didn't."

She couldn't stop staring at him, a terrible clenching feeling in her chest. "You were going to sacrifice yourself?"

"Call it what you like, Jericho dead was the whole point. My life didn't matter."

No. He was wrong. He was *so* wrong. "Elijah—"

"But things have changed," he interrupted before she could protest. "If your father's empire is going to be taken down, someone has to take control of it, and logically that person is me. And I can't do that if I'm dead or in jail."

It should have been some comfort that he wasn't going to throw his life away, and yet it wasn't. Instead a great feeling of sadness sat like a boulder in the center of her chest, weighing her down. Was this really how he wanted his life to go? An endless revenge quest for the wife he'd lost years ago?

It made those tears rise again, clogging in her throat, that aching sadness getting heavier and heavier. Sadness for him and for what he'd lost. For what his life had become. For what his life would be after this was all over. Because if he was going to take down what her father had created, then there would be no peace for him. No rest.

"You can't," she said before she could think better of it. "Elijah, when is it going to stop?"

"When is what going to stop?"

They'd come out onto the Esplanade now, the glittering blue of the river in front of them, the skyscrapers behind. He was scanning around at the crowds of people moving up and down the walkway, or standing to look at the view, or sitting on the benches lining the riverside.

"This need for revenge."

He stilled all of a sudden and his sharp-edged gaze came to rest on her. For a moment the walls behind his eyes dropped away and she could finally see the grief and rage that burned inside. The fuel he'd used to burn away the man he'd once been.

"Never," he said softly, almost gently. "It will never stop."

Violet couldn't speak, her throat locking up entirely, the sadness crushing, and she didn't know why.

Of course you know why. You haven't just fallen for him. You're in love with him.

Oh excellent. She'd fallen in love with her captor. A man who had revenge running through his veins instead of blood. A man who would destroy himself pursuing it because he could not let the past go.

Like you're any better yourself.

Hell, she knew that. Constantly moving, constantly flitting from one thing to another, pursuing academia because she had to fill the hole inside with something. A hole that had only gotten wider now that she'd found out about her father. Who knew how long it would take her to put that behind her? And apart from any of that, hadn't she come here with Elijah for revenge herself?

He'd glanced away from her, tugging her closer. Putting his phone in his pocket, he drew her over to the edge of the walkway closest to the river, where a wooden railing stood between the walkway and the river's edge.

There were a couple of tourists beside them, looking at the view and pointing out various landmarks on a map they held between them. On a bench not far away was a man in a tan overcoat, reading a paper, a young couple beside him laughing and talking.

It was a beautiful day and it felt like all of New York was out here enjoying it.

A normal day.

She watched the crowd move past, feeling battered by the emotions tangling themselves up inside her. Grief for Elijah. Hurt for him too. Fear of what was going to happen, both to herself and to him. There would be no good outcomes, would there?

"Good morning, Mr. Hunt." The voice was light, male, accented.

Violet turned and saw that an older man in a black coat had appeared out of the crowds and was now standing beside Elijah, his arms resting casually on the wooden railing. He was of average height, nondescript, his narrow, sharp face directed toward the view in front of them.

She stared at him. Holy shit, was this Jericho? Europe's shadiest crime lord? Jesus, he looked like someone's bachelor uncle.

"Jericho, I presume?" Elijah's tone was arctic. He'd changed his grip on her, his fingers now tight around her upper arm as if holding her there to prevent her escape.

"Yes," the man said. "That is one of my names."

Elijah had turned around so his back was to the railing, looking at the crowds moving along the walkway. "Prove it."

The man laughed. "Tiresome of you. Why should I?"

"Because I'm not giving Miss Fitzgerald to any random prick."

The man was smiling, his attention on the water in front of him. "In that case you have my word."

"Your word?" Scorn dripped from Elijah's voice. "I don't give a shit about your word. Not when you've broken it once already."

"Ah. You're annoyed I changed the meeting time." Jericho shifted against the railings. "Really, Mr. Hunt, did you expect me to obey all your commands like a good little dog? I'm not that kind of man."

"I don't care what kind of man you are. If I asked for a personal meeting with Jericho, then I expect a personal meeting with Jericho."

The man turned to look at Elijah. He was smiling pleasantly, a smile that didn't quite reach his eyes. "Let's move all this posturing along, shall we? Firstly, I don't like surprises, and learning of Fitzgerald's death was a surprise I didn't need. Secondly, I assume the reason you contacted me in the first place is that you've decided you're taking over your boss's operations and want the same trade concessions he asked for in exchange for the woman."

Elijah didn't speak, letting the silence sit there in a way that was familiar to Violet.

She supposed she should be appearing scared and trying to pull away to make sure she looked like Elijah's unwilling captive. It wouldn't take much since she was definitely quite scared already. And yet there was something off here, something she couldn't quite put her finger on.

Jericho hadn't even looked at her, not once. Strange when such a secretive man was willing to meet with Elijah just so he could get his hands on her.

"The strong silent type, I see," Jericho went on when Elijah remained quiet. "Useful in an employee. Except you don't seem the kind who follows orders well, Mr. Hunt."

Elijah shifted and Violet felt herself pulled slightly in front of him, so she stood between him and Jericho. This time, the man glanced at her and then away again, completely without reaction.

"I told you I wanted to meet with you alone," Elijah said coldly.

Violet blinked, surreptitiously scanning the area. She hadn't noticed anyone but the general public.

Jericho lifted a shoulder. "You can't expect me to come without some sort of protection."

"Send them the fuck away."

Jericho lifted a brow. "You're in no position to make demands."

Elijah moved again and Violet felt something cold and hard pressing into her side. She stiffened, her heartbeat suddenly veering out of control. It was Elijah's gun.

"Send them away or I'll shoot her." Elijah's voice was flat and uninflected, terrifying.

Do you trust me, Violet?

He wouldn't shoot her, he wouldn't. She did trust him.

Jericho frowned. "That seems . . . drastic."

"You think I won't? She's nothing to me."

Violet knew he wouldn't harm her and yet fear threaded its way through her bloodstream all the same. Turned out acting the part of frightened captive wasn't so difficult after all.

"If she dies, you won't get your trading concessions," Jericho pointed out.

"Then I guess it all depends on how badly you want her." Elijah pressed the gun harder against her. "Make a decision, prick. You have five seconds."

This was a bluff. That's all it was.

What if it isn't? What if you're not worth more than his revenge?

No, she couldn't think that. He'd promised her she'd be safe and she believed him.

Jericho was silent for what seemed like far longer than five seconds. Then he sighed. "Very well, if it'll make you happier." He straightened and made a flicking gesture with his hand. Instantly the tourists leaning against the railings moved away, as did a man taking pictures off to their left and the man in the overcoat on the bench.

Violet shivered. They'd been surrounded and she hadn't seen a thing.

"Now, shall we get to the point?" Jericho sounded bored. "The woman comes with me."

Elijah's hand tightened on her upper arm, his body a warm, strong presence at her back. "Come and get her then."

A crowd of rowdy teenagers obviously out on a school trip was coming closer, shouts and catcalls echoing in the air.

"Certainly," Jericho said. "Put your gun away first."

"Sure." Elijah's voice was calm.

And suddenly Violet found herself pushed out of the way as he lurched toward Jericho, looking like he'd tripped over something. His free hand came out, flailing, gripping onto the other man and pulling him close as if he was stopping himself from falling.

Jericho cursed, starting to pull away, his hand reaching for something in his overcoat, but it was too late.

As the crowd of schoolchildren moved level with them, Violet heard the sound of a muffled report. Jericho's eyes widened and his mouth opened as Elijah slid an arm around him. It looked like he was suddenly unable to stand.

Elijah frowned, looking deeply concerned. "Are you all right, sir?" he asked, his voice carrying despite the noise of the school group. Jericho's mouth moved but no sound came out. He'd slumped heavily against Elijah, the color slowly draining from his face.

Elijah glanced once at Violet, a clear warning in his eyes, then he lifted his head and started looking around at the crowds as if for help. "Someone call nine one one," he said loudly, his tone a little desperate. "This man needs a doctor."

People began to stare as Elijah helped Jericho over to the park bench where the man in the tan overcoat had been. The young couple looked up in alarm and scooted clear to make way. Then the young woman began talking and moving in to help while the man took his phone out of his pocket.

A small crowd began to gather, blocking her view of Elijah and Jericho.

Her heartbeat was loud in her head and she knew she should probably get clear and wait somewhere quiet for Elijah until the fuss had died down. Except she didn't want to. She wanted to stay near him, make sure he was okay. Because it was obvious what had happened. He had shot Jericho. He'd finally taken his revenge.

Are you sure you want to stay? It's over now. Perhaps he won't want you anymore now that he's gotten what he wanted.

She didn't like that thought, it made her feel small and cold. Made her conscious of that hole inside her, the hunger that craved him and his heat. That made her so vulnerable.

Trying to calm her breathing, she backed away from the knot of people around the bench. But the cold feeling wouldn't go away and she couldn't work out why she was now even more terrified than she had been before, especially since the danger was over.

Then she backed into someone standing beside her.

She began to turn, her mouth already open, an apology at the ready. But a hand came up and covered her mouth and nose, pinching hard and cutting off her air.

Fear burst like a star in her head, a scream building in her throat. A scream that had no outlet. Her lungs burned and bright lights seem to explode in her vision.

Her last thought before the blackness came was that being kidnapped was getting really old.

CHAPTER SEVENTEEN

Elijah moved away from Jericho, using the press of the crowd around the park bench to surreptitiously fade into the background. The woman who'd been sitting on the bench with her boyfriend had taken over, and she must have had some kind of medical training because she was issuing instructions while her boyfriend called an ambulance.

It was too late, though. Jericho would be dead within minutes.

But as Elijah faded into the crowd, he couldn't shake the feeling that it had been easy. Way too easy. A simple feint that Jericho had fallen for and now the guy was dead. It could not be that simple.

Something had been "off" about the whole interaction, and he couldn't quite put his finger on why. He hadn't missed that Jericho hadn't once looked in Violet's direction, not until he'd put her in front of the other man. Only then had Jericho looked. And even then it had been a simple once-over. Not the response of someone who was desperate to get his hands on her, that was for certain.

Unless he was bluffing, which could be one explanation.

Yet still. That didn't explain the niggling in his gut that told him he was missing something.

You've had that feeling once before, haven't you?

He ignored the thought, walking away from the crowd around the bench, wanting to put as much distance between him and Jericho as he could. It wouldn't take long for people to figure out the guy had been shot, and probably they'd soon start looking for him.

He scanned the area as he walked, trying to see where Violet had gone. He'd given her a warning look as he'd caught Jericho, hoping she'd understand that he wanted her well away from the area. And it looked like she had, because he certainly couldn't see her anywhere.

More crowds had started moving in and he could hear sirens. The ambulance would be here within minutes and no doubt the cops too, which meant he couldn't be anywhere in the vicinity. Looked like Violet wasn't either, because he sure as hell couldn't see her.

Fuck. Where had she gone?

He kept his head down as he continued moving away from where he'd left Jericho, at the same time expanding his awareness of his surroundings, a little trick he'd learned while employed with Fitzgerald. But still he couldn't see her.

You remember this, don't you?

That fucking snide voice again. That cold, familiar feeling.

He tried to dismiss it. Perhaps he should double back, see if she'd gone in the other direction? Except that would bring him back past where Jericho was, and that would be a huge mistake.

He kept walking, bringing out his phone and dialing the number of the burner he'd given her before they'd left the apartment that morning. There was no response.

The cold feeling began to freeze into small kernels of ice, sharp edges digging into him.

Those flunkies of Jericho's were still out there . . .

Elijah stopped and turned, looking back the way he'd come.

A large crowd had gathered around the park bench. Wouldn't be long before the EMTs arrived. He spotted the dark uniform of a cop already shouldering through the crowd, which was pretty much his cue to get away as quickly as he possibly could, and yet . . . no Violet.

Where the *fuck* was she?

He turned back around, the ice beginning to settle in his blood, clogging his veins.

This is what happened to Marie, remember?

Jesus. Like he could forget. They'd been out to dinner and were on their way out to get a cab. She'd had to make a detour to visit the bathroom and he'd told her he'd wait outside for her. He'd waited five minutes, then ten, then fifteen. Getting more and more annoyed by how long she was taking. Never once had it crossed his mind that something was terribly wrong. Not until he'd gone back to look for her and no trace of her had been found. No one at the restaurant had seen her go into the bathroom, no one had seen her come out. She'd just . . . vanished.

He'd never seen Marie again.

Fuck, no. This was not happening, not again. Not to Violet.

A burst of adrenaline flooded through him, making him want to take out his Colt and start shooting. Making him want to grab someone—anyone—and demand they tell him where Violet was. A stupid and dangerous thing to want, because obviously that wasn't going to help the situation, but nevertheless. He would not stand by while a woman he cared about was taken from him. Not again.

He wasn't Kane Archer, first oblivious to the danger and then powerless to do anything about it. Weak and ineffectual, who'd believed the lies Fitzgerald had told him, the bait that had gotten Elijah to work for him. That once he'd proved his loyalty, his wife would be returned to him.

He was different now. Stronger. And that was not going to happen, not to Violet. If anyone—anyone at all—hurt her, they were looking at a death sentence. And he would be their fucking executioner.

Elijah, when is it going to stop?

Her voice seemed to echo in his head from out of the blue, but he shook it away. He didn't care about whether it would stop or not. If they'd hurt her, they would pay. That's all there was to it.

He began to walk on, this time not bothering to keep his head down, scanning the faces of the people around him, looking for spiky blonde hair and vivid blue-green eyes. For a lovely, passionate mouth and a strong, determined jawline. Looking every-fucking-where.

But she'd gone. She'd just fucking gone.

Rage started to rise, so strong and so hot, melting the ice, causing a red haze to cloud his vision. A real goddamn worry, since uncontrolled rage wasn't going to help anyone, least of all Violet.

Christ, he needed to get his head back in the game. Put a lid on this anger. Try and figure out a plan to find her, not walk around aimlessly trying to see if he could spot her.

Except he couldn't seem to get a handle on his emotions, especially that cold, cold feeling. Almost like . . . fear.

You should have kept a better eye on her. You should have talked through a plan with her in the taxi on the way here. You should have kept her close.

But he hadn't done any of those things. Fuck, he should have learned his lesson by now.

And then someone said very distinctly from behind him. "Mr. Hunt. We need a word with you." The voice was accented and female, and he was going to ignore it. Until she added, "If you don't stop, I'm afraid I'm going to have to shoot you."

The rage swelled inside him, demanding an outlet, and he turned sharply, his Colt already in his hand. He only just had the presence of mind to keep it low and out of sight of the crowds moving around him.

Two women were standing in front of him, one tall and blonde, dressed in a dark suit. The other small and silver-haired, wearing a black beanie and a leather jacket. Familiar women.

Eva King and Katya Ivanova. Jesus, he just couldn't get rid of these people, could he?

Not bothering with pointless questions such as what were they doing here and why were they following him, he said instead, his voice freezing, "I suggest that you don't fuck with me right now, ladies. Not unless you want to end up dead."

Katya held her gun low, like he was doing, solidly pointing it at him, her green eyes utterly emotionless. "We are not interested in your threats, Mr. Hunt," she said flatly. "We only want to get Violet back."

Yeah, well, he wanted to strangle them both, the rage and frustration rising higher and higher. "Then you'll have to find her because I don't have her."

Eva's gray eyes narrowed. "So you gave her to Jericho?"

He didn't bother asking her how she knew about Jericho, she must have conducted her own searches after he'd gotten away from Zac's little basement prison. "No. She was supposed—" he stopped abruptly, wondering why the hell he was bothering to explain himself to these two when he could be searching for Violet. Because every minute he stood here was another minute that she could be hurt, she could be lost, she could be getting killed . . .

"Get the fuck out of my way," he growled and started

heading toward them, not giving a shit about the gun pointed in his direction. Because there was only one thing concerning him. Violet.

Katya moved suddenly in front of him, blocking his path, the muzzle of the gun pressing into his stomach insistently. "I'm sorry, Mr. Hunt, but you need to tell us what you've done with Violet. According to our tracking device she's on her way—"

"What tracking device?" he interrupted, totally ignoring the gun pressing into his gut, his whole body going still as a sudden surge of an emotion he couldn't put a name to flooded through him.

"The tracking device Zac put on Violet's sweater when she left his place." Eva's voice was very calm. "We've been tracking her since this morning."

The sound of the crowds moving around them had dulled, as if he'd gone deaf, every sense he had narrowing down on the small woman standing behind the Russian. His heartbeat thumped, fast and insistent.

"Where is she now?" The question came out as a demand, but by then he was past caring.

Eva frowned. "You don't know? Didn't you just have the meeting with—"

"See that crowd over there?" He nodded his head sharply in the direction of the park bench where he'd left Jericho. "I shot that motherfucker. They're probably working on him now, but they won't save him. If he's not dead already then he soon will be."

"But if he took Violet," Katya began.

Elijah cut her off again. "No one took Violet." He met her impassive green gaze. "In fact, I had no intention of giving Violet to that asshole, I just wanted to kill him, and I did. Now tell me where the fuck Violet has gone."

Eva gave him a considering look, and he was on the point of moving against Katya, of shoving her pissy little gun away and going over and forcing the information out of Eva himself, when she abruptly pulled her phone out of her leather jacket. Then she looked down at the screen. "Violet's moving up toward Midtown," she said. "Fast too. In a car probably."

"Give me the phone," Elijah grated, only barely keeping hold of his temper.

Again a quick, cool glance from those quicksilver eyes, measuring him. "Why? Are you worried about your investment?"

"If you don't give me that phone now, I will take you and your friend here apart with my bare hands and screw the fucking crowds."

There was no fear in Eva's eyes. Only that measuring look, a kind of understanding even, which he just didn't get at all considering he'd just threatened to kill her.

"You'll have to survive my bullet first," Katya murmured. "And considering I have you at point-blank range, that might be a little difficult to do."

But Eva said quietly, "It's okay, Katya." And taking a step forward, she held out her hand with the phone in it.

Elijah didn't bother to even glance at the Russian woman, grabbing the proffered phone and staring down at the tiny, fast-moving dot on the screen. Violet. Being taken . . . somewhere by fuck knows who.

The rage boiled up inside him again and he almost crushed the phone in his hand. Then he realized Eva was speaking.

"Gabriel, Alex, and Zac are on their way to get her," she was saying. "And since Katya and I were down this end of Manhattan, we were stuck with getting you."

Those pricks were already on their way to get her? While he was stuck here? Fuck that.

Gripping Eva's phone and completely ignoring Katya, he began to move off the Esplanade toward the streets where he could flag down a taxi and follow that rapidly moving dot.

"Wait," Eva ordered sharply.

He ignored her.

"You're going after her?" Eva was now following him, walking quickly to catch up, Katya behind her.

He didn't want to waste time talking to her or to her friend. There was only one thing that seemed important—getting to Violet. Christ, he didn't even know if she was alive. With that tracking device in her sweater, she could be dead and he could be following her body.

Beneath his rage, fear threaded like a cold current through a hot spring.

You could lose her.

No. He wasn't going to lose her. He wasn't going to lose her like he lost Marie.

"We have a car, Mr. Hunt," Katya said unexpectedly.

He didn't bother turning around. "Then fucking take me to it."

"Zac and the others will get her." Eva's voice was slightly breathless. "They're already on their way. Why don't you—"

He stopped and turned around, so suddenly that she was forced to backtrack to prevent from bumping into him. But he didn't care. He stared at her, allowing the rage to finally fill him up so that there was no cold anywhere. No fear. Nothing that could make him weak because right now he couldn't afford to be weak. "*I* will get her," he said forcefully, savagely. "Not them. Me." He stared at Eva then at Katya, letting them see the burning rage inside him. "She's *mine*. And I will kill anyone who gets in my way, do you understand?"

Violet came slowly to consciousness feeling like she had the world's worst hangover. Her head ached and her mouth was dry, and she felt vaguely dizzy. And when she opened her eyes, her vision was blurry, and she had to blink hard to clear it.

She was sitting in a ratty old armchair in a tidy but very low-rent apartment. Threadbare carpet and dingy wallpaper, a chintzy couch that had clearly seen better days, and a battered wooden coffee table covered in white rings from a thousand different cups.

Where the hell was this? And what the hell had happened to her?

Last thing she remembered was that crowd gathering around Jericho and then backing away, only to have someone's hand cover her mouth and nose, and then . . . nothing.

She looked down, expecting to see bonds of some kind, but her arms and legs were free. She also seemed to be alone in the room.

Weird. What kind of kidnapping was this?

Putting her hands on the arms of the chair, she began to push herself out of it. She froze as a man walked through the doorway that led off to another part of the apartment.

A tall man. He had blond hair, deep tawny at the roots, then fading to gilt at the tips. Much like her own. But his eyes weren't the same color as hers. His were as green and gold as fall leaves.

He was impossibly, stunningly handsome.

But then he always had been.

Halfway out of the chair, Violet's arms refused to work and she collapsed back into it, a curious roaring in her ears. She couldn't stop staring. Was she going to faint? Certainly it felt like it, which would just be ridiculous considering what she'd endured over the last few days and all without passing out like a Victorian virgin.

Then again, it wasn't every day that you saw a dead man.

He didn't speak, coming over to her chair and standing in front of it. His clothing was simple, dark charcoal trousers and a deep-green business shirt open at the neck, no tie. He had his hands in his pockets, the look on his face impossible to read.

Her voice wouldn't work, and she had to try at least three times before she could even make a sound. "Th-Th-Theo?"

There was a long moment where he didn't speak, just looked at her. And then slowly, he smiled, the heartbreaking, breathtaking smile she remembered from years ago, the adored older brother who helped her with her homework on his visits back home from college, who'd taught her how to play poker and how to ride a bike. Who'd vanished without a trace sixteen years earlier.

"Hey Peanut," he said quietly.

Tears filled her eyes and she had to grip the chair arms tightly to stop from bursting into sobs.

You were right. All this time you were right.

She wanted to throw herself into his arms, but something inside her held her back, as if she was afraid that touching him would break the spell. That he would vanish in a puff of smoke as soon as she put her arms around him, the way he had so often in her dreams.

In a fluid movement, Theo sank down on his haunches in front of her chair, his hands now clasped loosely between his knees. He was watching her carefully and she simply stared back, her gaze roving over his handsome face, cataloging the changes the years had wrought.

When he'd been twenty-one, he'd been fresh-faced, a golden boy with his angel face and his stunning smile. The privileged son from a high-society family, Ivy League and blue blood all the way through. Nothing could touch him, nothing could tarnish him.

Sixteen years had passed, and he still had those looks,

but time and experience had definitely tarnished them. There were lines around his eyes and mouth, walls thicker than a bank vault behind those green-gold eyes, and the easy, friendly warmth he used to project was gone. That beautiful smile was still there and yet there was an undercurrent of danger to it, of menace. Like a sleeping tiger, beautiful to look at, but liable to take your hand off if you touched it.

He'd looked like an angel once. Now this angel had clearly fallen far from grace.

What had happened to him? Where had he been? And why the hell was he here now?

"You have questions," he said, his voice was gentle and deep, the Theo she remembered.

Violet had to clear her throat. "Oh, only a couple of thousand."

His smile softened, but for some reason it didn't reach his eyes. "I can imagine."

"What happened, Theo?" She leaned forward, nearly trembling. Now that her voice was working, she couldn't seem to shut up. "Where did you go? What happened to you? Why did you let us believe for so long that you were dead?"

"Curious, Peanut? You haven't changed." The smile curving his mouth didn't waver. "Did you get the memory stick?"

The change of subject was so sudden, she at first couldn't process the question. "Memory stick? What—" And then she stopped, remembering what was in her pocket. "Yes. I did. But I haven't had a chance to see what's on it."

"Information. I even updated it."

"You were the one who accessed the storage locker weren't you? I was so sure it was you."

"Actually, an associate of mine accessed it. But the

intention was the same. To update that stick and to leave you a hint that I was still alive."

And he was, wasn't he? Crouched down in front of her, very much alive.

"You should have called me," she began. "You should have—"

"There were reasons I couldn't," he cut her off calmly. "Believe me there were a great many reasons, all of which I can't explain to you now, though I wish I could." Slowly, he rose to his full height once more. "But this isn't the time or the place."

Violet stared at him, her heart thudding. Okay, apart from her dead brother who was apparently not dead after all, there was something not quite right about this whole situation. Something she couldn't quite put her finger on. "What's going on? Why am I here? In fact, how the hell did I get here in the first place?"

"Some employees of mine brought you here."

"But how did you find me? I mean—"

"Violet," Theo said quietly and with such absolute authority that she fell silent. "Listen to me. I don't have time for long explanations, but you have to know I've been trying to get you out from under Dad's thumb for a while now."

"What?" She couldn't quite process that one either. "Get me out? How?"

Her brother's gaze was impenetrable. "He wanted to use you, do you understand? You were his princess and he wanted to marry you off, firm up alliances to strengthen his empire."

Something froze inside her. "How do you know that?"

"I know a lot of things." He smiled again, faintly, though this time the smile was the one she remembered, full of warmth, making his eyes glow. "Don't be afraid. I know my methods to get you here were drastic, but I had to change my plans quickly after Dad was killed." The smile faded and she had the sudden impression that she was teetering on the edge of a chasm she hadn't realized was right beneath her feet. A chasm he'd led her right up to.

"Theo," she said, her voice echoing strangely in the room. "What's going on?"

He didn't answer immediately, reaching into his pocket and taking out his phone, looking down at the screen. His thumb moved, tapping out something. "I can't tell you everything, but now that I've got you, I'm going to make sure you're safe. You need to leave New York, get out of here for a while."

Shock coursed through her. "Leave? What are you talking about?"

Theo pressed another button then pocketed the phone and looked at her. "You can't stay. Dad's little empire is in chaos now that he's gone and there are a thousand people out there who wouldn't mind taking control of it. And because you're his daughter, some of them will try and use you as their ticket to power."

The shock was icy cold. "Me?"

"You're a useful bargaining chip, not to mention the fact that certain people will expect you to know things." He lifted one golden brow. "If you think the past few days were a one-off, think again."

Her brain struggled to process what he was saying, because how did he know what had happened to her the past couple of days. "I don't . . . Theo . . ."

He held her gaze, a strange sympathy in his eyes. "I know about Elijah, Vi. I know he held you captive."

She opened her mouth to reply, but nothing came out.

"Did he hurt you?" The question was soft.

"N-No."

"Good. Well, you're safe now. I'm organizing a jet to take you out of the country, get you out of circulation for a while. No need to worry about passports and things, I've got that covered."

"Theo."

"I thought since you liked France, you'd prefer to take another holiday in Paris. I've arranged accommodations and—"

"Theo!"

For a second his eyes glittered, cold and hard, as if there was another man looking at her. A man who was not used to being interrupted and did not like it one bit. Then the cold thing was gone, and he was her brother again. "I know this is hard, Peanut. You'll just have to trust me."

Oh no, hell no. He couldn't just appear back from the dead, give her no explanations for anything at all, and then tell her she was leaving the country for an enforced vacation. No fucking way. She was sick of feeling like a goddamn chess piece, a pawn that other people pushed around on a board for their own ends, playing their own games. Games that she knew nothing about.

Violet pushed herself out of the chair, her heartbeat thudding. "No," she said. "I'm not going anywhere. Not until I get some answers."

He stared at her, a steady, assessing look that was somehow quite cold. As if he was trying to decide whether she was an enemy or not. "Answers to what?" There was only mild curiosity in his tone.

"Oh come on, seriously? Answers to everything. Like how do you know all this stuff? How did you know I was with Elijah? That we'd be in Battery Park? Do you even know what we were there for?"

"Yes," he said quietly. "You were there to meet Jericho."

Jesus Christ, she could really do without anymore shocks today. "And how the *fuck* do you know that?"

His mouth quirked and for an instant, he was again the brother she knew. Warm and funny, teasing. "Keep up, Vi.

I thought you would have worked it out by now. I always told you not to take anything at face value."

And the realization poured through her, stealing her breath like a plunge into an arctic stream on a cold winter's day. There was only one reason he'd know what had happened in Battery Park. And who she and Elijah had gone there to meet. "No," she said. "You can't be him."

His expression softened, becoming impossibly gentle. "I can. "

"But . . ." She shook her head, unable to make sense of it. "Elijah shot him. He was . . . dying."

"That wasn't Jericho, Peanut." A sudden, terrible weariness flickered briefly in her brother's eyes. "I'm Jericho."

CHAPTER EIGHTEEN

The SUV had barely come to a stop in the small alleyway before Elijah threw the door open and leaped out, his Colt already in his hand. Eva had told him that the tracking device was broadcasting from the building across the street and that Gabriel, Alex, and Zac were already there.

Fucking bastards. He knew he should be grateful to them and that without them there was no way he'd be able to find her. That it didn't matter who got her as long as she was safe. But he wasn't grateful. He wanted to be the one to find her.

Especially since you were the one who got her into this mess in the first place.

The thought lingered uncomfortably in his head as he tore across the street, not giving a shit about the horns that sounded as he dodged traffic.

He couldn't escape the fact that he'd been the one to use her, and though he'd vowed he'd keep her safe, he hadn't been able to make good on that promise. She'd been taken anyway.

Fuck, he was a dumb bastard. If anything had happened to her . . .

This is what happens when you care. You should never have let her get close.

Ruthlessly he shoved that thought to one side. He

couldn't dwell on his feelings or otherwise now, he had to find her first.

Pushing open the doors of the redbrick apartment building, he stepped into the foyer. Only to find Woolf, Rutherford, and St. James coming out of an elevator, their faces hard and set.

"Where the fuck is she?" Elijah demanded, tightening his grip on his Colt.

There was a look of pure fury on Woolf's face. "She wasn't there."

"What do you mean 'she wasn't there'?"

Rutherford held out his hand and sitting in the middle of his palm was a tiny wire, fine as silver thread. "The tracking device. They removed it and her phone, and left them for us to find as a decoy."

The ball of ice sitting in the pit of Elijah's stomach began to grow sharp spikes. "Then where the fuck is she?"

Woolf was staring murder at him. "Don't you know? You were the one who was intending to use her as bait for this Jericho cocksucker. Did you give her to him?"

Elijah met the other man's gaze, trying to keep his own anger and gradually deepening fear in check. There was a flame in Woolf's eyes, burning hot.

He wants the same as you. Violet safe.

It seemed too strange to acknowledge that he and this bastard shared a common goal because he wasn't used to sharing. Then again, hadn't he been doing the same with Violet the past couple of days? If he could let her help him, then maybe he and this prick could do the same.

"No, I didn't," he said coldly, resisting the urge to lift his gun and just start shooting. "In fact I wanted to protect her."

Woolf laughed, the look in his eyes feral. "Really? Wonderful fucking job you're doing of it so far."

"Jesus," St. James sighed. "How about we concentrate

on the important stuff instead of comparing dick sizes? Like figuring out where the hell Violet is?"

Rutherford folded his fingers over the bit of silver wire, clenching his hand into a fist. "Where's Eva? I have an idea about how we might be able to track what happened to Violet."

Elijah didn't want to, he really didn't, but his gut instinct was telling him that if he wanted to get to Violet, he was going to have to work with these people. He'd have to keep his rage in check and put his gun away.

Fuck. He'd been on his own too long. This kind of working together shit was foreign to him.

"She's out in the alley across the street." He did it—he put away the Colt, despite the anger that pulled at him, the desperate feeling that every second he stood here was another second lost, another second that might find Violet closer to death.

Like Marie. You waited too long. You were passive too long.

Without another word, he turned toward the doors to the apartment building and went through them, not caring whether the others followed him or not.

No more waiting. No more fucking around.

Katya and Eva were still beside the SUV, looking worried as Elijah strode up to them.

"Where's Violet?" Eva demanded.

"They took the tracking device out and left it there," Elijah snapped. "Rutherford said he had an idea about how you could track her."

Eva's gaze flickered behind him and he heard the footsteps of the other men approach. "Yeah, I know what he means." Then, to Rutherford, "You want me to see if I can hack into a cell phone tower and get a signal?"

"I'm not asking, angel," the clipped English voice behind Elijah said. "I know you can."

A smile flashed over her face, bright as summer lightning. "Give me a couple of minutes. The laptop's in the car."

Elijah turned to face the Brit, while Katya moved over toward St. James, blonde brows drawn down.

Rutherford's gaze was completely expressionless.

"Cell phone towers?" Elijah asked him. "You want to track a cell phone signal?"

"Yes. We might be able to see who was entering or exiting the building around the time the tracking signal stopped there. If we're lucky there'll only be a couple of people, and we can track their signals."

"Then we find them and hopefully find Violet?"

"We'll certainly find whoever put the tracking device there, which'll give us a lead."

The only lead they had. Which meant he was stuck here until Eva managed to work her IT magic. Fucking great.

"Who took her?" St. James asked. His tone was neutral, but Elijah didn't miss the undercurrent of threat.

"How the fuck should I know?" Elijah pushed his fingers into the pockets of his jeans to stop them from reaching for his Colt. "I met with Jericho. Shot him like I meant to. Next minute she was gone."

"Had to be him," Woolf growled, pacing like a caged animal. "Who else could it be?"

"This asshole just shot him," St. James pointed out. "How could it be him?"

But a suspicion that had been slowly turning over in Elijah's brain suddenly solidified into fact. "It wasn't him," he said roughly and with extreme reluctance.

Fuck. How could he have been so stupid? He'd known something wasn't right, but he'd wanted to take that shot at the man who'd been instrumental in his wife's death, had been so desperate that he'd ignored his instincts completely.

Woolf stopped dead, looking at him. "What do you mean 'it wasn't him'?"

Elijah made himself go on. "Jericho wanted Violet, don't ask me why, I don't know and I didn't care. As far as I was concerned, she was bait and if he wanted her, that's all that mattered. But when I got there and I met him . . . something wasn't right. He didn't even look at her. Not even once, and that's not what a man does when he wants a woman."

The other men were silent, but Elijah could feel the force of their combined attention like the pressure of a hand pressing down on him.

"I demanded proof of who he was," Elijah went on, "but he refused. Then he demanded Violet. And I knew if I gave her to him, I'd lose the fucker."

"So what? You shot him anyway?" Woolf's voice was heavy with scorn. "You shot a minion and then Jericho took her all the same."

The big, spiked ball of ice was like razor wire now, cutting into him.

You lost her. You wanted revenge and you lost her.

And it hurt. It just fucking hurt and he didn't understand why. This felt like when he'd lost Marie, a woman he'd loved . . .

Elijah shut down the thought before it had had a chance to take root and grow. Crushed it flat. Killed it. There was no love. Love led to destruction and he would never let it near him again.

"Yes," he said coldly, flatly, staring into the other man's dark eyes. Challenging him. "Which means it's up to me to take her back."

"Fuck that," Woolf spat. "I'm her half brother—"

"And I'm the one who's been dealing with Jericho up till now," he interrupted, his voice harsh. "I may not have met him but I know him and his operation better than any of you. You want Violet to have the best shot at getting out? Then you'd better let me get her."

There was a tense, highly uncomfortable silence.

Woolf was looking at Elijah like he wanted to shoot him right where he stood. Yeah, well, the feeling was fucking mutual.

"He's right, Gabe," Rutherford said unexpectedly. "We don't know Jericho, we don't know his men or the way he operates."

"And this prick does?" Woolf stood there glowering, fury gathering about him like a storm.

Elijah ignored it. "I know better than you. Fitzgerald's been dealing with him for the past six months, like I told you before."

"Yeah, and what the fuck do you know anyway?"

A very good point, not that Elijah would let Woolf know that. Because truth was, he didn't really know. No one did. Because Jericho never dealt with anyone directly—he was famous for it—only operating via a series of go-betweens.

So what the hell did you think was happening in Battery Park? Did you really think he was going to front up?

But he'd had no choice to believe it, had he? He'd wanted to believe . . . because as soon as he'd seen that fucker, he'd seen the finish line. The end to all this rage, this pain, this grief he couldn't get rid of no matter how hard he tried. No matter how deeply he managed to convince himself.

He'd seen the moment he could pull that trigger and it would finally all stop. Marie would be avenged and at last, at last, he could end it. He could rest. Find peace.

But it wasn't the end, was it? Not when they'd taken Violet.

You have to find her. You'll never find peace until you find her.

No, he wouldn't. Because she was his peace.

A part of him fought the realization, the knowledge that

settled down through his bones and into his soul. Fought desperately. But he couldn't deny it, not anymore. In the brief time they'd had together, she'd changed him and changed him irrevocably. Her caring, generous spirit and her courage. The way she touched him like he was precious, even after everything he'd done to her.

He wasn't the same. And though this couldn't be love, not when he'd made so sure that love would never be part of his life again, he needed her. If this was ever to stop, if all of this was ever to end, he needed her.

Elijah met Woolf's dark gaze. Held it. "What do I know? I know that I'll die before I let anything happen to her. And I'll die to protect her if I have to. That good enough for you, motherfucker?"

Surprise flared in the other man's eyes and a long, dense silence stretched out between them.

Then Woolf said, "Yeah, asshole, I guess that'll do."

It was reluctant, but it was something.

The silence was broken by the sound of the door of the SUV slamming as Eva got out, carrying her laptop. "And I think we have a winner." She was grinning. "Anyone feel like visiting Alphabet City?"

"What's in Alphabet City, angel?" Rutherford folded his arms.

Eva came over with the laptop, pushing the screen back a little so everyone could see. "There was only one cell phone signal that entered the building just before the tracking device stopped moving, then exited it just after. And that's this one here."

A map rotated on the screen, the orientation spinning as Eva's fingers moved on the track pad, manipulating then zooming in on the location.

Elijah stared at the map, memorizing it, then finally, he reached for his Colt. "I'm going and I'm going alone." He stared around at the rest of them. "Anyone got any fucking objection?"

Violet felt like the earth had shifted beneath her feet, as if she'd been in a violent earthquake and the landscape that had once been familiar had now changed beyond recognition.

And the ground was still moving.

"No." She said it reflexively, her voice sounding tinny and strange. "That's ridiculous."

The terrible weariness in her brother's eyes lingered for a moment, then his long, gold lashes descended. When they lifted, the weariness was gone, replaced by a gentle understanding that almost broke her heart. "I'm sorry, Peanut. But it's true."

Her mind reeled, unable to process it. Theo was Jericho. A crime lord heavily involved in the sex trafficking business, drugs, and who knew what other crimes.

It just . . . didn't make any sense.

"Why?" she demanded suddenly. "How? Elijah told me that Dad wanted to give me to Jericho, that he was trying to—"

"Yes," Theo interrupted, that gentleness lining his tone as soft as cotton balls, as if she was fragile, breakable, and he was trying to keep her safe. "That's what I meant when I said I've been trying to get you away from him for months. I was going to give him some new trade routes in exchange for you."

Horror unreeled through her at the words 'trade routes.' Like they were talking about actual goods and not human beings. "I didn't need you to get me away." Her voice shook. "And certainly not at the expense of people's lives!"

He didn't protest, just looked at her with terrible sadness. And she understood that part of her had been waiting for him to deny it, to tell her it wasn't true. But he didn't.

"Some things are worth the sacrifice," he said softly, as if that explained everything. "He would never have let you go, Vi. Surely you know that."

Maybe she did. Maybe deep in her soul she'd always known. But her life in exchange for all those women? Those 'trade routes'? No. Never. " 'Trade routes,' Theo? You do know what Dad wanted those routes for?"

He smiled, rueful. Sad. "Of course I know. What do you think I've been doing for the past ten years or so?"

Her throat closed up, grief crushing in her chest. "Why?" She could barely get the words out. "Why would you do such a thing? Why would you involve yourself? That's not the Theo I know."

"That's the thing, Peanut," he said softly, his expression full of dreadful sympathy. "I'm not the Theo you knew. Not anymore."

At that point a man came through the doorway, some big guy in a suit, the coldest expression she'd ever seen on his face. "We need to move, sir," he said, his voice tinged with some kind of European accent Violet couldn't place. "We've already been here too long."

Theo glanced at him and then said something in what sounded like German. The man responded, but Violet couldn't follow what either of them was saying. She'd picked up quite a bit of French while she'd been in Paris, but German not so much.

"What's happening?" she demanded as the man, clearly a henchman of some kind, began to turn away. "I'm not going, you do realize that, don't you?"

Theo was looking down at his phone again. "I'm sorry, Vi, but you don't get a choice."

Violet opened her mouth to tell him exactly what she

thought of that when the front door of the apartment burst open with a crash and all hell broke loose.

The big man in the suit reached for a handgun in his jacket, starting to raise it in the direction of the doorway. But he had no chance to get a shot off before he was suddenly dropping without a sound, a dark red wound in the center of his forehead.

Violet, frozen in shock, stared as Elijah stepped into the room through the remains of the door, his Colt in his hand, lethal fury twisting his scarred face and glittering coldly in his black eyes. He looked immediately in her direction and she saw the fury turn and change, morphing into savage satisfaction. But that Colt of his was moving, his arm coming up, aiming at the tall, golden figure of her brother, who strangely hadn't moved a muscle since Elijah had first kicked the door in.

And Violet knew without a shadow of a doubt that Theo would be next to get a bullet right between the eyes. So she didn't even think. "Stop!" she screamed at Elijah, throwing herself between her brother and the muzzle of that gun. "Don't!"

Surprise flashed briefly over Elijah's face, but he didn't lower the Colt. "Get out of the way, Violet," he ordered.

"No." She was shaking as she met his terrifying gaze, a mass of emotions tangling in her chest, far more than she could ever hope to sort out. Only one thing was clear: she couldn't allow Elijah to kill her brother. "I won't let you hurt him."

Behind her, Theo was silent. As if he was waiting for something.

Elijah's dark brows arrowed down, his gaze sharpening on her. "What are you doing? You were taken and I—"

"I know," she interrupted, trying to make her voice sound steady. "It was Theo, Eli. Theo was the one who took me."

For a second there was only a heavy, dark kind of silence as Elijah stared at her, then focused his gaze on the man she was protecting, his quick mind obviously sorting out the implications of that statement.

"Theodore Fitzgerald." It wasn't a question, his tone devoid of inflection.

"Yes," Theo said levelly. "Good afternoon, Mr. Hunt. I see you've found us."

Something twisted in Elijah's face. Something dark. "You took her." Another non-question.

"Yes," Theo repeated. "I did."

"Eli," she began. "You can't—"

"You're him." The rough edge in Elijah's voice was full of heat and fury. His gaze was no longer sharp and cold, but burning with a kind of black fire that Violet found both utterly terrifying and totally mesmerizing at the same time. "You're fucking Jericho."

How he knew, she had no idea. But he did.

"Elijah," she said.

"Get the fuck out of the way, Violet." Death lurked in each word, in his eyes. Merciless, ruthless. Because this was what he'd come here to do. What he'd been trying to do for the past seven years. Claim his revenge.

"No." She stayed exactly where she was, staring at the man she'd fallen in love with so quickly and so very hard. "He's my brother."

"He's a monster." Elijah didn't look at her, his gaze firmly on the man at her back. "He helped your father murder my wife."

She wanted to turn around, see Theo's face, demand to know whether this was true or not. But she didn't.

You don't want to know.

Grief choked her. Theo was all she had of her family. The only one who'd ever been there for her, the only one who'd ever loved her. She couldn't let him die, she just couldn't.

What if Elijah's right? What if he's a monster like your father was?

"I . . . I can't let you kill him." Her voice was hoarse, unsteady. "He's all I've got."

Elijah's gaze shifted, focused on her. And something intense gathered in his expression. "No, he's not. You have me."

Her breath caught and for a second it felt like the ground hadn't finished moving under her feet after all, was in fact still shifting, rearranging the landscape once again. Theo didn't say anything, though behind her she could sense his attention sharpening.

"You?" she croaked. "What do you mean?"

There was movement behind her, the sound of her brother taking a step closer. "You want her?" Theo made it sound like a casual question. "It'll be over my dead body."

Elijah's smile was frightening as he pointed the Colt. "That's the general idea."

"No." She moved more fully in front of Theo. "Please, Elijah. Don't do this."

But Elijah wasn't looking at her now, his gaze wholly on her brother, and there was such hate in his eyes. Such fury. It made her heart twist in anguish for him. "Two years she was in that fucking Russian brothel," he said in a cold, dead voice. "That's what your cocksucker of a father told me. He also told me that you were the one who sold her there. You made the deal. And you were the one who let her die after a client slit her throat."

Tears blurred in Violet's eyes. His wife. He was talking about his wife. The woman he'd failed to protect and had been taking the blame for ever since. And she waited again for Theo to say no, to tell Elijah he had nothing to do with it. But again, he was silent.

"Now's the time to pay, you fucker," Elijah went on, toneless. "Now's the time you go down."

It would be easy to step aside. To let this man take the revenge that, surely, he was owed. Yet she wasn't going to.

She had no altruistic reasons. No lofty motivations. She didn't have a wronged past and she had no one to avenge. She only loved her brother and didn't want him to die, no matter what he'd done, no matter the murders or rapes or any other evil he'd committed. Because he was the only family she had left and she couldn't bear to be alone.

You have me.

But, no, she didn't have him. She could never have him. Elijah may have been a killer, but there was a nobility to him that she'd never had. He was doing this out of love, out of love for his wife. Because he'd been a victim. He'd been manipulated and used, and so had Marie.

But Violet hadn't. All she'd had was a shitty family life. She hadn't been tortured or murdered or raped, and neither had she known anyone who had. There was no nobility in her, there never had been. She was a pampered Manhattan princess enacting a petty rebellion against her family because they never paid her any attention. She had no excuse, she hadn't been anyone's victim. She'd only wanted to feel connected to someone. Only wanted to feel not so alone.

But maybe there was a reason she was. Maybe the monster that had lived in her father, that now lived in his son, lived in her too. The dark hunger, the need. The hole in her soul.

Elijah had told her there was nothing wrong with her, and she'd wanted to believe it. But in so many ways, it was easier not to. In so many ways, it was safer to accept what she knew deep down inside.

There was no hope for her.

Because surely only a monster let another monster live for their own selfish reasons.

"No," she said thickly, again. "I'm sorry, Eli. I can't let you. If you want to kill Theo, you'll have to kill me first."

Elijah stared into Violet's blue-green eyes, searching for any kind of understanding. But there was none. There was only pain and the kind of determination that he'd recognized in her so many times before. She meant this. There would be no moving her.

Getting into the room where Violet was had been easy. He'd decided against going in the front, since it was likely the roof would be less heavily guarded, a hunch that had paid off. There had been an easy route from the roof of the building next door and the door that had led down into the apartment block's stairwell had had a paltry lock that had given the moment Elijah kicked it.

There had been no one watching the roof or the stairwell. Clearly Jericho was not expecting visitors.

Eva had tracked the phone to a particular apartment, and Elijah had managed to get rid of the four guards who had been watching that floor without too many problems. He'd checked the bodies for ID but hadn't managed to find anything. All of which just added to his suspicions that Jericho had indeed taken Violet.

He'd debated briefly the merits of kicking the door in and then had decided to hell with it, he wanted Violet and that was the most direct route. So he had, shooting what must have been the owner of the phone he'd been tracking before the guy had even managed to get a shot off.

Then he'd had eyes for nothing but Violet, because there she was, standing in the middle of the dingy apartment, her face white, but alive. And the relief had nearly brought him to his knees.

He hadn't failed her. Which meant he could save her.

Then he'd realized she wasn't alone.

Now, the dead man who was apparently Theo Fitzgerald

was staring back at him, looking like he'd just stepped out of the pages of *GQ* and so fucking smug, Elijah wanted to pull that trigger and Violet be damned.

He could. In fact, she didn't even need to die. He could just reach out and take her, pull her away and shoot the prick.

But clearly the asshole had had the same thought, because he reached out and put a possessive hand on Violet's shoulder, pulling her back. Holding her. "I wouldn't," he said calmly. "She meant what she said."

Violet's expression didn't change, no matter that her brother seemed to be using her to protect himself.

"Hiding behind your sister, prick?" Elijah didn't lower the Colt. He wanted to shoot so badly it was all he could do not to pull that trigger. "I guess that's what Jericho does best after all. He hides and lets other people do his dirty work for him."

Jericho's expression didn't alter, remaining calm. "You should never have involved yourself, Mr. Hunt. You should have given her to me and let me keep her safe."

"What, with you? Safe like Marie was safe? I don't fucking think so."

There was no flicker in that green-gold gaze. No hint of remorse or guilt or even sympathy. There was nothing at all. "Be happy with your trade concessions. That's all you're going to get."

"I don't want your fucking trade concessions," Elijah spat. "I never did. All I wanted was your father's head. And then someone took that, which means I'll have to settle for yours."

At last, a flicker of what looked like regret passed over Jericho's golden-boy features. "I suppose I should have seen this. Nevermind, can't be helped now. You won't shoot me, Mr. Hunt. Not if you want Violet to live."

"You happy with this?" He looked at Violet, staring into

her eyes, wanting to see that sympathy he knew was there, that understanding. But there was nothing but pain and that fucking awful determination. "Your brother using you to protect himself?"

An emotion shifted and changed in her eyes, more hurt. "Like you never did the same thing."

And he felt that, the barbs on the words catching at him, tearing at him. Because of course it was true. He had used her. All this time, that's exactly what he'd been doing.

"Violet," he said, unable to keep the desperate sound out of his voice. "Princess . . . I need this. Let me have it."

But her expression shuttered. "No. You're not killing him, Elijah."

"You want me to hurt you? Is that what you want?"

"But you won't hurt me." A bright spark of agony glowed in her eyes, suddenly sharp. "That's the thing Eli. I know you'd never hurt me, because I know you're a good man, a just man. And I'm . . ." She stopped, that little spark glowing brighter. "You told me once that all of us are monsters deep down, even me."

Oh, fuck. No. "Violet, you're not—"

"I'm a Fitzgerald, Eli. And us monsters have to stick together."

"Bullshit," he said, hard and certain and sure, not wanting those words lingering in the air, not even an echo. Because they were wrong, so wrong. "You're not a fucking monster. If anyone's the monster here it's that asshole standing behind you. And me. I'm the one you should be pointing the finger at."

"Okay," Jericho said unexpectedly. "I think I've had about enough of this." And with a smooth movement, he stepped around Violet and pushed her behind him.

Giving Elijah an unimpeded target.

"Theo, no!" She pulled at his arm, but he ignored her, keeping her behind him.

To anyone else there was a bored look in those green-gold eyes, yet Elijah knew it wasn't. He saw deeper than that. Because he knew men like this, had worked with them many times over the course of the years with Fitzgerald. It wasn't boredom. It was emptiness.

The look of a man who'd sold his soul to the devil.

Whoever Theo Fitzgerald once was, he wasn't this man standing in front of him. Like Kane Archer, Theo Fitzgerald was dead.

"If you're going to fucking shoot me, you'd better shoot me." Jericho's gaze was level and there was no fear in it. He looked like he'd stared death in the face one too many times and had come to terms with the fact that there was nothing to be afraid of.

Perhaps he even welcomes it.

No, he didn't want to acknowledge this bastard, he really didn't.

"My pleasure, asshole." Elijah lifted the gun. "This one's for Marie."

And then he made a mistake. He glanced at Violet, standing behind her brother, and saw the tears streaming down her face. She didn't make a sound.

She was his peace, but he wasn't hers. He only caused her sorrow. Pain. He only hurt her. And if he shot Jericho, he'd keep on hurting her. Her brother's death would be a wound that wouldn't heal, and he knew all about those kinds of wounds.

He'd promised he wouldn't hurt her again.

What about Marie? What about that promise? Didn't you want peace?

And his heart cracked, a great jagged line going right down the middle of it. Because he knew there would be no peace for him, no matter what he did. Killing Jericho would lay Marie to rest, but it would shatter Violet. Letting him live would spare Violet, but he'd have to live with his wife's death forever.

He stared at Violet, at her vivid eyes, her wet cheeks, and her soft, lush mouth. Bright and beautiful and alive. Hurting so much already. And he knew there was no choice to make.

Marie was dead and had been for a very long time. He couldn't save her. But he could give Violet this. Heal a little bit of her pain. It would only be fair after everything she'd given him.

Slowly, Elijah lowered the Colt. He looked at Violet one last time, memorizing everything about her so he could keep at least the memory of her to last him.

Then he turned and walked out the door.

CHAPTER NINETEEN

Violet wiped futilely at the tears, scrubbing them all away with vicious swipes of her hand.

She shouldn't be crying, not now she'd made her choice and picked a side. And it was the right choice, she knew that in her heart. Pity her heart kept insisting it was broken and shouldn't be making any sort of choices right now.

Theo was speaking on his phone to someone, his voice completely calm as if he hadn't just faced down a man intent on putting a bullet in his brain. He was again speaking in German and it sounded as if he was issuing instructions.

Violet tried to pull herself together, tried to ignore the way her chest felt like it was full of broken glass. Elijah was gone and she'd understood the moment he'd given her that final look, as he'd lowered his Colt, that she wouldn't see him again.

There had been such pain in his eyes. He'd looked at her as if he was a man standing on a desert island watching his last chance of rescue disappear over the horizon.

You have me, he'd said. The closest a man like him would ever come to laying out his heart.

And yet in the end, it hadn't been her who'd left.

She wrapped her arms around herself, shivering. Even now there was a part of her that wanted to go after him, throw herself at his feet and tell him that yes, she had him. And he had her. That he didn't have to hurt again. Pity she was such a fucking coward.

I need this, princess. . . . Let me have it.

But he hadn't taken it. Why not? What had stopped him?

"A car will be waiting by the curb when you get downstairs," Theo was talking to her, his deep, smooth voice so achingly familiar, and she had to struggle to pay attention. "It'll take you to Teterboro, where I have a jet waiting."

Ah yes, that's right, he wanted her out of the country. Ostensibly to keep her safe.

She lifted her chin, studying his handsome face, noting the tightness in his jaw and the lines around his mouth. Marks of grief and pain. There were shadows in his eyes, too. Shadows that she hadn't seen before.

You were the one who made the deal. And you were the one who let her die when a client slit her throat . . .

Had he really been the one who'd let Elijah's wife die? Who'd sold her to a brothel? Who operated behind a cloud of secrecy, the power pulling the strings on a vast, shadowy human trafficking ring?

"How could he not know?" She wasn't sure she'd said the words aloud until she heard them echo in the silence of the apartment.

Theo glanced at her. "Who?"

"Dad. How could he not know it was you?"

"Because I made sure he wouldn't." He'd put his phone away, reaching for an expensive-looking overcoat that was slung over the back of the threadbare couch.

"Why not? Why are you doing this?"

He put on the overcoat, shaking his head. "You need to leave now."

"Answer me!" She took a couple of steps toward him.

"I spent years looking for you, Theo. Do you know that? I was convinced you hadn't died, I was positive. Shit, searching for you has driven me for years and now here you are, and you won't even answer a few of my questions?"

There was no anger in his eyes, only a regret that tore at what remained of her heart. "No, Peanut, I won't. Because I don't have the answers for you, at least not the ones you want to hear. Now come on, it's time to go."

"Tell me!"

He only shook his head and the look on his face was like a parent with a demanding child. Patient yet firm. Laying down the law. "I can't. This is not your fight, Violet, it's mine." Turning, he went over to the kicked-in door and stood there, his arm out in a strangely old-fashioned gesture. "After you."

She remembered him like this. Her pushing him to play with her or talk to her back when they'd been children, and him always so patient, refusing to be pushed. He'd never gotten angry either, no matter the tantrums she'd thrown and the tears she'd cried. She'd been like the wind, battering at him, while he'd been a rock, standing firm. Completely unaffected.

No wonder you liked what you did to Elijah. You affected him.

But there was no point thinking of Elijah. Just like there was no point pushing Theo. She'd get nothing out of him, not if he didn't want to talk.

So she closed her mouth and shut up. Went over to the door.

Theo looked down at her, and she thought for a minute he was going to give her a hug, but he didn't. And there was something radiating off him, a kind of warning that suggested hugging him would be unwelcome. So she kept her arms wrapped tightly around her middle, trying to ignore the cold stealing through her.

"Once you get to Paris, lay low for a while," he said quietly. "You'll have everything you need there for a few weeks. I'll let you know when it's safe to return." He paused, his gaze roving over her, the look on his face impossible to read. "Good-bye, Violet."

She must have said good-bye too but she couldn't remember exactly as she'd walked down from the apartment to the foyer in a daze.

There was a car at the sidewalk, like he'd promised, and a man waiting next to it, ready to drive her away.

She got into the backseat without a word and the driver started the car, pulling out into the traffic.

Soon she'd be away from here, flying back to France. Away from the heartache that was her life, the reality of her world crashing down around her ears. If she closed her eyes, she could even pretend that none of the past week had happened. That she was still the daughter of a wealthy New York businessman, still puzzled by her brother's disappearance, still dressing to annoy her mother, still living off her trust fund, and still flitting from place to place, thing to thing, never settling on anything.

Still Violet Fitzgerald.

But no, she wasn't that Violet anymore, was she? She'd been changed. Irrevocably. By a man with black eyes and a scarred face. Who'd not only pulled her out of the stupid little box she'd been living in, but destroyed the box completely. He'd stripped her of her façades and forced her to confront who she really was inside, the person she was when all the layers had been ripped away. A selfish woman, like her father had been selfish. Thinking only of herself and her own loneliness.

Violet watched the traffic and the buildings sliding past outside the car window, her chest sore and her eyes gritty, like they had sand in them. And she couldn't get out of her head the sight of Elijah's face. The sharp pain in his obsidian eyes that cut her like razors. But she'd chosen her side, she'd chosen her brother.

You have me.

Elijah's voice echoed in her memory. She couldn't get that out of her head either, couldn't stop herself from wondering that if she had him, who did he have? But then, she knew the answer to that. He had no one.

Tears filled her eyes, the scene outside the car window blurring. How long had he been alone? Seven years. And what would he do now? He'd let Theo live, had given up his revenge, and now he was faced with the task of cleaning up the mess her father had made by himself. And all because of her.

He'd given up everything he'd been working toward for so long, for her.

And she'd taken it away from him.

The tears slid down her cheeks and a sudden wave of fury gripped her, so tight she could hardly breathe. Because here she was, sitting passively in this car, letting herself be taken away by yet another man. Letting herself be used the way they'd all used her at one point or another. A pawn of her father, of Elijah, and now of Theo.

And you're still a pawn. You think that move back there was you choosing a side? That wasn't a choice. That was reflex.

She swallowed. Fuck, she was so sick of this. Sick of being taken. Sick of being rescued.

Perhaps it was time she did some rescuing of her own. But not herself, because quite frankly, she didn't deserve it. Didn't need it. But there was another person who did. Who had no one to save him. No one but her.

It didn't matter what he'd meant when he'd told her that she had him. What mattered was that he needed to know that he had her. And if he didn't want her, then she'd just have to live with that.

The car slowed as it approached an intersection, then came to a stop for a red light.

Violet waited a moment.

Then she pulled open the door very, very quietly and slipped out.

Elijah stood in the middle of Gabriel Woolf's downtown office, his arms folded, not making any move to break the silence that filled the room. A silence so thick you could have cut it with a knife.

Before he'd gone to get Violet, he'd agreed with the others that they'd meet back at Gabriel's office on the fiftieth floor of the Woolf Construction building. He hadn't wanted to. What he'd wanted was to take her back to his own apartment and keep her there, possibly forever, but naturally enough Woolf and his friends wouldn't have been happy with that arrangement.

They were even less happy about it now that he hadn't actually gotten Violet at all.

Behind him huge windows gave a magnificent view out over Manhattan, the sun glittering off glass and steel, the concrete jungle in all its glory. But he didn't turn around to see it. He didn't give a shit about views. Not when all he could see were the tears sliding down Violet's cheeks. Not when he knew that walking away had been one of the best things he'd ever done. And one of the hardest.

"You bastard," Woolf said furiously at last. "I can't believe you left her with him."

"You expected me to drag her kicking and screaming from the building?" He met the other man's gaze head-on. "She was free to make a choice and she made it."

Pity it wasn't the one he wanted.

"You didn't seem to find that a problem last week." Woolf's voice was a growl.

Fuck, they wouldn't understand and he wasn't going to

explain it to them. He could barely explain it to himself. Giving up the work of nearly a decade for one lovely woman's tears.

Giving up the one chance he had—because he knew there'd never be another—to avenge Marie's death. And all because he couldn't stand to hurt Violet.

He was a fucking liability, that's what he was. Soft and weak and vulnerable. His ex-boss would have laughed himself sick if he'd known what his hard-as-nails henchman had fallen to.

Anguish stirred inside him, and a despair he'd been trying to keep at bay the whole time he'd made his way from the broken-down apartment building in Alphabet City to Woolf's office. But like blood in the water, it crept out, staining everything.

He wouldn't see her again. And not because that was actually what he wanted, but because she'd made her choice and he had to respect that.

Us monsters have to stick together.

Why she thought she was a monster he had no idea, because a woman less likely to be one he'd yet to meet. Nevertheless, that didn't change the fact that she hadn't chosen him. Not unsurprising, given all he'd done to her and yet it still hurt, a subtle pain that worked its way inside him, like a splinter heading straight for his heart.

But, shit, he had to ignore that. He had things to do. An empire to take over and bring down. Yes, it would be that much harder with Jericho still alive, but he'd do it anyway. At least he'd try.

After all, it wasn't as if he had better things to do.

"Yeah, well, I changed my mind." He stared at Woolf, his fingers suddenly itching to do violence. "I already took her choices from her once before, I'm not doing it again."

"So you thought leaving her with her fucking monster brother was a better idea?"

"He wouldn't hurt her."

"And how the fuck would you know that?"

The rest of them were staring at him, accusation in their eyes. And he couldn't blame them. He'd walked out and left Violet with one of Europe's most secretive and notorious crime bosses. Who also happened to be the brother who'd supposedly died sixteen years earlier.

And the brother who'd been trying to rescue her all this time. Because it was all so clear now, why Jericho had wanted her so badly. He'd been trying to get her free of her father the only way he could. So no, he wouldn't hurt her.

"He won't," Elijah said. "Jericho spent a long time trying to get her free. He wouldn't do all of that just to get rid of her now." He paused, looking at all of them in turn. "He's her brother, you do understand that don't you?"

Woolf cursed under his breath and flicked a glance at Honor, who'd been waiting in his office with the rest of them when Elijah had finally gotten back.

"Yeah, I didn't see that coming," St. James muttered.

"None of us did." Rutherford was leaning against Woolf's desk with his arms folded. "You didn't ever find anything about him, did you, angel?"

Eva sat next to him on the edge of the desk, her legs swinging. "Nope. Nothing at all. It's like he doesn't exist. Jericho I mean, not Theo."

Katya was by the door, frowning at Elijah. "You said his father never knew he was dealing with his own son?"

"He didn't." Of that Elijah was positive. Fitzgerald had had no inkling and in fact had spent a good many resources trying to find out who Jericho was, since the man had hated mysteries. Which in many ways made it odd that he'd accepted Theo's disappearance without any argument, especially when a body hadn't turned up. "He tried to find out but came up against the same dead ends. Jericho didn't want to be found and so he wasn't."

"Except we found him," Woolf murmured. "We know who he is."

Katya shifted. "We need to be careful. If he's kept his identity secret for that long, he's not going to be pleased that we know."

"Good point." Rutherford glanced at the small woman on the desk beside him. "I think perhaps a leave of absence might be a prudent thing."

"What? You mean run away?" Eva scowled, obviously annoyed with the idea.

"Jericho is a bigger fish than Fitzgerald ever was, angel," Rutherford said quietly. "He's got more resources and his empire, from what we can see, is . . . massive. I don't want you in harm's way if he decides to make sure his identity stays secret."

"But Theo wouldn't . . ." Honor stopped. Her face was pale, worry clear in her eyes. "I mean I know him. At least I used to."

"Forget what you know," Elijah said curtly. "Whoever he once was, he isn't now. Not after years spent building that kind of empire." And he knew, better than anyone, how true that was.

Woolf had put his arm around Honor's waist. "Zac's not wrong, baby. I'm thinking you might be better off out of New York too."

She shook her head. "I can't. I've taken a lot of time off work as it is and I don't have the staff to take the load like you all do."

"I'm not talking outer space here," Woolf said. "The lodge in Colorado has internet, you know that. You can work from there. Shit, that's what I do."

"Alexei," Katya's voice was quiet. "Perhaps you should—"

"Do you think you could wait till we're in private before you undermine my masculinity, Katya mine?"

St. James didn't sound at all offended, only amused, his mouth curving in a private kind of smile. "Anyway, I don't need to go anywhere. Not when I have my own personal ninja to protect me."

There were lots of undercurrents in the room that Elijah found difficult to follow. The emotions that ran between all these people were deep with warmth and there was a tenderness in the way they looked at one another that, strangely, made him feel angry. Made him feel as if he was missing something.

Fuck, he had to get out of here, away from all this cloying emotional bullshit.

"Protect yourselves how you can," he said coldly. "Are we done here?"

"Seriously?" St. James's blue eyes had narrowed. "You just land this information on us and then fuck off? What about Violet? What about Jericho?"

"What about them? Violet is safe and Jericho is probably halfway back to Europe by now."

"So you're just letting him go?" Woolf was looking at him now. "After all that shit about revenge and taking him down, you're letting him get away?"

"Yes." He didn't bother to explain himself. The other man wouldn't understand. "I have work I need to do here."

"What work?" This from Honor.

"Fitzgerald left one hell of a power vacuum and someone's got to fill it." He looked at them each in turn. "That someone's is going to be me."

There was a silence.

Eva gaze was full of silver sparks. "If you're going to take over that pile of shit, then perhaps we'll just shoot you right now and save ourselves a whole lot of bother."

"I don't want his fucking empire." Elijah held her gaze. "I want to take it down. Hell, I started the process of dismantling it years ago. It just needs a couple more years before it goes down completely."

"Why not let the police do it?" Katya asked.

"Because half the fucking police were in Fitzgerald's pocket. They want to keep it going for their own ends, make no mistake. No, it's got to be done from the inside, which means it's got to be me."

Another silence.

But they all agreed, he could see it in their eyes.

"What about Jericho then?" Eva said. "We're just going to let him go? Run away like a bunch of scared kids?"

"I didn't say we were going to let him go, angel." Rutherford unfolded his arms, reaching down to put a hand on her knee. "What I meant was that we should lay low while we work on a plan to take him down."

Something twisted in Elijah's chest, the memory of Violet's tearstained face.

He's my brother.

"Fuck, yes," Woolf said roughly. "We can't let him get away with this shit."

Once, Elijah would have agreed. But not now. He wanted no part of it, not when any move against Jericho was a move against Violet.

He turned to the door without a word. He had to get out of here, he had stuff to do.

"Elijah." Woolf's voice.

He stopped, didn't turn around.

"Are you with us?"

It was a gesture, he understood. An olive branch of sorts. An invitation to be part of the plan, to join with them at least for a little while.

But while he appreciated the sentiment, he wasn't going to. He'd been on his own path for almost a decade and it was better that he walked it alone. That's how he worked best after all.

"No," he said flatly. "I left Jericho alive for Violet. If you want to take him down, that's your business." He moved to the door and pulled it open.

"And Fitzgerald's empire?" Rutherford this time. "You might need help."

"I won't."

He stepped through the door and pulled it shut after him.

CHAPTER TWENTY

Violet had no money and no phone, so she walked, trying to keep her head down in case any of her brother's minions were out and about.

She'd timed her escape from the car just about perfectly, the lights changing to green as she'd gotten out which had meant the driver had been unable to chase her without abandoning his car in the middle of the street and causing a big traffic jam.

She'd run hard and fast after that, sticking to crowded places with lots of people at first, then dodging down alleyways. She'd gotten lost a couple of times, riding the subway a lot had meant she'd never really gotten a clear picture of how the streets of Manhattan connected in her head.

But even lost, she'd pressed on. Walking and walking and trusting that eventually she'd figure out where she was.

It was strange to realize that she was finally free. That for the first time in a week or so, she wasn't anyone's captive. Shit, she could go anywhere: back to her own apartment or to Honor's. It would have been the intelligent thing to do, after all. Go get a change of clothes, some money, a phone.

Yet somehow all of those things seemed unimportant.

There was only one thing that mattered and that was

finding Elijah. Making sure he was okay. Letting him know that she was there for him. Whatever happened after that felt kind of insignificant.

It shouldn't have taken her that long to get from Alphabet City to the West Village, but what with her getting lost and trying to keep a low profile, it felt like a long time before she finally started to recognize some of the streets.

By then the sun had started to go down as the afternoon shambled on into evening. It had gotten cold too, clouds rolling in and the temperature plunging. It would probably snow again, which was just great timing considering all she wore was a sweater and jeans.

The long shadows of evening had well and truly closed in by the time she eventually approached the hulking brick edifice of Elijah's apartment building. She went up the stairs, shivering as the wind began to pick up, realizing as she came to the securely locked door that she had no idea how to get in.

There was a buzzer off to the side, so she pressed it then waited. But nothing happened. She tried a couple more times with the same result. Okay, so crap. He wasn't there. Which meant she either had to wait here for him or find somewhere else to go.

She turned around, scanned the street up and down a couple of times, some part of her hoping that he'd magically turn up right about now. But the street was empty, no sign of him.

Well, she could go home or go to Honor's, it wasn't like anything was forcing her to stay here and wait for him.

Yet she didn't move. Because she didn't want to leave. She wanted to stay here, wait for him, be there for him when he came home, whenever he came home. And whether that took a couple of hours or whether that took all night, she knew that's what she was going to do.

You're crazy. You might freeze to death out here.

Well, yeah, she might. But how else was she going to find him?

She let out a small breath and sat down on the icy stone steps, wrapping her arms around herself. And prepared to wait.

The sound of footsteps brought her to consciousness, making her aware suddenly that she was cold, so cold it felt as if she was encased in solid ice. She opened her eyes, unable to remember when she'd closed them.

It was fully dark, the cold, clear light of the street lamps shining on sidewalks sprinkled with a dusting of fresh snow. A black shadow of a man stood on the steps in front of her, looming like a mountain.

The cold must have somehow frozen her solid because she couldn't move and she couldn't speak. She could only stare up at the shadow, her heart beating furiously as his features began to come clear.

Black eyes. A twisted, scarred mouth. Blunt, brutally handsome features.

Elijah.

Relief burst like fireworks, surging through her blood, making her feel weak and trembly and pathetically like crying.

He didn't say anything as he looked down at her, and she couldn't have said what was going on in his head. His expression was absolutely opaque.

Then abruptly he bent down and scooped her up in his arms, his warmth, after so long sitting in the cold, almost making her gasp aloud. His hold was gentle and she allowed herself to rest against his chest, looking up at him as he unlocked the door and got them both inside, heading toward the elevator.

He stayed silent as the elevator came and they went up. And she felt no need to say anything quite yet, content just to rest against him and absorb the heat of his body, letting the familiar scent of him surround her. She had no idea what he would say when he got her into his apartment, but of one thing she was clear. She wasn't going to leave. She wasn't going to leave him ever again.

He got her into the apartment a minute or two later, kicking the door shut behind them, and she thought he might carry her over to the couch and put her on it, but he didn't. He set her back on her feet the moment the door closed, then he leaned back against it, folding his arms.

The look in his eyes was the one she knew so well, cold, hard, sharp. Glittering with all that icy anger he carried around inside him. "What the fuck are you doing here, Violet? I thought you and your monster brother were sticking together?"

She swallowed, her throat suddenly thick because she'd known she'd hurt him back there in that apartment. She just hadn't realized quite how badly till now. "Well, I thought so too. And then I thought that perhaps I'd made the wrong choice."

He stared, his dark eyes roaming over her, giving her back nothing at all. "Why? You think I'm any less of a monster? I've spent seven years in hell, princess. I'm not coming out clean."

She still felt cold, the feeling settling down deep into her bones, even though the apartment's heat had obviously been on. But she ignored the sensation. She didn't matter, not right in this moment. Only he did. "I know that," she said clearly. "And I don't care what you've done or where you've been. I'm not here because you're less of a monster than Theo. I'm here because you don't have anyone who's there for you but me. You need me, Elijah. So that's why I'm here."

He watched her, his gaze completely cold. "But I don't need you, Violet. Not anymore."

It might have hurt if she hadn't realized then that his

whole body was taut, a leashed and furious energy radiating from him, like the wash of a stormy ocean contained behind a high seawall.

She knew what that energy was: the force of his emotions, the press of them, and he was trying to hold them back the way he always did, encasing them in ice. Imposing on them his usual savage control. And he wouldn't break—he'd been containing them too long to let them crack now.

But she knew how to handle this. He was a wild creature. A beast. And the only way to tame a beast like him was to lay her heart out on her sleeve and feed it to him.

"That's a shame," she said hoarsely. "Because I need you."

"No, you don't." There was a strange kind of tension in his voice. "You have your brother. You have your friends. You don't need me."

"But I do. My brother is . . ." She blinked back the sudden prickle of tears. "I don't know what he is. A monster, sure. And yes, I have my friends, but . . . they don't give me what you give me."

His mouth twisted. "I give you fucking nothing but pain."

That he meant it was obvious. It broke her heart. "No," she said forcefully. "You don't."

"I kidnapped you, shot at you. Fucked you up against a goddamn wall." He'd pushed himself away from the door now, his hands dropping in fists to his sides, the tension pulling tight. "You slit your wrists to get away from me and then, when you needed me to protect you, I wasn't there!" His voice had risen, echoing in the vaulted space of the apartment. "I was going to kill your fucking brother, but I didn't. And you know why? Because I couldn't bear to cause you any more pain, Violet. I just . . . couldn't fucking bear to see it." His chest heaved and for a second she saw the anguish in those midnight eyes. The same anguish she'd glimpsed back when he'd held that gun to her brother's chest. "That's all I give you, princess. That's all I ever give anyone. So I repeat. Why the *fuck* are you here?"

She couldn't stand still any longer. Couldn't hold herself back. She walked over to where he stood, coming up so close. Not touching him, but getting into his space so he knew she wasn't going to be backing down.

"You destroyed my world," she said fiercely. "But I'm glad you did. Because my world was a fucking lie. My whole life was a fucking lie! And yes, that hurts, but it wasn't you who lied to me, who pretended to be something they weren't. It wasn't you who faked their own death and let me believe it. You never lied to me, Elijah. You always told me the truth. And sometimes the truth hurts but I'd take that any day over a lie." Her breathing was fast and hard, and she didn't look away. Holding his gaze so he could see that she was telling the truth too. "I've been wearing a blindfold all this time and you ripped it away. You made me see myself. You made me see that I'm stronger than I ever thought possible." She wanted to touch him, but she didn't. She had to lay her heart out for him and see if he would bite. "I'm flawed, Elijah. There's something bad in me, something hungry. And I wanted my brother to live, despite knowing what he's done, because that bad thing in me doesn't want to be alone. Because he's all I have. And I was so stupid not to listen to you when you told me that I had you. So fucking stupid." She let the emotion thicken in her voice, didn't hold it back. "I chose the wrong person. I should have chosen you. So that's the truth of why I'm here. I want to choose again. I want to choose you."

His face was set, iron in every line. He was a man constructed entirely from hard materials, iron and granite and jet. A man of stone and metal. "Why?" A metallic, cold sound.

Violet didn't blink. Not once. "Because I'm in love you, that's why."

No one had said that to him for a very long time. Not since Marie, the night before she'd disappeared, whispered with tenderness in his ear after they'd made love and before she'd gone to sleep. And he'd said it back, carelessly, holding her in the night. Never dreaming that would be the last time he'd do any of those things. Make love. Hold a woman. Tell a woman he loved her.

Now another woman was saying those words, looking up at him, turquoise eyes vivid in her small, pale face. Telling him she needed him. Telling him she loved him.

And he could feel that somehow those words were changing him, reaching inside him and rearranging him, creating a different kind of landscape from anything that had gone before.

He didn't know what to do or how to respond. He wanted to tell her she was wrong, that she couldn't love him because he wasn't any longer the kind of man a woman fell in love with. But he couldn't seem to get the words out. He didn't have the language, not anymore.

She loved him. How did that work? After everything he'd done? After all the pain he'd put her through. He didn't understand.

But you want it.

No, he didn't.

Yes, you do.

She didn't touch him, only looked at him, not pushing. Waiting. The next move was his and he knew it.

He'd left Woolf's office and spent the afternoon visiting various contacts, letting them know, some subtly and others not so subtly, that he was now in charge. Letting them know who the big boss now was. Getting them to spread the word.

It would take time and no doubt there would come some protests, but he'd started the process of taking over Fitzgerald's empire. Soon it would be his. And once it was, he could destroy it.

He'd taken what satisfaction he could from that as he'd come back to his apartment, as he'd walked up the steps and seen the small shape of a woman curled up beside his front door. And for the first time in years he'd been genuinely shocked.

And then he'd gotten angry. So fucking angry.

How dare she come back here. How dare she wait for him. After he'd come to terms with the fact that he would never see her again, how dare she come here and screw everything up.

He should have left her there or put her in a taxi and sent her away. But he'd found himself bending to pick her up, everything in him wanting to hold her again, feel her warm body next to his for the last time. She'd been so cold he couldn't leave her there.

A mistake. Because now she was here, telling him what he'd done for her. Telling him she loved him. Making him want everything she said to be true so badly he could barely breathe.

A tear slid slowly from the corner of her eye, down over the sweet, soft curve of her cheek. "Say something," she said in a hoarse voice. "Don't keep me in suspense, Eli. If you want me to go, I'll go, but please . . . just say something."

But it had been too long since he'd felt anything at all for him to be able to talk about it, and he'd lost the hang of it anyway.

He didn't know what to say but his heart knew what it wanted.

Elijah lifted his hands and took her face between them. And covered her mouth with his own.

He could feel her gasp, taste it on his tongue, along with the flavor that was all Violet. Sweetness like honey with a faint tart edge. It made him dizzy and at the same time soothed something deep in his soul.

He kissed her deeper, harder, letting his hands stroke down the side of her neck, to her shoulders. Then further down over the elegant bow of her spine to the curves of her ass, sliding his palms over her and easing her against him.

She was shaking, her hands pushing against his chest.

He should say something. He really needed to.

He let his mouth trace the line of her jaw, kissing down her neck to the soft hollow of her throat. And he lifted his lips a fraction, inhaling her soft, musky feminine scent. "You're my peace, princess." His voice was raw and ragged, and he should probably have said more than that, but he couldn't. Those were the only words left to him. "You're my peace."

She went still in his arms. "Oh, Eli . . ." His name on a long breath.

And the tension went out of him suddenly, as if a weight that had been pulling him down had been cut. And he put his arms tightly around her, holding her as a weird feeling of lightness swept through him. It was strange, alien, and he had to turn his face into her throat, opening his mouth and nipping at her, desperate for something to ground him.

Violet shuddered as his teeth closed on the delicate tendons of her neck, and he felt her palms press flat to his chest.

Hunger filled him at the pressure of her hands and the taste of her skin on his tongue. A biting, clawing need that he accepted without question. And there were more words he wanted to say after all.

"You're right, I do need you," he whispered, like a vow. "And that's why I'm never letting you go. Never ever."

Then he picked her up in his arms and carried her through the doorway into the hall and down to his bedroom. Setting her onto the bed he'd once shared with the woman he'd loved most in the world.

She was gone now, nothing was going to bring her back. And he'd thought that once Jericho was dead he'd finally be able to let her go. But it wasn't revenge that'd helped him do that.

It was Violet.

Carefully he took off her clothes, a slow unveiling of her perfect golden skin and soft curves, and he wanted to let her do the same to him, but by then he was too desperate. Instead he tore off his own clothes and pushed her back onto the bed, pausing only to find the condom box he'd stashed in the nightstand and grabbing one for protection. Then he was easing into her, sheathing himself in her tight, wet heat, feeling her legs close around his waist and her arms around his neck. Surrounding him.

And he closed his eyes, resting for a moment.

Because he was home.

EPILOGUE

Elijah got the call just as Violet arrived back at the apartment. She'd been out helping the latest batch of women rescued from an underground brothel down in the south, near New Orleans. Another link in Fitzgerald's filthy chain broken.

Turned out Violet was good with the victims, gaining their trust and helping them adjust to freedom again. But then, as he'd found out in the past month or so, she was good at a lot of different things. Helping take down bad guys was just one of her skills.

She raised a brow at him as Zac Rutherford's voice spoke down the other end of the line. Only a few, cryptic words.

"We're going to send someone to get him, Hunt. A contact of mine who's managed to infiltrate his organization."

Elijah smiled at her then turned away, so she wouldn't see the darkness he knew had entered into his eyes. Because he understood exactly who Rutherford was talking about. "I didn't agree to this," he said curtly.

"Your agreement was not required. This is a courtesy call only."

"And if I want to stop you?"

"You're welcome to try, but I don't advise it."

The line abruptly went dead as Rutherford cut the call.

Elijah cursed silently.

So, they were going to move against Jericho. He'd been kind of expecting it for weeks, but he hadn't been sure when it was going to happen or how they were going to do it. And a large part of him had been debating whether or not he'd actually try to stop them.

Weird that he should want to save the man he'd been so desperate to kill.

But then that's what love does to a man, isn't it?

He stared at the blank screen of his phone for a moment. Love. Holy Christ.

"Hey." Warm arms slid around his waist, soft, feminine heat at his back. "Who was that?"

He turned, his heart beating faster, his cock ready and willing as it always was when Violet was around.

The smile turning her beautiful mouth started to fade, her brow creasing. "Something's up, isn't it?"

"Yeah, something's up." He couldn't tell her about the Nine Circles and their plans for her brother, not yet. But he could tell her something else. Something that had been building for the past month that he hadn't the words for. At least not until now.

He slid his hands into the short strands of her golden hair, holding her there, keeping her still. "There's something I forgot to tell you."

She blinked. "What? If you forgot to tell me we're out of coffee, I may be forced to kill you."

"No." He smiled. It still felt strange to do that. "I forgot to tell you I love you."

Her mouth opened, the color deepening in her cheeks, something glittering in her eyes. A diamond. A tear. And maybe she was going to say something of great importance, but he didn't let her.

He kissed her instead.

Love. It didn't destroy. It saved. It had saved them both.

And now it was going to save her brother.

Read on for an excerpt from the next book by
JACKIE ASHENDEN

IN BED WITH THE BILLIONAIRE

Coming soon from St. Martin's Paperbacks

The look on his face hadn't changed, the lazy smile still curving his mouth, his eyes still cold. Strange when he felt so hot and when he smelled . . . good.

What the fuck are you thinking? He's evil. He was the one responsible for taking Thalia. And you're going to kill him.

"There won't be any deals," he said in that same purring voice. "I take what I want when I want it. And the only reason I haven't taken you right now is that I don't want you."

Temple took a small, silent breath. She hated being restrained, hated being helpless, and his grip was very, very strong. It wasn't anything she couldn't break, though to do so now would be a mistake and would only cause him to be even more suspicious of her.

She eased the tension from her arms, looking up into his face. And sure enough, she couldn't see any of what she'd come to recognize as lust there, not even a flicker. She made a small movement with her hips, and yeah, despite the fact that she was nearly naked, there was no telltale hardness pressing against her there either.

Fuck.

His smile widened as if he'd read her mind. "Looking for something?"

Okay, so this was unusual. She wasn't vain, but again,

men were simple. If a nearly naked chick got in their laps, they were usually pretty interested. But this man? Nothing. Why not? Did crime lords lose the ability to get it up after a certain length of time?

Temple raised an eyebrow. "Did you forget your little blue pill?"

He laughed, a soft, deeply sexy sound that had her almost shivering. "Or maybe you just don't have what it takes to be in my bed."

She let her lashes fall. "Hey, I can be whatever you want me to be."

"I'm sure you can." His grip tightened on her wrists and he lifted his free hand to a lock of her hair, twisting it absently around his fingers, that scalpel-sharp gaze running over her. Dissecting her. "But if you don't know what I want, you can't be anything at all."

"Give me a hint and I can try."

His gaze narrowed. "You don't like this. You don't like me holding you like this."

She had to fight not to show her shock. She'd perfected the art of hiding her feelings, of never letting anyone see what she didn't want them to see. And she couldn't imagine how this man had managed to spot what she herself was only barely aware of. How the hell had he managed that? She was sure she hadn't let anything slip.

Discomfort built inside her, but she ignored it, trying to think about how to respond instead. If he didn't want her, she had to figure out how to make him, because currently the only thing holding him here was the fact that she wasn't acting like all the rest.

She needed him to want her and badly enough to keep her, at least for a little while. Until she'd gotten the information she needed from him. Then she'd kill him as she'd promised Zac Rutherford and his friends she would. Kill him and collect the money she was owed.

Jericho was always going to be her last contract. And her most satisfying.

Temple looked at him from underneath her lashes. "I wouldn't have thought it would matter to you what I like."

He stared at her for a second, bright and sharp as a blade. "It doesn't," he said. Then he smiled again, like a tiger, lazy and hungry. And the finger in her hair pulled suddenly tight, a small shock of pain flashing over her scalp.

She couldn't stop the soft gasp that escaped her, nor did she miss the sudden flare in his eyes as she did so. "So," she said, and this time the breathlessness was completely unfeigned. "I guess pain is what you want?"

He let the lock of red hair fall, his hand dropping to the side of her neck, his finger stroking lightly, gently down the side of it. And though she didn't want it to, the touch sent goose bumps rising all over her skin. "Not in particular. I was just proving a point."

"Let me go and I'll prove another."

"Really? What point would that be?"

"That I'm sitting here for a reason. And it's not because you don't want me." Her throat had gone weirdly dry, his finger stroking up and down the side of her neck. She could feel the touch acutely.

His finger moved again and this time didn't stop, brushing over her throat and down further to the swell of her left breast. And in spite of all the years she'd spent expertly hiding and controlling her responses to just about everything, when he opened his hand and cupped her breast, for the second time that night all the air escaped her lungs in an audible rush.

And the bastard, the fucking bastard, saw it all with those cold, clear green eyes while that maddening smile lingered on his mouth. "Interesting," he murmured, studying her like a scientist. "You want me, little girl. Don't you?"

Her nipple had hardened beneath the pastie and he wasn't even doing anything, just cupping her breast gently in one hand. Fuck. How had that happened? She didn't want him. He was the very last man on earth she'd ever want. And this—*all* of this—was just pretend.

So just go with it and fucking pretend.

She fought to keep her breathing even, to keep her head clear. It seemed that he liked her wanting him, that her responses were fascinating to him, so why not? She had to hook him somehow didn't she? And being different to all the rest seemed to be the way to do it. Which meant . . . perhaps she should just keep going.

"M-maybe I do." The stutter was a nice touch. Pity it was utterly unfeigned.

He examined her closely. "I think there's no maybe about it." With a flick of his finger, he got rid of the pastie covering her nipple, then brushed his thumb over it.

She trembled, a lightning strike of sensation arrowing through her. Shocking her. And a small knot of something she didn't recognize at first, curled tightly in the pit of her stomach. Then she did. Panic.

His thumb made another pass over her nipple, a second jagged bolt of lightning flashing through her body. And before she could stop herself, she'd broken his hold on her wrists and had leapt from his lap, coming to stand in front of the chair, her hands raised, ready to fight.

Jericho stared at her for a long moment, his expression utterly impenetrable. Then he leaned back in the chair, his elbows resting on the arms, long fingers loosely linked. "Something tells me you're not a stripper," he said mildly.

Her heart was thundering in her head in a way it had never done before, not even when she'd taken her first kill and she couldn't understand what had gone wrong. What the fuck did she think she was doing?

Focus.

She inhaled silently, forcing herself to get a grip, then she lowered her hands. "Actually. I'm . . . .studying dance. I was stripping for extra cash." The backstory she'd concocted. A poor college student doing what she could to get by. "I didn't like being touched so I took a few self-defense lessons."

The cold look in his eyes glittered. "And here was I believing you weren't scared."

"I wasn't." Fuck. She was going to have to give him the truth. It was either that or she lost the thing that had drawn him to her in the first place. "I'm just not used to . . . wanting a complete stranger."

He didn't reply, his intense green-gold gaze moving over her, right from the top of her head down to the soles of her stripper shoes. Reassessing her. Again. "What's your name?" The sensuality had gone from his voice completely now, nothing but hard authority in each word.

Briefly she debated telling him it was whatever he wanted it to be, but she wasn't stupid. She knew the time for flirtation had passed. Shit, she'd fucked up majorly. "Kirsten," she said, going with the name she'd settled on for her current persona.

Jericho was up off the chair in a sudden, fluid movement, coming towards her so fast she forgot she was wearing eight inch stilettos, nearly stumbling as she shifted instinctively into defensive posture. He caught her around the waist, hauling her up against him, one hand fisting in her hair and pulling her head back.

Every instinct she possessed told her to move, to bring her knee up to his groin then twist, pulling out of his grip. A hand on the back of his neck, jerking down then another knee to his face. That would take him out, easy. And it would all give her away completely, because those kinds of moves you didn't pick up via self-defense lessons.

So she had to fight to stay where she was, to let him tug

her head back, her hands pressing against the hard, hot wall of his chest.

"You're lying." His tone was casual, at odds with the ruthless way he held her. "You're lying through your fucking teeth." His smile was mirthless, cold, and if she hadn't been who she was, *now* she might have been afraid. "So let's try that one again. What's your name?"

She stared up at him. This was a test. He was pushing her, trying to frighten her, and she knew that because Jackson had done the same thing when she'd first started training with him.

Now's your chance to fix things. Do not *fuck this up.*

"Temple," she said, meeting his gaze. "My name is Temple."

He narrowed his eyes, not relaxing his hold on her one bit. "Temple? What the fuck kind of name is that?"

"The one my stupid mother gave to me." No lies this time. Only the absolute truth. "She wanted to call me Shirley Temple because of my curls. But my father didn't like Shirley, so they compromised with Temple."

The expression on his beautiful face was unreadable, but his gaze was like a laser beam, stripping her down layer by layer. Studying. Dissecting. Assessing.

Then all of a sudden, he smiled. Fierce, bright and sharp. The tiger in all its fearsome glory, making her heart miss a beat at the savage beauty of it. His hand in her hair tightened, almost painfully so. "Pleased to meet you, Temple," he murmured.

And before she could move, he bent his head and kissed her. Hard.

Temple's mouth shut tight under his, her slender body going rigid. Then, as if she'd changed her mind, she relaxed, leaning against him, her mouth becoming soft, opening up, letting him in.

She tasted of peppermints from the breath mints his men gave all the girls before they danced for him, and yet there was another, subtle flavor there as well. Something sweeter, darker. That took his curiosity and twisted it, deepened it.

But he hadn't kissed her because he'd wanted her. He'd kissed her to see what she'd do.

The way she'd pulled away from him before had been unexpected and he hadn't missed the briefest flicker of shock in her eyes; she hadn't meant to pull away either. And he didn't think it was because she didn't like him touching her. No, he'd smelled the delicate scent of feminine arousal, felt the hard little bud of her nipple. Seen her fascinating amber eyes darken, the pupil widening.

She'd been turned on. Yet something about it had panicked her and he didn't buy that it was because he was a stranger. If she'd been afraid and cowering before then sure. But she hadn't been. So it was something else.

And then there was the way she'd broken his hold and sprang off his lap like a singed cat, landing on the balls of her feet despite the ridiculous shoes. Her hands had been up in a classic martial arts pose too, and her bullshit about self-defense lessons was exactly that. Bullshit.

There was something "off" about this girl and he was going to find out what it was.

She was hot against him, her palms pressing against his chest, the softness of her breasts pressing there too. Her hair felt like skeins of silk in his hand, her skin like satin. He had his other hand on the curve of one buttock and he stretched out his fingers, squeezing, feeling the taut muscle beneath. She shuddered in response, her body arching against his.

Years since you've kissed a woman.

Yeah, it had been. Though how long, he couldn't remember. But Christ, her mouth. So soft. So hot. That dark, sweet taste elusive, tantalizing . . . another shift inside him, a crack running through the walls he'd placed carefully around his desires. Fuck. Who was this woman and where was all this curiosity coming from?

She definitely wasn't lying about wanting him, he already knew that. And she hadn't lied about her name either, at least not the second time. He'd used intimidation to try to scare her, but she'd told the truth about the fact she wasn't scared of him. Which only left one other way to get under her guard. Sex.

Of course he could just send her away like he'd initially intended, find another girl to rescue. But his gut told him she was a threat, and his gut was usually right about these things.

You could just kill her.

Finally he lifted his mouth from hers, keeping his hand tight in her hair, looking down at her. She had high, slanted cheekbones and a determined little chin. A finely sculpted nose. Her features were elfin, cat-like. There was a flush to her cheeks, her pupils dilated. Her mouth was small and pouty from the kiss.

A pretty thing.

But then, he'd killed pretty things before.